BENEATH
THE
SURFACE

ALSO BY SIBEL HODGE

Fiction

Duplicity
Untouchable
Where the Memories Lie
Look Behind You
Butterfly
Trafficked: The Diary of a Sex Slave
Fashion, Lies, and Murder (Amber Fox Mystery No 1)
Money, Lies, and Murder (Amber Fox Mystery No 2)
Voodoo, Lies, and Murder (Amber Fox Mystery No 3)
Chocolate, Lies, and Murder (Amber Fox Mystery No 4)
Santa Claus, Lies, and Murder (Amber Fox Mystery No 4.5)
Vegas, Lies, and Murder (Amber Fox Mystery No 5)
Murder and Mai Tais (Danger Cove Cocktail Mystery No 1)
Killer Colada (Danger Cove Cocktail Mystery No 2)
The See-Through Leopard
Fourteen Days Later
My Perfect Wedding
The Baby Trap
It's a Catastrophe

Non-Fiction

A Gluten Free Taste of Turkey
A Gluten Free Soup Opera
Healing Meditations for Surviving Grief and Loss

BENEATH THE SURFACE

SIBEL HODGE

THOMAS & MERCER

Text copyright © 2017 by Sibel Hodge
All rights reserved.

Published by Thomas & Mercer, Seattle

www.apub.com

Amazon, the Amazon logo, and Thomas & Mercer are trademarks of Amazon.com, Inc., or its affiliates.

ISBN-13: 9781611099492
ISBN-10: 1611099498

Cover design by @blacksheep-uk.com

Printed in the United States of America

A lie doesn't become truth, wrong doesn't become right and evil doesn't become good, just because it's accepted by a majority.

— Rick Warren

Prologue

I often wonder what would happen if everything we hid under the surface showed on the outside. Our thoughts and feelings, events that have shaped us, things we've done; the evilness that lives in some people. And if it was laid out on our skin, visible for all to see, how greatly would it affect our lives? How different would our decisions be?

Some say that evil shows in the eyes. But when you see photos of people who've committed atrocities in the news, most of the time they look normal, like someone who lives next door. They don't have 'psychopath' tattooed across their forehead. There might be no obvious sign that differentiates them from your best friend or your work colleague or a family member.

Dean Hudson didn't look evil. He didn't look like the sort of person who'd massacre his family and then kill himself. There was no inkling of what lay beneath his average teenage exterior. When you saw photos of him, his eyes were sparkling and kind and happy. And that was the whole point, really. I just didn't realise it then.

The last time I'd seen Dean was fourteen years ago, when he'd been a cute three-year-old who was quick to light up with a cheeky smile.

And I couldn't believe I was there, behind the cordon blocking off the street, watching the police and forensic officers going in and out of Jess's house. The same Jess who'd spilled Slush Puppie on my favourite dress when we were both six. Who'd done hilarious impersonations of people we knew. Who'd opened her heart and her life to me from that first day at junior school. Who'd cried so much when I left Ashfield that she had hiccups for hours. We'd been best friends before life got in the way. Before she got busy with Dean being in nappies. Before she'd become wrapped up in how he'd said his first word. Before she got so involved in mother and toddler groups. Before I'd moved to London to start my career and to prove myself – to escape this town and the weight of my parents' disappointment. Before our lives moved in different directions and there was always something getting in the way. Before we drifted apart.

It felt like a whole lifetime ago now as I stood next to the other reporters and camera crews and morbidly fascinated neighbours, feeling every inch the vulture my kind had been accused of being in the past.

Despite everything that had happened, this was never going to be just a story for me.

But sometimes it's better to stay blind. Because what lies beneath the surface can be deadly.

Chapter 1

'I thought you were covering the Fire Station's charity bake-off,' Brian shouted over to me through the thick crowd of people who were gossiping and speculating about Jess, Stephen, and Dean. Brian looked every inch the clichéd veteran lead reporter for the *Ashfield Post* – mid-fifties, his shirt straining round a belly cultivated by booze and fry-ups, broken veins on his red nose, jowly cheeks. If I stayed here too long would I end up like him?

I tried to ignore him and blinked away the tears that I'd been steadily willing not to form, but he jostled through the throng in my direction.

'I hope you're not trying to muscle in on *my* story.' Brian looked down his nose at me with a sneer that said exactly the same thing I'd overheard him saying to Neil, our boss, after Neil had hired me: *What's some fancy-pants from one of the London papers doing down here?*

Brian didn't like me. Fine. I didn't like me much, either. But I hadn't come back to be liked. I'd come back to get my head sorted out. Get a job and move on. Any job. Even if it meant covering bloody fetes and Fire Station bake-offs. It was only supposed to be a stepping stone until something better came along. But I was still waiting to step in a different direction.

'Well?' Brian glared at me.

'I know them,' I whispered, my throat scratchy, my gaze frozen on the house, before I corrected myself. '*Knew* them.'

'The ones who got sliced and diced?'

I narrowed my eyes, my mouth twisting with disgust and fury. 'Is that going to be your headline?' I thought about Jess's mum, Barbara. The woman who'd fed me peanut butter and jam sandwiches and home-made fudge all those times. Who always had a warm hug for me. Who took me along on shopping trips with Jess whenever she could. Barbara had been there for me in ways my own mum never was and never would be. Had Barbara heard the news yet or was she out somewhere, shopping, browsing in a book shop, or at the supermarket, looking for something tempting to eat for dinner, obliviously carrying on with her life? Blissfully unaware of the horror that was going to shatter her? I pictured her collapsing, devastated, broken. Her daughter, son-in-law, and grandson gone in a few horrific moments. How do you ever get over something like that?

A TV news crew were setting up their equipment at the side of the cordon, ready to record the outside of 14 Draper Avenue. The smoked salmon and cream cheese baguette I'd had earlier curdled in my stomach. I desperately craved a drink to steady my nerves. I pictured the empty wine bottles in my bin at home. Had I finished off the whole of my stash last night? If so, I'd definitely need to get some more to make it through tonight.

'So? What do you know about them?' Brian elbowed my shoulder.

'We were friends for a long time.' My gaze followed an anchorwoman running her hands through her hair before refreshing her lipstick, wanting to look picture perfect as she broadcasted to the world the awfulness of what had happened.

'Great. You can give me some background info for the story then.' Brian leaned close to my face. I got a waft of beer breath and curry.

I reeled back.

'I bet their kid always seemed like a psycho, right? Creepy. Getting into trouble. Fights at school. Nicking things. Probably a gang member, or into black magic. Cult stuff, maybe. Or one of those emos. It's always the way.' Cynicism shot through his voice as he thought about the ways to spin the story.

I could see Brian's headline now: 'Monster Slaughters Family'. I wasn't going to give him anything. At that moment I *couldn't* give him anything either, even if I'd wanted to. The Dean I knew wouldn't have hurt a fly.

I scanned the crowd of reporters and rubberneckers, looking at the excitement and shock on their faces. Some people were filming the comings and goings of number 14 on their phones. One man in a baseball cap and black bomber jacket with badly acne-scarred skin stood slightly apart from the crowd, carefully watching the building and texting on his mobile phone – probably telling his wife or girlfriend he was going to be late home because something terrible had happened and he just had to get a good look.

The clicking of camera shutters in unison drew my attention away from the man and back to the house. The photographers had focused on a detective with grey hair and a grey beard exiting number 14, stopping the gossip dead in its tracks.

The anchorwoman shouted over to the detective standing outside the house, wanting to get a police statement. Brian and the rest of the press fired out questions, calling the detective by name: DCI Turnbull. He ignored the questions and spoke to a forensic officer suited in white overalls. Then a younger detective emerged from the house and said something to DCI Turnbull, who nodded gravely and re-entered the house. The other detective glanced over at the crowd and our eyes met in a flash of recognition.

Will Jackson. The nausea I felt cranked up a notch. A memory flashed into my head of the last time I'd seen him. Me pulling on my underwear, feeling ashamed, embarrassed. Will telling me how he'd liked me all through school. How he wanted to see me again even though I was going to London. The excuses I'd made about how a long-distance relationship would never work. Better that than have to look at the happiness on his face and tell him it was a drunken mistake. As mistakes went, though, that one was far from my worst.

He looked more handsome now with just a few extra lines around his eyes, which were made prominent when he squinted at me. But there was a haunted expression etched into his features that had never been there before. A five o'clock shadow graced his jawline. His swarthy skin was now pale, washed out. I guessed mine would be, too, after seeing what was inside that house.

Will glanced away. He ran his hands over his face as if to wake himself up – get himself together again. He took a deep breath, his chest expanding, then disappeared back inside number 14.

'You'd better get back to the office and file the bake-off piece,' Brian said to me with a gleam in his eye. 'Some of us have important stories to write.'

I fought the urge to tell him to stop acting like a spoilt two-year-old. But I couldn't afford to lose this job, and he and Neil were good friends, which was why Brian lorded over the other staff at the *Ashfield Post*, even though anyone with a brain and a grasp of the English language could've written better stories than him. And besides, I needed to find out more about what had happened here, and I'd bet Brian didn't have a history with Will.

~

I drove back to the office in a numb haze, pictures of my past flashing into my head. Stephen and Jess's wedding reception. Cradling Dean in my arms two days after he was born. Kissing his skin and fine hair, like velvet beneath my lips. Dean presenting me with a messy drawing that was meant to be Jess, Stephen, and me. Jess laughing so hard at something that she doubled over with a stitch . . . Jess was always laughing. Even when things didn't go right she still kept her wicked sense of humour.

I trudged up the stairs to the first floor, gripping the banister to support my shaky legs, and I saw Neil at his desk at the far end of the room, his doorway open, typing manically on his laptop.

He didn't glance up as I entered and stood in front of him – just held a finger up and said, 'One sec. Gotta quickly do this.' More frenzied typing, then he finally edged his gaze upwards and smiled. 'Ah, Holly. Have you done the bake-off thing?'

I swallowed. 'Not yet, no.' Now I was here, I didn't know what to say. Speaking it would make it real, and I didn't want it to be. The words lodged in my throat like a hard object.

'Right. So what's up, then?' Neil prompted me.

'The murder at Draper Avenue.'

'*Massacre*,' Neil said. 'That will sell more copies, and God knows we bloody need to at the moment. Advertising revenue is down thirty per cent. We need a gory murder round here to get the circulation up.'

'Let me write the story.'

'You?' He raised two unkempt eyebrows at me. 'Sorry, no can do. Brian's on it.'

I gripped the edge of Neil's desk. 'I understand that, but I knew the family. Jess and Stephen Hudson. Dean. I want to make sure it's covered sensitively.'

He sat back in his chair, rocking it back and forth slightly, watching me. 'How well did you know them?'

'Jess and I went to school together. We were best friends for a long time. The last time I saw her was fourteen years ago, when Dean was three.' I bit my lip to stop the tears forming.

He tapped his fingertips on the desk for a moment, then shrugged. 'Well, you can give Brian a bit of background about them, but it's not like you can add anything to recent events, is it? Not if you hadn't seen them for years.'

'Yes, but . . .' I trailed off. Maybe he was right. I didn't have a clue what had been going on in that family lately. Was Dean into drugs? Or cults, like Brian had speculated? Had there always been a psychopath lurking beneath the friendly, placid little boy I'd known? But even if any of that were true, I didn't trust Brian to write a story that wasn't sensationalist, designed to sell more papers. 'Look, I know Jess's mum. I can find out what was going on recently. I'm sure she'd talk to me rather than Brian or any of the other press. We could get an exclusive interview that the nationals might syndicate. I can get the real story from her. Maybe a human interest piece about how teenagers can't cope with the stress of—'

'We don't need a human interest piece. We need shocking headlines and drama. Anyway, there's going to be a press conference later at the police station. Brian can get most of what he needs there. Just talk to him about the background information. What did the parents do?'

'Jess was a housewife. Stephen was a plumber. They were a regular family.' Or were they? How did I know Stephen wasn't abusing Dean? That Dean hadn't just snapped and killed them because of it? Were there dark secrets lurking behind closed doors that I never knew about? Never suspected? Just because I'd known them well once didn't mean I knew the real them. Fourteen years was a long time.

Neil took a slurp of coffee from the mug on his desk and nodded to himself. 'Good, good. Regular family means it could happen to anyone. That'll make it more shocking.'

I blew out a frustrated breath. 'Something pretty drastic must've made Dean stab his parents to death and then hang himself! Don't you want to find out what?'

'Not really. We're just reporting the news. The *Ashfield Post* doesn't do *human interest* pieces or bloody psychiatric evaluations. We're not an investigative journalism national, we're a small-town rag. You need to get your head out of the sky. You're not in London any more, Toto.'

I clenched my fists, digging my nails into my palms, fighting the swirl of emotions scrambling to the surface. 'Look, I've been here a year now and—'

'Exactly. So you know how we work. It's Brian's story and that's the end of it. Best get back to your own stuff. I need that piece by the end of the day.' He started typing again, dismissing me.

I opened my mouth to say more, but I knew it would be useless and so shut it again. 'OK.'

I threaded through the cubicles to my desk in the corner next to the toilets. I dumped my handbag beside my laptop and slumped down in my chair, tears pricking behind my eyelids. What did I know about journalism, anyway? I'd worked for *Pizzazz*, a women's magazine focused on celebrity gossip, the latest fashion trends, and hair and beauty tips. I wrote features about how to have the best orgasm and which ten beauty products were essential this summer. And when I'd thought there must be more to life than that, when I'd wanted to write serious articles, I'd got a job at the *Daily Insider*, one of the national newspapers, hoping that the ridiculous agony column, travel, and book and film review columns would be a foot in the door to *real* investigative reporting. But even that hadn't worked out how I'd planned. And here I was now, back in the town I'd wanted to escape at eighteen, tail between my legs and trying to get back on my feet. Maybe I was fooling myself. Just because you wanted something so badly, didn't mean it was ever going to happen.

But this wasn't about a job, anyway. Even if I wasn't allowed to write an in-depth story that wasn't judgemental and sensational, this was about finding out what had really happened to the Hudson family and how it all went so tragically wrong.

And no matter what Neil thought, he couldn't stop me asking questions.

Chapter 2

We've got a BIG problem.

I'm hearing it right now. It's nothing we can't handle. It'll blow over. They won't make the connection.

Orders?

Watch and wait. Let me know about any developments immediately.

Shall I dig into the coppers' backgrounds? See if they can be bought if the situation escalates?

Everyone can be bought for the right price.

Chapter 3

By the time I'd written up the bake-off story that hardly anyone would read or give a shit about, it was just after 5 p.m. Neil and Brian were chatting quietly in Neil's office when I walked in to tell Neil I'd emailed the story to him.

Brian treated me to a smirk, as if they'd been talking about me.

'Great. Thanks.' Neil grinned. 'I want you to cover the Women's Institute garden tea party on Monday,' he said.

Yippee.

'That should be right up your street.'

'Why?' I threw him a questioning look.

He glanced me up and down, and I could only infer that he thought I'd find it interesting just because I happened to be a woman. I fought the urge to call him a sexist bastard and nodded compliantly. 'No problem. Have a good weekend.'

'Yeah.' Neil stood up and grabbed his jacket from a coat stand in the corner of his office. 'You up for a pint?' he asked Brian. 'Thank God it's Friday!'

Brian chuckled, slapping Neil on the back lightly. 'Always, mate.'

I rolled my eyes as I walked out. I got in my car and a hollow feeling gnawed inside me as another solitary evening stretched out in front of me. I hadn't even thought about Jess for ages – I'd been too wrapped up in myself. Guilt clawed at me. I'd been back here a year and hadn't phoned her – hadn't popped round in an attempt to rekindle our previous friendship. It wasn't as if my social life was exactly full. Nowadays the most exciting thing I got up to was a night round at Zoe's watching *Frozen* with Leigh falling asleep on my lap.

Deep down, maybe it was because I hadn't wanted Jess to see me as a hopeless failure. I'd left here with such high hopes of a glittering, exciting career and came back with nothing. But what if I *had* got in touch with Jess again? What if we'd picked up where we'd left off as best friends? Could I have stopped what had happened in that house last night? Could I have spotted the warning signs? Told someone what Dean was about to do?

I rubbed at the throbbing ache in my forehead as I watched Brian and Neil exit the building, laughing about something, and head down the road to the pub on the corner.

I wanted to phone Jess's mum, Barbara, and tell her how sorry I was, but I didn't have her number any more, and besides, it was probably too early for that. She'd be distraught – maybe even sedated. It would have to wait a little while longer.

Wine. I needed wine. Lots and lots of it.

My mobile rang as I stared into the darkening evening through my windscreen, debating whether to head to the off-licence, which was closer, or the supermarket, where they had better special offers.

It was my brother, Miles. 'Where are you?' He didn't do pleasantries. No saying 'hi' and asking about my day. That was the trouble with him. Miles was self-centred, selfish, and prone to arrogance. He was the one who'd always done well. He always knew what he wanted and it fell into his lap effortlessly. Miles got to go to private school when Zoe and I didn't. Dad had always been working or too distracted for him to take an interest in Zoe's and my upbringing. Dad hadn't got involved because he'd been more interested in making the money that Mum loved to spend. In Dad's absence, Miles had become Mum's golden boy. She'd had a clear idea of the kind of child she'd wanted, and both Zoe and I were found sadly lacking. Miles was the favourite who could do no wrong. Now he had a wife, a gorgeous daughter, and a Porsche. He earned stacks of money and went on holiday four times a year.

Or was I just jealous that Miles had got everything he'd wanted out of life and mine seemed to be moving further and further backwards each year?

'I'm in my car,' I muttered. 'And how are you? How are Tania and Hayley?'

'Did you forget?'

'Forget what?'

'The *barbecue*!' He sighed. I could practically see him rolling his eyes.

'Did you hear about the Hudsons?' I asked him. It must've been all round town by now.

'The Hudsons? You mean Jess?'

I told him what had happened.

He was silent for a moment, which he rarely ever was. Miles always had an opinion on everything. 'I've been in meetings all day out of town and now I'm rushing around mingling with guests. I mean, it's terrible news, but you might as well still come. You'll only be moping around at home getting drunk on your own otherwise.'

I didn't feel like socialising but I did need a drink. And Miles would have plenty.

He started to speak again when the phone must've been snatched off him and I heard my sister's voice.

'I'm so sorry about Jess and Stephen and Dean,' Zoe said. 'I heard it on the radio as I was driving to Miles's. Are you OK?'

'Yeah. I suppose. It's just . . . I don't really feel like coming to the barbecue now. I won't be good company.'

Zoe lowered her voice to a whisper. 'You can't leave me here with this lot. You have to save me. If I hear Miles telling his mates how much money his bonus was *one* more time I'm going to throw my drink over him.'

Despite everything, I laughed.

'Anyway, Leigh wants to know where her auntie is. She's drawn you a picture.'

I thought of Leigh's blonde curls, so like mine. Her sticky kisses. Her sweet innocence. I wanted to give her a big hug, let her know we didn't live in a world where bad things can happen in an instant. And I didn't really want to go home to my empty flat and think about the Hudsons and drink alone. I wanted to blot it all out for a while.

'Please? For me?' Zoe pleaded.

'OK. I'm on my way. See you in ten.' I hung up and drove to Miles's five-bedroomed mock-Tudor house.

Luckily, the weather had been mild and sunny lately, meaning everyone was milling around in the garden and not huddled under umbrellas or making a dash to the kitchen as the British summer skies pelted down rain and turned the garden into a soggy quagmire. Not that Miles had something as plain and cheap as an umbrella, anyway. There was a marquee set up at one end of the garden that was big enough to house a couple of football teams.

As I made my way through the side gate I spotted Zoe immediately, chatting with Miles's wife, Tania. Tania looked stunning, as always. Hair in a stylish up-do pinned with grips that had flowers on the end, courtesy of her weekly appointment at the hair salon. She had flawless make-up, gelled nails in a sparkly silver colour and she wore a tight, sequinned dress that I knew cost five hundred quid because she'd told me. Zoe, on the other hand, had come straight from work after picking up Leigh from the childminder, with no time to change out of the smart navy pinstripe pencil skirt and beige silky blouse she'd got from Primark.

'She's here!' Tania raised her champagne flute at me and kissed me on both cheeks. Her face was flushed from alcohol – probably expensive champagne, knowing them. 'Let me get you some Moët. You're playing catch-up now. I'm pissed already!' She teetered off on dangerously high Louboutins.

I plastered a smile on my face and leaned in to hug Zoe. 'Hi. How's it going?'

'Oh, you know. Same old, same old.' She gave me a half-smile and pulled me towards her for a hug. 'I'm so sorry about the Hudsons,' she whispered in my ear.

I felt tears well up and blinked to push them away. I didn't want to fall apart with an audience. I pulled back, sniffed, and said, 'Where's Leigh then?'

'Over there.' Zoe pointed towards my four-year-old niece wearing a Disney Princess dress and a smear of chocolate on her cheek, running round and round the old willow tree at the end of the garden with Hayley, Tania and Miles's eight-year-old daughter.

'They're going to be sick at this rate.' Zoe grimaced.

I spotted Miles hovering over a state-of-the-art gas barbecue that looked big enough to cook a whole donkey on. There were fillet steaks and lobster tails sizzling away. Nothing as banal as burgers and sausages for Miles.

Tania teetered over and handed me a full champagne flute. 'Here you go. Just what the doctor ordered.' She laughed. It was an in-joke, since Miles worked for a pharmaceutical company as a sales rep, touting drugs to doctors' surgeries and hospitals. 'You OK? You look a bit pale.'

'Yeah. It's been a bad day.' I swallowed a couple of mouthfuls of bubbly, the chilled alcohol freezing my throat. 'Did you hear about what happened earlier?'

'Oh, no! What? You didn't get sacked again?' Tania asked.

'I wasn't sacked. I left,' I said. Sometimes I wondered if Tania's put-downs were as innocent as the wide-eyed, smiley presentation they were always delivered with, or whether she'd just picked up the arrogance from Miles and didn't really register the impact of her words. Don't they say couples take on each other's traits? I was sure she'd never been as high-maintenance and bitchy when she and Miles had first started going out with each other, but then there'd been the distance from London between us and so I hadn't actually spent much time with them until I'd moved back.

She put a placating hand on my arm. 'Yes, yes, of course. Sorry.'

'I *meant* what happened with Jess and Stephen and Dean Hudson.'

'Oh! The murders, you mean?' Tania shrugged carelessly. 'I heard someone talking about it a minute ago but I didn't know them. Anyway, must mingle. Food will be ready soon.' She strutted away without asking me anything else. Tania was cut from the same mould as Miles now. If something didn't affect them personally, they weren't interested.

I drank some more champagne and the glass was almost empty. Why did they make champagne flutes so damn small? I glanced around for more – I spied a bottle on a table nearby and grabbed it to top up my drink. 'They think Dean killed both Jess and Stephen before killing himself.' I told Zoe what else I knew so far, which was precious little, really. According to the brief press announcement by DCI Turnbull outside Draper Avenue earlier, the house had been locked from the inside when it all happened, with no sign of forced entry. They were keeping all lines of enquiry open while forensics did their stuff, but at this stage it looked as if no one else had been involved.

'That's absolutely awful!' A hand flew to Zoe's mouth.

I glanced over at my nieces giggling happily, remembering Dean at around the same age as Leigh. What made a child kill their parents?

Zoe put her hand on my shoulder. 'Did you ever contact Jess again when you moved back here?'

I swallowed. 'No. It's been fourteen years . . . I . . .' I downed my new glass of champagne and topped it up again.

Zoe hadn't touched hers yet. She eyed my glass with a worried look but didn't pass judgement. But, really, fuck it. It was the weekend and I'd had bad news. I needed a drink.

'I didn't get in touch with Jess when I moved back, and now I keep thinking . . . why didn't I? I should have.'

'I'm really sorry.' Zoe squeezed my shoulder tighter and glanced over towards Leigh and Hayley. Was she thinking the same thing as me? Wondering how Dean could've slaughtered his parents? 'I saw Dean about two weeks ago. He had an appointment with us.' Zoe had been working as a receptionist and secretary at a psychiatrist's practice for the last six months since Leigh had started preschool. 'I hadn't seen him there before. It was only after he gave his name and I checked his address that I knew he was Jess's son.'

'What was he there for?'

She raised her eyebrows. 'I can't tell you that. You know patient records are confidential. But, to be honest, I didn't even check the system to find out.'

'How did he seem?'

'Well, he didn't seem like someone about to kill his parents! Typical teenage boy, I suppose. Slightly spotty, hunched shoulders. Very polite, though.'

I wondered if the appointment meant anything significant. Had Dean been depressed? Been having suicidal thoughts or psychotic rages?

Before I could say anything else, Leigh, who was waving madly at us, broke away from Hayley. We waved back as Leigh ran towards us, sweaty fringe plastered to her forehead. She barrelled into me, almost sending me flying. I was more unsteady than I thought. The champagne had worked its magic well. I stumbled backwards but stayed upright and gripped on to her arms around my waist.

'Auntie Holly! You're here! I drew a picture of a pot-a-mouse for you!' She grinned up at me as I planted a kiss on the top of her hot head and laughed.

'A *hippopotamus*.' Zoe smiled at her daughter.

'Mummy, I feel sick.' Leigh suddenly released her vice-like grip on me and put her hand to her mouth.

'Uh-oh. I'm not surprised, the way you've been flying around that tree chasing Hayley. Come on, let's sit you down and get you some water.' Zoe held her hand out to her daughter and then led her into the kitchen.

I watched them go, wondering again if I'd missed my final chance to ever have kids, before a horrific picture blasted into my head – Jess fighting off Dean as he tried to kill her. Dean's face contorted with rabid rage. Stephen already bleeding out on the floor. Was that how it had happened? I didn't know the full details yet, and I wasn't about to phone Brian's mobile and ask him if he knew any more. Better to go straight to the source. And I knew where Will lived. I glanced at my watch. It was just after 8 p.m., and I thought Will would still be at work, sifting through the evidence, trying to work out why Dean had done what he'd done.

I was so deep in thought I didn't see the guy approach until he was by my side, holding out a bottle of Moët to top up my glass. I snapped back to the present as he said, 'You're empty.'

The metaphor of my life.

I pushed the thought away and forced a smile. He wasn't tall, but he was all wide shoulders and rugby-player thighs beneath butt-hugging jeans and a black shirt. He had blondish hair – short at the sides, swept back on top – and golden-brown eyes.

'Thanks,' I said as he filled my glass to the top.

He put the bottle on the grass beside us and looked at me with a slight smile, head tilted. 'I'm Martin.'

'I'm Holly.' I nodded as if I was stupidly agreeing with myself. I smiled self-consciously. Felt awkward. After Richard, I hadn't dated anyone. My love life was a train wreck and I wasn't about to add to it. I didn't know how to make small talk with attractive men any more. I wasn't interesting enough now. I'd lost that flirty, self-confident, happy side of myself, and I was worried about looking like a complete idiot.

His lips curled up at the corners. 'I work at Tragatech – with Miles.' He offered some words for me to grab on to.

'Ah. I haven't seen you at one of Miles's dos before.'

He shrugged and took a slow sip of his drink, eyes intensely focused on me, as if he were mentally undressing me. There was something about him – a hungry, animalistic vibe rolled off him.

I flushed under his scrutiny, hoping it was just the champagne making me hot. 'So you're a sales rep, too? The same as Miles?'

He chuckled. 'No. I'm a numbers guy.'

'Like accounts?'

His lips twisted into a grin. 'More like logistics. And you? You're a reporter, Miles said.'

Martin had been asking about me? 'Well, I wouldn't call it that yet. I work for the local paper, but so far the most interesting thing I've covered is a pet cat being reunited with its owner after getting stuck down a manhole.'

He smiled again in response. The garden was starting to spin slightly.

I scrabbled around in my brain for something funny to say – something the old Holly would've said. 'Oh, and I did a piece on the local Allotment Society's organic marrow-growing competition. They set a record apparently. You wouldn't believe the size of them.'

He laughed. Deep and scratchy. 'Sounds . . . interesting?'

'Boring as hell.'

'We all have to start somewhere, I suppose.'

'Yeah, but marrows?' I rolled my eyes and laughed.

Miles made a big announcement that the food was ready, waving his tongs around with a beatific smile on his face, like he'd just announced he'd personally solved world poverty, not grilled a couple of slabs of fancy meat and seafood.

'You hungry?' Martin asked.

I glanced up and met his gaze. *Another metaphor?* 'I am, actually.' I hadn't eaten since the baguette at eleven. The news of the Hudson family had – not surprisingly – obliterated my appetite, and now I was ravenous. But as we walked towards a large table in the marquee overflowing with food, Martin's hand guiding me with a light touch on my back, the sight of the blood-red juices flowing from the meat made me stop short, nausea welling up. An image of the Hudsons on an autopsy table flashed before my eyes, blocking out everything else. What a tragedy.

No – 'tragedy' wasn't the right word. I didn't know what the right word was for something so terrible.

'Are you OK?' Martin asked.

I waved a hand through the air. 'Mmm. Just . . . a bit of a bad day, actually. You go on and get something. I'm just going to . . .' I stumbled away from him into the kitchen, wanting space – solitude – before the tears started. Leigh and Hayley had disappeared by the time I got inside, and the place was now empty.

I made my way into the downstairs bathroom and splashed water on my cheeks and wrists to cool down. I wiped my face and stared at my reflection, thinking how awful it was that Jess and Stephen couldn't have known when they'd got up this morning that it would be their last day on earth. Had Dean planned it all in advance? How could it have happened?

I pressed a palm to my forehead. Took a few deep breaths. *I have to get out of here and speak to Will.*

When I opened the door and walked up the corridor I saw Miles in the kitchen, staring down into his heavy crystal glass filled with expensive scotch, a pensive look on his face. His jaw was clenched tight.

'Not enjoying your party?' I asked, walking towards him.

He'd been so lost in his own thoughts that my voice made him jump slightly. But then the look was gone, quickly replaced with a confident smile I was sure had to be part of his winning sales repertoire. 'There you are. Didn't think to come over and say hi, then?' He jutted his cheek towards me so I could kiss it.

I leaned in and did the perfunctory peck against his jaw. 'Sorry, I was . . . I got caught up with Zoe.'

'And Martin?' He raised an eyebrow. 'I saw you two chatting.'

'Are you trying to set me up or something?'

'You could do worse than him. He's bloody loaded.'

I rolled my eyes. In Miles's world someone's worth was measured by their salary and how many designer clothes they wore. He frequently liked to tell Zoe and me how Tania didn't need to work because he earned in an hour what she could earn in a day.

He scooped a crostini into a dish of caviar and popped it in his mouth. 'Mmm, this is good. Tania had it delivered from Fortnum and Mason. Try it.' He passed me the dish with the crostini in it.

God help me.

'Look, I've got to go, Miles. Thanks for the invite.'

His face puckered into a frown that said I'd personally ruined his evening – he'd mastered using that little boy pout to get his own way with Mum and had never grown out of it. 'But you only just got here! The evening hasn't even started yet. It'll be much better than going back to your poky little flat and getting pissed on your own.'

'I'm not feeling too good.'

'Oh. Time of the month? God, Tania's a bitch when *that* happens.'

'Oh, fuck off, Miles,' I snapped, but my angry remark just slid off his back. 'My friend was killed today!'

He paused for a moment, turning away from me to look through the window at the guests outside. 'Well, I'm going back to the party. Take a pill if you don't feel well. There are loads in the box.'

Miles had plenty of access to free samples of various medications via his job. He handed them out to doctors like candy in a bid to encourage them to prescribe his company's drugs. He kept a huge box of stuff in a kitchen cupboard – high enough for the kids not to be able to get at it, but still, I wouldn't feel comfortable with that amount of drugs in the house, legal or not. I was pretty sure Miles and Tania didn't just use them for medicinal purposes, either, so he couldn't exactly talk about my drinking.

'Say goodbye to Tania and Zoe and the kids for me,' I called out to his retreating back.

He raised a hand in acknowledgement but didn't turn around.

I slipped out the front door, left my car where it was parked on the street, and walked to Will's house. When I'd left for London, Will had been living with his parents, but Jess had told me years ago he was renting the house off them after they'd moved into an assisted-living flat. I just hoped he hadn't moved in the years since.

I looked at the end-of-terrace house on a quiet street. As houses went, it was bland. All blocky square concrete with no interesting features. The whole street had been built in the fifties and owned by the council for years until the houses were sold to tenants. My parents had always called it the 'wrong side of town' in their snobbery. A light shone behind the window in the lounge, so hopefully he was home.

Walking up the front path, I remembered the last time I'd been here. The drunken night in town with Jess – my leaving party. We'd met Will and some of his mates in the White Hare. Was it me or him who'd made the first move? I can't remember now. The years have blurred the lines. Will was two years older than me and he'd had a crush on me since school. Jess had joked that he'd worshipped me from afar all that time, but he'd always been a bad boy, living on the edge of danger. He'd been involved in fights at school and smoked weed. Rumour had it he'd stolen cars and other things, too, so I'd always given him a wide berth, not wanting to get dragged into that kind of thing. But that night in the pub, fuelled by alcohol, I'd thrown caution away, and it had suddenly seemed like sleeping with Will was a great idea. I'd wanted to leave Ashfield on a high. The sex wasn't even that great, and then afterwards, when Will had said he'd always wanted a relationship with me, there'd been something about him that had made me think it was too risky to trust my heart to him. Plus, I had a career to think about. New, exciting friends I wanted to make. Places I wanted to go. All that crazy nightlife to experience. And I hadn't wanted to be tied down to Bad Boy Will Jackson from this backwater old town. He was the least likely person from school I ever thought would become a policeman. But he'd obviously worked out his hard edges and turned over a new leaf. He'd followed a different path. Good for him. Maybe I could, too.

I rang the doorbell and hoped it wouldn't be answered by a woman.

Moistening my lips, I ran a hand through my hair as a shadow appeared behind the obscured glass in the front door.

And there he was. Will Jackson. The older, better-looking, ruggedly sexy Will Jackson.

He leaned against the door frame, the tie he'd been wearing earlier outside the Hudsons' house discarded, the top few buttons of his white shirt undone, showing a smattering of chest hair. He didn't even look surprised, although he wasn't smiling. His face was neutral. 'Holly Gold.'

'Will Jackson.'

'I thought it was you earlier.'

'I came back.'

'I know. You look well. How are you?'

'Great,' I lied. 'How are you?'

Up close, he wasn't just better looking – he was absolutely gorgeous. His shoulders had filled out, and his blue eyes had developed a deeper intensity, holding me captive.

He shrugged slightly. 'Busy.' He paused, his gaze roaming my face. 'So . . . you're a detective sergeant now. Wow!'

'I know. I guess I grew up.' He looked me up and down. 'You, too, by the looks of it.'

'You should be really proud of yourself.'

'Thanks,' he said, and I detected a note of something in his voice. Weariness, perhaps. Still, if I'd been in his shoes today, dealing with the aftermath at Draper Avenue, I'd feel the same. 'I know you work for the *Ashfield Post*. Is that why you're here? You know I can't say anything other than what's already been put out by DCI Turnbull or the press office.'

I briefly wondered *how* he knew where I worked. He didn't strike me as the type to devour the local paper, reading my crappy contributions and spotting my byline on them.

'This isn't about the *Ashfield Post*. It's completely off the record. I'm not even covering the story.'

He paused, glancing up at the ceiling for a second then back to me. 'That's what reporters always say.'

'This is about a friend of mine. You knew Jess, too, so you must know how it feels. I want to understand how it could've happened. I mean, Dean? He was a cuddly, sweet little boy. I don't know how he could've done it.' A sudden dizziness took over. Maybe it was the champagne I'd drunk on an empty stomach or the pictures in my head of the Hudsons refusing to go away. I held on to the edge of the wall outside the door.

'Are you OK?' His eyes flooded with concern and warmth. Or was I just seeing what I wanted to see, as usual?

I nodded. 'The last time I saw Dean, he was three. He was into his toy garage and Matchbox cars. I just can't equate that boy with someone who'd murder his family and then kill himself.'

'Fourteen years is a long time. People change. People do all sorts of things.'

Don't I know it.

'Yes. People change. People make mistakes. People do things they shouldn't. But this is a whole different ball game.'

Will pursed his lips, as if thinking. 'Do you want a coffee?'

I smiled. I pushed my hand away from the wall and swayed a little, consciously trying to stay steady on my feet. 'Coffee would be good, thanks.'

He stood back to let me in and then shut the door. I followed behind him into the kitchen at the back of the house. Luckily, he didn't see me bang my shoulder against the wall in the corridor as I swerved awkwardly. I'd drunk more than I'd realised.

The kitchen had been modernised since the last time I'd been there, and even though it looked budget rather than the coldly sterile, top-of-the-range design I'd just come from, it was homely and cosy.

I leaned against the worktop, watching him grab a jar of coffee and mugs. The muscles of his shoulders strained against his shirt as he poured boiling water and milk into the mugs and stirred their contents.

'Have a seat.' He turned around and tilted his head towards the small breakfast bar along one section of the wall that I knew overlooked the back garden, even though the blind was closed.

I sat on a high, padded stool and swung myself around to face him as he sat, too. 'Are you sure there's no mistake? Did Dean *really* kill Jess and Stephen then take his own life?'

Will sipped his coffee. 'We're still waiting for the Home Office pathologist reports and forensic analysis, and the results of other enquiries, but from our reconstruction of the crime scene, it looks that way so far. I'm sorry.'

'Why did he do it?'

'We don't know yet.'

'Did Dean have mental health problems?'

Will gave me a pointed look. 'I can't tell you anything else.'

'How's Barbara coping?'

'How do you think?' he said sadly. 'She's devastated.'

25

'Does she still live in their old house?'

'Yes. Her husband died a few years back and she retired a little while ago, so all she's got left in her life now is that house and her cat,' he said sombrely.

I stared down at my mug, wondering what questions to ask next. *This is why you're* not *a journalist, you stupid cow. You're only good for writing up rubbish no one's interested in.*

'I really can't say any more right now. I'm sorry.' Will paused, taking a sip of coffee and watching me over the rim of his mug. 'So why *did* you come back? Wasn't writing articles about how guys can give women better orgasms fulfilling enough any more?' The corners of his lips quirked up.

'You read that?' I didn't know whether to cringe or wonder why he'd been going through a women's magazine in the first place. I wondered hopefully if he'd been keeping tabs on me since that night. Trouble was, I overthought things too much now. Of course he'd moved on since that one-night stand. He wouldn't be interested in me any more. Especially not the person I was now. I bored myself.

He stood, towering above me. 'Look, it's been a long day. I really need to get a few hours' sleep before I'm back at work.'

'Of course.'

He walked me to the front door and I was all too aware of the heat of his body behind me.

I stepped out into the dark night and felt very cold. I walked down the path and looked back over my shoulder.

Will stood in the doorway – which surrounded him like a picture frame – still watching me.

Chapter 4

I ignored the pounding in my head when I woke at 7 a.m. the next morning, dry-mouthed and bleary-eyed, forcing myself to go to the gym as punishment. The trouble was however much I ran, I could never outrun myself.

I walked to Miles's house to pick up my car first, then headed for the small converted warehouse that passed for a gym round here.

I ran fast on the treadmill as I watched the news on one of the screens dotted around the place. Not surprisingly, the Hudsons had featured as one of the main items they repeated in an endless loop of headlines. You couldn't keep a crime like that contained to just a small town. Words like 'slain', 'slaughter', and 'bloodbath' were bandied about. There were interviews with neighbours of Jess and Stephen who were 'completely shocked' and 'had no idea what kind of monster lived on their street'.

The more I watched, the harder I ran, until my calves cramped and my thighs trembled and my breath came in irregular pants, lungs screaming with effort. My head felt as if it were about to explode.

'Sick bastard,' the man running next to me said out loud when a photo of Dean appeared on-screen. It was probably taken in the last few years. Dean stared angrily at the camera, his eyes hard and cold, head tilted in a defiant gesture. Of course they'd picked one that made him look deranged, but really the photo probably only showed a split second in which he'd been caught off guard, like we all are sometimes. Where had they got that from? Maybe one of his friends or his social media page.

I pressed the downwards arrow to slow my pace until the treadmill stopped, not bothering with a cool-down, and rushed into the changing rooms to stretch in private, ignoring the few other women in there. I hit the showers and got changed, then drove to Barbara's house.

A group of reporters and camera crews were lined up outside her three-bed semi-detached house, filling up the street. I spied the man in the baseball cap with the bad skin again. Brian was there, too, even though it was a Saturday morning and he didn't usually work then. I caught him laughing carelessly with another guy as I drove past.

The road was so full of cars and TV news vans that I had to park a couple of streets away and double back on foot. I heard the rowdy hum of conversation in the air even before I rounded the corner again.

Poor Barbara.

I pushed through the crowd that was hungry for all the gory details, ignoring the quick-fire shouted questions about who I was and paying no attention to Brian's voice saying, 'Oi! This is *my* bloody story! What are you doing here?'

I knocked on Barbara's door and waited. The curtains in the lounge were closed. Was I as bad as them all for being here?

No, I told myself. I'm not after a story. I just want to comfort my friend's mother. Give her my support. That's all.

I knocked again but there was no response. Of course not. Even if Barbara was up to visitors, she wouldn't open the door to who she thought was the press.

I thought about going down through the gate at the side of the house and knocking on the window at the back. I'd been through that gate before hundreds of times with Jess, preferring to spend time at her house instead of mine. Barbara was easy-going and fun. Being a vet, Barbara had always brought home cute animals to foster, too, which I'd loved making a fuss over. But it felt wrong of me to walk through the gate now, so I opened up the letter box instead.

'Barbara, it's Holly Gold. I'm so sorry. I just wanted to . . . let you . . . give you my condolences.' For someone who was always using words, I didn't have a clue what to say. What sounded good enough? Nothing.

I heard no sound. No movement from within. The house was silent.

And then there was a noise. It could've been a sob. Could've been a hiccup.

'Holly?' Barbara's voice croaked out from somewhere within.

'Yes. It's me. I understand if you want to be alone, but if you need anything, just . . . you can call me. I wanted to tell you how sorry I am.'

Another painful sob. Then she called out, 'Come round the back.'

I closed the letter box and walked along the side of the house, towards the gate, making sure not to catch Brian's eye. I tried the latch but it was bolted from the other side, so I waited, hearing the sound of Barbara's back door opening, her shuffling footsteps on the path, and then the bolt being drawn back.

Not surprisingly, Barbara looked awful – raw eyelids, swollen face, her jaw-length hair, which was normally tongued to perfection, flattened to her head.

I enveloped her in a hug. Held on tight. She felt fragile beneath me.

'Barbara.' I rubbed her back gently as she clutched me to her silently for a minute or so.

She pulled back abruptly and wiped her eyes, sniffing. 'Come in.' Her shoulders sagged as she shuffled back into the house as if her body were too heavy to keep upright. I hadn't been in her house for years – not since I was eighteen. The night of my leaving do I'd called for Jess before we'd gone into town. The place hadn't changed much since then. A familiar smell of home-cooking and Barbara's lavender body spray filled the air, etched into the seams of the place over the years.

She sank down on to a chair at the kitchen table, her body slumped, as if her spine had turned to jelly. A black cat jumped on to the windowsill outside and miaowed to be let in, but Barbara didn't seem to hear it. I sat next to her and took her hand.

'Those people out there are vultures,' she snapped, her eyes watering with unshed tears. 'I've even had to unplug the phone. They keep ringing and ringing! They won't leave me alone!'

'Didn't the police send a family liaison officer to help you? They could deal with all that for you.'

She nodded and then shook her head. 'They tried to, but I refused their offer. I don't want a stranger here, watching me, fussing around, spouting false sympathies.' She groaned. 'I can't believe this has happened.' Her face looked empty, hollow, pale. A ghost of the woman she'd once been. 'I mean, at first I thought there had to be some mistake. It's just . . . it's bad enough that they're all gone, but the police are saying . . . they think . . . that Dean was responsible. How can that be?'

'There has to be some mistake.' I squeezed her hand, trying to sound more confident than I felt. 'I don't see how Dean could do something like that.'

'I spoke to the police a little while ago and they said it's true.' She took a shuddering breath and pressed her free hand to her chest.

I shook my head slightly.

'They said their forensic people have worked out what happened. Dean killed Stephen first while he was asleep in bed.' Her hand withdrew from mine and cupped round her mouth. She breathed hard, her shoulders rising and falling, the tears she'd been keeping in check finally let loose, streaming in rivulets down her cheeks and dripping on to the table.

'Can I get you something? Water? Something stronger?'

She waved my offer away and started again, speaking fast, as if she had to get the words out in one go. 'They said Dean stabbed him five times in the chest. And then Jess was . . . they said Jess must've woken up. She was twisted over, you see, half lying out of the bed. They said Dean stabbed her in the back three times.' She closed her eyes briefly. 'I think she was trying to get away.'

I clenched my hands in my lap, saliva flooding my mouth.

'And then . . . a short while after he'd done it, Dean hung himself.' She pulled a tissue out of her sleeve and wiped her nose, then crumpled the tissue in her hand. 'I was the one who raised the alarm. I was supposed to go shopping with Jess. I went to the house and knocked on the door and there was no answer. I . . . I tried the spare key I've got, but the door was deadbolted from inside. I . . . I couldn't get in. I called the police. I knew something was wrong. She wasn't . . . she wouldn't answer me.'

I thought that the door being locked from the inside was the only good piece of news. If Barbara had seen what had happened in that house she'd never get the image out of her head. But even then, as I knew too well, the imagined images could crush you just as fiercely.

I moved my chair closer to hers, unsure if I should reach out again. When I was a kid, Barbara had hugged and kissed me and made me feel secure and loved. I'd thought of her as my second mum – the one who was ready with encouragement and kind words and smiles and freshly baked scones. I'd *wanted* her to be my mum, instead of the stone-cold one I had, who only cared about Miles and barely tolerated Zoe and me. Since Dad passed away, I'd hardly kept in contact with Mum any more, but moving back to Ashfield meant I saw her sometimes at Miles's house. Our relationship was strained to say the least. Zoe was better at forgiving and forgetting than me. Or maybe Zoe maintained a relationship with Mum for Leigh's sake – she is Leigh's grandmother after all. Maybe I, too, would've felt differently if things with Richard had worked out the way they were supposed to. Maybe I'd have put aside all the bad years with Mum for the sake of my son or daughter to have a relationship with their gran.

I wanted to take Barbara's pain away, but I felt useless. No one could do that. All I could do was let her talk, if she wanted to, and just be there for her.

'I don't understand,' she continued. 'I don't understand how it could've happened. Dean was . . . he was such a lovely lad. Polite, a good student, helpful round the house. He was bubbly and funny. He had his moments, of course, like all teenagers do, but he was a good boy. Why would he do it?' She stared at me blankly. 'There was nothing . . . nothing to indicate he could do something like . . .' She inhaled a shuddering breath. 'I knew him. I *did* know my grandson. So how . . . how . . .' She broke off and wailed loudly.

I rubbed her hand. 'When did you last see Dean?'

'Last weekend. They all came here for Sunday dinner. They were all fine. All seemed to be getting along as usual. There were no arguments or anything.'

'But something must've happened to make him snap. Was Dean involved in drugs? Or had he got in with a bad crowd?'

'No! Of course not. He was a good boy!'

'I'm sorry. I'm just trying to make sense of it, too.'

'He was definitely not into drugs. And there was no bad crowd at his sixth form college. It's one of the best in the county. A lot of their students go on to Oxford or Cambridge. They're all intelligent, hard-working kids.'

I didn't point out that that didn't mean there couldn't be bad apples – or that there could be drugs around the college, for that matter. How many kids took drugs without their parents knowing? There were so many emotions flying around as a teenager, so much pressure from peers, so many temptations to try something new and risky, to want to feel grown-up, to fit in.

'But . . . he'd been working too hard,' Barbara said. 'They put so much responsibility on kids these days. As well as his AS level work, they make them do an extended project, too. He had hardly any spare time any more. He even had to give up his hockey training.' She paused to wipe her nose again. 'Dean was really stressed about his mock exams, worried he was going to fail them. Did you know there was a girl at their college who committed suicide about a year ago? She couldn't cope with the pressure of it all. Dean didn't know her – she was in the year above – but it still shook him up. They had a memorial service for her at the college and he was really upset after he came back.'

'How awful.'

'He wasn't sleeping properly. He was too anxious. Jess said he was up all hours, locked in his room when he wasn't at college, cramming in revision, writing essays. He wasn't eating properly. She suggested all sorts of things to him. Tried to get him to take breaks. Go for a walk. Go out with his friends at weekends to clear his head and switch off. He was always conscientious, but it was like he was obsessed with wanting to do well. He wanted to go to Cambridge and study medicine. Even that Sunday, when they came here, they only stayed long enough to eat dinner because Dean wanted to get back and revise.'

I wondered if the stress of college work had been enough to make him do what he did. Surely not. If he was stressed or agitated, or even depressed, and had been thinking about suicide, surely he would've just killed himself, not taken his parents with him. But what if he'd taken some drug to keep him going so he could study harder? What if it hadn't agreed with him – made him psychotic?

'That must be why.' Barbara's voice dragged me from my thoughts. 'The stress made him act irrationally. Must've made him snap. If that college was responsible for the other girl's death, it could be the same now. They can't get away with that, can they?' Barbara said. 'They can't just . . .' She let out another sob, throwing her head into her hands.

I leaned towards her, wrapping my arms around her shoulders, letting her cry until the shudders subsided. Eventually, she pulled away, stood up and snatched several tissues from a box on the worktop next to the microwave in quick succession. She blew her nose, threw the tissues in the bin, and switched on the kettle with her back to me.

She made tea in a proper teapot, just like she always used to, covering it with a tea cosy she'd knitted herself, and brought it to the table with two mugs and a carton of milk. She poured out a stream of amber liquid into both mugs with a shaky hand and pushed one towards me.

I topped mine up with milk and remembered what Zoe had said about Dean visiting the practice where she worked. 'Did Dean see a doctor to get something to help him sleep or to talk about some problems? Was the stress about his exams making him depressed, do you think?'

She stared at her tea like she couldn't remember making it. 'Jess was really worried about him. First, she insisted on him taking vitamins. It was obvious Dean was run down with it all. She knew how important it was for him to sleep, but he was only snatching a few hours here and there. It was making him moody and argumentative, obviously, but I don't think he was depressed. She suggested first that he speak to his tutors or the college counsellor if he was so worried about the work, but he didn't want to. She approached the subject several times with him, but he said he didn't want any kind of mark on his records that showed he couldn't cope. He didn't want to be a quitter because all his mates were coping with it OK. He thought he'd be labelled a failure if he admitted there was a problem.'

I knew that feeling well.

'So Jess made an appointment with this doctor. He sees adults, but he's also an expert in child psychiatry. Jess thought talking to him might help Dean, and Dean *did* seem a bit brighter after the first session. This doctor gave Dean something mild to help him sleep. We all thought Dean would be more able to cope with everything if he wasn't so tired all the time. But the tablets didn't seem to help with that and he stopped taking them last week.'

I took a sip of tea. 'What else did the police say?'

'I don't think they're interested in *why* Dean could've done something like that. Now they've got the evidence that it was definitely Dean and not an intruder, it seems like they're just going to wrap it up and move on to the next thing. Now they've got their suspect and they can't prosecute him they don't seem interested. But I *want* to know *why*! Someone's got to be responsible for making him do it, and I think it's the college's fault.' She pushed her tea away and turned to me, her eyes narrowed with anger and so much more. 'Will you help me find out? You're a journalist; you know what questions to ask.'

'I'm not a journalist.' *Probably never will be at this rate.* 'If anything, I'm a columnist or crappy feature writer.'

'But you're used to researching, aren't you? If the college is to blame, if drugs are to blame, if it's something else, I *need* to know what turned Dean into a . . . what made him do this. And if the police won't dig beneath the surface and find out, then you're all I've got. I've got nothing left now – at least help me find some answers.' She reached her hand across the table and clutched my arm. '*Please.*'

I thought about my stupid pride stopping me from getting back in touch with Jess after I'd returned to Ashfield – how life had got in the way over the years and made us lose touch in the first place. I thought about how I'd been wallowing in self-pity, never feeling good enough. Why hadn't I just picked up the bloody phone and called her? Helping Barbara was the least I could do in return for all of her kindness over the years. I placed a hand over hers. 'Of course I will, if that's what you want.'

She gave me a fleeting, grateful half-smile. 'She missed you, you know. When you fell out of touch. She thought you were living the high life in London with new friends and a glamorous job. She didn't think she was good enough for you any more. She thought you'd find her life boring.'

I stifled my own sob then. How stupid I'd been. Now I *wanted* the cosy family life Jess had had. The newborn baby in my arms, the familiarity of a kind husband coming home at the end of the day, rather than the excitement that eventually fades to dullness, and the back-stabbing and empty promises of people who tell you what you want to hear to keep you in line. 'Oh, God, it was nothing like that at all. My life wasn't as glossy as the pages of that magazine. I really missed Jess, too.'

And now it was too late to tell her.

Chapter 5

I left Barbara's house armed with a list of four names belonging to Dean's closest friends. Barbara had only known the address of one of them because she'd dropped Dean off there on her way home from Jess and Stephen's house a few months ago.

I pushed through the crowd of press outside her house who called out questions and took photos. Their numbers had dwindled a little since I'd been inside. In a few days they'd be gone, having moved on to the next sensational story.

Brian grabbed my elbow as I passed him. I shook him off and stormed down the street towards my car, but he followed.

'Let's get one thing straight. Just because you had some flashy job before doesn't mean you can try to muscle in on my assignments.'

I stopped walking and turned to face him. He was red faced, as usual. The smell of alcohol was practically oozing out of his every pore. But then who was I to talk?

'The Hudsons were my *friends*, you fucking heartless bastard! I'm not muscling in on any story. I'm not even writing a story! I'm trying to find out what happened.'

'Yeah, right! Maybe that's why you've never made it as a *proper* journalist. Too caring and happy-clappy, are you? Well, let me tell you, there's no room for *heart* in this job.' He sneered. 'I know exactly what you're trying to do here.'

'Well, you're wrong. Don't judge me by your own standards.' I carried on walking, leaving him standing there.

'It won't work, you know!' he called after me. 'Neil and I go way back. Don't think you can take my job!'

I let out an angry growl and walked faster. Maybe I shouldn't have sworn at him. I wasn't doing myself any favours, and I was sure my words and actions would all be reported back to Neil over a pint. But at that moment I didn't even care. Fuck the lot of them.

When I climbed into my car, I slammed the door shut and leaned back against the headrest just as my mobile phone rang. I pulled it out of my bag and accepted Zoe's call.

'Hi,' my sister's cheery voice sang down the phone. She was always happy, even at 5 a.m. when Leigh had been teething and she'd had no sleep all night. Zoe didn't give a shit what people thought. Not in the arrogant way of Miles, but in an I'm-comfortable-in-my-own-skin kind of way. I wished I could be more like her. I *had* been like her before Richard. We'd had to be, growing up with a distant dad and a mum who didn't care. Had to fend for ourselves emotionally. But now I'd lost myself and didn't know who I was these days. 'I just wanted to find out how you were after everything that happened yesterday with Jess and that.'

'Thanks, Zo. I'm still shocked and pretty upset. The thing is, I don't know if I've got the right to be, though, after all this time. It's not like we were close any more.'

'Don't be silly. You feel what you feel. It is how it is, that's it.'

'Thanks. I've just been to see Barbara. It was horrible.'

'Poor woman. All her family just wiped out like that. Has she got anyone with her?'

'No. Her husband died years ago. I didn't like to ask her about Stephen's family, but she didn't mention them and I didn't want to pry. Some people prefer to be on their own at a time like this, don't they?' I said, speaking from experience.

I heard Leigh call out '*Mummy! I've finished!*'

'Look, I've got to go. But I wanted to know if you fancied coming round for lunch or something?'

'Thanks. Maybe I'll pop round later. I'm going to speak to Dean's friends and find out if they knew what was going on with him. Barbara thinks the college is responsible for what happened.'

'The college?'

'Dean was under a lot of stress and not sleeping.'

'That's very worrying. But I know what she's saying about the pressure in education these days. They're doing exams for four-year-olds in school now. It's ridiculous! Whatever happened to kids being kids?'

'Barbara wants some answers. And I do, too.'

'The college isn't going to admit to any kind of negligence.'

'I know, especially if there are now two teenage suicides linked to the place.'

'Two?' she asked.

I told her about the girl in the year above Dean that Barbara had mentioned. 'They'll try to sweep it under the carpet. But I said I'd help her. She's desperate.'

And so am I. I have to prove I can at least do something right. And I have to do it. For Jess.

'OK, I'll let you go then. Just turn up if you feel like it. I'm in all day and I've got plenty of food.'

'Thanks.' I hung up and turned on the local radio.

'*A police investigation is still continuing in connection with the brutal and gruesome murders at Draper Avenue, Ashfield. The bodies of Jess and Stephen Hudson were discovered at the house, along with their son, Dean, early on Friday morning. A police spokesman said forensic examination of the scene is still ongoing.*

'*And in other news, all train services from Ashfield Station have been suspended due to a suspected suicide. Witnesses reported a young woman jumping in front of a train at 10.30 a.m. Officials have not yet identified the woman. We'll have more updates as they come—*'

I switched the radio off before they could say any more, unwilling to listen to another story about death and suicide, and drove the rest of the way in silence.

~

Howard Becker was apparently Dean's best friend and went to the same college. He lived in an executive house in a neat cul-de-sac with two cars parked on the driveway. I sat in my car outside for a moment, letting potential questions roll around in my head. I must've sat there too long, looking suspicious, because the front door opened and a man in his late forties strode down the front path with a face like thunder.

'If you're the press, you can get lost right now,' he shouted out, loud enough for me to hear with the windows closed. 'My son's not talking to anyone!'

I got out of the car. 'I'm sorry to disturb you, Mr Becker. I'm a friend of the Hudsons.'

The creased look of anger on his face took a little while to deflate.

'Dean's gran, Barbara, wanted me to try and look into why it happened. She gave me your son's name. I understand he was good friends with Dean, and I just wanted to speak to him and see if he can tell me what was going on with Dean lately.'

'Howard's too upset to speak to anyone else. We had the police here for hours yesterday. Sorry, but I can't help you. Please give Barbara my condolences. It's a tragedy.'

I nodded, not wanting to push it any further. Brian's voice echoed in my head: *There's no room for* heart *in this job.* Maybe he was right and I didn't have what it took to follow up a real story. Mum's words filtered through, too: *You'll never amount to anything.* I shook them away and concentrated on Mr Becker's face.

A voice called out then from the half-open doorway behind Mr Becker and a teenage boy appeared.

'Dad? What's going on?'

Mr Becker turned around. 'Get back inside the house, Howard.'

Howard eyed me carefully before turning around and sloping back inside.

'I don't want anyone blaming my boy – writing rubbish about how he should've seen some sign and missed it.'

'That's not my intention at all. Maybe I can give you my number and you can call me when Howard's feeling a bit more up to it.' I scrabbled inside my bag for my pad and pen. 'Barbara just wants to understand how something like this could've happened. I'm trying to help her.' I scrawled my name and number down and held it out to him.

Mr Becker looked at the paper flapping in the breeze between my fingers like it might catch fire.

'If it were your grandson, wouldn't you want to know why?' I said.

He didn't answer, but he did reach out and take my number before returning to his house.

I got back in my car. I'd been hoping Howard could've told me the addresses for the next three friends on my list because Barbara hadn't been sure where they all lived. It would've helped if I could've got access to Dean's address book or phone, but I was sure the police would still have those.

I pulled my mobile phone from my bag and searched Google, looking for the name Moffatt on directory enquiries, which was the surname of another friend of Dean's. I didn't think it would be a particularly common name, but there was no listing. Next, I logged into Facebook and pulled up Dean's page. If I could find the pages matching the other friends' names that Barbara had given me, I could message them and see if they'd talk to me.

I hadn't been on Facebook for at least a year. Not since I'd moved back here. What would I have said? *Split up with boyfriend who happened to be my boss who happened to be using me #feelingshit. Quit my job and will probably never get the chance to be a serious journalist #failure!*

Dean's page had no privacy settings so I was able to access everything. I scrolled through the entries on Dean's wall. His last post had been three months ago – a video of a teenager tearing his hair out while revising. There was a photo taken at college four months ago of Dean and some friends, arms around each other and smiling. I recognised Howard. Dean looked happy, although it was easy to hide emotions behind a smile. I'd been doing so for a long time. Was that before college work had got him so stressed and anxious? Before he'd thought about killing his parents and himself? Or had he known then what he was going to do? I stared at the photo for what seemed like ages, hoping it would give me an answer. I was so engrossed in it that the knock on my window only registered as a vague background noise at first.

The second knock jerked my head up.

Howard stood beside my car in a sloppy T-shirt and jogging bottoms, pensively shifting his weight from one foot to the other. His eyes were bloodshot.

I opened the door and stepped out, glancing from him to his front door, thinking his dad would appear in a minute and haul him back inside. 'Hi, Howard. I'm Holly. Did your dad tell you I wanted to talk to you?'

'No. I heard what you said to him.'

'Does he know you're outside with me?'

He shook his head. 'Nah. Said I was going for a walk. Come on.' He stuffed his hands into his pockets, shoulders hunched up to his ears, and strode around the corner of the cul-de-sac.

'I'm sorry. Barbara said you and Dean were good mates.' I hurried to keep up with him.

'I can't believe it,' he said. 'It doesn't make any sense. I'm really fucking confused.' He glanced warily at me out of the corner of his eye, as if I was going to berate him for swearing.

'I can't believe it, either,' I said as he cut through a tiny alleyway tucked in between two houses that led to Cooper Park. You wouldn't have even noticed the gap if you didn't know about it. 'But I hadn't seen Dean since he was little so I didn't have a clue what was going on with him lately.'

He pulled a packet of cigarettes from his pocket and lit one. He glanced at me again, as if expecting me to tell him off, then said, 'Want one?'

'No, thanks.'

We walked along the edge of the park towards an empty play area with slides and swings.

'It's just mental, isn't it?' Howard took a hard drag on the cigarette and blew out a long stream of smoke.

'Was there anything about Dean's behaviour that suggested he might do something like that?'

'Course not!'

'OK, maybe not kill his parents, but did you ever think he was suicidal or depressed?'

'No! He didn't talk to me about feeling . . . you know, like he was going to do something bad. And I feel shit. Like I should've seen it. Like maybe it's all my fault because I . . .' He glanced away from me, across the park. He sniffed and wiped his nose on the shoulder of his T-shirt. 'Maybe I could've stopped it.'

'How? How could you have if you didn't think anything was wrong? It's not your fault. If Dean didn't talk to you, how could you know?'

'But I feel like I should've seen it coming.'

We reached the swings. Howard sat down on one, puffing away vigorously. I sat next to him. We both stared straight ahead at a line of trees, obscuring the high street in the distance.

'Barbara said he was worried and anxious about college work. He was studying really hard for his mocks. Do you think that could've been enough to tip him over the edge?'

'Dean always had to work more than me. He was intelligent, yeah, but he had to study hard to get the same grades.'

'You were in competition with each other?'

'No. Nothing like that.'

But maybe it was like that. Maybe kids were always in competition with each other. I knew that from my own childhood. Miles was the favourite I could never live up to, no matter how hard I tried. When you're a kid, a teenager, there's so much pressure coming at you from all angles. I suppose when you grow up and finally become an adult you forget just how much. Or the pressure festers away and grows into something else.

'He was studying hard. He got kind of obsessed over it. He wanted to go to Cambridge. Wanted to be a doctor. The last few months he kept talking about not being good enough. He got an F in an assignment recently and freaked out. He didn't want to fail his mocks so he was hitting the books properly mental. He didn't come out with me any more. We stopped playing NHL 15 online.'

'What's that?'

'It's an ice hockey game on Xbox we'd play – he'd be at his house and I'd be at mine.'

'Right,' I said, making a mental note to look at Dean's laptop when the police had finished with it. Maybe he'd visited some suicide chat rooms. Or maybe he was talking to someone else online about how he'd felt recently.

Howard took one final draw on the cigarette and threw it on the ground, stubbing it out with the toe of his trainer.

'When did you last see Dean?' I asked.

He swallowed hard, his Adam's apple rising and falling. 'Thursday. At college.'

And Dean had killed his parents and himself in the early hours of Friday morning. It was hard to believe there were no signs at all.

'Did he seem . . . I don't know . . . agitated? Or angry? Or down?'

Howard chewed on his lower lip for a moment. 'He was a bit weird. He said he was really tired. He wasn't sleeping properly and he'd got some tablets from the doctor but they weren't helping so he stopped taking them. I walked to college with him and it was like he was a bit manic. Really hyper. Walking fast, eyes all over the place. I was telling him he'd missed a good party at the weekend and it seemed like he wasn't really listening to me. He'd just add a few yeses and noes to the conversation, but it was mostly me doing the talking. It seemed like he had his mind on something else, but we had a mock exam that morning so I thought he was just going through some last-minute study questions in his head. 'When we got to college we dumped our kit in our lockers. Fraser and Alfie were there, but they were both taking a different exam so they disappeared pretty much straight away.'

Fraser and Alfie were both names Barbara had given me. 'Did Dean speak to Fraser and Alfie?'

'I think they just said hellos. Nothing major. Then Dean and I headed for the exam room. We were in there two and a half hours. Dean was sitting at the front and I was at the back, so by the time I got out he was nowhere to be seen. I thought he would've waited for me. We had free study periods for the rest of the day, but we would've usually walked home together.' He pulled out another cigarette and lit it.

'So you didn't see him again?'

He shook his head, staring down at the ground, kicking it with his heel.

I put my hand on his shoulder. 'It's not your fault.'

'Yeah, right.'

'Was Dean being bullied?'

'No. Course not. He was popular. Everyone liked Dean. Besides, he was a hockey player – before he gave it up because of studying. But still, he was fit. He could handle himself.'

'Was he having problems with a girlfriend?'

'He didn't have a girlfriend. I mean, he had friends who were girls but nothing . . . you know . . . romantic.'

'Did Dean take drugs?'

Howard flinched but didn't look at me. 'No.'

'He never tried anything? Not even a spliff?'

Howard took a puff of his cigarette again. With his free hand he scratched his elbow hard.

'Howard? If you know something, please tell me. Maybe he took something to help him stay awake so he could study longer. It wouldn't be the first time someone's done it. It could've been something that didn't agree with him. Or maybe it was some dodgy mix that affected him badly enough to do something like that. Gave him some kind of psychotic trip.'

'Look, we did weed a couple of times in the past. That's it. Nothing heavy. He wasn't really into that kind of thing. Neither am I.'

'When in the past?'

He shrugged. 'Once at a party about a year ago. The other time was with Fraser a few months ago, but I wasn't there.'

'Where did the weed come from? Who got hold of it?'

He avoided my questioning gaze. He just said, 'He didn't do drugs, all right?'

'But there must've been something – something that tipped Dean over the edge. You don't murder your parents and kill yourself for no reason.'

'I don't know why he did it!' He threw the cigarette down next to his last one, grinding it viciously into the ground.

'There was a girl at your college who committed suicide last year, wasn't there?'

'Yeah. She was in the year above.'

'Did it affect Dean badly? Did he become obsessed about it or anything?'

'We were all shook up. It was horrible. But he wasn't, like, brooding about it or anything. We didn't even know her. We'd just seen her around.'

'Do you know why she did it?'

He shrugged. 'I heard she couldn't take the pressure.'

'Of the college, you mean?'

'I heard her parents were pushing her too hard. She had a breakdown.' Another shrug, then he added, 'Obviously.'

I swung myself in the seat slowly, hanging on to the metal chains. 'Do you think the college pushes its students too hard, then? Puts too much pressure on you all?'

'The work *is* hard, yeah. But that's just the way it is. If we want to get into Cambridge or Oxford we've got to step up the game.'

'And Dean was struggling with the work,' I said.

Howard's answer was a slight nod.

'Was it his parents pushing him to do well?'

'No. It was Dean. His mum said he should do whatever made him happy. I think she thought all this stressing Dean was doing wasn't worth it. She wouldn't have minded him dropping out and getting a job. My parents are a lot worse than Dean's, believe me.'

'Did he ever tell you how he felt about his parents? Did he complain about them? Slag them off?' I thought about Jess and Stephen. She was the most easy-going, chilled person I'd known, apart from Zoe. Stephen had always seemed kind and fun with a sarcastic, dry sense of humour.

I didn't think it was a front. That's how they genuinely were. It wasn't like they were cold and distant and uninterested in Dean.

Howard glanced over at me, his forehead knitted with what looked like worry – or guilt.

'What? What did Dean say?'

His gaze slid away, back to the ground. 'Just, you know, the usual things. I moan about my parents all the time. Everyone does it. Doesn't mean I'm going to kill them!'

I could relate to that. I was still complaining about my parents now. It was human nature. Even the best, most functional of families pissed each other off from time to time. 'But what exactly did he say?'

'Normal stuff. He moaned that his mum was stifling him. That he didn't have any privacy because she kept coming in his room and cleaning it all the time. That his dad kept wanting to take him on 'boys' days out' and he didn't want to go any more. That they didn't understand him. Like I said, normal.' He blinked a couple of times, as if trying to stop tears forming. 'But what he did – that's not fucking normal.'

Chapter 6

I headed off to see the only girl on Barbara's list: Keeley Moffatt. Howard told me she worked in a bakery in town called Right Bites so I parked in the pay-and-display car park and walked down the high street, wondering if she would've called in sick after what had happened.

The queue was almost out the door when I entered the shop, the smell of yeast filling the air. My stomach rumbled as I eyed the doughnuts and chocolate eclairs. I hadn't felt like eating breakfast this morning, and after my early bout of exercise, I was pretty sure I was just running on adrenaline and the early-morning caffeine hit I'd had before leaving home.

There were two members of staff working behind the counter: a middle-aged woman with her hair piled up underneath a netted cap and another girl, late teens, unsmiling and moving mechanically to fill orders. She had the obligatory hairnet over a topknot and no make-up on. She was pale and delicate-looking, as if the effort of packing cakes and sausage rolls was too much for her. I watched her as the queue moved slowly along. When she handed some change to one of the customers, they complained she'd given them the wrong amount. She apologised and stared at the till for a moment, as if disorientated. The woman who was next in line huffed and tapped her foot impatiently.

Eventually, the girl counted out the right change, the customer left, and we all edged forward by one.

'What can I get you?' the girl asked when it was my turn, not quite meeting my eyes.

'Are you Keeley?' I smiled.

She looked at me properly then. 'Yeah.'

'Do you have time to talk? It's about Dean.'

She blinked rapidly, as if she were about to burst into tears – or worried about something. Nervous, maybe?

'I'm a friend of the family.'

She glanced to the older lady behind the counter who was bagging a sliced white loaf.

'I'm . . . working. I can't talk now.'

'Do you get a break? We could talk then.'

'Uh . . . OK. I guess.' She looked at her watch. 'I'm due a break in half an hour.'

'Great. I can wait for you. Can I get a doughnut and a white coffee, please?'

She put a doughnut on a plate and turned around to the coffee machine. She rang up my purchase at a till on the end of the counter and I placed my money in her hand, her skin cold against mine.

I spied a seat in a corner and pointed in that direction. 'I'll be over there when you get a sec.'

'OK.'

While I ate and drank, I tried to process everything Howard and Barbara had told me, rearranging it in my head again and again. So far Dean sounded like he'd been conscientious, hard-working, and focused, but had become obsessed about doing well and getting into Cambridge. So he'd dabbled in a couple of spliffs, but what teenager hadn't? Or was Howard covering for him? I wouldn't know until Barbara got the post-mortem results back to see if there were any drugs in his system. Dean had stopped going out with Howard and his mates. Stopped playing games online. Stopped hockey training. Holed himself up in his room. Were these signs of depression, or something else?

I was checking my phone when Keeley appeared in front of me. She'd removed her hairnet and had a denim jacket on over her uniform.

'You knew Dean, too?' she asked.

'Yes. And his parents. His gran wants to understand what happened. She asked me to speak to his friends. Are you OK talking with me?'

'Yeah. I suppose. But not here. Can we go outside?'

'Sure.' I stood up and followed her out. 'How about we sit over there?' There was a wooden bench a little further along the street and we made our way over to it.

She sat down on the edge of the bench, shoulders rounded, hands stuffed into the pockets of her jacket in much the same posture as Howard.

She looked at me, her forehead creased. 'I didn't *want* to come to work today,' she said, as if I'd accused her of being heartless for carrying on with life as normal. 'I can't really think straight at the moment. But if I don't come in they'll probably sack me and I need the money.'

'I spoke to Howard Becker and Barbara. They said you were friends with Dean. I'm just really trying to find out why he did what he did.'

'I've got no idea! I'm really shocked. I never would've thought he could *do* that! It's proper bad.'

'How long have you known Dean?'

'Since secondary school. We used to hang out sometimes. He was really sweet. A good laugh. How could I have been so wrong about him?' She chewed on her bottom lip, a pained expression twisting her face.

'Were you just friends, or was it more than that? Were you seeing him?'

'We . . . um . . . we were friends.' But her voice had a wistful edge to it.

'Did you want it to be more than that?' I said gently.

A brief look flashed across her face. Worry? Revulsion? I wasn't sure.

'Yes, I suppose. But what does that make me? That I thought a murderer was fit? I feel terrible.'

'Did Dean give you any inkling of what he was about to do?'

'No way! I keep thinking this is all a bad dream. That it hasn't really happened and I'm going to wake up. There was nothing he ever said at all that . . . I swear!' Her eyes widened.

'It's OK. I believe you.'

'I hadn't seen him for about a month. I didn't go to the college. Not brainy enough for that. Whenever I suggested hooking up lately he said he was too busy with revision.'

'Did you ever go to his house?'

'Yeah. But not for ages.'

'How did he seem with his parents?'

She frowned slightly. 'I don't know. They all seemed to get on all right. His mum was really nice. I only met his dad a few times because he was always at work, but he seemed OK.'

'Did Dean ever talk to you about his parents? Were there any arguments he told you about? Or do you think he was angry at them for something?'

She shook her head. 'No. He never said anything like that.' She picked at the pink nail varnish she wore, sending chips of it fluttering down on to her knee.

'Did he ever mention suicide?'

'No. Never. The last time I saw him he was fine. Really.' She stopped picking and swiped at her cheeks, at the tears that were now beginning to fall.

'I'm really sorry, Keeley.'

She sniffed. 'Yeah. Me, too.'

'Did Dean ever mention doing drugs?'

She chewed on her thumbnail and ignored the question, shuffling in her seat with what appeared to be discomfort.

'You won't be in trouble if you tell me. But it may have had something to do with things.'

'We smoked weed at a party a while back. With Alfie and some others. But that was it. Dean said it was a mug's game.' She looked at her watch and stood up, not quite meeting my eyes. 'I've got to get back now.'

'OK. Thanks for talking to me. If you think of anything else – anything that might've happened with Dean – could you give me a ring?' I ripped a piece of paper from my pad and scribbled my number for her.

She took it and stuffed it in her pocket. She stared at the ground for a moment. 'Can you love someone and hate them at the same time?'

I thought of Richard and was about to say yes, but it was too late. Keeley had already walked back into the bakery.

Chapter 7

Fraser's house was an arty modern new build – an infill of land nestled between two older large houses. It wouldn't have looked out of place on the TV programme *Grand Designs*, but to me it was ugly. All windows and obtrusive angles. It seemed cold and uninviting and lacked privacy.

I rang the bell and the door was opened by a teenage lad wearing a hoodie and jogging bottoms. He was overweight and had angry red spots on his chin.

'Hi, are you Fraser Childs?'

'Yes?' he said uncertainly.

'My name's Holly. I'm a friend of the Hudsons. *Was* a friend,' I corrected. 'Dean's gran has asked me to speak to his friends and try to find out how something like this could have happened. Would it be OK to talk to you about Dean?'

'I don't know.' He glanced behind him. There was another lad there, too, hovering in the background. Skinny, short, about the same age. 'My parents aren't here.'

'Would you prefer me to come back when your parents are here?'

'Um . . .'

The other lad stepped forward so he was shoulder to shoulder with Fraser. 'What do you want to know?'

'I'm just really trying to get some more information about Dean and what he was going through.'

The skinny lad and Fraser exchanged a look. Skinny shook his head. Fraser shrugged at him then turned to me. 'I suppose it would be OK.' Fraser stepped out of the house, closely followed by the other boy. He sat on the bonnet of a shiny new Mini. 'This is Alfie.' He cocked his head at Skinny.

I smiled at them. 'I actually wanted to speak to both of you. Barbara and Howard said you were both friends of Dean.'

'Yeah, but we don't *know* anything,' Alfie said, a defensive note in his voice. 'And the police have already asked us loads of questions.' He folded his arms across his chest.

'But you both saw him at college on Thursday, didn't you? How did he seem?'

Fraser glanced at Alfie for a brief moment before turning back to me. 'I don't think he even said two words. I thought he was nervous about his exam.'

I looked at Alfie. He didn't say anything.

'Howard thought he was acting a bit weird,' I said.

'We didn't see anything,' Alfie snapped. 'And we don't know anything. He was obviously fucked in the head and good at hiding it.'

I ignored his animosity and carried on addressing Fraser, who seemed more open to talking. 'Did Dean ever mention suicide? Or having any violent thoughts towards his parents?'

'No way!' Fraser said.

'Do you think he could've taken something before the exam?'

'Define "something",' Alfie said, but I'm sure he knew exactly what I meant.

'Apparently, Howard thought Dean was very agitated and hyper. He hadn't been sleeping well. Do you think he might've taken some type of drug to help him stay awake for the exam?'

Alfie glared at me. 'You can't ask us stuff like that! You've got no authority. Come on, Fraser.' He walked up the path, then stopped when he realised Fraser hadn't moved. He turned back, treated me to another angry glare, then went inside the house.

'I'm not trying to get you into trouble,' I said. 'This is obviously very serious. And something *made* Dean do it. His gran just wants to find out what.'

Fraser inhaled a breath and fidgeted with the zip on the front of his hoodie, sliding it up and down. 'I know it's serious. And we don't want to get tarred with the same brush. These things stick, don't they? And we're going to Oxford, Alfie and I. We don't want to be caught up in something like this. It's bad. Really bad.' He tugged on the zip so hard I thought it would break. 'I feel terrible. We all do. We were mates with Dean, yes. We'd known him since secondary school, but I'm telling you there was nothing that happened – ever – that made me think, "Yes, Dean's going to murder his parents one day!" He was a great guy. And now he's not. Now he's just a fucking psycho!'

'Nothing happened at all? There must've been something that might explain his behaviour.'

'You can't explain it. It's unexplainable,' Fraser said, pushing himself to his feet and leaving me standing there.

Chapter 8

I drove to the supermarket and perused the aisles, hoping for some inspiration. Cooking for one was just sad. Plus, my appetite had deserted me again. When I'd been with Richard, I'd gone through a learning-to-cook phase. I'd wanted to be a woman who could do everything. Contentious and professional reporter by day, domestic goddess by night.

That was before, of course. Before I'd told him about the baby and he'd wanted nothing to do with me. Before he'd admitted he'd been seeing his ex all along behind my back and work had become too uncomfortable to stay there any longer. Before the realisation kicked in that he'd just been using me. And then the miscarriage, which had sent me back to Ashfield to try to get my head together.

I didn't really want to go home now to my pathetically empty flat, where the loneliness seemed to suffocate me more and more each day. I could've gone to Zoe's for some company and food, like she'd offered, but I wanted to get on my laptop and do some research.

I grabbed some meagre essential supplies and a few microwave meals and I stocked up on wine, watching the couples plodding round or the families with kids in tow, trying to stop the jealousy taking hold.

When I got home, I poured a glass of chilled white wine and fired up my laptop. While I waited for it to boot up, I pricked the plastic wrapper on a single portion of lasagne and shoved it in the microwave.

Eight minutes later, the steaming dish on a plate beside me, I googled Downs Road Sixth Form College. The college's website came up, but I saved that for later. I forked in a mouthful of pasta, which had all the consistency of soggy cardboard and the taste to match, and clicked on the next link, which was a student chat room.

Someone had posed a question about whether Downs Road was a good college or not. I scrolled through the replies. One person had written that it had a bad record for pressuring students. Another poster agreed. Someone else asked 'How much pressure?', which remained unanswered. Another comment said it produced the most pretentious people they'd ever met. There was a further post about how Downs Road had a bad record for suicide and drugs. And another comment saying 'If students can't cope with the pressure they shouldn't be there in the first place!', which resulted in several heated replies between the posters. Another person said their sister had gone to Downs Road three years ago and she knew five people in her year who'd had breakdowns because of the stress. Someone else mentioned the name of the girl who'd killed herself last year. Emma Tolley had hung herself after leaving a suicide note saying she couldn't cope with life.

I opened a new tab and googled Emma Tolley. There were several reports from the local papers online and comments from the family, calling for better mental health awareness strategies for young people. Emma's parents said they hadn't recognised any warning signs of depression and hadn't realised anything was wrong with their daughter until she took her life, so they'd never taken her for any counselling or medical treatment. They blamed themselves, but I wondered if the college had played an underlying part in the tragic ending. According to the inquest, Emma's death had been ruled as suicide, although the coroner hadn't mentioned stress being a factor. I tried to find some contact details for Mr and Mrs Tolley, in case they could give me any insight into what Dean had done, but it was reported that they'd moved to an unknown location in Spain after their bereavement in an attempt to start a new life.

I attempted another bite of the lasagne, chewed through the stodge and pushed the dish away. I reached for my wine and took a good gulp as I looked at the college's website, searching for any counselling services they offered students. There were several boasts about them being committed to safeguarding and promoting the welfare of their students, and a big blurb about how they were creating and maintaining a safe and secure environment in which the students could learn and develop whilst encouraging them to actively talk about any concerns they had regarding health, safety, and welfare. There was a whole page dedicated to their Student Services Team, which was there to support students through many aspects of college life, whether they were feeling unwell, unsure about anything or just needed someone to talk to. The college came complete with Wellbeing Advisers and an in-house counselling service.

It sounded good in theory. But what if the students didn't admit they needed help? They could've been too afraid of failure – too embarrassed to talk to someone about how they were feeling. Until it was too late.

Next, I looked up teen suicides and found several worrying articles. One was about a cluster of suicides that had happened within two years in a town in Wales; such clusters were defined as multiple deaths occurring in close succession or location. 'Copycats' who became obsessed with death and the suicides of their fellow students. Dozens of teenagers had killed themselves in what was called an 'epidemic'. Experts were unsure whether an 'Internet cult' or 'backwater town malaise' was to blame, or whether the massive international attention the suicides garnered had romanticised the increasing number of deaths to such an extent that it became contagious. Such clusters were apparently rare, but not new. Experts couldn't agree on a single reason for it happening.

Another article was from the USA, about an elite school where the ten-year suicide rate was way higher than the national average. During 2015, five students had killed themselves, and twelve per cent of the students surveyed in one report said they'd 'seriously contemplated suicide' during the last twelve months.

It would be easy to assume that the kids who'd killed themselves had clear mental health or social issues, or were obviously struggling, but it didn't appear so. They were popular, athletic, full of life, privileged, and seemingly unfazed by their schoolwork. A suicide note left by the last student, Cameron Hicks, said his death had nothing to do with school, social pressures, or friends and family. In fact, there was no clear reason for him doing what he'd done. The only possible anomaly with Cameron was that he never seemed to sleep. When Cameron's parents had asked him why he was up at all hours, his reply had been 'doing homework', but his best friend was quoted as saying that Cameron was 'super intelligent. He didn't need to worry about the work. It all came easy to him.'

Parents of these students were obviously desperately worried because if it could happen to kids who outwardly appeared to be coping, how did they know theirs wouldn't be next? Some began to question what the high-achieving environment was doing to their kids.

A psychologist had said that even teenagers who appeared to be thriving were not necessarily navigating successfully through adolescence, stating that kids are frequently able to hide their failures – whether real or imagined – from parents and teaching staff. Another expert described a growing mental health crisis amongst schools and colleges, going on to say that very accomplished students were falling apart. He added, 'There is a lot of literature that shows academic pressure can cause anxiety and depression, which can then cause suicidality.'

The head of the school and other staff and administrators were also worried about suicide clusters. The school district had put together a new, comprehensive suicide awareness toolkit to try to manage the escalating problem. The school head said, 'One thing that increases the risk for kids is another student's suicide. And a student could be ruminating about it for a long time, but a seemingly ordinary and inconsequential event can sway them into following through.'

But even a psychiatry professor and expert on suicide said, 'We don't really have a good idea of why people kill themselves.' And although Cameron's parents had become obsessed with attempting to piece together every bit of information about his behaviour during the weeks before he died, looking for some kind of explanation, they eventually realised they might never find the main cause or get a satisfying answer, and would have to live with many unresolved questions.

I sat back in my chair, picked up my glass, and stared at the screen, the parallels between Cameron and Dean strikingly clear. I'd forgotten how hard being a teenager was. But then, being an adult wasn't any less stressful, was it?

I could understand Dean's studying being a huge factor in his suicide, along with the lack of sleep, but what about the murder of his parents? Surely the pressure of college couldn't be the *only* reason. Barbara had said they'd all got on well together. Howard had told me they had the usual tiffs that all families do, but there was never anything serious. So *what* had made him do it?

I typed in 'children who killed their parents' and had to refill my glass of wine before I had the stomach to look through the hits.

Thankfully, parricide seemed to be incredibly rare, but the information I could find on previous crimes carried no single underlying theme that pointed to a particular cause. One girl's parents had refused to let her see an older man she was obsessed with, one boy was jealous of his sibling, one boy did it for money – his parents being multi-millionaires – one boy had been abused by his father and his mother had done nothing to help, another girl had been sexually abused by her father, one boy was schizophrenic.

Had Dean been abused? No, surely not. I couldn't see Stephen doing anything like that, but how could you know for certain? Jess had met Stephen on the night of my leaving do when we were eighteen. While I'd been chatting to Will, Stephen had been flirting with Jess in the corner of the bar. But then I'd disappeared to London, only returning for the weekend every few weeks to catch up with her and Zoe. Dean had been an accident early on, but even though Jess and Stephen were still young and in a new relationship, they were ecstatic. And it had worked out for them. They clearly loved each other to bits and doted on Dean when he was born. For the next three years, I'd witnessed their happy relationship whenever I came back to visit – until the journey from London became a chore and I began to prefer going clubbing with my new friends than listening to conversations about nappies and teething. Until the hangovers on a Saturday morning kept me in bed until noon – far too late to bother driving the two-hour trip to Ashfield and back for one night. Until shopping for new clothes became far more important. My life had moved in a different direction and it hadn't included Jess any more. Slowly, the phone calls between us got fewer and fewer or went unreturned. Jess made friends with other new mums and our friendship fell off a cliff.

In all the articles I found about parricide, though, the people who'd killed their parents hadn't taken their own lives afterwards. They didn't seem to be filled with remorse. So what was the trigger for Dean to do both? What poison had been festering away inside him, and what was the catalyst for it to be unleashed?

I did another search: 'children who kill their parents then commit suicide'. This time I didn't find any articles. The only hits were about parents who'd killed their kids and then themselves, not the other way around.

I grabbed a pad and wrote down several thoughts on the page.

Did Dean blame his parents for something? Abuse?

Did he take some kind of illegal drug that didn't agree with him?

Was the lack of sleep making him hallucinate?

Did Dean have some kind of mental health issue or depression that he'd hidden from his parents?

College/lethal amount of stress?

I chewed on the end of my pen and stared at the list, the news report on the radio flashing into my head about the young woman who'd thrown herself in front of a train.

A horrible thought hit me then, and I desperately hoped that what Dean had done hadn't set off a chain reaction of cluster suicides in Ashfield.

Chapter 9

I woke up the next morning on the sofa with a crick in my neck, my shoulders stiff and aching, my head fuggy, an empty wine bottle in my lap.

I wandered into the kitchen for water and headache tablets and spotted the congealed pasta, still in its plastic container where I'd left it on the worktop. I dumped the stinking mess in the bin, my stomach lurching.

I made coffee and toast and ate standing up, staring out of the window down to the communal car park at the back of my flat, wondering what to do next. It was Sunday. No chance of talking to anyone at the college today, and the hours stretched out in front of me. I could go to the gym, but I couldn't be bothered. I could take a walk, but that didn't interest me, either. I could go shopping, but I had to watch my pennies now. My salary at the *Ashfield Post* was rubbish. I had some savings, but I didn't want to delve into them. Best to save them for an even rainier day than today. I wasn't about to give Mum the satisfaction of rubbing my nose in how much of a mess I'd made of my life or turning me down if I asked her for a loan. Even though Dad had left everything to her when he'd died on the understanding that his assets would be passed on to Zoe, Miles, and me when she went, I had no doubt she'd leave it all to Miles. Or spend it all in the meantime, keeping her in the lifestyle she'd grown accustomed to with Dad.

I texted Zoe to see if she was at home, then jumped in the shower. By the time I'd finished and got dressed, she'd texted back saying she and Leigh were heading to Cooper Park. I said I'd meet them there.

It was only a ten-minute walk so I went on foot, hoping I'd catch a bit of sun on the way, and the fresh air would clear my head. I'd noticed lately my skin was pale with dark smudges beneath my eyes. My hair looked limp and faded from its usual glossy sheen. I was washed out. I heard Mum's voice in my head: *You'll never meet a man looking like that!* I pushed it away and carried on walking.

As I neared the park, my phone signalled a text. I retrieved it from my bag and read the message through. It was Miles, asking if I wanted to come over for Sunday dinner. As much as he did my head in, I was glad of the invite. At least it meant a few more hours out of my flat. I fired back a quick *Yes, thanks.*

When I got to the park, I spotted Leigh on the smaller climbing frame, confidently taking steps along a beam that led to a slide. Leigh was fearless in the way that four-year-olds are – before bad things and accidents happen to change the way they look at the world. There was a row of kids behind her, all waiting their turn on the slide.

A huge beaming smile lit up Leigh's face as she whizzed down and then rushed towards Zoe. 'Did you see me, Mummy?' She threw herself at Zoe's waist.

Zoe bent over, arms tight around her little girl, and kissed the top of her head. 'You did great.'

'Auntie Holly!' Leigh noticed me walking up and then rushed towards me. It was my turn for a stomach hug.

I lifted her up and spun her round, peppering her face with kisses. 'I've missed you, gorgeous!'

'I'm not a gore-just, silly!'

I laughed and set her back down on the ground.

'Watch me again!' Leigh rushed back towards the climbing frame.

Zoe put her arm around me and kissed my cheek, one eye on Leigh, her usual smile in place. 'All right?'

'Yeah,' I said, even though I wasn't. It was the standard reply. No one wanted to listen to someone moaning about their life the whole time.

'How did you get on yesterday? Talking to Dean's friends?' she said as we watched Leigh navigate the walkway again.

I told her what little I'd found out. 'Actually, I wanted to ask you about accessing Dean's medical records from your practice. Can Barbara do that, as next of kin? Dean might've talked about being depressed or having trouble coping.'

'Yes, she can request them. There's a form she'd need to fill in at the office. I can get one for you to give her, if you like. It'll probably take about three weeks, though.'

'Three weeks! You mean she can't just go down there and ask to see them?'

'No. There's a load of bureaucracy involved. It takes a while to be approved.'

'I don't suppose you could just have a quick look at his records, could you?'

Zoe raised her eyebrows, a silent refusal.

'OK. Sorry. I shouldn't have asked. But three weeks is a long time.'

'I'm sorry, too. It's a tragedy.' She slid her arm away from my shoulder. 'Did Miles text you about dinner? That might take your mind off things.'

'Yes. Two invitations in two days. What's going on with him? Anyone would think he liked us.'

'I don't know. Maybe he's getting mellow in his old age, feeling guilty about all the times he got the favourite treatment.'

'Or maybe he just wants to gloat again about how perfect his life is and how crap ours are.'

'Oi!' She poked me in the arm. 'My life's not crap. I wouldn't have it any other way. Anyway, there are good things about being single. You don't have to wax, for starters.' She chuckled.

'OK, it's just mine that's crap. Anyway, you know what I mean.' I forced a smile at Leigh tumbling down the slide, pushing down the familiar broody feeling that seemed to be getting worse since the miscarriage. I was just a withered-up, wrinkled aunt now. I felt a rush of envy of Zoe, and then the inevitable guilt that followed hot on its heels. 'Anyway, at least Mum won't be there, poking holes in my life and having digs at us.'

'Yeah, she phoned me before she left yesterday. Mmm, I wish I was going on a three-month cruise to Australia,' she said wistfully. 'She's doing her best to spend everything Dad left.' She laughed and put her arm around me again, squeezing me to her. 'Still, money won't make you happy, eh?'

I felt a twinge of jealousy for Zoe's calm attitude and perspective – for her life with Leigh. She might not have had much money, unlike Miles, but she had everything she wanted. She'd been through something similar to me with her ex, who hadn't wanted to know her as soon as she'd told him she was pregnant. He'd buggered off God knows where and she hadn't heard from him since. But Zoe had just got on with things. What was wrong with me? Plenty of people break up with their boyfriends, plenty of people have miscarriages, plenty of people move on with their lives afterwards. So why couldn't I try to make the best of things and be happy?

We spent an hour at the park, then stopped off at a newsagent on the way back to Zoe's house. I perused the tabloids on a shelf near the door as Leigh pulled Zoe towards the sweetie aisle. Several papers had picked up the Hudsons' story and plastered it on their front pages.

The headlines ranged from 'Teen Kills Parents' to 'Butchered Family Tragedy!'.

Zoe came back and put a hand on my shoulder. 'I never read them.' She eyed the papers.

'Maybe that's why you're so happy.'

She grinned and pulled me outside. We headed back to her flat with Leigh high on sugar and Zoe just high on life, and I spent the afternoon playing games with Leigh and watching *Tinker Bell* twice while Zoe caught up on washing and ironing and housework.

At five we all bundled into Zoe's car and drove to Miles and Tania's house. Leigh disappeared with Hayley straight away into Hayley's bedroom, giggling and stomping around upstairs like a herd of baby elephants. Zoe and I followed Tania into the kitchen.

'We'll have to make do with Prosecco or Châteauneuf-du-Pape, I'm afraid. The champers from the party has all gone.' Tania held a bottle in each hand, looking immaculate as always, even though she had an energetic eight-year-old to look after. She had full make-up on, as usual – I didn't think I'd ever actually seen her without it. If the house was burning down, I was pretty sure she wouldn't leave it until she'd put her face on.

I mentally slapped myself then. Was I just jealous of her, too? I wanted the husband, the gorgeous child and, yes, the money and holidays – not having to worry about buying anything would be pretty nice. I'd thought with Richard that's where my life was headed. How wrong could you get?

But Jess and Stephen had had all that, too, and look how that turned out.

Miles wandered into the kitchen, designer shirt and jeans on, feet bare, still slightly tanned from their recent trip to their holiday home in Saint-Tropez. He gave Zoe and me a perfunctory kiss on the cheek. It was wet and cold against my skin. 'How are my two lovely sisters?'

'You never call us lovely,' I said. 'And you never ask how we are. What are you after?'

'Nothing!' He put on a fake upset look. I didn't think anything upset Miles. Things slid off his back as if no one could possibly ever say anything that criticised him. 'Can't I ask how you are without you snapping at me?'

'I wasn't snapping,' I said. 'It was a joke. Ha ha.'

'God, you're so moody lately.' Miles rolled his eyes at me. 'Have you been drinking already?'

'No. And I've got reason to be moody.' I jerked my head towards one of the national papers on the table. The words 'Family Slain in Tragedy' stared back at me.

Miles said, 'Have you found out anything else from the police? You know that copper Will, don't you? Wasn't he the one who used to fancy you at school? Do they know why Dean did it?'

I averted my eyes from the newspaper and bit my lip. 'He won't tell me anything else. I've already asked him.'

'Surely a good journalist is supposed to work their charms on potential sources.' Miles raised an eyebrow at me. Another little put-down.

'Will is obviously very conscientious about his job,' I said. 'Anyway, I'm still looking into what happened. Barbara's asked me to help her find out what was going on with Dean.'

'And how are you going to—' Miles was cut off by Tania interrupting.

'Let's not talk about things like this at the dinner table! The kids'll be down soon.' Tania scrunched up her nose with distaste and pushed a glass of Prosecco into my hand. 'It's too depressing.'

'You need to improve your small talk if you're ever going to meet someone.' Miles tilted the edge of his glass in my direction. I heard echoes of Mum in him all the time. 'Martin was asking about you on

Friday night after you'd gone.' He gave me a smug smile and winked. 'Leave it to me and I'll sort your love life out for you.'

With everything that had happened, I'd completely forgotten about Martin until then.

'Maybe she doesn't want to meet anyone,' Zoe said, sticking up for me, as always. '*I'm* perfectly happy on my own.'

Tania pulled a casserole dish out of the oven and set it on the worktop. A waft of orange and garlic drifted towards me. 'Pheasant in an orange and chestnut sauce,' she announced proudly.

'I gave him your number,' Miles said to me.

'What?!' I said, eyes wide. 'Why did you do that without asking me first?'

He sighed and pulled a face, as if I were being ungrateful. 'What's wrong with that? You've been moping around since you moved back here, moaning about never meeting anyone again and getting all broody. It's getting really boring now. He's the first guy who's shown an interest in you in ages, and you're not getting any younger, are you?'

'Miles!' Zoe glared at him.

'Oh, so sorry to bore you!' I said. 'I don't know why you invited me if that's the case. I'll just let you get on with your dinner then, shall I, without *boring* you? Then you can just talk about me behind my back instead.'

Zoe put a hand on my shoulder. 'Don't go. Miles is just being a prick, as usual.'

The bickering was normal for our dysfunctional family, but I was still oversensitive about the whole thing. Had been ever since the miscarriage.

'You could do a lot worse than Martin – oh, yes, you already did. With Richard.' Miles had to get that little dig in there.

I clutched the stem of my wine glass – thought about throwing the contents over his head.

'Stop getting so touchy about everything,' Tania said to me over her shoulder as she strained a steaming pan of petits pois. 'Miles is doing you a favour in trying to set you up with someone. You need to get out and start dating again.'

As if that was the answer to everything. Dating wouldn't fix the gaping hole inside that seemed to have been slowly engulfing me for the last year. I was trying, though, even if it didn't look like it.

'Yeah, but you can't just give out my number to people I don't even know.'

'He could be a crazy psycho or a stalker.' Zoe frowned at Miles.

'No, he's not. I play squash with him. He's got a senior position at Tragatech.'

'Oh, right. And psycho killers don't play squash or have good jobs?' I snorted.

He tutted. 'Don't be ridiculous. There's no pleasing some people, is there?'

'Martin's nice,' Tania said. 'I talked to him for ages on Friday.'

'Look, it's very' – I tried to think of the right word: *Scary? Nosy? Interfering?* – '*nice* that you're both taking such an interest in my love life, but—'

'Zo, can you call the girls?' Tania butted in as she pulled out a dish of bubbling dauphinoise potatoes. 'Dinner's ready.'

Zoe nodded, flashed me a what-can-you-do look, and headed out of the kitchen.

I poured more wine and stopped talking, not wanting a row on top of everything else. I didn't speak much again until the kids had finished their meals and were wriggling in their seats, giggling and pleading with Tania and Zoe to let them leave the table to go and play Chef Piglet, whatever that was. I remembered Zoe and me being exactly the same at that age. With two years' difference between us, we were always close. We'd even had a secret language that had seriously pissed off Mum. Miles was five years younger than Zoe.

I was helping Tania and Zoe clear the table when Miles announced, 'We're off to Antigua in three months.' His cheeks were flushed with wine. He had a cheek talking about my drinking when I'd seen how much he could polish off.

'Wow, sounds amazing,' Zoe said. 'I'd settle for a caravan in Devon if it meant having a holiday.' It was tough for her bringing up Leigh on her own and working full-time. Like me, she didn't have much disposable income either. 'Don't suppose you've got room in your suitcase?' she joked.

Miles lounged back in the chair and crossed one foot over his knee. 'A perk of the job. Tragatech's top sales reps have been invited with their families, along with some of our big customers. Throw a couple of medical guest speakers in and they call it a conference. But most people will be taking advantage of the all-inclusive bar and the sunbeds.'

Tania's face lit up with a huge smile. 'I can't wait! Think I might try diving when I'm there. And the company pay for free spa treatments. *And* there's a kids' club! Hayley will love it.'

'Your boss is going, actually,' Miles said to Zoe.

'Dr Baird? I'd noticed the week's holiday pencilled in the diary, but I didn't know he was going there.'

'Yeah. He's taking his wife and kids.'

'And Tragatech pays for it all?' I asked.

Miles nodded.

'Why has Dr Baird been invited on a Tragatech conference?' I frowned.

'He's one of our high-volume prescribers in the area. Plus, he's involved in some research for Tragatech.'

'So he gets to go on an all-expenses jolly to the Caribbean for prescribing loads of your drugs?' I asked Miles incredulously.

'A *medical conference*,' Miles corrected me.

'How do you know what he prescribes to which patient, anyway?' I asked.

Miles tapped his nose. 'Confidential.'

I rolled my eyes at him. 'So what's he like?' I asked Zoe, leaning my elbows on the silk tablecloth.

'He's very sweet,' Zoe said. 'He's got a nice way with the youngsters. He does treat adults, too, but he's a child specialist.'

'He's a good guy,' Miles said to me. 'You should make an appointment with him.'

'What for?' My shoulders stiffened defensively.

Tania glanced at Miles slyly, as if they'd been talking about me. 'A miscarriage is heartbreaking on top of splitting up with Richard and the stress of getting a new job and coming back here. We don't think you're moving on with anything.' Tania looked back at me with her usual wide-eyed innocence, but it felt like she'd stabbed me with a knife.

'And it's obvious you've been depressed since all that shit in London,' Miles added.

'You should get some happy pills,' Tania said. 'Hey, why don't you ask for some Caprixanine? It's Tragatech's new wonder antidepressant that's going to make them billions, so Miles will get some mega bonuses soon.' Excitement lit up her face. She'd probably already worked out what they were going to spend the money on. 'Everyone's raving about it. You'll feel better again in no time.'

'I think that's Holly's call to make, don't you?' Zoe said. 'Stop badgering her. People get over things in their own time.'

'Just because you think taking pills is the answer to everything, doesn't mean I do,' I said. 'And besides, I'm OK. I'm coping.'

'Are you?' Miles raised his eyebrows. 'So why do you keep ringing me up late at night, drunk, crying, upset about everything?'

'I did that once!'

'A lot more than once!'

I looked at Zoe. I'd called her in a drunken state, too, and not remembered doing it in the morning. She offered a supportive smile but didn't say anything.

Miles poured more Prosecco into his glass. 'Anyway, if you play your cards right with Martin, you could be coming to Antigua, too. Maybe a holiday would cheer you up instead.'

'I'm not going to shag someone just so I can get a trip to Antigua. Anyway, doesn't Martin work in accounts or something? How would he wangle a trip there?'

Hayley ran into the room then, closely followed by her shadow, Leigh, and asked if she could have some ice cream.

'Only one scoop,' Zoe said to Leigh, glancing at Tania. 'I don't want her buzzing all night.' Zoe stood. 'Come on, I'll get it for you.'

'I could get you a job at my place,' Miles said to me. 'Even a secretary gets paid more than a reporter at the *Ashfield Post.*'

My defensive hackles rose again. First off, Miles didn't even know how much I earned, which was – I had to admit – pitiful. And secondly, he always wanted to be in control. But maybe he really was just being the concerned brother for once, so I let it slide. 'Thanks, but I'm OK at the moment.'

He shrugged. 'What big stories are you working on at the moment, then?'

'I'm covering the WI's garden tea party tomorrow.'

He was sipping his wine and snorted, nearly spitting it out. 'Sounds . . . thrilling.'

'Oh, shut it.' I slapped his arm gently and yawned. 'Anyway, I'd better be heading off. I've got a lot to do.' I wanted to do some more research on teen suicide and think about how best to approach the head of the college.

'What, checking out how to spell "millefeuille" for your article?' Miles joked, then ducked when my hand veered towards his head.

I stood up. 'Thanks for dinner.'

'Don't say I never do anything for you.'

'You didn't. Tania did.'

'Seriously, though. If you want a job, we're always recruiting admin staff. Let me know. I'll put a word in for you. I got Zoe her job.'

'No you didn't!' Zoe said. 'You *told* me there was a job going there when you went to Dr Baird's practice. You didn't apply for it or wow Dr Baird at the interview, did you?'

'Thanks,' I said to Miles, but I couldn't think of anything worse than being tied to an office all day.

'Do you want a lift?' Zoe asked me. 'I'll be leaving as soon as Leigh's finished watching Hayley's DVD.'

'No, it's OK. I'll walk.' I needed some fresh air to clear my head and sober me up.

When I stepped outside it was dark. I swung a left out of Miles's driveway and headed along the street, concentrating on walking in a straight line. I rounded a corner on to the next street and was halfway down it when I felt the weird sensation of being watched. The hairs on the nape of my neck rose.

My eyes scanned both sides of the street, but it was deserted. There was no one in the gardens of any of the nearby houses, either.

I whipped my head around to look behind me, my hair flying into my face as I did so. There was a split second when I thought I saw a shadow at the corner of the road, but when I batted the hair out of my eyes the street was empty. I was alone.

Miles was actually right about one thing. I really did need to stop drinking. I was hallucinating now.

Chapter 10

I was in the office the next morning at 9 a.m., munching on a Polo as I transferred some articles on to the *Ashfield Post*'s website. Brian appeared half an hour later, looking hungover. At least it wasn't just me.

I said hi. He glared at me in response and sat down at his cubicle in the corner, opened his laptop and started typing.

'Good weekend?' I asked, trying to be friendly.

He grunted in response.

'Who was the young woman who jumped in front of a train on Saturday morning?' If anyone would know more about her, Brian would. He had contacts all over the place. I'd thought about asking Will for more information, but he hadn't wanted to tell me anything about Dean, so I didn't think he'd be willing to speak to me about this woman either, and I'd heard nothing further about it on the local news.

'Girl,' he corrected. 'She was sixteen. Rachel Tucker,' Brian said without glancing up.

'What do you know about her?'

'Why? What's that got to do with the WI tea party?'

I suppressed my irritation. 'Who was she? Did she go to Downs Road College?' I wondered if Rachel had known Dean and heard about what he'd done. Maybe it had prompted her to take her own life, too. Brian ignored me, or pretended he hadn't heard me, so I asked, 'Do you know why she did it?'

He shrugged. 'Why do any of them do it? She must've been seriously messed up in the head.'

I sat back, chewing on the end of my pen, wondering what had gone through Rachel's mind in the hours, minutes, seconds leading up to her jumping in front of that train. I knew about depression. I was being swallowed up by something that felt overwhelming. Felt like I was cracking open at times. But that was normal after what had happened to me, wasn't it? Life *is* sometimes shit. It can't always be sunshine and smiles. It knocks us down and then kicks us when we're in the gutter. But even though it was hard to drag myself out of bed sometimes and put one foot in front of the other, I'd never thought about ending everything, like Rachel and Dean. I knew, eventually, it had to get better. I just had to work through things. Be more like Zoe. Not let everything overpower me. I *was* working on it. After what Miles and Tania had said last night, I'd seriously been debating making an appointment with Dr Baird and talking about how I felt, instead of getting some antidepressants like Tania had suggested. I'd always dismissed the idea of medicating myself into euphoria. How could that fix what was hurting? What happened when I stopped taking them? In the long run, I knew I had to change the thoughts deep inside my head, and I didn't think a pill could fix that.

'Do you know anything else about her?' I asked.

Another shrug. 'Not much. I'm only doing a small piece. Don't have time to dig into it. The Hudsons story's taking all my time.' He treated me to another glare, as if daring me to challenge him.

I wondered if Neil would let me look into Rachel's death. Teenage suicide was something that I could get my teeth into for a human interest piece. Even if Neil wasn't interested in it for the *Ashfield Post*, I could write it freelance and pitch it to some papers. Why hadn't I thought of doing that before? But deep down I knew why – I didn't want to fail again. I couldn't handle more rejection.

A bubble of something I hadn't felt in a long time rose to the surface. A frisson of excitement. I scribbled 'Rachel Tucker' in my pad and collected up my bag and camera. 'Right. I'm off to the tea party.'

Brian ignored me and carried on typing.

'See ya, Holly,' I muttered to myself and left.

I had allowed myself an extra ten minutes to get to the house where one of the WI members was hosting the event so I could phone Downs Road College and make an appointment with the head. I doubted they'd admit that they hadn't spotted possible mental health issues with Dean, nor any possible liability stemming from a lack of emotional support for him, if indeed there was any on their part. Barbara didn't think Dean had seen a counsellor there, although it was possible Dean hadn't told anyone if he had – embarrassed, perhaps, at the thought of people seeing him emotionally bereft or unable to cope with work that his friends found easy. Not wanting to appear lacking or inferior. I could relate to that completely. And teenage boys are notorious for keeping things to themselves. The head wouldn't reveal any confidential student-related information to me, even if I did say I was looking into things on behalf of Barbara. With two suicides and several breakdowns under her belt, she probably had a large team of expensive lawyers on speed dial in case anyone threatened to sue them, but I wanted to get a feel for the place. Luckily, Mrs Hedges, the head, could fit me in at 3 p.m.

The next couple of hours passed in a blur as I sipped tea and nibbled on scones and cucumber sandwiches and spoke to a lively bunch of women. I took photos and scribbled notes about the history of their organisation, what projects the local band of charitable ladies had completed over the years, and anecdotes about guest speakers they'd had.

I returned to the office to write up a glowing, sparkly piece that would make Emmeline Pankhurst proud. The atmosphere inside was oppressive. Neil kept shooting me suspicious looks through his office doorway, but I didn't know if that was in response to me telling him I had an urgent dentist's appointment at three so I could go to the college or whether Brian had been complaining about me again.

My mobile phone rang as I was about to leave for Downs Road. It was Barbara.

I lowered my voice as I said, 'Hi. How are you?'

'Not so good.' She sounded sore-throated and hoarse, the abundance of tears she'd shed evident in her voice. 'I spoke to the coroners' officer this morning. They said an inquest was being opened today for Jess and Stephen and Dean. They said I didn't need to go – that it would be a very short, routine hearing and would be adjourned pending further enquiries. And now the police have just called. They're going to come here at five o'clock to speak to me. Could you . . . I mean . . . would you be here with me? I know I won't be able to take in everything that they say.'

Anger pushed its way to the surface. Why hadn't Brian or Neil mentioned the inquest was being opened today? While I'd been eating bloody finger food, I bet Brian had been at the coroners' court. It would've only been a five-minute or so hearing, with the police giving a short statement of fact, but even so, I should've been there, too.

I pushed the anger away as I realised I should've checked myself when the inquest was being held. What a stupid idiot! I was sure Brian and Neil hadn't told me on purpose, but still, I had to start taking responsibility for my own failures. I mentally slapped myself, fighting the urge to glare at Neil as I grabbed my bag and walked out of the office to my car. 'Of course I will, if that's what you want. I was going to call you later anyway and let you know what happened when I spoke to Dean's friends.' I quickly filled her in on what they'd told me. 'I'm going to see Mrs Hedges from the college in a minute to build up a picture.

I'll come straight round after I speak to her. Then we can have a chat before the police turn up. Are the reporters still there?' I unlocked my car and slid behind the wheel. I transferred the call to loudspeaker as I drove out of the car park and on to the main road.

'A few stragglers. I can hear them laughing.' Her voice cracked with bitter anger. 'They make me sick! Preying on people at their most vulnerable times.'

A twinge of guilt niggled at me. But I wasn't like them. I wasn't a hack for one of the tabloids, cashing in on people's grief. I wasn't much of anything, really.

'They're saying Dean's a monster. Evil. A psychopath! But he isn't! He wasn't! I need to clear his name, Holly. I need to find out what made Dean do something like this, because he was . . .' She let out a loud wail.

'I know, Barbara. I know. I'm working on it, OK?' I said softly. 'And I wanted to ask you something, actually. Did Dean know a girl called Rachel Tucker? Did he ever mention her?'

'Rachel Tucker?' There was a pause as she thought. 'No. I've never heard the name. Why?'

I didn't want to tell Barbara about another suicide just yet in her already fragile state. 'It doesn't matter. Um, can I get you anything from the shops on my way over? Milk? Bread?'

She exhaled a deep breath, as if she were trying to pull herself together. 'No, I'm all right. I haven't had any appetite, anyway, but I didn't want to run the gauntlet and push my way past those parasites, snapping pictures of me as I go by. Shouting out their obscene questions.'

'OK. I'll see you soon.'

'Thank you, Holly. Thank you so much.'

~

Mrs Hedges was tall and rail thin. She had small, dark eyes and reminded me of a crow. Her thin blonde hair was up in a neat chignon. I'd once written an article for *Pizzazz* with a step-by-step guide to styling the perfect chignon. By the looks of it, she'd read that article. It felt like that person who wrote such frivolous rubbish was from a past life now. When the glamour of the magazine had faded, I'd realised I wanted to do something that made a difference. Write serious, thought-provoking, gritty human interest pieces. And I hadn't written a single one. But maybe now was the time to change that.

Rachel Tucker's name flashed into my head again. I'd try to speak to her family and attempt to get them to tell their story so I could write something sensitive and poignant. Hopefully, I'd get one of the broadsheets interested. If I wanted to be that kind of investigative journalist, then I had to step up, get my arse moving, and stop wallowing in so much self-pity and bitter insecurity. I had to actually *write*! It was time to stop blaming everyone else for the way things had turned out.

When I stepped into Mrs Hedges' office, she rounded her desk and held out an elegant hand. 'Very nice to meet you, Mrs Jennings.'

I'd plucked that name from thin air, thinking my best way to get any information would be posing as a prospective parent.

'Likewise.' I gave her a friendly smile.

'Please, sit. Would you like some coffee or tea, perhaps?' She returned the smile. It was confident, composed. Then she sat opposite me and crossed one thirty-deniered leg over the other at the ankle, her knees to one side.

'I'm fine, thank you.'

'All right, then let's get started, shall we? You mentioned to my secretary that you were researching prospective sixth form colleges for your son?' She slid her fingers together and rested them against her flat stomach.

'Yes. He goes to Ashfield High.' It was the same secondary school Dean had gone to.

'It's an accomplished school. We've had many students from there over the years. And what AS levels is he interested in studying?'

'Chemistry, maths, biology, and physics. He wants to go to med school at Cambridge afterwards.'

'A wonderful career choice. Again, many of our students have gone on to do just that. Our students are also required to do an Extended Project Qualification, along with their other choices.'

I nodded. 'Downs Road has an excellent reputation for getting results, but I am a little concerned regarding some recent things I've heard about student suicides and breakdowns. I understand, because of the level of education here, it will be more of a pressured environment, but what measures do you have in place to protect the students' welfare?'

'Yes, there have been two devastating incidents involving former students. But I don't believe they were connected to their education. And, unfortunately, as child psychiatrists will tell you, you cannot predict teenage suicide in many cases.'

Mrs Hedges had only mentioned two – Emma Tolley and Dean – so I presumed that Rachel Tucker hadn't been a pupil here.

'We take the utmost care and responsibility, firstly with the selection criteria for this college, and secondly in making sure that while students are here, they have access to our exemplary range of wellness advisers and in-house counsellors, should they find themselves in difficulties.' She didn't blink, didn't falter in any way. Her voice was smooth and her response quick, as if she'd rehearsed it. Or said it many times to real prospective parents.

In theory it sounded good, but would only work if the student *wanted* to share their problems. What if they went undetected by tutorial staff?

'I'm worried that the pressure of this college may be too much for my son – that he might struggle to cope.'

She smiled again. 'We conduct various interviews and psychological assessments before we even consider a student for Downs Road. And, of course, their GCSE results must be of the highest standard. There are many students wishing to attend the college, so we have to be highly particular about any places we offer. We have exemplary educational results, but I can assure you, we provide the highest level of care to all our students.'

'And what measures do you have in place to detect that a student is suffering difficulties once they start here?'

'Obviously, their work is a strong indicator – if they're falling behind or failing to understand lectures or coursework. All of our tutors are highly regarded and are well trained to spot any difficulties arising before they might spiral out of control.'

I thought about Howard telling me Dean had got an F recently. Had his work suffered in other subjects and the staff hadn't picked up on it? Had he acted normally in class? Or had he been withdrawn? Distant? Hyper? Manic? Falling asleep? And if so, why hadn't the tutors realised something was wrong?

'My concern is that my son is incredibly conscientious and driven to do well. He wouldn't want to be seen as a failure or quitter if he was having trouble coping with the work. In fact, he would probably go the other way. He'd become obsessed about working harder, particularly as he's not academically gifted in a way that others can be who find this level of work easy. He has to work at it.'

She nodded, head tilted, a sympathetically understanding expression on her face as I carried on.

'In that respect, it could appear from his schoolwork that he was coping very well, but in reality, he could be highly stressed, and I'm worried that the pressure could lead to depression.'

'As you probably know, Downs Road is affiliated with Cambridge University, so the standard of education and expectation is very high, and yes, there are pressures for students who are not suited to this environment or this level of academia. You know your son best, of course, and perhaps Downs Road isn't right for him after all. I mentioned that the tutors are highly trained to spot students getting into potential difficulties, but this must be a responsibility of the parents also. We're all in this together!' She raised a fist in a mock rallying gesture.

But Jess and Stephen weren't in it together. Not any longer. Part of me wanted to smack that self-satisfied smile off her face. 'I was wondering if you'd put any additional measures in place recently to prevent possible copycat suicides following the tragedy with Dean Hudson.'

Her smile faltered a little at the mention of Dean's name, but she recovered quickly. 'We don't believe there will be any "copycat" suicides, as you put them. As I said, we're confident that all the measures we have in place are more than sufficient to deal with any problems students might face. Did you have any other questions?' She asked, clearly wanting to steer the conversation in a different direction.

I clenched my jaw for a moment and then asked, 'Do you have any problems with drugs on campus?'

She shook her head vehemently. 'Absolutely not. We have a zero tolerance policy when it comes to drugs. We haven't found any students in possession of drugs in the ten years we've been open. And if we had evidence that a student was taking drugs, they would be automatically expelled.'

'OK,' I said. 'Well, thank you for your time. You've given me a lot to think about.'

'You're very welcome.' She picked up a glossy brochure and held it out to me. 'Would you like to peruse this in your own time?'

I took it, staring down at the photo of the old building that housed the college. I knew from their website it had been erected in 1855 as an orphanage. The mission statement tagline on the front was 'A World-Class Centre of Learning'.

She shook my hand again before walking me towards the door. 'If you have any further questions, feel free to email my secretary and we can take things from there.'

We said our goodbyes and I walked off down the corridor, my shoes clicking on the parquet flooring, the sound bouncing off the stone walls.

I'd just got into my car when I saw Brian pull up in his Ford Focus, no doubt hoping for a quote from the college about Dean. I sank down in my seat so he couldn't see me, kept my gaze on him until he'd headed inside and then started the car.

As I pulled out of the gates on to the main road, I spotted Howard Becker walking away from the college. I pulled up alongside him and lowered my window.

'Hi, Howard.'

He looked over at me and stopped walking. 'Oh, hi.'

'How are you?'

He glanced around at a few other students milling out of the college gates before walking up to my window. 'OK, I s'pose.' He sighed. 'Still can't get my head round everything.'

'You and me both.' I gave him a sad smile. 'Can I ask you a quick question?'

'Yeah. What's up?'

'Did Dean know a girl called Rachel Tucker? She was sixteen. I don't think she went to Downs Road.'

He scrunched up his face for a moment, as if thinking. 'I don't think so. I've never heard of her. Why, who is she?'

'I don't know yet. But thanks, anyway.'

He shrugged.

I spotted Alfie and Fraser exiting the college then. Alfie called out to Howard, who turned around and acknowledged him with a jerk of his chin.

Howard turned back to me. 'I'd better go.'

'Yeah. Thanks again.'

I drove off, watching them in my rear-view mirror as Alfie slapped Howard playfully on the back.

This time Barbara's street was quieter. There were a couple of male reporters outside who, judging from their rumpled suits and messy haircuts, belonged to the tabloids. The acne-scarred guy was there again.

I thought about mowing through them to park on Barbara's drive but didn't want to draw attention to myself until the last minute, so I parked a little further along the street.

I overheard their conversation about football scores as I approached. One of them laughed at the other. Business as usual for them. Another day, another tragedy, but, hey, life goes on.

I pushed past one who was actually leaning on the front wall, inside the boundary of Barbara's driveway, accidentally-on-purpose catching him in the hip with my heavy handbag. 'Have some respect,' I muttered. 'And you're on private property!' I glared at him until he shuffled back on to the pavement.

'Did Barbara Acres know her grandson was a psycho?' Acne Guy called out as the one I'd hit rubbed his hip.

I treated them all to another glare and called through the letter box to let Barbara know it was me. Whirring clicks of a camera shutter went off at full speed as they took photos of the back of my head.

Barbara's shadow approached the front door and she called out, 'Go round the back. I don't want them taking photos.'

I ignored more shouted questions as I made my way through the side gate that Barbara unlocked for me.

'Bastards,' Barbara muttered, locking the gate behind me.

I walked through the kitchen door, then turned and gave Barbara a hug. The smell of her perfume from the first time I'd seen her on Saturday had been replaced by something stale and sour. Maybe it was my imagination, but she felt like skin and bone underneath her rumpled dress.

I pulled back and looked at her properly. Her face was even puffier than before, eyes almost sunken into their sockets.

'Has anyone been here to support you?' I asked. 'Stephen's parents? Friends?'

'I've spoken to Stephen's parents, but they haven't been particularly supportive. They're blaming me for what Dean did. I don't want them here. I can't even deal with myself at the moment, let alone company.'

'Shall I make you a cup of tea?' I asked her.

'No. I'll do it. I need to keep busy.' She abruptly stepped away from me, taking mugs out of the cupboard, filling the kettle, moving like an old woman. As she turned on the tap, the water came out full blast, spraying up over her dress. She yanked the tap off, threw the kettle in the sink with a clatter, and clasped her hands over her face. 'I'm hoping the police are coming to tell me they got it wrong. That it was someone else who did it.'

'Come on, let's sit you down.' I put my arm around her shoulder, led her towards the table, and guided her into the chair.

I sat opposite and just let her cry. Tears welled up in my own eyes and I pushed them away, trying to be strong for her. I knew the agony of losing a child, even though I had never held my son or daughter, never heard them speak their first words, take their first steps, get married, have their own kids. But I could relate to the emptiness left behind. The sadness, the loss, the grief, the raw devastation. And I knew nothing I could say would make the situation any better, any more bearable, particularly given who was responsible for Jess's death.

Barbara's black cat entered the room and wound its way around her ankles, purring. She bent down absent-mindedly and stroked its head. This was obviously a new addition to the family. I didn't recognise it from when I'd been here as a teenager, when there had always been various dogs and cats in the Acres household – abandoned strays that Barbara had taken in from the veterinary practice. The cat nudged my hand for a stroke and I obliged, but then it got bored and padded to its food bowl in the corner of the room.

My gaze drifted towards the table. There was a cardboard box on top of it with various bits and bobs inside. Next to it was a pile of photo albums, one of them left open at a page showing Dean when he was much younger – probably ten or eleven – sitting on a wall with the sea in the background, holding a toffee apple. His eyes were crinkled at the corners with a cheeky grin.

How could Barbara ever come to terms with something like this?

I watched her falling apart, unable to help her. And eventually, when her sobs stopped, she wiped her eyes with the back of her hands and looked up at me.

'What did Mrs Hedges say?'

'She spouted from the brochure. Exemplary, prestigious school, great results, superb student welfare in place. I didn't really expect much else. I certainly didn't expect her to say they'd ever neglect their duty of care.'

'But do you think they did? Do you think they're to blame?'

'I don't know. If a student appears to be coping on the outside and they're hiding it well, how could the college know for certain? Especially if Dean never spoke to a counsellor there.' I rubbed at a vein pulsing in my temple. 'I think you should apply for Dean's medical records from his doctor. It's possible Dean discussed something with him when he went to get the sleeping tablets.'

'Do you think there could be some kind of medical malpractice? Failure to diagnose a mental health condition or . . . something? There has to be *something* that caused this to happen!'

'Again, I don't know yet. But you're entitled to see his notes, although it seems like it will take several weeks to get hold of them.' I reached out and squeezed her hand. 'But nothing is certain yet. Maybe the police really are coming to tell you Dean wasn't even involved in it at all. Maybe they've found new evidence someone else was in the house that night who murdered them.'

The doorbell rang then. Barbara's eyes widened with terror at what news the police would bring.

'I'll let them in.' I left her there, wiping at her eyes again, trying to compose herself, and opened the front door.

The straggling reporters had left, probably moved on by the two policemen who stood on the doorstep.

'Holly.' Will looked surprised. 'I wasn't expecting you.'

'Barbara wanted me to be here.'

He nodded solemnly and turned towards the older man beside him. 'This is DCI Turnbull.'

I recognised DCI Turnbull from outside the Hudsons' house. He held out his hand for me to shake.

I took it and explained, 'I'm a friend of Barbara's.' I held the door open and stepped aside. 'Come in.' I led them into the kitchen.

Barbara stayed seated. She met DCI Turnbull's gaze and said, 'I'm almost afraid to ask what more information you have.'

'I'm sorry we're meeting again under these circumstances, Mrs Acres. Is it OK to sit?' DCI Turnbull said.

Barbara nodded.

'Do you want a drink?' I hovered by the kettle. Both of them refused.

DCI Turnbull sat down opposite Barbara, adjusted himself in the chair, and leaned his elbows on the table. I sat opposite Will. He'd been clutching some plastic bags and put them on the floor beside his feet.

'Once again, we're very sorry for your loss, Mrs Acres,' DCI Turnbull said.

'Barbara. Please, call me Barbara,' she muttered.

He cleared his throat. 'As you're aware, we've been conducting a thorough forensic examination of the scene, along with post-mortem examinations, and enquiries into what transpired leading up to the tragedy that occurred early Friday morning.'

Barbara gasped when he said 'post-mortem'. She clenched her fist to her mouth for a moment, then let it fall uselessly to the table. 'Please say that you were wrong. Dean wasn't responsible. That it was someone else. It was an intruder who did it. Please!' Her eyes implored him.

DCI Turnbull paused for a moment. 'I'm very sorry to tell you that there were no signs of anyone else being involved in the tragic incident with your family. As I informed you previously, we believe Dean was responsible for his parents' deaths before he took his own life.'

'Oh . . . G . . . God.' She hiccupped the words out.

Even though it was what the police had already told her, Barbara had still been clinging to the possibility that Dean was innocent, holding on to a life raft of hope. I knew all about hope. And when the hope was gone, helplessness was the only thing left.

I put my arm around her, rubbing her shoulder.

'Were there any drugs in Dean's system?' I asked.

'No,' Will said.

Barbara's mouth hung open, her face a frozen mask, unable to speak.

'Did you speak to his doctor? Dean's friends? The college?' I asked. 'Did you find any specific reason for why Dean did it?'

DCI Turnbull placed his hands flat on the table. 'From our enquiries, we haven't found anything concrete that explains why he snapped that day. There was no suicide note discovered that could point us in a certain direction. It could've been a combination of hundreds of possible things.' He paused, looking at Barbara with obvious sympathy. 'Dean was stressed with college work, under pressure and not sleeping. I've spoken to mental health professionals with experience of similar incidents and it's unfortunately common for relatives to never find an exact answer to what triggers something like this. We spoke with Dr Baird, who Dean recently went to see, and he'd diagnosed Dean as suffering from depression. Unfortunately, the depression escalated into the terrible events that took place.'

'But he didn't seem depressed. He was just tired – overworked,' Barbara insisted.

DCI Turnbull inhaled a slow breath. 'As you can imagine, people with depression are often prone to suicidal thoughts.'

I sat back in my chair and took a deep breath. 'Suicidal, maybe, but how many go on to murder their parents?'

Will kept his eyes on me as DCI Turnbull spoke. 'We're satisfied we know what happened in the house. But we could spend years investigating the *why* and never reach a conclusion. We're not looking for anyone else in connection to the murders. And as a result of all of that, we'll be closing the police investigation soon and everything will be passed to the coroner who will hold the full inquest, which won't be for several months yet.'

I glanced at Barbara. She still appeared frozen in place in complete shock, her face lost and vacant.

'We're returning some things we took from your daughter's house.' Will lifted the heavy-duty plastic bags he'd placed at his feet and removed items one by one. A laptop with stickers of various emojis on it, peeling at the edges. A mobile phone. What looked like some school notebooks. 'These belonged to Dean.'

Barbara reached out and gently touched the laptop.

The last item Will pulled out was a set of keys, resting them down on the table with a jangling sound that spoke of finality. 'Our forensic officers have finished examining the house now so . . .' He trailed off. He looked between me and Barbara, but Barbara seemed in her own world of devastation. 'I can give you the name of a cleaning company, if you like.'

I pictured the blood everywhere. In Jess and Stephen's bedroom. Splatters up the walls, on the sheets. A pool of it seeping out of their bodies on to the mattress. Bile rose in my throat and I swallowed – kept swallowing until I'd pushed the image away. 'Yes, that would be a good idea. I'll sort it out.' I looked at Barbara, who was having a hard time

91

coping with breathing, let alone arranging anything as gruesome as cleaning her daughter's house.

DCI Turnbull pressed his hands on the table and stood. 'Again, I'm very sorry for your loss. We'll leave you in peace.'

Peace is the last thing Barbara will find for a long time to come, I thought as I followed them along the corridor.

DCI Turnbull said goodbye and headed down the path towards their car parked on the street.

As Will was about to leave, I clutched the arm of his suit jacket. 'Is that really it? How can you leave her without any answers?'

He stared at me, his eyes filled with a mixture of sympathy and resigned tiredness. 'I'm afraid we don't have the resources or the remit to investigate things further. It's up to the coroner now. And I'm under strict instructions from my boss that the investigation is to be closed.' He jerked his head in DCI Turnbull's direction, who was now sitting in the car. 'I can completely understand if Barbara is looking for someone else to blame – some kind of negligence by the medical services or the college that took place – but I didn't find any evidence of that, and anyway, that's not our job. It would be a civil matter, not a criminal one.' He glanced down at my hand and covered it with his own.

'Did you find any signs that Dean was being abused? Or was there any violence at home? He must've blamed Stephen and Jess for something, mustn't he? He must've been so angry about something.'

'No. We found no evidence of anything like that, and I'm satisfied that there was no abuse. Dean seemed a normal teenage boy who was under pressure to succeed. And although Jess and Stephen wanted their son to do well, I don't think they were pushy parents. I think a lot of the pressure was of Dean's own making, something *he* made for himself. Something in his own head. And that pressure snowballed into depression, murder, and suicide.'

'Does that make it even scarier then?' I asked, more to myself than Will. 'That it could happen to anyone?' I slid my hand from his arm, balling it into a fist. 'There was another suicide a year ago. A girl called Emma Tolley who went to the same college as Dean. And the day after Dean did what he did, another teenager, Rachel Tucker, jumped in front of a train. Do you know anything about that? It seems a bit strange that two teenagers killed themselves in Ashfield within two days of each other.'

'Unfortunately, it's not the first time a teenager has committed suicide and it won't be the last. The coroners' officer is dealing with Rachel's death. There aren't any suspicious circumstances. And I can't see how Emma Tolley's death relates to any of this if it happened a year ago. Why? What are you getting at?'

'I don't know, really. I know teen suicide happens, but is this the first time one of them took their parents with them?'

He sighed. 'Look, I'm sorry, I'd love to help, but I can't do any more. It's more than my job's worth. I'm not exactly my boss's favourite person right now.'

'What do you mean?'

He looked away and ran a hand through his hair, then let his arm fall to his side, looking embarrassed.

'What is it?'

He blew out a breath and lowered his voice. 'A little while ago, I was on track for promotion to DI, but then I . . .' He glanced away. 'I cocked up a high-profile investigation and now I have to do everything strictly by the book. I can't risk poking my nose into things I'm not supposed to be investigating. It's going to be a long time before I get another shot at DI, and I have to follow orders to the letter in the meantime.'

No wonder he'd looked weary when I'd asked him about his job before. It must've taken him years of hard work and dedication to advance to that level, and now the opportunity for promotion had been snatched away from him. I'd been there, done that, and bought the bloody T-shirt. 'I'm sorry.' I reached out and touched his arm again. 'If it's any consolation, I've made more than my fair share of mistakes, too.'

He gave me a half-smile, then pulled a business card from his pocket and pressed the card into my hand. 'Here's my number. If Barbara needs anything or has any questions, get her to ring me. Or if you need to speak to me, just call, OK?'

I nodded and then closed the door behind him before rejoining Barbara.

She stroked the laptop, the sticker making a clicking sound as it curled and uncurled when she ran her finger against it.

I looked at the cardboard box on the table. Inside I spotted a sweatshirt folded up and a maths textbook. 'Were these Dean's?'

She nodded. 'He left them here that last Sunday when they were round for dinner.'

I peered into the box and spotted a packet of tablets nestled in the corner. 'Are these the sleeping tablets Dean was prescribed?'

'Yes. They were in the pocket of his sweatshirt. He said he'd stopped taking them because they didn't work. Probably forgot they were in there.'

I picked out the packet and read the name on the front: 'Caprixanine'. It was the name of the antidepressant Tania had told me about. I opened the cardboard cover and pulled out the blister packs inside. Seven tablets had gone. I sighed helplessly, stuffed them back inside the box and put it on top of the sweatshirt.

'You think you know your family,' Barbara said, still stroking the laptop as if she were in a trance. 'You think you know your kids and grandkids. But you don't know what they're doing behind your back. When they're out with their friends. What they talk about with other people. What they feel. What's going through their heads.' She opened one of the photo albums and flicked through to a picture of Dean when he must've been about seven or eight. Long curls reached down to the top of his shoulders and freckles were scattered across his nose. 'He went through a phase of not wanting his hair cut. The teachers kept on at Jess, saying it looked messy, but she wouldn't back down and make Dean get it cut. Of course, the next year short hair was in, so he went from one extreme to the other.' Barbara pressed her fingertips to Dean's hair. 'I was going through them, looking for some kind of sign. Looking for something in him I'd missed that I should've seen. I could've stopped it if I'd known. I could've . . .' She snatched her hand away from the picture and pressed it to her mouth.

'It's not your fault, Barbara.' I squeezed her hand.

'You expect to lose your parents, but not your child. Not your grandchild. Or your son-in-law. Not your whole family, wiped out suddenly with no warning. You can't brace yourself for something like this. And it's not something you can ever get over. I know I'll have to carry on. Put one foot in front of the other and just get through the days. But what kind of existence is that? It hurts. It hurts so much.' She pressed a palm to her sternum as if the grief were really a physical pain.

I didn't know what to say because she was right. I couldn't imagine how hard things would be for her from now on, but thankfully she didn't seem to want an answer from me. Now she'd started talking, the words poured out of her.

'And even though Dean did this, I still love him. I can't turn off my feelings. I can't erase the last seventeen years. And I don't know whether that's right or wrong. I don't know anything any more.'

Chapter 11

What's happening with that Tucker girl?

Routine investigation. Nothing to worry about.

Good. I want to keep it that way.
And Dean Hudson?

Police investigation will be closed. But I'm monitoring the situation.

Let me know if anything changes.

I've got it covered.

Chapter 12

I left Barbara after she'd said she needed some time alone. I'd taken Dean's laptop, his phone, and Jess's house keys, at Barbara's insistence. Even if the police were no longer looking for answers, Barbara still wanted me to find something to explain Dean's actions.

I needed a drink so badly my mouth watered and my hands trembled. It had started after Richard and the miscarriage. I hadn't been sleeping well and was exhausted with it all, with grief, with self-loathing, with life. Sometimes I thought I saw my baby crawling around the floor in my flat or lying on my bed, just at the edge of my vision, but when I turned my head the vision was gone, cruelly snatched away from me. Maybe it was just wishful thinking, a projection of what I wanted so badly to be real. Or maybe the sleep deprivation was making me hallucinate. Even when I did manage to fall asleep, I had recurring dreams in which my baby was crying out to me, alive, only I couldn't get to her. In my vivid dreams, she was always a little girl. Her screams were so real that they woke me in a cold sweat, tangled beneath the sheets, the thumping of my heart mixing with the visceral pain of losing her all over again when I realised I was alone. So I turned to alcohol to blot everything out – to escape from myself for a while. Being anaesthetised felt much better than being awake. I didn't see Miles or Mum enough for them to even notice things were spiralling out of control at first, and I'd been hiding it from Zoe, until the day I couldn't hide it any more.

Zoe had turned up unexpectedly at my block of flats one Sunday afternoon when Leigh was on a play date, and one of the other residents who was just leaving the building let her in, so she hadn't needed to use the intercom entry system. Zoe used her spare key and found me lying in a pile of vomit on the lounge floor, empty wine bottles scattered around, the kitchen bin overflowing with even more. I'd hit that infamous rock bottom and it was screaming loudly in my face. I'd been scared of admitting to Zoe how bad things had got, how the strong Holly had now become weak and pathetic. But she'd made bucketsful of coffee and given me a pep talk in her usual compassionate way. She'd let me ramble on for hours, pouring out my heart and the tears. I don't remember every encouraging word she'd said that day, but I remember the last thing: *I know losing a baby is horrific, and things* may *get harder before they get easier. But it* will *get better. You just have to make it through the hard bit first.* A few days later, Zoe bought me a self-help book about dealing with grief. There were five stages, apparently: denial, anger, bargaining, depression, and acceptance. I was still stuck on the page about depression, both literally and figuratively. I'd made a promise to myself then to work harder at getting thorough this. And I'd broken that promise many times.

Today, that familiar pull of alcohol was too hard to ignore. I needed a drink to get rid of the images of Jess and Stephen and Dean in my head, but I had nothing to drink at home so I drove to the supermarket and headed straight to the alcohol aisle. I put three bottles of red wine in my basket and headed to the checkout, thinking how in the midst of tragedy, life was still casually going on around me as normal. But then life was fucked up. Everything was fucked up. I fought the urge to rip off the bottle top there and then and swig it down on the way back to my car.

Of course, I didn't. I put the bottles carefully in a plastic bag as if they were more precious than gold and carried them to the car park, the anticipation of that first glass sweet in my mouth.

As I approached my car there was a man crouching next to my front bumper, his hand reaching up underneath it, a trolley laden with shopping bags at his side.

I hurried over and said, 'Can I help you?'

He stood up abruptly. 'Sorry. Is this your car?'

'Yes.' I spotted a new scratch on the black plastic bumper about five centimetres long. 'Oh, God. What's happened?' I leaned over to inspect it closer.

'I'm really sorry. I put the trolley behind my car to load up my shopping. I took my eye off it while I opened up the boot and it just wheeled off.' He winced sympathetically. 'Straight into your . . . er . . . bumper.' He pointed to the scratch. 'I couldn't grab it in time.'

I ran my finger along the scratch, sighing.

'I'll pay for the damage, of course,' he said hastily.

I stood up and looked at him. He was about my age, clean cut, dressed in a suit. He bit his lip sheepishly. 'I always get the one with the wonky wheel that has a mind of its own. I'm really very sorry.' He pulled out his wallet. 'Um . . . I haven't got a clue how much it would cost to repair it.' He pulled out two fifty-pound notes. 'Maybe if I give you this and then you can take my number? If it's any more, give me a ring and I'll pay the rest.' He held the notes out in the space between us.

I looked at the money. Looked at the scratch again. It wasn't that bad. The car was six years old anyway and wasn't pristine. I licked my finger and rubbed it over the scratch. The bumper turned dark with saliva and then lighter as it dried. You could hardly see it, really, and I felt guilty taking money off this man. Most people would've just driven off and not said anything.

'Look, you can't even really see anything. Let's just forget about it.'

His forehead wrinkled with what looked like surprise, or relief, maybe. 'I'd feel really bad if you don't take something for it.' He wiggled the notes at me.

I waved my hand. 'No, don't worry about it. It's not bad enough to bother doing anything about it.'

He pursed his lips, head tilted slightly, big blue eyes fixed on my face. 'Well, if you won't take any money for it, at least let me apologise properly and take you out for a drink.' He smiled. It was a nice smile.

I opened my mouth, about to say no. And if it hadn't been for the last awful few days, or Miles and Tania's digs about my life, or the loneliness closing in around me, then I might've done so. But I needed a distraction to take my mind off everything – to try to blot out the images of Jess and Stephen dead in their bed that were seared into my brain. He was nice looking, and he seemed really kind and considerate. And it had been a long time since someone had smiled at me like that.

I don't know if the word 'Yes' that slipped out was more of a surprise to him or me.

'Right. Great.' He grinned. 'So . . . er . . . when?'

A brief thought flitted into my head that he could be a psycho, but it disappeared as quickly as it arrived. Someone who could've done a runner after scuffing another car but stayed around to pay for it didn't strike me as psycho material. 'Are you busy tonight?' Did that sound too desperate? Too needy? I didn't know how to date any more. Didn't really know how to be, how to act. I was always worried once someone got to know me they'd find me sadly lacking. Like Richard obviously had.

'Erm . . . actually, no. Tonight would be great. There's a nice wine bar in the high street called Fredos. How about I meet you outside at eight?'

I looked at my watch: 6.30 p.m. Plenty of time to do something with myself. 'OK.'

'Um . . . here's my number, just in case.' He reached inside his wallet again and handed me a business card.

I took it and read 'Andrew Watson, Construction Project Manager'. 'That's me.' He blushed. 'Obviously.' He flashed an awkward smile. 'So. I'll see you at eight?'

'Yes.'

'Right. Good. And I'm really sorry again about your car.' He scrunched up his face.

We said goodbye and I unlocked my car, dumped my bag in the passenger footwell and closed the door before I could shout out to him that I'd changed my mind.

He gave me a wave as he wheeled the offending trolley back to his own car, and a blush heated up my cheeks all the way home. What had I just done?

I jumped in the shower and shaved my legs before trying on five different outfits, examining myself in the full-length mirror in my bedroom. I settled for a black summer dress and leopard print wedges that hadn't seen the light of day since Richard. Tonight I wanted to be the old Holly – fun, popular, interesting, unchained with worries about myself.

I traced black eyeliner around my eyes, brushed on black mascara, applied pink, shimmering lipstick, and accessorised with some dangly gold earrings and a chunky necklace before spraying on some vanilla perfume. A final look in the mirror reflected someone confident and sexy. I'd forgotten who she was. If only it was as simple to overwrite the damage inside as it was to cloak and disguise the exterior.

I stepped outside into a warm summer evening ripe with possibilities and walked to Fredos. When I arrived, Andrew was already waiting outside for me, dressed in smart casual jeans and a Paul Smith shirt, his aftershave lingering in the air between us. Something musky and sweet. He was smooth and polished, his light brown hair swept back, eyes bright and buzzing with energy.

'Hi.' He beamed a smile at me, showing perfectly white teeth.

'Hi, yourself.' I moved my mouth into an equally bright smile. *See, it's easy. All you have to do is act like you're special.*

'You look amazing.' His gaze met mine.

Warmth flooded through me. 'Thanks.'

We went inside and he bought a glass of wine for us both before we sat at a quiet table at the back of the wine bar. For the next hour, we made small talk with a surprisingly easy flow. I was way out of practice, but it helped that he was chatty and asked a lot of questions. As things seemed to be going so well, he suggested we move on somewhere for a bite to eat.

'Buying you dinner is the least I can do, really, after trashing your car.' He smiled at me.

The alcohol on an empty stomach suddenly made me brave. 'OK, why not?'

'Great. Do you have a preference for food? Italian? Chinese? Indian?'

'Italian would be nice.'

'There's a nice Italian bistro in Bloomfield. It'll only take us about ten minutes to get there. Or if you want to stay in Ashfield, we could go to Pizza Express, although I did want to take you somewhere special to make up for everything.'

'I don't mind. You choose.' I wanted someone to make the decisions for me for a change. The weight of the decisions I'd made in the past rested firmly on my shoulders. I wanted to be led tonight.

'The bistro it is, then. I'll drive.' He stood up and I followed him to the car park at the rear of the wine bar. He put his hand on my elbow, guiding me to a navy blue car, all shiny paintwork and cream leather seats.

He opened the passenger door for me and I slid inside.

We snagged a table in the corner of the bistro, complete with the requisite red and white chequered tablecloth and candle centrepiece with drips of age-old wax down the edge of the glass wine bottle.

The waiter sounded authentically Italian as he handed out menus, told us the specials, and took our drinks order. He returned shortly afterwards with a bottle of wine Andrew had chosen, and while Andrew tasted it and nodded his approval to pour, I couldn't help watching him, mentally comparing him to Richard, to Will. He was nothing like Will's rugged darkness or Richard's unwavering confidence.

'I have to admit that I actually know you work for the *Ashfield Post*.' Andrew glanced up from the menu and grinned sheepishly.

I frowned slightly, trying to place him. 'We've never met before, have we?' I would definitely have remembered him.

'Your picture. It's on the paper's website. I read your articles online.'

I took a sip of fruity, mellow wine, my gaze on his, trying not to cringe. 'In my defence, I have to say it's not my finest work.'

'On the contrary, I think you manage to make even the most mundane events sound interesting.'

If only I could do the same with events in my own life.

I laughed. 'You're just being kind now.'

He chuckled. 'How long have you worked for the *Ashfield Post*?'

'A year. I used to work for a magazine and a newspaper in London before that.'

'Wow. Quite an achievement.'

I was about to say not really. The fluffy pieces for the mag seemed ridiculous now, and being a junior reporter for a newspaper was hardly the same thing as being the investigative journalist I'd wanted to be for so long. But I had to stop putting myself down. Tonight, the old Holly Gold had to be back in town, not the shell of her former self, so I took the compliment and clutched it tight. 'And what about you?' I asked. 'You're a building projects manager?'

'Yes. Probably not as interesting as your job, but it pays the bills.' He grinned. 'So, how come you're not attached? Or have you stashed your boyfriend or husband at home tonight?'

'There's no one stashed in the cupboard. Actually, no one would fit in my poky little cupboard, anyway.' I shrugged and sipped more wine. 'My last relationship didn't work out. How about you?'

'Divorced but no kids. I own my own house. And I have all my own teeth.' He flashed his teeth at me in a sexy smile.

'Teeth are always a bonus.' I grinned back.

'You must've covered quite an array of stories.'

I thought back to my portfolio of work. 'If only you knew.'

'I've been reading about that teenager who killed his parents. Terribly tragic business.' He shook his head. 'Must be awful when you have to write about things like that.'

Another picture of Jess and Stephen, stab wounds peppering their body, flashed into my head. I reached for my wine and realised it was empty. Andrew poured me some more from the bottle on the table. I took a sip, pushed the image away and concentrated on Andrew's lovely, open face. I hadn't eaten since breakfast, and the wine on an empty stomach had given me a welcome floaty feeling, my limbs feeling light and free. I was drinking too fast, but I needed it for the confidence hit.

'I knew them, actually. The family who were . . .' I trailed off, bit my lip and looked away, holding back tears.

'Really? Gosh, I'm sorry.'

I nodded a thank you. 'It's been a horrific week, as you can imagine,' I admitted, turning back to him, hoping I didn't sound weak and needy.

'It sounds like it.'

'Maybe we could talk about something else.'

'Absolutely. Perhaps I can take your mind off things for a while.' He treated me to a warm smile, tilting his glass and chinking it against mine. 'Let's eat, drink, and have a good time. Cheers.'

'Bottoms up.'

'What's it like being back in Ashfield after the hustle and bustle of London?' He settled back in his chair, head tilted.

'Quiet. I'm . . .' If I told him the truth – that I didn't know what direction I was heading in any more, that my life was empty – he'd probably run a mile. 'I'm not intending to stay at the *Ashfield Post* forever. I'm thinking of doing some freelance pieces and pitching them out. I want to write meaningful stuff, you know. Thought-provoking. Human interest stories.'

'Great idea. You could do that in your spare time and, when it takes off, then jack in the *Post*. It's never too late to have a change of direction.'

'And how long have you been a projects manager?'

'Years. It can make you tear your hair out sometimes, but I enjoy it.'

We shared a seafood pizza that was so huge the edges hung off the wooden platter dish. It was the best thing I'd tasted in a long time, although maybe that was due to the company and not the food. I was out in the land of the living with a good-looking, considerate guy, and it wasn't as scary as I'd thought it would be. Andrew didn't just know how to talk; he knew how to listen, too, thoughtfully asking questions as if I was interesting – as if I was worth knowing.

After we'd finished our meal, Andrew said, 'So, do you want coffee? Or would you like to go somewhere else for a drink?'

I'd had most of the wine, since Andrew was driving, so I didn't really need any more, but I was buzzing now. I felt happy and carefree in a way that I hadn't for a long time, the knots of tension dissolving away. I'd probably have a hell of a hangover in the morning, but I didn't want the night to end so soon. I needed Andrew to chase my demons away.

We chose a pub on Ashfield High Street and, making the most of the warm night by sitting in their crowded beer garden, he told me a story about a building project he was managing that kept going hilariously wrong.

I threw my head back and laughed. And then I couldn't stop laughing. Or maybe the story wasn't even meant to be funny, but I was drunk by then, and I didn't feel like sad, lonely Holly Gold any more. I felt on top of the world. I could do anything. Be anything.

'Sorry.' I giggled, my hand on Andrew's shoulder. 'I'm a bit pissed.'

He took my hand and held it. His fingers were thick, like sausages, the thought of which made me giggle again.

'You've got strong hands,' I said, stroking them, imagining his fingers running all over my body, picking out the shards of loneliness embedded deep beneath my skin. Sewing up the hole in my soul. I wanted to feel – just for a short while – skin on skin. The warmth of another body. Being sexy. Wanted. I yearned for that closeness with someone again. Longed to be held. Wanted to feel alive again, instead of the deadness inside me these days. Even if it was all meaningless. Why not? I was an adult. Maybe I should let myself go. I had to stop letting my past define me. And I was so tired of being alone.

'Do you want to go back to my place?' I whispered in his ear.

He pulled back slightly, his smouldering gaze on mine. 'I'm very flattered, but I'm not sure you'd remember it in the morning. How about I take you home instead?'

It felt like a slap, stilling me for a moment. I wasn't sure if I was disappointed in him or myself. I nodded, trying to hide the flame of embarrassment creeping up my neck, and stood on wobbly legs. Andrew's hand snaked around my waist to steady me as I meandered between the tables, bumping my hip on the edge of one as I passed.

'Oops, sorry,' I muttered to a seated figure, grabbing a bottle of beer just before it fell off their table and hit the floor.

'Holly?'

Wait. I knew that voice. I focused my bleary eyes on Will, sitting next to another guy.

Will looked between me and Andrew, a questioning expression on his face. 'Are you OK?'

I giggled again and leaned towards his ear, whispering slurred words. 'First night out in ages. God, I'm such a fuck-up! Don't worry, though, Mr Policeman. I'm not driving.'

'Come on, let's get you home.' Andrew tightened his grip against my waist and walked me out.

'Shorry,' I muttered, getting in the car.

'Don't worry. You've had some bad news. It happens.' Andrew reached over and fastened my seat belt for me.

'Bad life, more like,' I muttered. 'I just . . . wish . . . I'm . . . Oh, God. I haven't got a clue, really.' I rambled on some more, probably incoherently, as Andrew drove me home, following my directions.

When we arrived, he parked in the car park at the rear of my flat and walked me to the communal entrance.

He kissed me on the cheek and said, 'I'll ring you.'

I stumbled inside and up the steps. When I reached my front door, I attempted to slide my key into the lock, which kept moving out of reach for some weird reason. I groaned to myself.

He'd never call me.

Chapter 13

I didn't know which was worse: the raging hangover that felt like hundreds of fireworks were being let off inside my head or how I'd behaved with Andrew. The last part of the night was a blur, but I knew I'd been rambling on about total rubbish. He must've thought I was such a loser.

I pressed a hand to my banging forehead. 'Oh, God.' I fumbled around on the bedside table for my phone. What time was it?

8.15 a.m. I needed to be at work in forty-five minutes. I swung my legs over the bed and my stomach protested. Sweat broke out on my forehead. 'Oh, double God.'

Luckily, I made it to the bathroom just before I threw up. I cleaned my teeth, but the movement was too much for my pounding head, so I had to stop and brace myself against the edge of the sink for a minute before carrying on. I moved slowly into the kitchen and drank a pint of water with two painkillers, then curled up on the sofa and rested my head in my hands.

Right. Come on. Get moving, Holly. Get dressed. I still had two articles to write for the leisure section. One was a book review, which wouldn't take that long, and the other was a travel piece about Capri. I could easily call in sick and do them from home. Plus, I wanted to go through Dean's things and visit Jess's house – see if anything provided some sort of clue for Barbara.

I phoned Neil and told him I'd come down with some sort of stomach bug (the stomach part was true, at least), saying I'd email my pieces to him by the end of the day. He sounded quite pleased that I wasn't going to infect the rest of the staff and told me not to come back until I was better.

My phone beeped with an incoming text. I braced myself for a message from Andrew, telling me how out of order I'd been and letting me down gently, but when I opened the text the screen was blank. I checked the number and it wasn't one I recognised. Maybe someone had sent it by mistake. I deleted it, made a cup of tea, and forced myself to eat two pieces of dry toast in an attempt to settle my stomach.

I opened Dean's laptop as I ate. As it fired up through Windows, I worried it would ask me for a password, but it went directly to the home screen. Maybe the police's technical team had already removed any passwords when they'd been through it.

I clicked on the Google Chrome icon and then looked through Dean's history, which showed he'd recently checked Facebook, his email, Cambridge University's website, and a careers advice site. There were no suicide chat rooms. Nothing that spoke of how damaged his mind must've been.

I looked at the files stored on the laptop. There were many documents, a few films, and some downloaded music, but nothing else. Slowly, I went through the documents, which consisted of lots of notes and assignments for coursework, looking for any signs of morbid thoughts or emotions that may have been evident.

I glanced at the clock when I got halfway through. It was midday already. I stretched my neck, the pain in my head now a dull ache. I needed to get some of my own work done before I carried on.

I wrote a glowing book review, then pulled up several articles and photos online about Capri and put together something that even made me want to visit the place. By the time I'd finished it was late afternoon and I felt almost human again. I emailed the pieces off to Neil and heated up a carton of soup, my thoughts wandering back to Andrew. And . . . Will. I suddenly remembered he'd been in the pub at the end of the night.

I let out a groan and clutched my head in my hands. I *had* to stop drinking. I didn't know how many steps I was away from being an alcoholic, but I knew it wasn't a giant leap. I could stop. I would stop. Tomorrow, though. I'd do it tomorrow. Easy.

By the time the sky began to darken with a dusky glow outside my windows, I'd looked through everything on Dean's laptop, but nothing had jumped out at me. Next, I turned on Dean's Samsung Galaxy. Again, I wasn't prompted to enter a password. I was pretty sure a teenager would guard their privacy carefully, so it must also have been removed somehow by the police. There was an email icon so I clicked on it. Again it let me in with no password prompt. Either Dean had the tidiest inbox I'd ever seen or he'd deleted all his emails for some reason.

I scrolled through Dean's contacts but couldn't find an Emma or Rachel listed, so I looked at his texts. Most of them were between Dean and Howard, Alfie, and Fraser, his friends asking him to hook up and Dean begging off, saying he was studying. Some were from Keeley asking how he was and whether he was free to meet, but Dean repeated his excuses of college work. There were a few between Jess and Dean, his mum asking him to make sure he ate or took a break. Dean replying that he was OK and to stop fussing.

There were only a few photos in the phone's gallery: one a blurry picture of a desk, one a photo of a notebook. When I enlarged it, the notes were about maths equations. Maybe it was a fairly new phone. I checked the other apps and found nothing out of the ordinary.

Leaning back on the sofa, I stared up at the ceiling. Maybe Will and the psychiatrists in those articles were right and we'd never find a reason for Dean's actions. But I couldn't tell Barbara that yet – not until I'd tried my hardest. It wasn't like she could ever find closure, but perhaps an answer would stop her feeling so guilty that she could've done something to prevent it.

My phoned beeped with another text message on the edge of the coffee table. I rushed towards it, hoping and dreading that it was Andrew at the same time.

It was Zoe.

Hey you! How's it going? Got those medical record forms you were asking about for Barbara. XX

I replied: **Thanks, hon. Not sure if we'll need them now. Found out Dean had depression. Hope you and Leigh are OK. XX**

I clutched the phone in my hand, an empty, desolate feeling swirling inside me as I tried to work up the courage to go to Jess's house to look for . . . *something*. I knew the sight of their place would be devastating. The blood and carnage. The images that came into my head were bad enough, and they weren't even real. It would be so much worse if I actually saw the crime scene.

I chewed on my lip, wondering if I should go through with what I was thinking about doing.

Five minutes later, I swallowed my pride and dialled Will's number, his business card with the police crest resting on the arm of the sofa.

'DS Jackson,' he said, and then it was too late to change my mind and hang up.

'Hi, Will. It's Holly.'

'Hi.' He sounded distant, somewhere echoey. 'How are you? You were pretty drunk last night.'

I cringed inwardly. I remembered saying something to him as we'd left, but had no clue as to what. 'Yeah. Sorry about that. I think the shock of everything just caught up with me.'

'It's understandable.'

'Um . . . look, I was wondering . . .' I hesitated. 'I was going to go to Jess's house to have a look around.'

'We didn't miss anything at the house, Holly. We found nothing there that pointed to why Dean did it.'

'No, I'm not saying that. I just think maybe . . .' I didn't really know what I thought any more. This was way above my investigation skills. 'Barbara wanted me to have a look and just see if there was something there, you know. But I was wondering if you'd come with me. I know it's going to be awful in there.' Yes, I wanted him to hold my hand – wanted him to support me with his quiet air of solidity and strength. I was tired of doing everything alone. Especially something as horrific as this.

There was silence on the other end as he hesitated. 'I'm really busy at the moment. I—'

'It's OK. Don't worry. Course you are. I shouldn't have bothered you. I'm sorry. I know you're not supposed to be doing anything to jeopardise your job at the moment.'

'You're not bothering me. Look, can you give me a couple of hours? I'll meet you outside their house at eight.'

A thrill rushed through me. Relief? Or something more?

'Yes, of course. Thanks, Will. I'll see you there.'

'Will do. Oh, and Holly . . . you're not a fuck-up.'

Chapter 14

I stood on Jess and Stephen's doorstep, staring at the bright red front door. Apparently, Jess and Stephen had moved into the house five years ago. It was an average house in an average street in an average town. But now it was infamous. There had been so many photos of it plastered in the press lately. It was now known as 'The House of Horrors'.

'Are you really sure you want to go in there?' Will asked.

I glanced nervously at the keys in my hand. 'I have to.' And I slid them into the lock before I could turn around and walk away.

I stepped inside the narrow hallway and stopped, frozen, the smell of something metallic and rotting hitting me. I put my hand to my mouth.

'Are you OK? You've gone white.' Will put a hand on my shoulder.

I took a breath. 'I'm OK,' I managed to squeak.

The hallway looked normal: coats on a rack by the door, shoes kicked off carelessly at the bottom of the stairs – a pair of work boots that were probably Stephen's, a pair of Jess's sandals, and a pair of Converse that must've belonged to Dean. I knew I was going to see far worse upstairs, where the killing took place, but somehow the sight of all three pairs of shoes together, such incongruous items, wedged a splinter through my heart. How many times had they sat there together like that before Friday had happened? Hundreds? Thousands, probably. What had changed?

'You don't have to do this.'

I nodded vigorously but stepped into the lounge to our left.

'Everything happened upstairs so you won't see much down here,' Will said as I glanced around the room.

If you ignored the dusting of fingerprint powder everywhere you could imagine Jess and Stephen and Dean had been called away suddenly while they were in the midst of tidying up. There was a wine-coloured velour corner sofa unit sitting in a strange diagonal position in front of a large flat-screen TV on the wall. Underneath the TV were some storage units, and next to those were patio doors that looked on to the rear garden. Magazines were messily strewn on the coffee table. I spotted *Pizzazz* – the magazine I used to work for – the front cover promising exclusive photos of the year's best-dressed celebrities inside. There were DVDs, various remote controls, and CDs scattered on the floor. 'Did the police do this when they were searching or was it this messy before?'

'Our teams did it when they went through everything. And they *did* go through everything. I don't know what you're looking for.'

'I don't either.' I bent down and gathered up some DVDs. Action films, some romantic comedies, a couple of documentaries. How could everything be so normal?

We headed into the kitchen, and I stood in the centre and turned 360 degrees, taking everything in: a microwave, a stainless steel kettle in one corner of the worktop, a square wicker basket in the opposite corner.

I opened the fridge, probably to delay the moment when I'd have to go upstairs. There was a half-empty bottle of wine. Or was it half full? A memory hit me then – me on the phone to Jess after I'd left Ashfield and started at the magazine, worrying about how long it would be before I'd get the chance to do proper stories. Her telling me to just enjoy the ride. That everything would happen when it was ready. And to think of all the experience I was getting in the meantime. She'd said, the glass isn't half empty or half full, it's refillable.

Hot tears seared my eyelids as my gaze roamed the rest of the fridge's contents, evidence of everyday life: an unopened packet of salad leaves, jars of condiments, bottles of beer, milk, a packet of chicken breasts that had leaked through the polystyrene tray underneath and had dripped blood on to the shelf below in a pool of pinky-red. While Jess had been thinking of what to cook for dinner, had Dean been planning to kill them all?

My throat tightened and I slammed the door shut.

I turned to the kitchen drawers, opening them as Will watched me silently, leaning against the worktop. They were full of the usual stuff: cutlery, dishcloths, takeaway menus, phone chargers.

I moved to a pile of post on the worktop next to the wicker basket.

'There's nothing addressed to Dean there,' Will said, but I looked anyway.

A phone bill for Jess, a joint bank statement, a letter from Downs Road College with term dates for next year. I put them back and looked through the basket, which was full of medication. Paracetamol tablets, soluble vitamin C tablets, some drops to remove earwax, athlete's foot cream, plasters,

'Look, why don't we just go?' Will asked. 'There's nothing here, I told you. Dean was suffering from depression and it obviously must've escalated into some kind of psychotic episode. That's it. There is no other reason. I really don't think you want to go upstairs until the house has been cleaned.'

'But who hasn't suffered from mild depression at one time or another?' I said, unable to meet his eyes. 'Life *is* stressful. It throws things at us and it's natural to get down sometimes. But those people don't kill their whole family and then themselves. There had to be something that made things worse – a trigger of some kind.'

'I don't think this is going to do Barbara any good. It's just going to prolong everything,' he said firmly.

'Is it? Because I don't see how it's ever going to get any better for her anyway.'

'So, hypothetically, what if Dean had kept a diary and you found it? And it said that Jess and Stephen had argued with him that night. Maybe they'd called him lazy or useless, maybe they'd refused to give him some money, maybe they'd had a go at him for not cleaning up the bathroom after himself or maybe he'd been grounded for something. And then he'd written all of that down and killed them. Would that make it any better for Barbara? Would she blame her daughter or son-in-law or herself more or less? Is it really worth putting her through something like that?' He paused. 'Look, it was a terrible tragedy that no one could have foreseen. It shouldn't have happened, but it did. And all this running around looking for something you'll never find isn't going to help. You can never understand what really goes on in someone else's head.'

My shoulders slumped and I held on to the edge of the worktop for stability as I processed what Will had said, my thoughts turning this way and that.

He was right. It was over. There were no answers to find.

I nodded silently.

He took my hand in his. It was warm and strong and mine seemed to fit inside his perfectly. 'Shall we go?'

'Yes,' I whispered.

I held on tight as he walked me outside and then he let go, my fingers sliding through his until they met warm air.

'That guy last night,' Will said tentatively, his tone more of a question than a statement. 'Are you seeing him?'

'I doubt it.' *Not after the way I acted.*

He reached out and swept away a lock of hair from my cheek. I trembled inside and looked deep into his eyes, willing him to ask me out. Once, I'd turned him down. If he asked again, I wouldn't do so a second time. But I was too afraid of the rejection to ask him myself.

He dropped his hand to his side. 'Do you need a lift? My car's down there.' He jerked his head further down the street.

I shook my head, disappointment flooding through me. I looked away. 'No, thanks. I'll walk. It's not far. I think I need some fresh air, anyway.'

'Take care, then.'

'Thank you for coming with me tonight.' I turned and headed down the street. It was dark now, the street lights giving off an ineffectual sodium haze, my shoes quietly slapping against the pavement as I vaguely registered Will's car starting behind me. I thought about how I could try to help Barbara get through the next days and weeks and months, worrying about what I'd say to her. Maybe she could join some sort of support group. I wondered if she'd move away now, just like I'd done. Run away from all the reminders here.

It registered then that a car was travelling slowly behind me, its engine so quiet it hadn't penetrated through my thoughts for a while. I turned around. It was non-descript, black, the interior dark so I couldn't see the driver, travelling maybe five miles an hour. Was it Will, making sure I got home safe? Or someone searching for a particular address?

I increased my pace, heading towards a T-junction. I turned left. The car did the same, still travelling at a slow speed.

My phone rang. I stopped walking, fumbling in my bag for it. I answered and glanced back at the car. It had pulled in next to the kerb now.

'Hi, it's Andrew.'

'Oh, hi!' That threw me for a moment. He was the last person I ever expected to hear from again. I started walking as I talked.

'So I bet you had a raging hangover this morning!' He laughed. I liked the sound of it.

'Mmm. I'm sorry about that. It had been a really bad day and—'

'Don't worry about it. I thought you were pretty cute when you were drunk.'

I smiled. 'I hope I wasn't boring, rambling about all sorts of crap.'

'You? Boring? I don't think you could be. No, seriously, don't worry about it. I was wondering, actually, if you wanted to meet up again.'

'Um . . . yes.' My heartbeat quickened. 'That would be nice. I promise not to drink so much next time.'

'How about Thursday?'

'Yeah. Sounds good. Look, by way of apology, why don't I cook you something?'

'We always seem to be apologising to each other, don't we?' He laughed again. 'But I'd like that.'

'OK, well, how about you come over at seven?'

'Great. I'll look forward to it. Which flat number are you in?'

'Number sixty-five.'

We said goodbye and I hung up. I glanced over my shoulder again to see if the car was still there. The driver had turned off the headlights, but I was too far away now to see if there was anyone still inside it. I shrugged to myself. It was nothing. They'd obviously found the address they were looking for.

Chapter 15

I was in the office earlier than usual on Wednesday, firstly because I'd felt bad about calling in sick the day before, and secondly, the *Ashfield Post* was out today and I wanted to get a look at Brian's story about Dean.

I said good morning to Donna, the receptionist, and grabbed a paper from the edge of her desk where spare copies were always kept, reading the headlines as I walked up the stairs.

'Slaughter in Suburbia'.

Anger ignited inside me. I pushed through the double doors at the top of the stairs and walked past the empty cubicles to my desk, sat down, and read more.

It was slanted in a way that made Dean out to be a troublemaker, severely disturbed, with a possible obsession about black magic. Where the fuck had Brian dredged this bullshit up from? It was no more sensational than I'd read in the tabloids, but it felt like a betrayal. Brian and Neil both knew I'd been friends with the Hudsons.

I stewed at my desk, jigging my knee up and down, swivelling in my chair until Neil arrived.

'Morning,' he said to me, stopping by my desk. 'Was it a twenty-four-hour thing?'

I held up the paper, my face taut as I tried to keep calm. 'What's this?'

'That's our lead story and it's going to sell more copies than we've sold in ages.'

'But it's—'

'It's *news*, Holly. You know, a *news*paper sells *news*!'

'This isn't news. It's complete bollocks made up out of thin air! I could've written something much more sensitive and accurate.'

'Which would *not* help sell more copies.' He tilted his head, eyebrows raised, as if I didn't have a clue what I was talking about.

I heard the office doors open behind me but didn't look back.

Neil glanced over my shoulder, said good morning to someone, then addressed me. 'I think you should come into my office and we can have a chat.' He walked into his office, dumped his briefcase on his messy desk and sat down as I followed. 'Close the door, please.'

I tried hard not to slam it, but the glass surround still shook as it shut.

'Sit down.'

I sat.

He leaned forwards, elbows on the desk. 'I don't think this is working out.'

'Is there something wrong with my work?' I jutted my chin out with a confidence I didn't feel.

'No. Your work's good. It's your attitude. You've tried to muscle in on Brian's story. You—'

'It's not *Brian's* story. It's the Hudsons'. And Barbara Acres deserves more than that piece of—'

He held a hand up to silence me. 'I don't think you're cut out to work here. This isn't the right news media for you. And I'm not having petty staff squabbles getting in the way of me running this office. It's a small place. We don't cover the kind of stories you obviously want to do, anyway.'

I opened my mouth to speak, on the verge of saying I'd do better, toe the line – to beg for my job. But I'd been toeing the line for years and it hadn't got me anywhere I wanted to be. And I'd been trying to be *better* for years, but that wasn't working out so well, either. My life was a mess. I'd been moving in the wrong direction for too long, but I was the only one who could change things. I needed to just stop moaning about it all and stop being scared.

'You know what, you're actually right,' I said, sitting up taller.

Neil raised his eyebrows in surprise.

'I quit.' It was better than him firing me.

'Yes, I think that's for the best.'

'Do you want me to work a month's notice?'

'Actually, I think we can probably cover things until I find someone new.'

'Right. OK, then.' I stood, feeling weirdly euphoric.

'I'll give you a good reference. I still think you write a great story.'

'Thanks.' I held my hand out to shake his.

He leaned over and shook mine. 'Look after yourself, Toto.'

I gathered my meagre belongings together and stuffed them in a plastic bag I had in my bottom drawer. As I walked out of the building, I saw Brian getting out of his car.

'Going somewhere?' he called out.

I stormed towards him. 'I can't believe that piece of shit you call an article! How could you write such insensitive propaganda when you knew they were my friends?!' I yelled.

He snorted. 'You're so high and mighty, aren't you? What do you think this job's all about?'

'How about the truth?'

He smirked. 'What planet are you on?'

I narrowed my eyes at him. 'Anyway, I'm leaving. So, thankfully, we won't have to clap eyes on each other any more.' I turned my back on him and walked to my car.

'Yeah, I knew you couldn't hack it!' he called out triumphantly.

I stopped dead. Turned around. 'The only thing I can't hack is *ever* becoming like you. And at least I don't compromise my integrity!' I hit the button on my key fob to open the boot, dumped the bag inside then got in and slid behind the wheel. My anger was replaced by a sudden calm, my shoulders felt lighter, the dark clouds fluttering away. The calm morphed into a heightened sense of purpose as I started the car. Now I had no job, I'd *have* to concentrate on freelance work. *Real* stories about *real* issues that would hopefully connect with people on a heartfelt, emotional level. Stories that changed how people thought, or made them consider other viewpoints. Stories that raised awareness about worthy causes. The possibilities were endless.

And I knew where to start.

Chapter 16

I rang the bell of a small home on an estate of identical-looking houses and waited.

I was just about to leave when the door was opened by a haggard-looking man with grey stubble sprouting from his jaw, who looked like he needed about a year's worth of good sleep. He had a wrinkled dishcloth over his shoulder.

'Mr Tucker?' I asked, trying to avoid looking at the brown stain on the front of his shirt.

'Yes.' His voice oozed weariness.

'My name's Holly Gold. I'm a freelance investigative journalist' – *as of ten minutes ago* – 'and I'm researching a story about teenage suicide. It's going to be a very sensitive article, and I wondered if you'd be willing to talk to me about your daughter.'

He blinked rapidly, a deer-in-the-headlights, stunned expression, but didn't tell me to bugger off, so I continued.

'I'm really sorry about Rachel. I was hoping my piece might help other parents going through the same thing.'

He sucked in a breath. 'I don't know how I can help you. I still don't understand what Rachel was going through myself. It's all just . . .' He made a strangled noise in the back of his throat.

'I'm so sorry. I didn't mean to upset you. I know this is a very difficult time,' I blurted out, feeling guilty for turning up on his doorstep now. I shouldn't have come. *This* is why I'd never make a hardened journalist. Why I'd procrastinated so long. Why I'd always written fluff pieces. I was too worried about hurting people.

He swallowed hard, his Adam's apple bobbing up and down.

I was about to turn and leave when he said, 'Why don't you come in? Jenny's upstairs – my wife. She's been sedated. It would actually feel good to talk to someone. And if I can help another parent in the same situation, then at least something good will come out of it.'

He held the door open.

I stepped straight into the open-plan lounge and glanced around at a room in disarray. There was a duvet and pillow bunched up at one end of the sofa and piles of clothes at the other end. Empty mugs littered the small coffee table, along with an ashtray overflowing with cigarette butts.

'Sorry, it's a bit of a mess. I've been sleeping down here to let Jenny get some rest. I haven't cleared up yet.' He stared sadly at the sofa.

'Do you have anyone to help? Friends or family?'

'Friends have been bringing over food that goes untouched. They can't help with a broken heart, can they?'

He removed the dishcloth from his shoulder. 'Do you want a cup of tea?'

'Please don't go to any trouble, Mr Tucker.'

'It's no trouble. And call me Pete. Have a seat on the . . .' He picked up the pile of clothes on the sofa and looked around for an uncluttered space to move them to. The only free space was the stairs in the corner, so he left them there and then walked out of the room.

He returned a few minutes later with two mugs of tea, setting them down on the table next to all the empty ones. 'Sorry, I forgot to ask if you take sugar.'

'No, it's OK. I don't.' I perched on the edge of the sofa. 'Rachel was sixteen, is that right?'

'Yes. She was in her last year at Ashfield Girls' School. She wanted to be a model. We told her she'd have to finish her education before she started looking into that.' He smiled, walking towards a bookshelf at the back of the room. He picked up a photo and handed it to me.

Rachel was beautiful – eyes set a little far apart and a slight gap in her front teeth made her quirkily different, but no less stunning. Her hair was braided on one side, head tilted slightly, and she was smiling for the camera with a sparkle in her eyes.

'She was lovely. When was this taken?'

He sat next to me and leaned back against the sofa. 'Last year.'

'Can you tell me what your daughter was like?' I handed the photo back to him.

He looked down at the picture in his hands, his eyes watery with grief. 'She was always confident. Even when she was a little girl. But she wasn't one of those precocious kids, you know? She was a good girl. Thoughtful, helpful around the house. When she got to about thirteen she started taking an interest in how she looked. She experimented with hair and make-up and clothes. She loved fashion. She was always devouring those kinds of magazines and copying the models' looks. Obsessed with them. I'm sure I don't have to tell you what teenage girls are like.'

I smiled sadly. 'No. I was obsessed with the same magazines. But then I became obsessed with writing for one.'

'The next thing was, she thought she was fat. She started trying all these faddy diets and things. She either wouldn't eat anything or she'd binge a lot in one go. We didn't realise at first that we should be worried. Jenny thought it was normal for teenagers to be picky about what they ate. She'd gone through a similar phase at that age when she'd started noticing boys.' He placed the picture of Rachel on the coffee table in front of us, picked up the mug of tea, and rested it on his knee. 'But then Jenny started paying more attention and she discovered Rachel sneaking off after she'd eaten a lot and being sick. Jenny also found laxatives in Rachel's room. It always ended up in a big row.'

'Rachel was bulimic?'

'Yes.' He folded his lips in on themselves and blinked as if trying to keep tears at bay. His pain was raw and seemed to permeate the air. 'And it got so bad that nothing Jenny or I did helped. Rachel would still keep purging or binging. In the end we took her to see Dr Baird. He's a child psychologist. He has a really good reputation. We're not well off, but we wanted the best for our daughter. We wanted her to get well again.'

'Dr Baird?' A nervous feeling of anticipation swelled in my throat. 'Yes, do you know him?'

'I know who he is. When did she see him?'

'Three weeks before she killed herself. Rachel talked to him in private. She didn't want Jenny or I there. And he told her there was a terrific new medication that would help her.'

'Do you know what she was prescribed?'

He nodded, then stood and left the room. He returned carrying a white and blue box and handed it to me. 'These were in her handbag. She left it here when she . . . when she went out the day she . . .'

I stared at the packet. Caprixanine. The same tablets Dean had been given.

The anticipation turned to dread. 'Did Rachel take them?'

'Yes. You can see from the packet.'

I opened the flap and checked the blister packs inside. Twenty tablets missing.

'And then what happened? Did the tablets help her?'

'Rachel went downhill after that. She was jittery all the time. Up till all hours of the morning because she couldn't sleep. When she did manage to sleep, she had terrible dreams of killing herself. She started self-harming, cutting herself with razor blades, although we didn't find that out until after the post-mortem because she kept it hidden well. She refused to eat. Jenny and I were really worried so I called Dr Baird to tell him that Rachel seemed to be getting much worse.'

'And what did he say?'

'He told me Rachel was suffering from agitated depression as a result of her bulimia and that it would improve soon – that she should keep taking the medication. A few days later, she was dead.' He stopped abruptly and took a deep, shuddering breath. 'Rachel didn't leave a note. My wife and I were both at work that morning. My wife called her at around nine-thirty to check up on her and Rachel said she was watching TV. She told Jenny she loved her. Those were the last words Rachel said.' Tears streamed down his cheeks.

I reached out and touched his arm.

He looked at my hand for a moment and then shot up and walked out of the room. I heard him blowing his nose.

I thought back to the radio report about Rachel I'd heard after visiting Barbara on Saturday morning. I thought about the devastating news Pete and Jenny had received that Rachel had jumped in front of a train.

A few minutes later he returned and sat next to me, staring at the wall. 'Sorry.'

'You've got nothing to apologise for.'

'If we'd got her to Dr Baird sooner, maybe it wouldn't have happened. We should have taken her sooner. We left it too long.'

'You did what you thought was right for your daughter. You did what you could.'

'But it wasn't enough.' He clenched his fists, the desperation in his voice heartbreaking to hear. 'It wasn't enough!' He pounded his thigh with his fist.

'Had Rachel had any previous thoughts of suicide? Or had she ever self-harmed before?'

'No.' He shook his head. 'That's why it was such a shock.'

'Did you ever think her worsening symptoms could've been caused by the tablets?'

He gave me a confused look. 'Of course not. Dr Baird said they were a mild antidepressant. Millions of people take antidepressants every day. He said they were safer than aspirin. It was the bulimia that messed her head up.'

'There's been another suicide recently. You might've read about it in the paper.'

'I haven't had time to read the paper and we don't really watch the news.'

'A local teenager, Dean Hudson. He'd also seen Dr Baird and was taking Caprixanine. He wasn't suicidal and didn't seem depressed, either, but he murdered his parents and then took his own life. I . . . I knew the family.'

'How tragic.'

'Did Rachel ever mention Dean? Did she know him?'

Pete repeated Dean's name as he stared at the floor, thinking.

'Dean went to Downs Road College,' I offered.

He shook his head. 'No, I never heard Rachel mention him.'

I thought about suicide clusters again. Had Rachel *heard* about Dean on the news and that had triggered a suicidal reaction? 'Do you know if Rachel could've found out about Dean? Maybe on social media?'

'It's possible. She liked using Snapchat and Instagram. I'm sure her friends would've been talking about it if it happened in Ashfield.'

'How about Emma Tolley? Did Rachel mention her name at all?'

He shook his head.

I picked up the box of Caprixanine. 'Can I look at the information sheet inside?'

'Yes.'

I opened the box, but there was no patient leaflet inside. 'It's not here.'

'Maybe Rachel threw it away. Jenny and I always do. You can never get the tablets back in the box because the leaflet always bunches up and gets in the way.'

I heard a female voice calling Pete from upstairs then. The woman sounded in pain.

He shot off the sofa. 'That's Jenny. I have to go and check on her.'

I stood up. 'Of course. Thank you for your time. And once again, I'm really sorry for your loss.'

He nodded sadly. 'If you need to speak to me again for your article, that's OK. If I can help another parent spot the signs of bulimia before it's too late, then it will be something worthwhile.'

I shook his hand on the doorstep, my mind racing with questions that he couldn't answer. Was it possible that Caprixanine had made two people suicidal and one of them violently psychotic? Dean wasn't even taking them when he died and Rachel had only taken twenty. Could Emma Tolley have been taking them, too? Was Caprixanine to blame, or had all three teenagers really suffered from depression that escalated to tragic ends? It seemed like a hell of a coincidence to me.

A reason where there is no reason.

Chapter 17

I left Pete on his doorstep looking numb and bewildered and walked towards my car, scrabbling in my bag for my keys. I was just pulling my door open when I spotted a black car parked a little further down the street. I was useless at recognising makes of cars, but it was the same shape and colour as the one that had been kerb-crawling behind me the night before. The sun glinted on the windscreen so I couldn't see if there was anyone inside or not.

I shook my head to myself and slid behind the wheel. Of course it wasn't the same car. No one had any reason to be following me. There must be thousands of the same type of car on the road. It probably belonged to one of Pete's neighbours.

I pulled out my mobile phone and dialled Miles. The call went straight to his voicemail.

'Miles, it's me. Can you give me a ring back as soon as you're free? I wanted to pick your brains about something.' I hung up and drove home.

I let myself into my flat. It felt weird to be here in the middle of a workday, but also exhilarating, too. I was sure I was on to something that might explain Rachel and Dean's behaviour. Neither of them had been suicidal or violent before they'd been taking Caprixanine.

I booted up my laptop and typed in 'Caprixanine'. There were several articles hailing it as the new wonder antidepressant and it had been on the market for six months. Unlike the old selective serotonin reuptake inhibitors, or SSRIs, Caprixanine differed in its mechanism of action from all other antidepressants on the market and had been shown to be well tolerated without significant side effects, had a rapid onset of action, and patients could abruptly stop taking it without the need for a gradual reduction of dose. It was also non-addictive.

Then I stumbled upon the Medicines and Healthcare products Regulatory Agency, or MHRA, website. Under Caprixanine there were two PDF documents to click on. One was the patient information leaflet, which should've been in Rachel's box of tablets but had been mislaid or maybe thrown away. It was a two-page document and listed what it was used for: depression, anxiety, obsessive–compulsive disorder, insomnia, bulimia, post-traumatic stress disorder. There was also other information about the dosage, taking it with food or drink, driving or operating machinery while on the drug, contraindications, taking it while pregnant, and other drugs to avoid when taking it. There was one passage related to its use in children:

Caprixanine is not for use in children and adolescents under eighteen.

Patients under eighteen have an increased risk of side effects such as suicide attempt, suicidal thoughts and hostility (predominantly aggression, oppositional behaviour and anger) when they take this class of medicines.

I peered at the screen aghast, wondering how it was possible that a psychiatrist who specialised in children wasn't aware of this when he'd prescribed them the drug.

Further down, it listed several side effects. Common ones were insomnia, headache, nausea, diarrhoea, weight loss, yawning, dry mouth and indigestion. Uncommon ones were excess air or gas in the intestines, passing gas, itching skin, and abnormal dreams. Rare side effects were dizziness, heartburn, and loss of taste. And finally, very rare ones were sensation of spinning, stomach discomfort, upset or pain, and gastrointestinal bleeding.

At the end it said: *If you experience any side effects, talk to your doctor, pharmacist or nurse. This includes any possible side effects not listed in this leaflet. You can also report side effects directly via the Yellow Card Scheme,* and gave the website of the MHRA. I clicked on the link and it was indeed a form to fill in for patients reporting side effects.

Next, I looked at the second PDF file, which was a much longer document. Sixteen pages of what was called a 'Summary of Product Characteristics'. It listed a lot of the same information as in the leaflet, along with more details. But again, the use of this drug in youngsters caught my eye:

Caprixanine is not recommended for the treatment of depression in patients aged less than eighteen years since the safety and efficacy of Caprixanine have not been established in this age group. In clinical studies in children and adolescents treated with other antidepressants, suicide-related behaviour (suicide attempt and suicidal thoughts) and hostility (predominantly aggression, oppositional behaviour and anger) were more frequently observed than in those treated with placebo.

There was a section that talked about 'Undesirable Effects'.

The most commonly reported adverse reaction was nausea. Adverse reactions were usually mild or moderate and occurred within the first two weeks of treatment. The reactions were usually transient and did not generally lead to cessation of therapy.

I read through lots of other information that had simply been expanded upon from the information leaflet. Near the bottom was a table showing adverse reactions observed in clinical trials, with five lines quoting some of the drug's effects in different parts of the body. The only thing listed under 'Psychiatric Disorders' was that abnormal dreams were common. Underneath were several paragraphs about 'Clinical Efficacy and Safety', which gave very brief information about clinical trial results. It seemed that Caprixanine had been tested on 2,200 patients in four double-blind, placebo-controlled, six- to eight-week fixed-dose studies. The document went on to list different statistics, but the gist of it was that Caprixanine was a very effective drug that was superior to any old-type SSRI antidepressant on the market, had very few side effects in general, and was suitable to be discontinued abruptly with no withdrawal problems.

Next, I typed in 'Dr Baird' and found many articles about him being an expert child psychiatrist. He'd published a lot of medical papers that had been quoted by others. He appeared to be a highly regarded doctor. So why was he giving Caprixanine to under-eighteens if it wasn't considered safe to do so?

I tried to find statistics on people taking antidepressants, but most of what I found wasn't current or definitive. I discovered some numbers from a couple of years earlier that made my head spin. A huge chunk of the population took psychiatric drugs, with kids under five years old being the fastest-growing market.

I sat back and chewed on my lip, thinking about Emma Tolley again. Her parents hadn't noticed any depression prior to Emma killing herself, but she had never sought any medical help. Caprixanine hadn't even been available on prescription a year ago, so if the theory building in my head was right, then Emma's suicide couldn't be connected to the other two and was a completely separate tragedy.

I turned my attention to Tragatech's background next. They weren't just an international pharmaceutical company – they also owned several other huge corporations that manufactured agricultural pesticides and poisons, food additives, GM crops, veterinary products, and industrial chemicals. They'd been involved in several price-fixing and drug monopoly schemes by refusing to let other companies produce generic versions of their drugs during several epidemics and scares because they didn't want to lose profits. Their actions meant that many patients couldn't get access to life-saving medications in time.

There were mentions of other scandals, from dumping toxic waste to fuelling the misdiagnosis of various psychiatric disorders through aggressive marketing and close ties to psychiatric associations. Somehow they'd never been held to account, and maybe this was because they were reported to donate heavily to political and lobbying campaigns. They were listed on the Forbes Biggest Public Companies List as having a 2015 market worth of $218 billion.

My phone rang then as I peered at the laptop's screen. It was Miles. Just the person I needed.

'You wanted something?' He sounded distracted.

'Hi, Miles, *how are you?*' I said sarcastically, trying to point out his lack of a warm and cosy greeting.

'What? I'm all right,' he said shortly. 'I'm busy. What did you want?'

Sometimes it felt like I had to make an appointment if I wanted to speak to my brother. 'I wanted to ask you about Caprixanine.'

There was a pause on the other end.

'Are you still there?'

'I'm driving.'

'Haven't you got hands-free?'

'Why do you want to know? Did you go and get some antidepressants?'

I didn't correct him. 'So what can you tell me about it? Tania mentioned it was Tragatech's new wonder drug.'

Another pause. Then he said, 'Get out of the fucking way, you tosser!' which I assumed wasn't meant for me. 'Hang on.'

I heard static, and when he spoke again the reception was tinny, as if he had put me on loudspeaker. He seemed reluctant to talk, as he let out a sigh before launching into a spiel that sounded like he was reading from a sales brochure. 'It's a new, innovative, first-in-class antidepressant. Its efficacy and safety are mind-blowingly good. It's incredibly well tolerated, has far fewer side effects than leading previous treatments and has a rapid onset of effect. Considering there are about

350 million people worldwide suffering from depression, this is a *major* breakthrough. It means patients don't have to suffer the horrible side effects of the old SSRIs any more.'

'But it's only supposed to be prescribed for adults, right? So does that mean a doctor prescribing it to under-eighteens would be considered negligent?'

There was another pause on the other end. 'What's that got to do with you taking it?' His voice had an uneasy edge to it.

'I didn't say I was taking it. So, would they be considered negligent?'

'Are you harping on about Dean Hudson again? Is that what these questions are about?' He shouted at someone else to hurry up.

I butted into his string of abuse at another driver and said, 'Can't you just answer the question for me? Would Dr Baird be considered negligent in that situation?'

'You're talking about off-label use and it's perfectly legal and very common.' He said offhandedly, back to being cocky again.

'Off-label. What does that mean?'

'It means prescribing a drug for a disease or symptom or patient population that it hasn't been approved for.'

'So you could prescribe a drug to adolescents that is meant for adults – that hasn't had any clinical trials carried out on its safety and effect in kids – and that's *legal*?' I frowned incredulously.

'Yes. Probably about seventy-five per cent of drugs prescribed for children haven't been tested on them. It's *normal*.'

'And does the doctor have to inform the patient about this off-label use?'

'No.'

'No?!' I was momentarily gobsmacked.

'It happens with many different drugs, all the time. A drug isn't given blanket approval for everything, only for specific treatments. And getting approval for a new disease or group of people is time-consuming and costly.'

'But . . . that means that the public are acting as guinea pigs, then, surely. If you don't know whether a drug works or not for a particular group of people or disease, or even what the side effects are, then effectively the drug company and prescribing doctor are carrying out a clinical trial on them without them knowing or having informed consent, right? And the—'

'I can't discuss that with you.'

'Why not?'

'Because there's a confidentiality clause in my contract. I can't discuss those kinds of things with any old Tom, Dick or Harry,' he said in the same tone you'd use to talk to an idiot.

'Look, I'm trying to get answers for Barbara. You know that.'

'You're not a bloody doctor! Dean Hudson was mentally *ill*! You didn't *know* him. You hadn't seen them for years so you have no clue what you're talking about. And I don't think you're in any frame of mind to be helping someone else when you can't even help yourself. Do you?'

'What's that supposed to mean?' My voice rose.

'You're a fucking drunk, Holly! And you're acting completely irrationally! You need to sort yourself out. I called your work first because I thought you'd be there and they said you'd walked out. Are you mad? Why did you do that?'

'Long story. But anyway—'

'Have you really got the motivation to work for yourself?' he said.

I bristled.

'What are you going to do for money without a wage?'

'I'll . . . look, I wasn't phoning to talk about my wages!' I ground my teeth and ploughed on. 'This isn't just about Dean. There was another girl, Rachel Tucker. She saw Dr Baird and was on Caprixanine. She was bulimic, with no history of depression or suicidal thoughts either, and she killed herself after taking three weeks' worth of tablets! Either Dr Baird's a really bad doctor or there's something wrong with the drug.'

'What are you, some kind of expert on mental illness now? Did you train for years to study it?' Sarcasm oozed from his voice. 'No. So you don't have a clue what you're talking about. A drug goes through rigorous testing and scrutiny by regulators before it gets approved. And if you go round saying things like that, you're going to damage your own credibility and get sued.'

'So you can't give me more information, then? Or *won't*, more like.'

'Don't be ridiculous. I'd get fired!'

I remembered then something Miles had said when I was at his house for dinner. 'You said Dr Baird did clinical research for Tragatech. Is that what he's doing with Caprixanine? Is there some kind of clinical trial going on for its use in adolescents?'

'What are you playing at, Holly?' His voice had a cold edge to it.

'Oh, sorry. I have a confidentiality clause in my contract and I can't tell you.'

He snorted. 'You phoned me!'

'And now I'm hanging up. Thanks for your *help*.' I stabbed the 'Off' button, fuming.

My head was exploding with questions that Miles obviously wouldn't answer. I needed to speak to a source who could help me navigate through the inner workings of the drug industry, so I turned back to my laptop. A little while later, by accidentally following another link, I came across many articles involving a prescription drug called Tiazal, going back to 2003. The drug was licensed by regulators in 1991 and prescribed in its thousands for adolescents to treat ADHD. It was made by Grafloxx Solutions, an American company, and they covered up known findings that the drug caused a dramatically increased risk of suicidality, self-harm, and aggression in under-eighteens. Clinical trial data was falsified or distorted by Grafloxx, and their PR and marketing departments spun a lie to healthcare professionals, promoting it to doctors as a safe and effective treatment for the attention deficit condition that had exploded in recent years, even though they knew it didn't work and caused deadly side effects. During the years it was prescribed, Tiazal was worth a whopping $65 billion to Grafloxx.

The drug regulatory bodies were also duped into believing the falsified data, which, when discovered, showed that children became suicidal whilst on the drug. No criminal charges were brought against Grafloxx because of legal 'loopholes', although they received a fine of $3 billion for fraudulently promoting the drug – small change for the company when Tiazal had made them so much profit. Several class action suits by families of children who'd killed themselves whilst on Tiazal had resulted in wins for the plaintiffs. The drug had finally been removed from the market in 2005, a whole fourteen years after it was licensed for sale and did untold damage.

The scandal had been exposed by Daniel Foster, an ex-drug sales rep for Grafloxx who turned whistle-blower. He was a Brit who'd worked for their American arm, and after it all came to light he'd returned home, turned his back on conventional medicine and retrained as a naturopath. A link to his website was listed. I clicked on it, found his contact number and called him, but it went to voicemail. I left a message, asking if he would be able to talk to me about the inner workings of the pharmaceutical industry. Then I hung up and stared at the wall, my stomach roiling with disgust and disbelief at how any of this was possible. It was unimaginable that Grafloxx had got away with putting the youth of society at risk for so long, or that so many kids had died while Grafloxx were getting fat profits. What kind of a society are we living in?

Chapter 18

We've got another problem.

What?

Not what. Who. A reporter who's asking questions.

It won't last. The Hudsons will be old news soon.

She's different. She knows the family. I've been watching her. I think she's made the connection.

Have you had ears on her?

Of course. A Trojan was sent to her phone via text. I'm listening, don't worry.

Name?

Holly Gold.

Gold? Is that a coincidence?

No. You're correct.

He'll keep her in line. He's too invested.

Or shall I silence her?

*Not yet. Watch. Listen. Remind him he's got a wife and kid.
We might need to send them a warning.*

Chapter 19

'Do you want dinner? I'm doing an amazing culinary creation of chicken nuggets, chips, and peas. It's the only thing Leigh will eat at the moment.' Zoe glanced affectionately over at Leigh seated at the kitchen table, drawing a picture. 'Is that a dog?' Zoe peered over Leigh's shoulder. 'It's very good.' She ruffled her daughter's hair.

'It's a cat-a-pillow,' Leigh insisted without looking up.

'With four paws?' I asked. 'Are you sure it's not a dogaterpillar?'

Leigh's frantic scrawling stopped and she looked up at me, bursting into loud, hysterical laughter.

I smiled. 'Glad I can make someone laugh these days.' I leaned over and blew a raspberry on her neck until she struggled to get away, giggling uncontrollably.

'So?' Zoe placed a hand on her hip, standing behind her daughter. 'Do you want to taste my Michelin star cuisine?'

'How can I refuse an offer like that? It's better than another ready meal at my place.'

Zoe turned to the freezer and dumped a packet of frozen nuggets into a baking dish.

'I quit my job today,' I said.

'What?' Zoe swung around. 'Really?'

I nodded, grinning.

'Good for you.' She grinned back. 'You weren't happy there.'

'Thanks. That's the complete opposite to what Miles said. I'm going to do some freelance work and see what happens.'

'That's great! Now you can get your teeth into things you really want to write about. It'll be good for you.'

I felt a grateful, warm rush of love for Zoe. She was the only one I could rely on to be supportive of me, even when I didn't deserve it.

She sprayed oven chips from a packet into the baking tray next to the nuggets and slid it in the oven.

'I think this calls for a toast,' I said, pulling out a bottle of red wine from the plastic bag at my feet.

Zoe looked between me and the wine, chewing on her lower lip.

'Don't worry!' I said, trying to disguise the lack of confidence in my words. 'I'm only going to drink socially from now on. It's all under control.'

'You know we're all worried about you. Even Miles, although he shows it in a strange way.'

I nodded and dipped my head, concentrating on opening the bottle so I didn't have to look her in the eye.

Zoe grabbed a couple of glasses and put them on the table for me to fill.

'Cheers to new beginnings.' I touched my glass to hers.

'Cheers!'

'Can I have some?' Leigh looked at Zoe's wine glass.

'No, this is special medicine for adults. Do you want juice?'

Leigh pressed her lips together and shook her head, pulling a face.

'So, what's your first story going to be about?'

'Actually, that's one of the reasons I popped round. You know I said I didn't think Barbara needed those medical records request forms any more? Well, I think she might. I wanted to drop them off to her tonight.'

'Oh, right. OK, no probs.' She frowned. 'I thought you weren't going to write about the Hudsons.'

'No, I'm not. I wasn't. I . . .' I glanced over at Leigh, not wanting her innocent ears to hear what I was going to say.

Zoe caught on and said to Leigh, 'Why don't you go and finish your drawing in the lounge, sweetheart? I need to quickly talk to Auntie Holly about grown-up things.'

'Ooo-kaaay.' Leigh gathered her pencils and paper together and trotted out the door.

I pressed my elbows on the table, leaning closer to Zoe. 'I wanted to do something about teenage suicides so I went to see a man called Pete Tucker. His daughter, Rachel, committed suicide on Saturday.'

'Rachel killed herself, too? I haven't seen the local news so I haven't heard anything about that.' She closed her eyes and shook her head. 'God, how awful. I remember her from when she came to the surgery with her parents.'

'Exactly. I found out she was Dr Baird's patient, too. And when I spoke to Pete, he said Rachel had bulimia, but she didn't seem depressed or suicidal *until* she started taking Caprixanine.' I told her what I'd discovered about the drug not being tested in children.

'Right.' Zoe's eyes narrowed slightly, a pensive expression on her face.

'And that's exactly what Dean was prescribed. And he hadn't been depressed, suicidal or shown any sign of violence before, either – or any kind of reason why he'd kill Jess and Stephen. What Rachel and Dean did was completely out of character, and I'm thinking it's a side effect of this drug.'

She was silent for a moment, watching me, chewing on her lip. 'And you want to do a story on it?'

'Well, yes, if there *is* a story. It would be pretty huge, wouldn't it? And it would also warn people of the dangers of this drug if there's a problem with it.'

She took a deep breath, pursed her lips into an O shape and exhaled, worry clouding her eyes. 'Look, I know something, but you *can't* say you got anything from me. I can't risk losing my job with Leigh to support.'

'Of course not. I'd always protect my sources, especially you. What do you know?'

She took a sip of wine and set the glass back on the table. 'After I found out what Dean did, I was being nosy so I looked at Dean's file.'

'And what did you find?'

'Dr Baird wrote that Dean had spoken to him at their session about feeling tired and stressed with college work and not sleeping, but there was no mention of him having depression or suicidal and violent thoughts. Nothing like that. Dr Baird had noted the prescription for Caprixanine he'd given Dean, but it was given for insomnia, and he'd asked Dean to make a follow-up appointment in a few weeks to see if his sleeping pattern had improved.' She took another gulp of wine.

'But Dr Baird told the police Dean *was* suffering from depression.'

'I know, that's why I thought it was weird when you told me that.' Two frown lines formed between Zoe's brows. 'I can't believe he'd lie, so there must be an explanation. Maybe Dr Baird got Dean's notes mixed up with another patient. Or maybe he was in a hurry and made a mistake or something.'

'Or maybe he thinks he'll get sued for negligence after what's happened, so he's now saying Dean *was* depressed. He might already know there's something wrong with Caprixanine. Miles said he's one of their big prescribers and does research for Tragatech. He could've been doing a clinical trial on his young patients.'

'No. He's done clinical trials for Tragatech before because he's an expert in his field, and there are reams of paperwork and protocols involved. He's not doing any trials at the moment, I'd know about it. And there were no consent forms or anything else about a trial in Dean's file.'

'What if it was a secret trial? Dr Baird's covering up something, I'm sure. And two of his patients taking the same drug have died within days of each other.'

'I spoke to Rachel when she came in with her parents. It had been really hot that day and I made a comment about the weather to them all, and then I just started chit-chatting because it was fairly quiet.'

I could imagine Zoe at work, making easy small talk, trying to make patients relaxed with that great big smile on her face.

'So, I was saying something like who needs a holiday abroad when we've got a great summer like this, and Mrs Tucker agreed, and Rachel said she was looking forward to going on a weekend away to a caravan park in Cromer a month later with her parents and a mate.'

'Not the kind of thing you're looking forward to if you're about to jump in front of a train,' I said.

'No. The thing is, any kind of adverse reactions while taking drugs have to be reported to the drug company or the MHRA by the doctor prescribing it. They can also be reported by the patient through the Yellow Card Scheme. I know Dr Baird has heard about Dean because we had a conversation at work about how tragic it was. He's probably heard about Rachel, too, but he didn't mention anything to me about her suicide. And I don't remember seeing a note about any adverse reactions when I looked at Dean's records.'

'Dean wasn't actually taking Caprixanine when he died. He'd stopped taking the drug.'

'Well, there you are then. It can't be a side effect. And that's why Dr Baird didn't file a report.'

'All the bumf on Caprixanine says you can stop taking it suddenly with no bad effects, but if it's never been tested in children, how can they be sure?' I raised an eyebrow. 'And if Dr Baird's covering up something, he wouldn't report it, would he?'

'But he's a highly respected expert in child psychology. I find it hard to believe he'd intentionally hide something dangerous. I'm sure it's just a mistake on his part not to mention depression in Dean's notes. Or maybe I missed it.'

I leaned forward and clutched her hand. 'Can you have another look? And also check Rachel Tucker's notes to see what you can find? Have a snoop around Dr Baird's office maybe?'

'You know I'm not supposed to.'

'But what if this drug *is* responsible? How many more kids might die? What if Leigh was in the same position as Rachel had been? Wouldn't you want someone to help?'

Zoe chewed on her fingernail, looking as if she were battling with her conscience. 'Who makes Caprixanine?'

'Tragatech.'

'Really? Then why don't you ask Miles about it?'

'I did. He said he had some kind of confidentiality clause that stops him talking about their products.'

'Pompous arse!' She took a deep breath, then said, 'OK. I'll see what I can find out.'

'Thanks.' I hugged her and, when I let go, Zoe called Leigh in to the kitchen to eat.

Leigh kept us entertained while we finished our meal. Afterwards, I gave Zoe another hug and was treated to a sloppy kiss from Leigh before saying goodbye.

I drove to Barbara's house next and found a parking spot directly outside. The paparazzi had gone now – off to pick the bones of another tragedy. Dean was yesterday's news.

I knocked on the door and called Barbara's name. This time, without the press watching and trying to photograph her every move, she opened the front door for me, looking like she might splinter into pieces at any moment.

I stepped forward to hug her. She felt as if she might crack beneath my grasp.

'At least the press have gone,' she said, pulling back. 'It doesn't feel so claustrophobic inside any more knowing they're not out here waiting for me. I'm sorry, but I really don't feel like company.'

'Of course. I understand. I just wanted to drop off the medical request forms for Dean's records to you. I think it would be a good idea to get hold of them as soon as you can.' I didn't want to tell Barbara my suspicions yet because I still wasn't sure myself. Somehow it seemed worse to get her hopes up about answers only for her to be slammed back to the ground again with a terrific crash if I was wrong. I needed to do more research before I said anything.

'Oh, right.' She stared at my hand holding out the form. 'But Dr Baird said Dean had depression. I've been going over and over it in my head, and it must be right. I've been fooling myself into thinking Dean was OK when he wasn't. He must've just taken a turn for the worse and none of us realised.'

'But we need to know for certain. There could be something in his notes that might help us find out.'

She stared at the form and then shook her head. 'I don't want to. I have to live with the fact that I didn't spot his depression. That I wasn't there for him when he needed me. That I could've prevented it and didn't.' She sniffed hard, her eyes glistening with unshed tears. 'I was wrong.' She shook her head slowly, a lone tear creeping down to her chin. 'It's my fault.'

I opened my mouth to say more, but no words came out. I couldn't argue with her – she was in enough distress as it was. I put my hand on her arm. 'Do you need anything?'

She shook her head. 'No, thanks. I'll probably go out to the shops tomorrow. I need to keep moving forward. Somehow. Don't you worry about me.'

But I *was* worrying about her. And Pete and Jenny Tucker. And all the other people who could be out there right now taking Caprixanine, a potential nuclear bomb ticking within their bodies.

Chapter 20

Miles was on my doorstep at eight the next morning, looking perfectly primped and preened. I, on the other hand, had fallen asleep on the sofa and felt like shit. I could smell the stale, yeasty wine sweating through my pores. When I ran a hand through my knotted hair it felt greasy.

He carried a wave of annoyance into the flat with him.

'Do you want a tea?' I asked, yawning.

'No.' He stood in my small kitchen, elbows crossed.

'So what do I owe this pleasure to?' I asked, but I could guess. Miles never just turned up at my flat. We didn't have the kind of relationship where he just popped in to see me for my sparkling company – especially first thing in the morning.

'This . . . *thing* you're thinking of writing.' He ran a hand through his hair. 'Zoe told me about it.'

'Thing? You mean story?'

'Yes. Whatever.' He waved his hand dismissively. 'Look, I can't have you on some kind of crusade against the company I work for, trying to dig up dirt where there isn't any. How would that reflect on me?'

My eyes widened. 'On you?'

'Yes! If you publish something negative about them, not only will you be on your way to getting sued, but if they find out I'm associated with you I could be out of a job. A *very good* job that I've worked fucking hard for.' He scowled at me.

'Right.' Anger niggled beneath my sternum. 'Why does everything have to be about *you*, Miles? And from what I've read about Tragatech, there's plenty of dirt already out there to find.'

He narrowed his eyes at me. 'What exactly are you trying to prove here? That you can actually write a story and see your name on the byline in all its glory? Well, you've had plenty of opportunities to in the past and failed. Are you so desperate to get noticed by the nationals that you'll concoct some wild conspiracy story? Why don't you just give up now and think about a different career?'

'Thanks for pointing out my failures. That's very kind of you. Any other brother would be supportive.'

'What do you think you know about Caprixanine?'

'What do *you* know, Miles?'

'I can't tell you anything,' he snapped. 'My confidentiality clause protects trade secrets.'

'So you won't give me any information about the clinical trials involved in its production? Or whether the company knows of any side effects not listed on the insert information? Or whether they've covered something up?'

'Don't be ridiculous, Holly. I'd lose my job.'

'But you know something, don't you?'

He tutted loudly and followed it up with an exasperated sigh. 'There's nothing *to* cover up. It's a perfectly safe, effective drug. It wouldn't have been approved by the regulators if it wasn't. And Dr Baird was prescribing it off-label for the benefit of his patients, in line with good medical practice. Do you think you know more than all the scientists and doctors and the MHRA put together?' He raised an eyebrow.

'What if there *is* a story here? What if Caprixanine was the reason Dean and Rachel Tucker did what they did?'

'Depression is *very* hard to recognise in some people,' Miles said in a tone that implied I was stupid. 'Often people hide it incredibly well from friends and family. There's nothing going on here that you haven't made up yourself. You need to stop this right now because you're going to make an idiot out of yourself and you'll never get another job. Why are you doing it? For attention?'

'Of course not! Isn't it *someone's* responsibility to find out if there is a connection before more people die?'

'There is no connection!' His eyes flashed angrily at me. 'You haven't got a clue what you're talking about. If you start down this path, you'll take me with you. Think about that when you're being ridiculed and your life is even more pathetic than it already is. And when Tania and Hayley and I are struggling because I can't get another job.' He stormed out of the flat, leaving me standing there, shocked.

The sound of the door slamming made me jump. I stood for a moment, wondering what the hell had just happened. It took a while for the words to filter through.

Was I jumping to conclusions? Or was there something very wrong with Caprixanine and Miles knew about it?

Chapter 21

I was glued to the laptop for most of the day, typing up my notes from the interview with Pete Tucker and trying to find more evidence that might help me. What I couldn't work out was that if Caprixanine was responsible, why weren't there any mentions of its negative effects anywhere? If psychiatrists and doctors throughout the world were prescribing it off-label and it was a bad drug, why hadn't it come to light, when it had been on the market for six months already? Was it because Dr Baird really was carrying out some kind of secret clinical trial?

Then I thought back to what I'd read about Tiazal. The deadly side effects of that drug hadn't come to light for *years*. And I'd never heard about Tiazal before in my life, so maybe it was easier to keep these things hidden than I'd thought.

It wasn't until I glanced at the time and noticed it was 4 p.m. that I remembered Andrew was coming round for dinner and I had nothing suitable in the house to cook him, unless he wanted cheese on toast.

I grabbed my handbag and drove to the supermarket, noting my petrol tank was only a quarter full. Well, it would have to wait until I was on fumes before I put more petrol in. Now I had no job, I had to be even more careful with money.

I walked up and down the aisles, looking for inspiration. I hadn't entertained anyone except Zoe and Leigh in the last year, and they were happy with a frozen pizza or a takeaway. I wanted to impress Andrew, but at the same time I didn't want to go overboard. He obviously liked Italian, and you couldn't really go wrong cooking pasta, so I chose some fresh tagliatelle, olives, vine-ripened tomatoes, shallots, and a ready-prepared green salad. Before I headed to the checkout, I grabbed some beers and a few more bottles of wine.

Laden with bags of shopping, I walked back to my car, deep in thought. It wasn't until I'd dumped the bags in the boot and opened the car door that I had the feeling of someone watching me again. Some sixth sense kicking in from our ancestors, maybe. I glanced around the car park, my skin prickling. There was an old man pushing an empty trolley towards the trolley park, a mum holding her daughter's hand and heading into the entrance of the shop, a young guy exiting, pulling off the cellophane wrapper of a packet of cigarettes. No one was looking at me, but I felt uneasy. It wasn't until I'd backed my car out of the parking space and edged out on to the main road that I saw a black car emerge from another space.

Was it the same car? Or was I being paranoid? Before, I'd thought there'd been no reason for someone to follow me, but now I wasn't so sure. Was someone watching me? And if they were, it could surely only be something to do with me asking questions about Dean and Rachel and Caprixanine.

I drove home, half concentrating on the road ahead and half checking my rear-view mirror, but I didn't see the car again.

After I'd lugged the bags upstairs to my flat, I dumped my handbag on the arm of the sofa and put the shopping away. I glanced at the clock and saw I had an hour before Andrew was due – plenty of time to rustle up what I had in mind. I chopped shallots and tomatoes and garlic and pitted the olives. I made the vegetable sauce before letting it cool to reheat later, grated some cheese, then hopped in the shower, feeling excited and nervous. It would be the first time a guy other than Miles and the plumber had been in this flat. And Andrew must've been pretty interested to have phoned me after what happened the other night. Maybe things really were looking up for me. It was about time.

I gave myself a confident pep talk in front of the mirror as I applied make-up and got dressed, then I tossed the salad with dressing.

At dead on seven my intercom buzzed from downstairs. I pressed the 'Answer' button in the lounge by the front door and Andrew asked if I could let him up. I released the 'Entry' button for the communal front door, smoothed down my hair, and peeked into the corridor, waiting for him to appear, a zap of nervous energy hitting me.

Andrew walked towards me with a bunch of flowers, a bottle of wine, and a huge smile.

'Hi,' he said. 'Hope I'm not late.'

I grinned. 'Dead on time, actually.'

He handed me the flowers. 'These are for you. Um . . . obviously.' He blushed, seeming as nervous as me, and it made me like him even more.

I bent my head to the beautiful arrangement of roses and inhaled. 'They smell lovely. Come on in.'

He followed me inside and glanced around the spartan lounge. Even though I'd been there a year, I couldn't call it home. It was bland and characterless with no heart. And I hadn't had the interest or energy to make it more cosy. Deep in my heart I'd spent all this time hankering after my old life in London, hoping one day to return, to get back with Richard, to try again for another baby, so I hadn't wanted to waste the precious little energy I had left on improving the place. I hadn't been sure how long I'd stay. But now I could see it through Andrew's eyes and it looked dreary and depressing, cramped and tatty. It hit me then that the past was well and truly out of reach. And maybe, for the first time, I thought that was a good thing.

'Have you been here long?' Andrew asked, his presence filling up the tiny lounge.

'A year.' I laughed to cover my embarrassment. 'So.' I wiggled the bottle of wine at him. 'Do you want a glass of this?'

'Thanks.' He nodded. 'Is there anything I can do to help with dinner?'

'No, it's all under control. You have a seat and I'll sort out the wine.' I swept my hand towards the sofa, headed into the kitchen, turned the kettle on to boil water for the pasta, then opened the wine and poured two large glasses.

I was about to take Andrew's in to him when my landline rang. I grabbed the handset from the tiny kitchen table and picked it up.

'It's me,' Miles said.

Maybe he was calling to apologise for his stand-offishness earlier, but if he was, it could wait until tomorrow now. Andrew was here and I didn't want anything to interrupt getting to know him; plus, I was still annoyed with my brother.

'Miles. I don't—'

'Is Zoe with you?' he butted in before I could finish the sentence.

'Huh? No, why?'

'I've just had a call from the childminder. She's got me and Tania down as first contact next of kin in case something happens with Leigh and she can't get hold of her. Zoe was due to pick up Leigh at quarter to six, just like always, and she hasn't shown up there yet.'

'Oh. Has Tania tried calling her?'

'Of course! Zoe's number keeps going to voicemail. I just tried Dr Baird's practice to see if she's still at work but it's closed now and on answerphone. I've also tried his mobile number, but that's on voicemail, too. I'll keep trying him.'

'Is the childminder absolutely sure Zoe didn't tell her she'd be late?'

'She's positive.'

I leaned my hip against the worktop. My sister was organised and thorough. If she was going to be late for some reason, I know for certain she would've told the childminder in advance. Zoe wouldn't want Leigh to get worried. Unless . . . 'Oh, no, I hope she hasn't been in an accident. I'll ring the police and check.'

'All right. Tania's going to phone round Zoe's friends to see if they've heard from her.'

As soon as I hung up I called the police to ask whether there'd been any accidents involving pedestrians. Zoe walked to work to save petrol since it wasn't far from her house to the high street practice. But there had been none, nor any other incidents that could explain why Zoe hadn't turned up.

I rang Zoe's mobile but, as Miles said, it went to voicemail.

Andrew walked into the kitchen then. 'I heard you on the phone. Is everything OK?'

'Um . . . sorry, you've walked in on a bit of a family emergency.' I explained that Zoe hadn't turned up and we were trying to find her.

His face dropped slightly but he recovered quickly. 'Sorry to hear that. Maybe she's broken down somewhere and her phone's dead?' he offered.

'She won't have her car – look, I think I need to go and drive around and have a look out for her. Maybe I can spot her somewhere. I'm so sorry, but can we rearrange tonight? I need to find out what's happened to her.'

He smiled again. It would've been heart-melting if I wasn't so frantic. 'Absolutely. I completely understand. Would you like me to help? I could drive you.'

'That's really sweet of you but, really, you don't need to do that. And I don't want to ruin your night.'

He nodded softly. 'OK. Then I'll . . . um . . . call you?'

'Thanks.'

He turned to leave and I thought how I kept sabotaging any possible relationship with Andrew before it started. He'd give up on me now, surely. Still, finding out what had happened to Zoe was more important. This wasn't like her at all.

I tried Miles's mobile to tell him what I was going to do but it was engaged. I got in my car and drove to Zoe's house. The lights were off and her car was outside. I opened the door with my spare key, shouting for her as I hurried from room to room, but there was no sign of her.

I headed to Dr Baird's practice next, which was a converted 1920s house right at the end of the high street, fidgeting as I waited at traffic lights and cursing slow drivers. When I arrived, I drove into the car park that went around the back of the building, but there were no vehicles there, and the lights in the surgery were all out. I parked haphazardly, made my way to the front door of the building and knocked loudly.

There was no reply. I knocked for a while longer, but no one answered.

I pulled my phone from my bag to call Miles and see if he had any news, and that's when I noticed a voicemail notification flag on the screen.

I played the message back and a current of dread scorched through my veins.

Chapter 22

'Holly, it's me.' Zoe's voice was barely a whisper on the line so I had to strain to hear it. It sounded echoey, as if she'd made the call from a cramped space. 'I did some checking and something seems a bit off. You know I said I'd looked at Dean's records before and they didn't mention anything about him having depression? When I checked them today, I found a completely new set of notes that say his symptoms showed moderate depression. They must've been changed *afterwards*. And I checked Rachel Tucker's, too. Dr Baird has put that he diagnosed agitated depression following on from the bulimia, but that could easily have been changed after she committed suicide, too. And there's something else . . . Rachel and Dean aren't the only ones. I found another two patients so far taking Caprixanine who've killed themselves recently. Maria Butterworth – she was seventeen, and the . . . Oh, shit, I've got to go!' The call terminated abruptly.

I played the message again. The second time I heard someone knocking on a door in the background when Zoe said she had to go. And I knew then, before rationality could kick in and tell me I was being stupid, that Zoe had stumbled on to something Dr Baird didn't want anyone to find out about. Zoe's call had come in at 4.25 p.m. I'd rushed out to the supermarket and forgotten to take my phone. And then I was busy getting ready for Andrew and hadn't even thought about checking it. If only I'd answered her, maybe she wouldn't have disappeared.

I called her again but it went straight to voicemail. I called Miles and he answered straight away.

'Have you heard from her?' he asked. 'I got hold of Dr Baird and he said she left work at the usual time – five-thirty.'

'Zoe left me a message this afternoon, and now I think something bad has happened to her. She found out something about Caprixanine and other patients.'

'What the hell are you talking about? Why would Zoe find out something, and what—'

'She was looking into Dean's and Rachel's notes. I asked her to.'

'You what?! You asked her to break patient confidentiality? You know she'll get fired if Dr Baird finds out. What's she going to do then? How will she support Leigh with no job? Honestly, Holly, you need to take a hard look at yourself. You're on some crazy destructive rampage and you're going to ruin everyone else's life in the process. What is wrong with you?' he yelled.

'Zoe told me Rachel and Dean weren't the only ones on Caprixanine who've killed themselves. What the fuck is going on, Miles, and what are you hiding?'

Miles was silent on the other end for a moment. 'Don't be stupid, Holly. You're jumping to all sorts of ridiculous conclusions. Like I said, there's nothing wrong with Caprixanine – it's perfectly safe. You're getting paranoid! I swear you're having some kind of breakdown. Have you been drinking again?'

'No!' I snapped, anger rising to boiling point.

'Zoe's probably just with a mate.'

'So why hasn't she called? Why has she left Leigh?'

'Her phone's probably run out of juice.'

'No way. She never lets her phone go below fifty per cent battery when she's not with Leigh. Something's happened to her. I'm going to call the police.'

'She's only been missing a few hours! You're totally overreacting.'

'Is Leigh still at the childminder's place? I'll go and collect her after I've spoken to the police.'

'No. Tania picked her up. She's playing with Hayley. But there's no need to waste police time. She'll turn up soon. She's—'

I hung up on him before he could finish and dialled 999.

Chapter 23

Two uniformed policemen turned up on my doorstep a couple of hours later. One didn't look old enough to drive. The other looked as if he was about to hit retirement age.

'So, how long has your sister been missing?' the older one, who'd introduced himself as PC Page, asked. He stood leaning against the wall while PC Hockley sat next to me, filling in a missing persons report.

I told them she usually left work at five-thirty and would've been at the childminder's place by quarter to six. It was now gone nine and still no one had heard from her. I told them my brother had called Zoe's friends, but there was no sign of her. PC Page checked with his control room that no incidents involving anyone matching Zoe's description had been received. I reiterated how she'd never just leave Leigh like that without letting someone know what was going on.

I thought about sharing Zoe's voicemail message with them, but although I was desperately worried about her, I knew she'd get into serious trouble for telling me confidential information about patients. Even then, I still hoped that Miles was right and there was some reasonable explanation for everything – that Zoe would call me in a minute and apologise for worrying everyone.

'So she's never done this before? Gone off somewhere leaving her daughter with the childminder and not told anyone where she was going?' PC Page asked.

'No. Absolutely not. But . . .' I chewed on my lip, worrying how much to tell them. I opened my mouth to say something that would explain the situation was desperately wrong without revealing that Zoe had been giving me information and that we'd been discussing private details of patients from the practice. What if I really was being paranoid? I had no proof of anything.

PC Page and PC Hockley stared at me, waiting for me to say more.

'I think something might've happened at Dr Baird's surgery. Something bad.'

'What do you mean?' PC Page frowned. 'Are you alleging Dr Baird is involved in your sister's disappearance?' He and PC Hockley exchanged a glance.

'I don't know! I just think something's happened to Zoe. Look, Dr Baird gave some patients this drug, and I think it made them violent and suicidal.'

PC Page's frown furrowed deeper. 'You're alleging Dr Baird is giving his patients illegal drugs?'

'No! It was a prescription drug. He prescribed it to his patients.' I explained about what had happened with the Hudsons and Rachel Tucker – how I'd found out they were taking Caprixanine and suspected it had deadly side effects.

'We're aware of the tragedy involving the Hudsons,' PC Page said. 'And I attended the suicide of Rachel Tucker and spoke to her family, but I don't see how they relate to your sister going missing.'

'Dr Baird is trying to keep it hidden.'

'Keep *what* hidden?' PC Hockley looked confused. 'The fact that he prescribed legal drugs to his patients?'

'No. Well, maybe, yes. I think he wanted to hide that the side effects made Dean do what he did and made Rachel kill herself.'

'Rachel Tucker was depressed. Dean Hudson was also depressed,' PC Page said, eyeing me carefully. 'Of course both incidents are very tragic, but it's not unusual for depressed people to commit suicide, Miss Gold. Dr Baird is a psychiatrist, is he not?'

'Yes.'

'So he's dealing with patients who are mentally ill and potentially a high risk for suicide.'

'No, there's something else going on here!' I said, realising that it sounded ridiculous to my own ears, so how could I expect them to believe me? 'There was another one. Another patient. Zoe found out a seventeen-year-old girl also killed herself after taking Caprixanine.' Shit, there was no way I couldn't tell them about the voicemail now. Not if I wanted them to take me seriously. 'She left me a voicemail message earlier. I think she was at work when she made the call. And at the end of it, she sounded scared. I think Dr Baird found out she knew what was going on.'

'Right.' PC Page hooked his thumbs into his fully laden equipment belt, leaning back on his heels. 'Can we listen to this message, please?'

I nodded and took my phone from my bag. I put it on loudspeaker and called up my voicemail.

'*You have no messages,*' the automated female voice said.

'What? It was on here earlier. I listened to it.' I stared at the phone for a moment before jabbing the buttons more vigorously. 'No, I can't have deleted it. I didn't delete it.' I glanced between PC Page and the phone, my forehead wrinkled with confusion. I tried the voicemail again, all too aware I was looking slightly mad.

'*You have no messages,*' the voice repeated.

I glanced up at PC Page, my mouth hanging open. He raised a sceptical eyebrow at me.

'I don't . . . I don't understand. I didn't delete it. There must be some technical glitch or something.' I rubbed a hand over my face. 'Zoe left a message. There *was* another patient!' I tried to wrack my brains and think of the name Zoe had mentioned in the voicemail. Marie? Maria something? I couldn't remember. My brain felt like scrambled egg. 'I can't remember who Zoe said.' I rubbed at my throbbing forehead.

PC Page glanced at the half-empty wine bottle on the table, which I'd drunk when I'd got home after looking for Zoe while waiting for the police. 'Have you been drinking tonight, Miss Gold?'

'Yes.' I squirmed in my seat. 'Just a little bit. But I'm not drunk! What I'm saying is right.'

PC Hockley looked to his colleague for guidance, clicking the top of his pen on and off.

'I'm sure your sister's just got held up somewhere, but we'll file the report and make some further enquiries,' PC Page said.

'No, something bad has happened, I'm telling you,' I said, desperation making my voice creep higher. 'She wouldn't leave Leigh and be out of contact.'

'I'm sure she'll turn up soon. It's probably just a misunderstanding. Try not to worry,' PC Hockley said, gathering his papers and pen together, along with the photo of Zoe I'd given him.

'So you'll speak to Dr Baird?'

'We'll be making enquiries with him to see when she left work, yes.' PC Page made his way to the front door and PC Hockley followed.

I thought about grabbing hold of PC Page's arm and explaining it again, slowly, so he'd understand, but all I had was suspicion. And they already thought I sounded drunk or crazy. If I pressed it any more they wouldn't take Zoe's disappearance seriously and do all they could to find her.

So instead, I watched them leave and closed the door, leaning my back against it, knowing they hadn't believed what I'd said.

And without Zoe and any of the information she could give to the police, how could I even prove anything?

Chapter 24

I spent a sleepless night on the sofa, wrapped in a blanket, waiting for news. I called Miles every half hour or so, but every time I did he snapped that if he knew anything he'd call me straight away. At 3 a.m. he said he was going to bed and told me not to phone any more.

I stared at the phone with disbelief. His sister was missing and he was going to *sleep*? I felt useless just sitting there so I walked around town, hoping to spot Zoe somewhere.

My head pounded as I trudged the streets, horrifying scenarios flitting through my mind: she'd been hit by a car and was lying in a ditch somewhere, bleeding to death; she'd been attacked, abducted. I desperately wanted to believe she was alive, but I had the horrible sensation that she was already dead – and that Dr Baird was involved.

Dawn was breaking when I arrived home, dejected and exhausted. I'd only seen a few late-night revellers staggering drunkenly home, an early-morning jogger, and a homeless man wandering the high street, rummaging in rubbish bins.

I scrubbed my hands over my face, dumped my bag on the kitchen table and made a strong coffee. I had a dreadful feeling that whatever the day was going to bring, it wouldn't be good news. Zoe would never stay out all night and not let anyone know where she was or arrange childcare for Leigh.

I watched the sun coming up through my window, my thoughts racing. I had to *do* something!

I phoned Dr Baird's surgery, but there was a message on the answerphone saying his practice was temporarily closed due to an emergency. Next, I tried Miles's mobile several times, but it was constantly engaged, so I tried his landline.

'Hello?' Tania picked up the phone within a few rings, her voice nervous.

'Hi, it's me,' I said. 'Have you heard anything? I've been trying Miles's mobile but it's always busy.'

'He's on the phone to work. He said something about an urgent teleconference, but I don't know if I believe him. He's holed up in the office upstairs and won't open the door.' She lowered her voice. 'Is there something going on with Miles? I mean, is he having an affair or something?'

'What? How should I know?'

'Even before Zoe went missing he'd been acting really weird.'

'Weird how?'

'I don't know. Secretive with his phone calls and texts. Not sleeping properly. He seems like he's miles away when I'm talking to him, and he's been really snappy.'

'Since when has he been like this?'

'I don't know. Since the barbecue, really. Do you think he's seeing someone?'

The memory of me walking into their kitchen that evening and catching Miles staring vacantly into his whisky glass appeared in my head. I'd thought the look on his face was unhappy, pensive, but now I thought it might have been something else. He'd looked haunted, trapped. And it was just after he would've heard about the Hudsons.

He'd also been uncharacteristically angry with me when he'd found out I was looking into Caprixanine, too. *Was* Miles having an affair, or was his strange new behaviour because he was worried or scared about something to do with Caprixanine coming out? Something he'd be implicated in?

'He hasn't told you anything about that new drug of Tragatech's, has he?' I asked.

'What? Only that it's going to be huge.' She didn't even ask why I wanted to know. She just replied, 'So do you think he could be having an affair then?'

I rubbed at the tension in my forehead. 'I don't know, Tania. I've got other things on my mind right now. Do you have the mobile number or address of Dr Baird?' I wanted to speak to him first-hand and see what he knew about Zoe going missing. Even though he'd told Miles she'd left work at five-thirty yesterday, I didn't believe Dr Baird. I wanted to ask him face-to-face.

'What do you want that for?'

'To find out about Zoe leaving work, of course!'

'Yeah. Of course. Um . . . I've got both somewhere. I've got a list of Miles's customers I send out Christmas cards to. Hang on.' She disappeared for a few moments and then returned and gave me a phone number and address.

I hung up and drove to Dr Baird's surgery, just in case. There were no cars in the car park and the door was locked. There was no answer to my repeated banging so I drove to his house in Bloomfield, the next village ten miles away from Ashfield.

Dr Baird lived in a well-to-do street of large detached older cottages. I parked on his block-paved driveway that was empty of any vehicles. The curtains were open in the downstairs windows, but the house looked dark inside, as if no one was home.

I rang the doorbell and looked around the front garden. There was no answer, so I rang again and knocked loudly, but there was still no sign of life.

I peered through a window to my right into his lounge, but it was empty. 'Dr Baird?' I called out. 'Zoe? Are you here?'

The only response I got was the trill of a nearby bird.

I looked in the only other front window into a second, smaller living room. Again I couldn't see anyone, so I walked down a path that led around the side of the building to the rear garden. I knocked on the back patio doors, leading into a kitchen. 'Dr Baird? Zoe? Is anyone home?'

Still no answer.

I exhaled a worried breath, took one last look through the doors and headed back to the car.

When I got home, I alternated between pacing the flat and sitting on the sofa, staring into space, worrying endlessly, fear for my sister gnawing a hole inside me as the hours passed. Eventually, I must've succumbed to an exhausted sleep, because I was jerked awake hours later when my mobile phone rang from inside my bag.

I lurched towards it, praying for good news.

The number was unrecognised, but I still cried 'Zoe?' down the phone.

'Zoe was just a warning,' a deep voice said, quietly and calmly.

Before I could properly register the words, the connection was abruptly severed and I was listening to silence.

A wave of panic engulfed me as I stared at the blank screen in my hand. Then a knocking on the door made me jump, the phone slipping through my fingers and landing on the carpet.

I froze, wondering if the same person who'd called was on the other side of my door.

'Holly?' a voice said, accompanied by another knock. 'It's Will.'

I pressed a hand to my chest, the thudding of my heart against my fingertips, and rushed to the door. 'Will! Is there any . . .'

I knew from the grave expression on his face there was news – and it wasn't good.

I stood in the doorway, limp, like a ragdoll. 'You've found Zoe?'

'Can I come in?'

I stepped back to let him enter and closed the door behind him, leaning my back against it for support.

'I'm very sorry to tell you that we found the body of a woman early this morning in some trees at the edge of the woodland area in Cooper Park.'

My hands cupped around my slack mouth.

'She had no handbag or identification on her, but I think it's Zoe. It's been a long time since I saw her around town so I can't be sure, but I need someone to come to the mortuary and ID the body now that forensics and the pathologist have finished.'

'Oh, God!' The room swirled around me.

'The woman we found was wearing a black skirt and white blouse. About five foot six with shoulder-length blonde hair. She has blue eyes and a small scar on her right palm.'

My stomach shuddered. I sank down on to the edge of the sofa. It sounded like Zoe. I traced a fingertip along my right palm, remembering exactly when Zoe had got that scar. She'd fallen off a wall at a friend's house when she was ten and slit her palm on a sharp rock. She'd milked it for ages, trying to get sympathy from Mum and Dad. Not that it worked. Mum told her not to be such a baby and Dad just gave her extra pocket money that week.

'Did she have a necklace on? A gold one with a purple stone on it?'

'No. She had no jewellery, but it could've been stolen, along with her handbag. We think it's a mugging at this stage. There were what looked like defensive wounds on her hands. It's likely she put up a fight.' Will towered above me, concern clouding his eyes. He reached out a hand and placed it gently on my shoulder. 'Is there someone else who could identify her if you don't feel up to it? Your brother, maybe? Or maybe your parents could.'

'Um . . .' I tried to get myself together, push through the swirling emotions and stand up, take a step forward. Breathe. 'Dad died five years ago. My mum's on a cruise somewhere. I'd need to reach her. But I'll phone Miles. He can come with me. Just . . .' I glanced around for my mobile phone, my limbs feeling numb. I grabbed it from the arm of the sofa, remembered the last call.

Zoe was just a warning.

I opened my mouth to tell Will about it but then stopped. I needed to talk to Miles first. He knew more than he was telling me. And I had to make sure it wasn't just some nasty prank caller messing with my head. Maybe Zoe really wasn't dead and it was some other poor woman they'd found.

I took a deep breath and called Miles.

He picked up on the third ring. 'No, I *still* haven't heard anything,' he said gruffly.

'Well, I have. The police are here. They think they've found Zoe.'

'Where is she? Why didn't she bloody call us?'

I glanced at Will, stared into his dark eyes. 'The woman they found . . . she's dead.'

'Oh,' he said, his pompous tone deflating.

'They want someone to identify her. Will you come with me?'

Silence for a moment, and then he cleared his throat and said, 'Yes. Where is she?'

'Where's the mortuary?' I asked Will.

'I don't know!' Miles answered me, back to his old self, but there was a hint of panic in his voice now.

'At the hospital,' Will told me. 'I can take you there. If you want, I can pick your brother up on the way.'

'The hospital,' I said to Miles. 'Do you want a lift?'

'No, I'll meet you there. I'll leave in five minutes.'

'OK.'

~

The mortuary was in the hospital basement, tucked away from the hustle and bustle of the rest of the building. Will led Miles and me along a corridor before pausing outside a door.

'If you just wait here a moment, I'll make sure they're ready for you.' Will entered through the door and closed it behind him.

I looked at the floor, unable to look at Miles. I fixed my gaze on a scuff in the grey lino, watching it blur out of focus the harder I stared.

Will reappeared. 'There are some visible injuries to her face,' he warned us.

An anguished noise involuntarily escaped my lips.

'I'll go. You stay out here,' Miles said to me.

'NO! I . . . want to see her.'

Will nodded solemnly and opened the door. Miles took the lead and I followed. Inside, a tall man in blue scrubs and white clogs stood next to the body of a woman on a trolley. There was a sheet pulled up to her neck and her hair was covered with some kind of plastic cap. I wanted to avoid looking at her face but I couldn't. My eyes were drawn there immediately – to the closed eyes and arched eyebrows and the bruising around her temple. The snub nose and plump lips that Leigh had inherited.

It was Zoe. My always-cheerful, kind-hearted, amazing sister.

I stared at her, unable to speak.

'Is this Zoe Gold?' Will asked.

'Yes,' Miles croaked out before rushing out of the room.

Tears bubbled to the surface and slid down my cheeks. I'd suspected it, but I'd still been fighting it. I couldn't believe she was really gone.

I felt Will's arm around my shoulder, holding me tight against him. 'I'm very sorry, Holly.'

I leaned into him and let out a groan of sadness. Pressure built up in my chest, sucking the air from my lungs. I had to get out of there. I couldn't bear to see Zoe like that any more, cold and lifeless.

'I need some air.' I extracted myself from Will and stumbled out of the door.

Miles was in the corridor, leaning against the wall, his head in his hands. He looked at me when I came out.

I glared at him, the sadness overtaken by incandescent rage. This was his fault. I was certain he knew something about Caprixanine that he was keeping secret and now our wonderful sister was dead.

I turned to Will, keeping my gaze locked on Miles's. 'This wasn't a mugging. There's something else going on. Something that made—'

Miles took hold of my hand and squeezed it hard. 'You'll have to excuse my sister. She's obviously very upset and isn't thinking straight.'

I tried to wrestle my hand away but he gripped it tight. 'What are you—'

'Come on. Let's go and get some air.' Miles practically dragged me by the hand up the corridor away from Will.

'What the hell are you doing?' I hissed at Miles, trying to get my hand out of his grasp, but he just held it tighter.

'Trying to protect you, that's what!' He marched me out of the hospital, through the front gates, and along the street.

'This is about Caprixanine, isn't it?'

'Shush! Keep your voice down.' Miles's gaze darted everywhere before spotting the entrance to a cemetery further up the road and dragging me in that direction.

His grip loosened on my hand as we entered the gates. I pulled my hand free but still followed, wanting to demand answers out of him. He strode towards an iron bench overlooking a row of graves. No one else was around.

'What the fuck is going on, Miles?' I spat out as I sat down so hard that the bench's thin metal slats bounced. 'I had an anonymous phone call before Will turned up. It was a man saying "Zoe was just a warning". I think someone's been following me in a black car. They know I'm trying to find out what really happened with the Hudsons and Rachel Tucker.'

Miles ran agitated hands over his face. He took a deep breath and held it before forcing the air from his lungs. 'You're losing the plot. You really are. You've become fixated with the Hudsons and now you're dragging everyone else into your . . . your crazy obsession!' His nostrils flared, eyes wide.

'How can you blame me? I know you're covering something up! Something that got Zoe killed. You'd better tell me what you know, Miles, or I'm going to Will right now.'

'Weren't you listening to him? A mugging, that's what he said. Zoe was killed by a *mugger*.'

'What, and you really believe that?'

He twisted on the bench, his gaze drilling into me. 'Do you even know what you're doing any more?' He leaned closer to my lips and sniffed. 'You absolutely reek of drink. You're an alcoholic and you need help.'

'I'm not cracking up! And I'm not an alcoholic.' I clenched my hands in my lap to stop them shaking. 'I know what *I'm* doing, as a matter of fact! I'm asking questions about Caprixanine. It has deadly side effects, doesn't it? But Tragatech doesn't want it to get out because it's their new wonder drug that's worth billions of pounds a year. I think Dr Baird is being paid off to cover it up. But what about you, Miles? What have *you* done? Did you know suicidal and psychotic behaviour was a side effect before you prostituted yourself to sell a dangerous drug for Tragatech? Because you want to keep your fucking mansion and holidays in the sun? So Tania can get her Botox and hair extensions and spa days?'

He sat back as if I'd slapped him, the anger seeming to disperse until his face had crumpled.

'Go on, tell me I'm wrong!' I challenged him with narrowed eyes, tears streaming down my cheeks now.

He didn't speak so I told him about Zoe's voicemail message that had disappeared.

'A disappearing voicemail?' He snorted. 'Do you know how mad that sounds?'

I ignored him and carried on. 'I'm going to find out about the other patients Zoe mentioned. How many people are already dead because of this drug? How many more people *will* kill themselves or someone else after taking Caprixanine? Do you want that on your conscience?'

'Think about how your behaviour might affect Leigh and Hayley,' he snapped, disgust flaring in his eyes.

'What's that supposed to mean?' I glared back at him, my heart pounding in my chest. 'How can you let them get away with this? You need to help me find evidence. They know. They definitely know what's going on or they wouldn't be following me, and they wouldn't have murdered my sister and sent me a *warning*!' I yelled out the last word, wiping at my eyes.

'You're insane.' Miles got to his feet, his jaw clenched.

I clutched his arm. 'You can get inside Tragatech and find evidence.'

'Shut up! Just shut up! You need to let it drop right now! No more nosing around, making up stories. No more, do you hear me? Because you're going to end up in the psychiatric ward the way you're going. I mean it! Stop it right fucking now! At the moment, you've got a choice. Don't make it so there's no choice.'

My eyes pinged wide open, rage curdling inside. 'What are you saying? That you're going to try and get me sectioned?'

His gaze darted sideways.

I stepped close to him, invading his space. 'You got our sister killed. The *least* you can do is help me.'

He stepped back, a vein pulsing at his temple. 'I did not. You're fucking disturbed and I'm trying to help you before it's too late.'

'Who is it you're really angry with? Me or yourself?'

'What?' he said, his bravado faltering slightly.

'I think you've got in too deep, haven't you? Why won't you tell me what's going on? Are they blackmailing you or something?'

'Don't be ridiculous.' He clamped his lips together tight and I was sure it was to stop them trembling.

'You're a coward, Miles – and a liar and a narcissistic, arrogant bastard.'

'And you've got no idea what you're doing.' His gaze skewered me to the spot until he turned on his heel and strode away, but not before I saw the tears glittering in his eyes.

'I haven't had any idea what I've been doing for years. Why should now be any different?!' I raised my voice to reach him across the distance between us.

Chapter 25

I couldn't breathe. I tried to suck in oxygen. Tried to slow my heart rate down. A pain blossomed beneath my sternum. Was I having a panic attack? I concentrated on inhaling and exhaling slowly. I needed to call Mum and tell her what had happened to Zoe. I needed to speak to someone other than Miles about something this big. I needed to call Will.

But should I? Was Miles right? Should I drop it right now before I ended up like Zoe? What about Leigh and Hayley? Would they go after them next in an attempt to stop me digging further? Is that what Miles had meant when he'd mentioned their names? And if so, how could I put their lives at risk?

I don't know how long I sat on that bench while thoughts rushed in my head on a manic loop.

Eventually, I walked home on unsteady legs, pedestrians blurring into one as they passed me by, but all I could see was Zoe and Jess and Stephen and Dean. Rachel Tucker and Barbara. The people left behind whose lives had ended the day their family members died.

I let myself into my flat, poured a glass of wine, and called my mum's mobile number. It rang four times before the voicemail kicked in, asking me to leave a message. I had no idea where she was on her cruise. She could've been in Australia or Timbuktu for all I knew about her itinerary, and the reception was sure to be sporadic out in the middle of the ocean. I left a message asking her to call me urgently and then sent her an email saying the same thing. I had to speak to her before Miles did because I knew he'd twist everything and make out like I was going mad.

I sipped my wine, staring into space and letting the tears and grief consume me.

Sometime later, my phone rang. The sky had darkened by then and a summer storm pelted heavy drops of rain at the windows. The air was thick with humidity.

I scrambled for my phone and answered.

'Hi, it's Will. I was just calling to see how you were.'

I swallowed, bleary-eyed, staring at the almost empty bottle of wine on the coffee table, rubbing at my eyelids with one hand. 'Thanks. I'm not . . . um . . .' I trailed off, unable to put into words how I was. 'I left a message for my mum. She hasn't called me back yet.'

'Is anyone with you?'

'No, why?'

'My shift's about to finish. Do you want me to come round and keep you company?'

'That would be really nice, thank you.'

'OK. I'll be there soon. Do you need anything? I could pick up a takeaway or something?'

'I don't think I can eat anything, but you go ahead and get something for yourself if you like.'

'All right. See you soon.' He hung up.

I put the rest of the wine in the fridge and made a strong black coffee with two sugars, gulping it down before splashing cold water on my cheeks at the kitchen sink.

By the time Will knocked on my door I'd downed another coffee and a pint of water and felt more awake. The sight of him on the doorstep, his eyebrows furrowed with concern, made me want to throw myself into his arms and stay there forever.

He gave me a slight smile and held up a carrier bag with some food in it. 'I got you something anyway. In case you're hungry later.'

I forced my lips into a grateful smile and we headed to the kitchen. He put the bag in the centre of the table.

'Do you want a drink?' I asked.

'What are you having?'

I wasn't drunk any more, just overwhelmingly tired with a terrible headache, but I needed a real drink if I was about to tell him what was going on. 'I've got wine or beer.'

'Wine is good.' He sat down, and I felt his eyes on me as I grabbed a couple of glasses and emptied what was left of the previous bottle of wine into my glass. Then I opened another and filled his. I sat opposite him, one leg tucked underneath the other.

'Do you want to eat?' I asked. 'I can get you a plate.'

He shrugged. 'I can eat later.' He sipped his wine and silence swelled in the room as I replayed the anonymous caller's voice in my head.

Zoe was just a warning.

I closed my eyes and pressed my fingertips to them until I saw stars, worrying whether to tell Will what I suspected. If I started down this path, what would happen to me or Miles or Tania, Leigh, or Hayley? If Miles had done something illegal he'd get into trouble, but then what further tragedies would happen to other families whose loved ones were taking Caprixanine if I didn't speak up? And why did I even care about Miles when he seemed to be intent on trying to twist things and keep me quiet, too? Had he really threatened to have me sectioned or was I reading something completely wrong into his words?

I let my hands fall to the table and blinked. 'There's something not right about this.'

'Well, something like this is never right.' Will tilted his head.

The thing is, I didn't really know where to start – what to say. It all sounded so far-fetched. And, yes, crazy and paranoid.

I reached for my wine and swallowed a huge gulp, feeling the anaesthetising effect trickling through me. I swallowed some more for courage. Will watched with an open, sympathetic expression on his face.

'It started with what happened to Jess and Stephen and Dean.'

'What did?' Will raised his eyebrows inquisitively.

'You know I was trying to get answers for Barbara? Trying to find out what made Dean do what he did? When Dean killed his parents, that night I saw Zoe and told her about it. She looked at Dean's medical records at the surgery. There was no mention in them then that his psychiatrist, Dr Baird, had diagnosed Dean with depression, just stress and insomnia. Dr Baird prescribed Dean some Caprixanine, which is supposed to be a new blockbuster drug for depression, but it hasn't been tested in adolescents, just adults.' I gripped my glass tightly.

'So, what? You're saying you don't think Dr Baird should be prescribing this drug to adolescents?'

'He's either prescribing it off-label or he's doing some kind of clinical trial.' I explained what 'off-label' meant. 'Anyway, I think a side effect of the drug is psychotic and suicidal behaviour. I think the drug made Dean kill Jess and Stephen and then kill himself – not any kind of underlying mental illness or depression.' I paused, waiting for his reaction – for him to tell me I was crazy or being stupid.

His face didn't change.

I paused, trying to find the right words to explain things. 'I spoke to Zoe about my suspicions and she checked Dean's records again to see if Dr Baird had noted any kind of adverse reaction to Caprixanine or filed some kind of report with Tragatech, the company who makes it, or to see if she could find anything about a clinical trial. She left a voicemail message for me before she was killed saying that Dean's records were altered after he'd killed his parents and himself. Dr Baird had added an entry to say Dean had depression.'

'How do you know Dr Baird hadn't had time to write up his full notes after seeing Dean the first time due to other appointments? And that he simply updated the records at a later date when he had time?'

'I don't. For sure.' I watched for Will's reaction, but his face was inscrutable. I bet he'd heard numerous bizarre stories during his career and wouldn't give away his thoughts just yet, so I ploughed on. 'But there was also another suicide. Do you remember I told you about a girl called Rachel Tucker who'd jumped in front of a train? Well, I spoke to her dad because I was interested in writing a story about teenage suicide. Dr Baird had also prescribed her Caprixanine. And in the message Zoe left, she mentioned another girl who killed herself after Dr Baird prescribed the exact same drug, and was about to tell me about another patient. Two people might be a horrible coincidence, but four? That's got to be suspicious!'

'What was the name of this girl she mentioned?'

'I don't know. I can't remember.'

'Have you still got this message?'

I chewed on my lip. 'No. It disappeared.'

'Disappeared?'

'I don't know what happened to it,' I said quietly. 'I didn't delete it. It just vanished from my phone. I think her name was Maria.'

'Dean wasn't taking anything when the tragedy happened. There were no drugs in his system.' He studied me carefully, head to one side, his eyes searching my face.

'I know, but I think because he stopped taking it suddenly, maybe it triggered some kind of psychotic state.'

Will didn't speak for a moment. He just stared at me with a quizzical look, as if I'd been speaking Russian all along. 'So you actually only know of *one* patient who was taking this drug when she committed suicide? Rachel Tucker?'

'And this other girl, plus another patient.'

'Whose names you don't know.'

I nodded numbly. 'But you could find out, couldn't you? You must get to hear about suicides at work. They would probably have been local.'

'I don't necessarily hear about sudden deaths that aren't suspicious. Usually, uniform would be first on scene and then, if it's a routine suicide, the coroners' officer would deal with it.'

'But you could find out,' I said, my voice thick with desperation. 'I know you don't want to risk doing anything to piss off your superiors but—'

'No, it's not that. I just don't think there's anything *to* find out.' He tapped his fingers on the table, studying me carefully. 'Are you aware that one in four young people in the UK experience suicidal thoughts?'

'No. But Dean and Rachel weren't suicidal before they started taking this drug. That's the whole point. Dean was suffering from insomnia and stress and Rachel was bulimic. It was completely out of character for them to do what they did. I think there's something very wrong with this drug that seems to trigger a terrible reaction in adolescents.'

'It was only *one* patient taking this drug when they killed themselves. A patient who was obviously seeking help for bulimia, which is a mental illness. And people with mental illnesses are much more likely to suffer from violent or suicidal thoughts.' He looked at me sympathetically. 'You can't be sure anyone else was taking this drug if you don't even know who they are.' He paused for a moment. 'Did you know that there is such a thing as cluster suicides?' His brow knotted with . . . what? Concern? Disbelief? 'There's a town in Wales where twenty-five young people killed themselves in a two-year period. They thought social media was to blame for glamorising death.'

'Yes. I know! But there's nothing glamorous about jumping in front of a train. Or murdering your parents before hanging yourself.' My voice rose, sounding almost hysterical. I took a deep, shaky breath. I had to calm down. Nothing was coming out properly. I had to try to explain without seeming irrational. 'Look, this drug is worth billions to Tragatech. And if they can hide the side effects for as long as possible so that they can prescribe it to kids, which is the new growth market for psychiatric drugs, it's going to be worth even more money. But if Zoe found four patients in Dr Baird's practice alone who've killed themselves recently, imagine the amount of deaths there'd be if this were being prescribed all around the world? And now, after leaving me that message, Zoe has been murdered in what was made to look like a mugging. I got . . .' I stopped and blinked away tears, determined not to fall apart. 'Just before you turned up this afternoon, I got an anonymous phone call on my mobile from a man saying "Zoe was just a warning".'

'Can you show me your mobile?'

I leapt up and went into the lounge to get my bag. I plucked my phone out and walked into the kitchen, scrolling through my list of incoming calls.

I froze in the kitchen doorway.

'What?' Will asked.

'The call. It's not showing up.'

'Let me have a look.' He held out his hand.

I walked towards him and put it in his palm. He scrolled up and down as I looked over his shoulder. The last call on there was to Miles.

He frowned slightly.

'What? You don't believe me, do you? There was definitely a call! It's disappeared. Like Zoe's voicemail message.'

He cleared his throat. 'I think you're obviously distraught with what's happened to Zoe, and that's completely understandable. Especially coming on the heels of the Hudson tragedy. And I think your mind's running riot, looking for things that aren't there.' He reached out and took hold of my trembling hand.

I sank down on to the chair next to him, staring into his eyes. 'I'm not looking for things. There *are* things going on. Look, Miles works for Tragatech as a drug sales rep. I think he knows something about it all. I confronted him and he got really angry.' I mentally replayed Miles's outburst earlier. Whenever he felt helpless or upset, he turned to shouting and hollering and blaming everyone else as a way to cope with his own feelings or inadequacies. 'I think he knows exactly what's going on with Caprixanine and Dr Baird and the patients, and he's covering it all up. At first, I thought it was because he has a damn good lifestyle from Tragatech's salary and perks, but I also think now, after what's happened with Zoe, that maybe he's scared. He didn't want me to speak to you about it all, but this is too much to handle on my own. And I . . .' My face crumpled with sadness.

Will squeezed my hand gently. 'I spoke to your brother earlier. He phoned me to say he was very worried about your mental health, but you'd refused his help. He said you'd been acting irrationally and were paranoid. He thinks you're having some kind of breakdown – that you've been drinking too much. Have you seen a doctor?'

'No! Miles is lying. There's nothing wrong with me. But I'm in way over my head here. I don't know what to do next or whether to do anything.' I sniffed, staring down at the table, willing myself not to cry, feeling like I was swimming underwater. The room closed in on me. The edges of my vision faded. What was happening to me? *Was* I going mad?

'Miles told me about the break-up with your boyfriend and the miscarriage. I'm very sorry. You've been under a tremendous amount of stress and emotional upset in the last year, and he said you've been having trouble coping with—'

'He had no right to tell you anything!' I slammed my wine glass down so hard on the table that the flat base broke away from the stem and wine sloshed out on to the table. 'Shit!' I yelped, surprised by my own force. 'Cheap rubbish,' I muttered, pouring out the wine into a new glass and dumping the broken one in the sink.

'Let me help.' Will pulled off several sheets of kitchen roll and mopped up the spillage on the table. Then he threw it in the kitchen bin.

I leaned on the edge of the sink, staring through the window at the car park below, my shoulders taut.

'Are you OK?' He took my hand in his.

I nodded. I sat back down opposite him and stared into my new glass.

He sat, too, and silence filled the room until he said, 'Zoe left work at five-thirty. I've seen the CCTV footage Dr Baird gave me, which clearly shows her leaving the front of the building on foot at 5.32 p.m. Unfortunately, there are no more CCTV cameras at that end of the high street to capture any of her further movements after that, but it's likely she took a shortcut through Cooper Park and that's where she met her attacker.' His hand drifted away from mine. 'Zoe was mugged, Holly. Dean was depressed and it escalated into a psychotic episode. Rachel Tucker was suffering from a mental illness. And Dr Baird is a well-respected child psychologist and a law-abiding citizen.'

'But the phone call! The warning about Zoe! And her message!'

Will took a deep breath and his unspoken words hung in the air. *What phone call? What voicemail? There's nothing on your phone.* He looked at me with a peculiar expression.

'But I must be right because someone's been following me, too. A black car. I didn't think much about it at first, but now I know it must be because I'm on to something.'

'Did you get a registration number?'

'No.' I cringed inwardly, dropping my head into my hands, the walls closing in on me further. I did sound mad.

Chapter 26

A warning was delivered but it wasn't exactly as planned. Dr B panicked.

I'll keep him in line. He likes the money too much.

The reporter's talking to the police. Shall I fix her?

Not yet. Might look too suspicious right now.
Pay off the copper NOW.
Remind the Golden Boy again how much he has to lose if he doesn't keep her in line.

Chapter 27

Will didn't leave until he'd made me promise I'd go and see a doctor. I lied and said I would, but in reality that was the last thing I'd do. I almost burst into hysterical laughter because seeing a doctor was how all of this had started. I made a decision then to stop drinking, though, once and for all.

I sat on the sofa, hugging my knees to my chest and staring into the darkness, knowing there was no way I could sleep. Tears streamed down my cheeks as memories of Zoe kept flitting into my head. My kind, sweet sister. The peacemaker. The one who always looked on the bright side of everything. The one whose warmth and compassion knew no bounds. And Miles wasn't the only one who'd got her killed. If I hadn't asked her to dig around in Dr Baird's notes, she'd still be alive. Guilt crushed my heart. I had to put Zoe's killers behind bars. Somehow.

I knew I hadn't imagined the threatening phone call or Zoe's voicemail message. I was certain of that. And if someone had gone to such extreme lengths to delete them and make it seem like I was unhinged, then the only reason for that could be because they were worried I'd expose Caprixanine. The question was: how had they done it? Who'd had access to my phone? I thought back over everything that had happened.

Andrew. He'd been alone with my phone in the lounge when he'd come for dinner and I was making final preparations for the meal in the kitchen. He must've put some kind of virus on it so he could access it remotely and wipe things off it to make me look crazy.

No wonder he hadn't called again. That chance meeting in the car park wasn't by chance at all. He'd engineered it to get close to me – to keep an eye on me.

And he knew where I lived.

I took the SIM card and battery out of my phone and rummaged in my kitchen drawers for a pair of scissors. I cut up the SIM card and put the shards in the bin, along with the battery and the phone. Tomorrow I'd buy another mobile. I also made a mental note to phone Mum with the new number.

I took a knife from the kitchen drawer, just in case Andrew came back, and wandered into the lounge. I slumped on the sofa, clutching the knife in one hand and chewing on my thumbnail with the other, trying to work out a plan.

I wanted to go to bed and pull the covers over my head – to stay there forever in a safe cocoon and never face the world again. I wanted to give in to the overwhelming grief and sadness and dread. I wanted someone else to take over now – for them to make decisions, find answers, keep everyone safe. But that wasn't going to happen. If Will didn't believe me, I was going to have to find some kind of evidence on my own. And that meant having another crack at Miles, even though I didn't want to speak to him again.

When I couldn't face any more thoughts about Zoe, I rested the knife on the arm of the sofa and turned on my laptop, searching for information on the third girl Zoe had mentioned in her message. Maria or Marie.

It didn't take me long to find something. Just a tiny paragraph was all seventeen-year-old Maria Butterworth warranted in the online version of the *Bloomfield News*. Maria had lived in a small village fifteen miles from here, which is why I hadn't heard the story through the *Ashfield Post*. Two months before Dean's murder–suicide, she'd taken an overdose when her parents were out.

My stomach churned. What kind of place must she have been in inside her head to do that?

I put a hand to my mouth as I read the scant details again.

And then there were three.

Chapter 28

At first light, I showered and changed and forced a bowl of cereal down to keep up my energy. I slipped the knife into my bag, along with some self-defence spray that I'd bought when I was in London, and drove to Miles's house, keeping an eye out for the suspicious black car. I didn't see anyone following me, but maybe they thought Zoe's murder and their warning were enough to make me drop things.

Tania swung the front door open. Even though it was only 7.30 a.m., she had full make-up on and her hair had been straightened. How could her appearance be a priority when her sister-in-law was dead?

'Hi,' Tania said, her crimson lips turning town at the edges in a sad expression. 'I was going to phone you last night and say sorry about Zoe, but Miles said you weren't up to talking.'

'Did he?' I forced my voice to sound neutral. More like he didn't want me to tell Tania about what was going on and his involvement in it. Because he *was* involved. I was certain. 'I wanted to phone and speak to Leigh, but I wasn't in a good place.'

'Come here.' She pulled me into a hug, something she'd never done before. Surprised, I stumbled forwards over the step and had to cling on to her to stop myself falling. 'I can't believe it. Miles is devastated. He's been locked in his office all night, drinking. I keep banging on the door, trying to get him to come out, but he won't.'

Devastated? Or guilty?

I pulled back, feeling awkward in Tania's stiff embrace. 'How's Leigh taking things?'

'She's confused, obviously. She—'

Leigh ran to the front door then, dressed in pyjamas that were too big and belonged to Hayley. 'Mummy!' she cried, an expectant look on her face. She stopped short when she realised it was only me, her face dissolving into tears. 'Where's Mummy?'

I scooped her up in my arms and let her cry as I brought her inside, glancing at Tania over Leigh's head.

'We told you, sweetheart, don't you remember?' Tania said, stroking Leigh's hair as she rested her head against me and sucked her thumb, tears dribbling down her cheeks. 'Mummy's with the angels now.'

'But when will they bring her back? I don't want to stay here any more. I want *Mummy*!' she yelled.

I sat down at the eight-seater glass table with Leigh on top of me, straddling my legs. I leaned back and looked into her eyes, my heart shattering, my own eyes welling up. I tried to fight off the tears, to be strong for Leigh. A thought flashed into my head that if Zoe was here she'd know exactly what to do, but, of course, she wasn't. So instead I did what I could to comfort Leigh by holding her tight and stroking her hair, rocking her gently.

'How about some juice, sweetie?' Tania asked Leigh, her forehead pinched with what looked like exasperation.

'Don't want juice. Want Mummy,' she said in a whisper, although all the exploding emotions seemed to have wiped her out and she was a dead, floppy weight in my arms, sniffling.

I brushed her tears away with my fingertips and sat rocking her for a while as Tania stared out of the window.

Eventually, Tania said to Leigh, 'Come on, poppet, why don't you watch a bit of TV, hmm?' She held out her hand and Leigh took it, eyes downcast.

We both walked her into the huge lounge. I picked up one of the many remote controls on the stand below a gigantic TV screen on the wall.

I jabbed at the buttons, but the TV didn't come on. 'How do you work this thing?'

'That's for the Bose system.' Tania picked up another remote and turned on the TV, then flicked through some channels until she found a cartoon station.

I kneeled in front of Leigh, who had thrown herself on the sofa, sucking her thumb again, something she'd stopped doing ages ago. She stared at the TV, but I wasn't convinced she was actually looking at it.

'I need to talk to you.' Tania touched my arm and jerked her head back towards the door.

I kissed Leigh's cheek and followed Tania back into the kitchen.

'How are you supposed to explain something like this?' Tania said when we were out of Leigh's hearing.

'I don't know.' I exhaled a breath, feeling so tired, as if my bones were melting inside me. 'Where's Hayley?'

'Still asleep. It took ages to get them off last night after what happened, so I thought it best to let her have a lie-in. Do you want tea?' Tania filled the kettle without waiting for an answer, looking eager to do something.

'That would be nice, thanks.' I didn't want one – I wasn't sure I could even get it down my closed-up throat.

'I've tried my best explaining to Leigh, but I'm not sure what else to say,' she said, a defensive edge to her voice, turning away from me. 'I mean, it's not really my responsibility, is it?'

I glanced at her rigid back as she shoved teabags into mugs. I wanted to scoop Leigh up and take her home with me to stay, but I wasn't certain she'd be safe there. Not after Zoe. And I'd never forgive myself if anything happened to her. For now, I thought the safest place was right here, even if it wasn't exactly a calm, happy environment at the moment, so I didn't offer to have Leigh, although I thought that's what Tania was hinting at.

When I didn't reply, she said, 'Your mum phoned Miles. She's on her way back.'

I didn't even have the energy to be annoyed that Mum had called him instead of me, the person who'd actually rung her. Then I remembered cutting up my SIM card. But even so, she could've called my landline.

'I think it's probably better if Leigh stays with her for the time being, don't you?' Tania said.

Not really, I thought. Surely it would be better for Leigh to be with Hayley and have a friend right now. And I wasn't convinced Mum, with her cold aloofness and no-nonsense, unsympathetic composure, would be a good thing for Leigh at all. When I was eight and my pet hamster died, all Mum had said was 'Good. It stunk and was noisy'. There was no sympathy. No attempt to understand my devastated loss. Sometimes I thought Mum was born without a heart.

'I don't want Hayley to fall apart,' Tania carried on. 'It's not good for her to see all this upset.'

I suddenly felt an exploding anger towards Miles. 'I'm just going to speak to Miles for a moment.' I stood up, clenching my fists.

'I don't think that's a good idea. He was pretty annoyed and upset with you when he came back yesterday. He doesn't need any more hassle at the moment. I'm really worried about him.'

'Really? And did he happen to mention *why* he was so annoyed with me?' I said, trying to dampen the furious tone in my voice.

'No, he just said you'd had a row. You didn't tell him I thought he'd been having an affair, did you?' She gasped.

'Of course not!'

'Good. I was jumping to stupid conclusions. He must just be stressed about work. And now he's really upset about Zoe, so I don't think you should . . .'

I ignored her and stomped up the stairs to the fifth bedroom that was decked out as Miles's office. I banged on the door. 'Miles, it's me. We need to talk!'

'Go away!' Miles's voice slurred from behind the door.

I tried the handle, expecting it to be locked, but it swung open. Miles sat in his high-backed white leather chair, feet up on the polished mahogany desk, a glass of whisky in his hand and an almost empty bottle in front of him. He wore the same clothes he'd been wearing when we'd identified Zoe yesterday. The blinds at the window were closed.

'Bugger off.' Miles's bloodshot eyes met mine with defiance.

'I'm not going anywhere until you agree to help me.' I stepped into the room and closed the door. 'I've told Will everything.'

'You stupid cow.' Miles's feet dropped to the floor and he sat up, although his usually confident posture was slumped. 'I warned you not to do that. Do you—'

'I'm not listening to that again. He didn't believe me anyway, and I've probably got you to thank for that!' I snarled. 'But Zoe was murdered and just left there like a piece of shit!' I spat out. 'Now, if you know something about Caprixanine, you need to tell Will before anyone else dies.'

'You're crazy, Holly. You're—'

'NO! *You* shut up for once in your bloody life. You always were a bad liar. Fuck knows why Mum always believed you, instead of me and Zoe. Just *tell me!*' I slammed my hand down on his desk.

Miles took another swig of whisky and stared at the blinds, ignoring me, probably hoping I'd go away.

I stepped forward and knocked the glass out of his hand. His eyes widened with indignation as it bounced on to the cream luxury carpet, spraying amber liquid everywhere.

'I hope you're going to pay the cleaning bill!' Miles glared at me.

I threw my hands in the air. 'I don't fucking believe you!' I yelled at the top of my voice.

Tania's feet hurried loudly up the stairs before bursting into the room. 'What the hell is all the shouting about?' Tania frowned at me.

'Nothing,' Miles snapped. 'Holly's lost the plot.'

'You should ask *him*.' I pointed to Miles. 'Go on, ask him what he knows and what he's done. Maybe he'll tell *you*.'

Tania's frown slipped and she looked confused. 'What do you mean?' she said to me uncertainly, then turned to Miles. 'Miles? What's going on?'

'Zoe was killed trying to find out about a side effect caused by one of the drugs Tragatech makes,' I told her. 'And God knows how many other deaths it could be responsible for. I think Miles was fully aware of the problems with this "wonder drug" he's been plugging so you two can carry on your bullshit, all-expenses-paid lifestyle!'

'What?' She blinked rapidly. 'Miles? Is that true?'

'Get the fuck out of my house!' Miles shouted at me, anger flaring in his eyes.

'Don't worry, I'm going. I don't want to be around you any longer than I have to. I hope selling yourself out is worth it! And if something happens to me, too, then it will be on *your* head!' I stormed out of the door, leaving Tania with her mouth gaping open.

I rushed down the stairs and took a few deep breaths in the hallway. Running the back of my hand over my sweaty forehead, I faked calmness and walked into the lounge where Leigh was sitting numbly, just as I'd left her. I crouched in front of her, stroking her hair away from her forehead.

I hugged her hard until she wriggled and squealed, 'You're too tight.'

I pulled back, my gaze flickering over her desolate face. 'I love you, sweetie.' I kissed her cheek. 'I'll be back to see you soon, OK?'

She nodded dully. I took another deep breath and stood. I walked towards the doorway.

'Do they have chicken nuggets in heaven?' Leigh said to my back.

I pinched my eyes shut but I couldn't stop the tears. They fell in a torrent as I let myself out the front door.

Chapter 29

I drove out of Miles's driveway, wheels spinning on the gravel. I felt light-headed and fuzzy, as if my body was no longer attached to my brain. Fury and adrenaline rushed through me. I hated Miles at that moment. He was the only one who could get into Tragatech and find evidence of what they were covering up about Caprixanine, but he'd made it clear he wouldn't get involved or even admit to anything. How could he stay silent now after what had happened to Zoe, his own sister? I knew Miles was a self-centred, self-indulgent prick, but this . . . well, this went beyond any lengths I ever thought he'd stoop to.

I had to pull over into a lay-by until my hands stopped shaking. Sweat trickled between my shoulder blades and dotted above my upper lip. I couldn't arrive at the Butterworths' house in this state.

I don't know how long I sat there trying to calm down, but all that time I kept an eye out for black cars or someone watching me. I didn't notice anything suspicious, so eventually I started the car and followed the directions on my satnav to Bloomfield.

The street on which the Butterworths lived had been given in the online article, but not the house number. I parked at the end of the

Butterworths' road and went to the first house. There was no answer to my knocking. At the next house the door was opened by an elderly man with a small mongrel dog beside his feet.

'Hi, I'm sorry to bother you. I'm looking for the Butterworths' house. They live on this street. I think I must've taken their house number down wrong. Do you know them?'

He nodded. 'Aye.' He leaned out of the door, pointing further up the road. 'Number sixty.'

I smiled. 'Thank you.'

'Terrible business, that. Terrible,' he said, shaking his head as he closed the door.

As I walked up to number sixty, I noticed that the small front garden looked neglected, the grass tall with brown patches left from the unseasonably hot summer. A terracotta pot housed a mass of twigs that used to be a lavender bush. A few newspapers sat on the front step. There was a 'For Sale' board just inside the boundary of the property. I didn't blame them wanting to move. I couldn't have stayed in the same house with a constant reminder of what had been lost, either.

I knocked on the wooden door and waited.

A tiny woman with lank hair greying at the roots, gaunt cheekbones, and weariness in her eyes opened the door.

'Hi, are you Mrs Butterworth?'

'Yes.'

'I'm really sorry to bother you, but I'm a freelance journalist, and I'm writing a piece about teenage suicide. I wondered if you'd be willing to talk to me about Maria?'

She blinked a few times, then cleared her throat. 'Um . . . I don't know. My husband's not here. What kind of thing are you writing?'

'It's going to be something very sensitive to raise awareness about the issue. I'm hoping it might help other parents spot potential risks in advance.'

She pressed her lips together as if she were thinking. 'Well, I wouldn't want another parent to go through this, so if you think it will help in some way, then, yes, I suppose so.' She wrapped the cardigan she wore more tightly around herself and shuffled backwards to let me inside.

I followed her into the lounge.

'Would you like a cup of tea?' she asked.

'Yes, please. That would be nice.'

She left the room and I glanced around. There were photos of a girl at various ages taking pride of place on a mantelpiece above a gas fire. I stepped closer to the mantel and peered at the Butterworths' daughter wearing a blue and white leotard, holding up a trophy, her hair pulled into a neat bun. There was another one of Maria on a high beam, her back arched and her arms high in the air in a perfect gymnastic pose. Several trophies were also on the mantel.

Maria's mum returned holding a tray with two mugs of tea and a plate of custard creams. She set the tray down on the coffee table and stood beside me. She picked up the photo of Maria on the beam. 'She was twelve there. She was always really athletic. I took her to her first gymnastics class when she was five and she fell in love with it. She won lots of county awards.'

'You must've been very proud of her.'

'We were.' Her voice hitched. She coughed to disguise it and set the photo back down. Then she perched on the edge of one of the armchairs and wrapped her arms around her stomach.

'I'm very sorry about what happened.' I sat on the sofa.

She looked down at her knees. 'Thank you. I still can't believe it. I still wake up every morning and there's that split second where it doesn't register at first. Then you have to go through it all over again.' She reached for her tea, her hands shaking – she cupped them around the mug.

'What else can you tell me about your daughter, Mrs Butterworth?'

'Call me Terri, please.' She clutched her mug so hard her knuckles strained against the skin. 'Maria was always a bubbly girl. She wasn't that academic, but she loved the gym, like I said. She was at Bloomfield High doing her AS levels. She wanted to be a coach.'

I removed a pad and pen from my bag as she talked and scribbled down notes about how Maria had been popular, had a lot of friends, was mad about One Direction.

'About seven months ago, though, Maria was walking home from a gym meet late at night. I thought she was going to walk back with her best friend who only lives on the next road, but Liz went to meet her boyfriend in the end, so Maria came back alone. She was . . .' Terri paused and swallowed hard. 'A man stole her bag.'

'She was mugged?'

'Yes. He ran up behind her and threw her on the ground. He hit her in the face before running off with her bag. It happened really quickly. Maria was so startled she never even got a good look at his face, so he was never caught. But that's when the trouble started.'

I couldn't ask outright if Maria had been seeing Dr Baird because Terri might become suspicious about how I knew, so I said, 'What kind of trouble? What happened?'

'Maria was worried about the man finding her and coming back to hurt her. She started having panic attacks. We tried to manage them, but sometimes they got so bad. She started having nightmares, too. So after a while we took her to see this psychiatrist.'

'And what was his name?' I said, the words almost sticking in my throat.

'Dr Baird. He was recommended by our GP.'

'And what did Dr Baird do to help with the panic attacks?'

'He prescribed her some tablets to help with them and gave her exercises to do when she was having one.'

'Do you know the name of the tablets?' I asked, even though I already knew the answer.

'Cap . . . Caprixine? Something like that.'

'Was it Caprixanine?'

She nodded. 'Yes, that was it.'

'And how did Maria get on after she'd seen Dr Baird and was taking the tablets?'

Terri chewed on her lower lip, her forehead wrinkled with anguish. 'Maria was a lot brighter. The tablets seemed to be helping calm her down and she was doing the exercises Dr Baird had given her when an attack came on. In fact, she hadn't had an attack for about a week, so my husband and I thought it was OK to leave her alone for the evening and go out to see some friends.' She rocked back and forth. 'That's when . . . it happened. That night she . . .' Her hands shook so hard some tea sloshed over the rim of the mug on to her jeans. She put the mug down clumsily on the table and her fingers flew to her lips. Tears fell down her cheeks.

My throat contracted with choking emotions. 'I'm so sorry.'

Terri blinked, expelling more droplets of tears. 'She found some of my old sleeping tablets and Ian's strong painkillers. He was prescribed them when he had a terrible disc problem with his back and had an operation. She . . . mixed them . . . and she . . . killed herself.' She hiccupped in gulps of air to get the words out.

I pressed my eyelids closed for a moment and shook my head. 'And there was no prior sign that Maria might do something like that? She didn't seem agitated or have suicidal thoughts before that?'

'No, never. I'd never have left her alone like that if there had been. We shouldn't have left her, but she seemed so much better. And it was exhausting for all of us.'

'What did Dr Baird tell you about Caprixanine?'

'Umm . . . I don't know. Maria saw him alone. She was too embarrassed to talk about things with me and Ian in the room. And I wanted to give her space . . . you know . . . to treat her like an adult.

But now . . . oh, God!' She shook her head and clamped her jaw tight, her mouth in a tight line, as if she were angry with herself.

'So he didn't discuss the treatment with you and Ian in private?'

'Well, yes, as Maria was under eighteen. He just said he'd prescribed her some mild tablets and some exercises for anxiety and panic attacks.'

'Did he mention any kind of clinical trial or research he was carrying out?'

Terri scrunched up her face in surprise. 'No.'

'Did Dr Baird tell you about any possible side effects of the drug? Or tell you they weren't approved for adolescents?'

She took a sip of her tea. 'Umm . . . he just said they were safer than aspirin.'

That phrase again. It was the same thing he'd told Pete Tucker. A dreadful feeling of déjà vu settled over me. 'Did you speak to Dr Baird after Maria took her life and tell him what had happened?'

'Yes. I spoke to him on the phone. He was lovely.'

'Did he explain why he thought Maria might have done what she did when she was never suicidal before?'

'Yes. He said that anxiety disorders can be associated with suicide attempts. He said Maria must have suffered an acute attack that triggered a suicidal reaction.'

'He didn't mention that Caprixanine might have caused the reaction?'

'No.' She looked at me oddly. 'They were perfectly safe, I told you. We followed his advice!' she wailed. 'We did all we could. It's not our fault. We tried! We . . .' She leapt to her feet, her lower lip quivering. 'Are you blaming us? You've got a cheek to come in here and blame me!'

'No, of course not. I'm sorry if you thought I was. That's not what I think at all. I think the drug Maria was taking was dangerous. It's not supposed to be used for under-eighteens. I—'

'That's ridiculous. If it was dangerous, people would know about it, and Dr Baird said it was perfectly harmless.' Terri pointed towards the front window. 'I want you to leave. Get out now! The press always twist things. That's what you're doing, isn't it? Trying to blame us? We *loved* our daughter!' she screamed in my face.

I quickly gathered my things and walked to the front door. As I opened it and stepped on to the street I heard Terri sobbing behind me, muttering over and over again, 'We loved her!'

I hurried down the street to my car, feeling terrible for upsetting Terri.

I knew how Dr Baird and Tragatech were getting away with it all now. How Grafloxx had got away with the deadly side effects of Tiazal for so long. It was easy to blame a psychiatric disorder for suicidal and violent behaviour, rather than the drug. It could take years before other people started asking questions.

But who would be the next to die in the meantime?

Chapter 30

Thinking of Tiazal made me remember Daniel Foster, the whistle-blower. He hadn't called me back and now my phone was out of action he wouldn't be able to, but I really needed to speak to him.

I drove back to Ashfield and parked on the high street. Ten minutes later, I'd bought the cheapest mobile phone with Internet I could find in the shop and a pay-as-you-go SIM card.

I drove home, unwrapped it and left it to charge. When the battery indicator showed one bar, I called Daniel's number again.

'Hello?' a cheerful male voice answered.

'Hi, is that Daniel Foster?'

'Yes.'

'My name is Holly Gold. I'm a journalist and I left you a message a few days ago. I'm—'

'Oh, yes! Sorry I haven't got back to you. I've been away. It was on my to-do list to call you today. You're writing an article and wanted to talk to me about Tiazal?'

'Yes. Is it possible to speak to you in person?'

'Yes. I have some free time tomorrow, actually, if you want to meet.'

'Absolutely.' I stood up and walked into the kitchen. 'You're in London, aren't you?'

'That's right.'

I tucked the phone between my shoulder and ear as I grabbed a pint glass and filled it with tap water. I wanted a glass of wine instead, but pushed the thought away. 'What time are you free?' I took a large gulp.

'Three-thirty? Is that any good for you? I have a little time then in between seeing clients.'

I stopped gulping quickly and swallowed. 'That would be good. Whereabouts?'

We arranged to meet at a coffee shop in London. I knew the area – it was only a couple of miles from the *Daily Insider*.

I paced up and down the kitchen, wondering what to do next. When my landline rang I jumped. The warning call I'd had about Zoe echoed in my head and I hesitated for a moment before answering.

'Hel—' I started to answer tentatively.

'I've tried ringing your bloody mobile and it's dead,' Tania said abruptly before I could finish.

'I had to get a new one today.'

She huffed loudly. 'I'm downstairs outside your flat with Leigh and I need to drop her off.' I sensed anger and impatience in her voice. 'I don't want to come up.'

'What's going on?'

'I need to get away for a few days and I'm taking Hayley with me. I can't take Leigh as well.'

'Did you ask Miles to tell you what's going—'

'I'm not getting into this now. Can you just come down?'

'Yes, hang on a—'

'Right. Good.' She hung up.

When I got to the communal entrance, Tania was sitting on the little wall outside, looking immaculate apart from her red face. She was smoking, something I hadn't seen her do for years.

'Where's Leigh?' I asked, confused.

'She's in the car with Hayley, playing on the iPad.' She jerked her head towards her shiny new four-by-four in the corner of the car park before throwing the cigarette on the ground. She thrust Leigh's *Frozen* rucksack towards me, not meeting my enquiring gaze. 'Her stuff's in here.'

'Right.' I took it, worrying whether Leigh would be safe here. I glanced back at the intercom entry system. Even if someone did get inside the building, I'd double-lock the door.

'I know you think I'm selfish and materialistic and maybe you're right.' Tania said, her chin jutting into the air, although it was wobbling, as if she were trying hard not to cry.

'Look, I'm sorry. I shouldn't have said that,' I said.

'Sometimes it's easy to enjoy the money and perks, but Miles . . .' She shook her head and stopped.

'What did he say? He knew about the side effects of Caprixanine and kept it quiet, didn't he?'

She closed her eyes for a moment, and when she opened them I saw the shimmer of tears. 'I can't talk about it,' she hissed, wiping her eyes. 'And I've got to go.'

'Whereabouts are you going with Hayley?'

She marched off towards the four-by-four and ignored me.

I followed behind and grabbed her arm. 'Tania! If you know something, you need to tell me before anyone else gets killed. You need to seriously look into what Miles is doing. I'm certain innocent people are dying over it. And you need to be careful, too.'

'Get off me!' Her voice was bordering on hysterical as she ripped her arm from my grasp and opened Leigh's door. 'Come on, poppet,' she said to Leigh. 'Auntie Holly's going to look after you until Granny comes back.'

I glanced at Leigh, who wiped her tired, sad eyes as she climbed out of the car. I kneeled down and wrapped my arms around her. 'All right, sweetie?' Which was a ridiculous thing to say. Nothing was all right, and it probably wouldn't be again. 'Hi, Hayley.' I forced a smile at her over Leigh's shoulder.

Hayley said to me, 'Why can't Leigh come with us?'

I narrowed my eyes at Tania, seething inside, wondering what Miles had told her – wondering how the hell she could keep it quiet, too, if she knew something.

She looked at me as she got inside the driver's seat. 'Because we don't know when we'll be back.'

Leigh held my hand as we watched them drive away, Hayley waving madly at us from the back seat.

I hugged Leigh tightly to me. 'Come on, then. Let's go upstairs. Maybe we can play some games.' I led her inside and she followed meekly.

After I got Leigh settled, I spent the afternoon trying to keep her entertained. I didn't know if it was best to have her confront Zoe's death or to try to brush over it. But I watched cartoons with her cradled against me. Made her a boiled egg and soldiers and coaxed her into eating something. Read her favourite story. Bathed her and read to her some more until she fell asleep at seven o'clock on my bed.

I watched her eyelashes fluttering against her plump cheeks, wishing she'd never have had to know the pain of the real world. Guilt sliced through me because my actions had culminated in Zoe's death.

The intercom ringing in the lounge shrieked in the silence. Sweat broke out on my palms as I walked towards the handset. What if it was Andrew coming to finish me off? What if he was the one who'd killed Zoe? I couldn't let anything happen to Leigh. But then, I doubted he'd pre-announce his arrival, unless he was hoping I still hadn't worked out his connection to Tragatech.

I hesitated, my finger hovering above the 'Answer' button. The intercom buzzed again, and I wished there was a video camera on the system.

I took a deep breath as my heart danced erratically in my chest. I leaned against the front door, wondering what to do.

A few minutes later my landline rang. I picked it up slowly and put it to my ear, bracing myself for that threatening voice again.

'Hi, it's Will,' he said. 'I've been really worried about you. I was trying to get you on your mobile all day. And I've just been pressing your intercom.'

I puffed out my cheeks with a breath of relief. 'I had to get a new phone. My old one . . . broke.'

'Is it OK if I come up?'

'Yes. Sure.' I buzzed him in, waited a few moments, then opened the front door and leaned against the door frame. When I saw him appear along the corridor, I wanted to run into his arms. It took all the strength I had to stay where I was.

'Hi.' He stood in front of me, his face oozing kindness and worry.

'Hi.' I looked up at him.

'Are you OK?'

I nodded, unable to speak, because if I did I'd probably crumble.

He followed me inside and closed the door.

I flopped down on to the small sofa. 'My niece is asleep in the bedroom so we can't be too loud.'

He sat next to me, his thigh brushing against mine, the heat from his body seeping into me. He twisted to face me, resting his arm along the top of the cushions. 'Is that going to be permanent?'

I rubbed my hands over my face. 'I don't know. I don't really know anything at the moment.'

'Did you make a doctor's appointment?' His gaze caught mine.

'Yes,' I lied and looked away. I wanted to tell him how I'd confronted Miles at his house about Caprixanine, but that he wouldn't tell me anything. How Miles had obviously said something to Tania that had made her want to disappear. How I'd spoken to Terri Butterworth. But it would probably only make me look more obsessed and mad. Instead, I asked, 'Have you got any leads on Zoe's killer?'

'Unfortunately not.' His arm grazed my shoulder.

I closed my eyes, wanting to rest my head against him, but a banging on the door made my eyelids snap open.

'Are you expecting someone?' Will asked.

I froze for a second, before a familiar dulcet tone barked out my name.

'Holly? Are you in there?'

I groaned and whispered, 'It's my mum.' How had she got inside without me buzzing her in? I cursed irresponsible neighbours for letting just anyone through the door. I shot off the sofa and opened the door.

Even though she'd been travelling for hours, my mother's hair was still immaculately neat in a jaw-length wavy style. Her tailored trousers had no creases in them and her perfume was still as overpowering as ever.

'I've just spoken to Miles and he said Leigh was here! I don't think a one-bedroomed flat is any environment for her to be in, do you?' She waltzed into the room. 'Especially when you seem to be having enough difficulties of your own.'

'Hello, Mum, how are you?' I said wearily.

'Who are you?' She noticed Will and narrowed her eyes at him.

'I'm a police officer. DS Jackson.' Will stood and held out a hand, which Mum ignored.

'What's she done now?' she demanded, her eyebrow quirking up as she looked at me.

'Nothing. I'm investigating Zoe's murder and giving Holly an update.'

Her face looked as if it had been slapped. 'Right. Well, have you caught the bastard who did this yet?'

Will glanced at me before answering her. 'Not yet. We're still working on things.'

'So why are you here and not out there looking for them?' She pointed towards the front door.

'We're doing everything we can.'

'And you think it was a mugging?' Mum tilted her head.

Will glanced at me for a second. 'Yes, we do.'

She looked at me. 'Miles told me you'd concocted some ridiculous conspiracy story about all this. Honestly, if it's not one thing with you, it's another. Even as a child you'd stoop to making up stories to get attention. You're a fantasist!'

I thought I could stay silent. I wanted to in front of Will, otherwise I would've been digging my own grave, making myself look even more on the verge of a breakdown. But the words slipped out before I could stop them. 'Why don't you ask Tania about it all? She's left him, you know. Miles knows something about Zoe's death and what's been going on and he's lying about it.'

'Are you drunk again?' She veered backwards.

'No!' I wanted to scream at her.

She gave me a disbelieving look. 'Tania hasn't left him. She's taken Hayley to her parents for a couple of days for a bit of a break away from all the upset.'

'Is that what he told you?' I asked incredulously. If that was true, then why hadn't Tania just told me that?

Mum held her hand up, palm out. 'Look, I don't have time for this right now. I'm tired. I've been travelling for *hours*. I want to take Leigh home and get her settled and go to bed. We can talk in the morning.'

'By talking do you mean talking *at* me and not listening to anything I have to say?' I muttered.

'I assume you have a card?' She turned to Will.

'Yes.' He fumbled in his pocket for a business card and handed it over to her.

'Good. I'll call you tomorrow, when I can think straight. Now, let me get Leigh and I'll take her back to my house. Poor little mite, being shoved from pillar to post.' She treated me to another glare, as if it were all my fault. 'I suppose she's in the bedroom?' She stalked towards my bedroom without waiting for an answer.

I thought about putting up a fight, but I was too tired. It felt like I'd been fighting her my whole life and getting nowhere. Nothing was about to change now.

She reappeared with Leigh in her arms. Leigh's sleeping head lolled against Mum's shoulder-padded jacket. I picked up Leigh's backpack and handed it to her, but she waved it off.

'I've got everything she could possibly want at my house.' She glanced a final time at Will. 'I'll speak to you in the morning.'

Will raised his eyebrows when she'd gone. 'She's a piece of work.'

'You have no idea. She's not good at confronting reality.'

'Look, I'm sorry, but I've got to shoot off, too. Work stuff.' He put his hand on my forearm. 'Will you be OK?'

I faked a smile. 'I'll be fine.'

'Can you give me your new mobile number in case I need to reach you?'

I scribbled the number down on a piece of paper and handed it to him. After he'd gone, I closed the door, rested my forehead against it and exhaled. Sadness and tiredness were etched into my every cell, but I had a restless energy I couldn't contain.

I tried to sleep, but it wasn't happening. Every time I closed my eyes, I saw images of Zoe again. I shoved the covers of my bed away and went into the kitchen. I grabbed a bottle of wine from the cupboard and loosened the screw cap.

Then I stared at it in my grasp. I could picture myself gulping down the first glass, welcoming the fuzzy feeling, waiting for it to obliterate the pain. Drinking the whole bottle. Opening another. Waiting for sleep to come and claim me so I wouldn't have to think about anything. Oblivion was waiting to clear everything away for just a short while.

My mouth watered as I clutched the bottle tight. My breath quickened. Sweat broke out on my forehead.

I put the bottle down on the worktop, staring at it, clenching and unclenching my jaw, fighting a battle beneath my skin.

I reached for it again, hands shaking.

Then I took off the cap and poured it down the sink.

Chapter 31

I burst through the door of the coffee shop, my face hot, fringe plastered to my forehead. The train had been delayed and then the Tube had been packed, so I'd had to wait for the next one. Having been back in Ashfield for the last year, I'd forgotten the stress and bustle of London life.

I stood by an array of cakes and sandwiches behind a glass counter, the smell of bacon sandwiches and fresh pastries hitting me. My stomach growled with hunger. The cereal bar I'd eaten on the train hadn't filled the hole.

I glanced around and recognised Daniel from the photo on his website. He sat in a booth in the far corner, dressed casually in jeans and a grey Fred Perry top, reading a thriller.

I wiped away the hair from my forehead and wound my way through the tables towards him. 'Daniel, hi. I'm Holly.' I wanted to smile, but my face wouldn't cooperate. How could I smile when Zoe was dead? Instead, I held out a hand. 'Thank you for taking the time to see me.'

He did smile at me, though, as he stood and shook my hand. 'Nice to meet you.'

'Can I get you another?' I eyed his almost empty cup of tea.

'Thanks. A green tea would be great.'

I nodded and headed to the counter. As I edged my way forward in the queue, I glanced over at Daniel, head bent over his book. There was no doubt he was good-looking in an outdoorsy way. Not that I cared what he looked like. It was just an observation, really. I guessed that all companies were going to pick sales reps who were attractive and personable. He glanced up from his thriller and our eyes met. I glanced quickly away and stepped forward in the queue.

My phone beeped with a text. I retrieved it from my bag and looked at the screen. It was another blank text. Was this the new equivalent of spam call-centre hang-ups on landlines? I put it back in my bag, instantly forgetting about it as I took another glance at Daniel and shuffled further along the queue.

Armed with our drinks, I returned to the table and set them down. He slid a bookmark inside the thriller, closed it, and put it on the bench seat next to him, on top of a brown A4 envelope.

'So, you said you're doing some research on the pharmaceutical industry for an article?' He leaned back against the vinyl backrest.

I blinked back the image of Zoe lying cold and lifeless on the mortuary table.

I must've delayed too long before replying because he prompted me with, 'Do you have some specific questions? I'm guessing it's something to do with Tiazal?'

'Kind of.' I didn't really know where to start. Will hadn't believed me, and now I was doubting what was real and what was fantasy.

I took a deep breath and told Daniel about Dean and what he'd done. About Rachel Tucker and Maria Butterworth. How I suspected Caprixanine was to blame.

'Aha! Tragatech's new wonder antidepressant!' He threw his hands wide in a *ta-da!* gesture, a sarcastic edge to his voice.

I carried on with my theory until I got to the part about Zoe – how I suspected she was murdered because she'd discovered something they wanted to keep hidden.

'I'm very sorry.' His lips pressed together into a solemn line. 'Are you sure you want to do this now? We can rearrange.'

'No. I'm OK.' I had to do this now. I was going to get to the bottom of things for Zoe, even if I died trying or lost my sanity along the way. 'Dr Baird has been giving Caprixanine to teenagers, either off-label or doing some kind of clinical trial or research involving adolescents for Tragatech. I think he's in Tragatech's pocket and he's covering up the side effects for them because the drug's making them a *lot* of money and will make even more if it's marketed to kids. It happened before with Tiazal, as you know, so do you think it's possible that it's happening again? That this drug is causing these terrible side effects? Or am I looking for things that don't exist because I want there to be a reason to explain things that can't be explained? I'm doubting myself because, if Caprixanine *is* responsible, I don't understand how it can even be available on prescription.'

He tilted his head slightly and blew out a breath. 'Because you think it sounds too incredible? Like something out of the pages of one of these?' He tapped his finger on the cover of the thriller beside him.

'Yes. But Dean wasn't taking Caprixanine just before he died, and the parents of Rachel and Maria haven't considered the possibility that the drug made their daughters suicidal, so am I making crazy connections where there aren't any? Were they really all suffering from a mental illness that made them suddenly and inexplicably act out of character?'

'What you've just described to me – suicidality, self-harming, violent and aggressive behaviour – could definitely be side effects of a drug. Most antidepressants on the market can have those same effects.'

He pushed his tea aside and leaned his elbows on the desk, lacing his fingers together. 'If there's a really bizarre side effect to a drug, like, say, your arm drops off, then people are going to notice that reasonably quickly, especially when there's a sudden surge of one-armed people who've taken a particular drug. But the problem with what you're describing is that suicidal ideation as a side effect of an antidepressant is very hard to detect or prove, since people with depression are at a higher risk of suicide than the general population because of their disease. And there is no biological test to measure whether a patient has any kind of psychiatric disorder or not.

'Also, suicide is generally quite rare, so you'd need a lot of people committing suicide while on a particular drug before you could detect an increased risk. Suicide and other adverse reactions, when reported, are not always coded or recorded accurately in health records or adverse reaction reports. And although there are mandatory laws or obligations in place for healthcare practitioners or drug companies to report side effects, there are loopholes that can have deadly consequences for patients.'

I'd got out a notepad and pen and started writing, but I was struggling to keep up. He paused while I jotted down some more, then I said, 'What kind of loopholes?'

'A lot of the reporting structure involves reams of paperwork designed to discourage HCPs – healthcare practitioners – from filing reports. Patients themselves often don't know they can report a side effect directly to the regulator in some counties. It's also common for patients and even doctors not to make a connection when certain drug-induced symptoms are similar to ones associated with a particular condition they're being prescribed for, or when they are things that happen naturally or frequently, like headaches or insomnia, for example. Any events that are reported can be misclassified or downgraded. A suicidal thought, for example, might be coded as "emotional liability". And there's no way to police the system. Typically, only one to ten per cent of adverse reactions are ever reported. And even when they are reported, generally they're only suspicions, which could take years to accumulate or analyse or prove.'

'And what about Dean? If he wasn't taking it when he died, could Caprixanine still be responsible?'

'I read the hype that said Caprixanine was suitable to be stopped suddenly without a withdrawal period, but I doubt that's true. It's entirely possible that the sudden effects of withdrawal itself brought on his behaviour. Patients are at risk from serious withdrawal side effects even months after discontinuation of antidepressants. Abrupt withdrawal can increase that risk.'

I tapped my pen on my pad. 'So it *is* possible, what I'm talking about?'

'Look, maybe it's best if I give you some background first. Then you'll understand how not only is it possible, it could be very probable.'

'Do you mind if I record our conversation?'

'Be my guest.'

I removed a small Dictaphone from my bag and placed it on the table next to Daniel. I'd bought it when I'd worked at the *Daily Insider*, hoping for that break that would get me working on the gritty stories. I'd never actually used it until I'd tested it at home before the train journey here to see if it was still working.

I pressed 'Record' and leaned closer to Daniel.

'When I started out in the pharma industry, I really believed I was going to be helping people get access to innovative new drugs, but the long-term reality couldn't have been more different. I was ambitious and driven, making sure I gained a huge array of medical education through reading journals and attending medical conferences and seminars so I could do my job better, and I worked my way up the ladder. I got sales awards and mega bonuses, but over the years, the more I learned, the more disillusioned I became. Ethical practices were becoming non-existent, marketing strategies were designed for one purpose only – to push drugs to maximise profits – and, quite honestly, my conscience and morals couldn't take any more.

'I couldn't continue to be a glorified drug pusher of meds known to kill thousands of people each year. The contribution I was making was harming innocent and trusting people. Tiazal was the last straw, but even more terrifying than that scandal is the fact that it's by no means an isolated incident. It's actually frighteningly common.' He took a sip of tea and cupped the mug with his hands, staring down at it. 'When I started asking Grafloxx questions about Tiazal, I was demoted and they cut my wages. Then when I blew the whistle there was a huge smear campaign by the company to discredit me. Luckily, they didn't succeed, but I did have to come back to the UK and start all over again.' He shrugged. 'Still, I'd do it all over again if it meant saving lives.'

'It must've been a nightmare for you.'

'Not as much of a nightmare as for the poor families who lost loved ones.' He pursed his lips gravely. 'I could talk for days about this subject and still have so much more to say, so I'll try to break things down for you as simply as I can. And it's probably best if I start with explaining the industry to you.'

'That would be a big help.'

'If I said the words "drugs cartel" or "drug dealer", what would you be thinking?'

'Probably about a criminal underworld warlord in Colombia, or a seedy gangster hanging around a street corner.'

'Exactly. But the pharma industry has the biggest, most lethal drug-dealing cartels on the planet. Here's an astounding statistic for you . . . prescription drugs are the *third* largest cause of death after cancer and heart disease.'

'Did you say the third?' I stared at him, wondering if I'd misheard.

'I did.' He shook his head incredulously. 'If an illegal drug was killing that many people, there would be a war on it like nothing you've ever seen, right?'

'Of course. No question.'

'I'm not saying there aren't many undeniable benefits to certain drugs. There are. There are also plenty of life-saving drugs out there, *but* . . . even those are held to ransom with companies having a monopoly on pricing. The industry isn't altruistic. They're not health*care* companies. They're huge corporations in the most powerful industry in the world, who commonly engage in bribery and kickbacks, corruption, fraud, and widespread crime.

'They're not in the business of selling drugs, they're selling *lies* about drugs, because pretty much everything we know about the medicines we're prescribed is what the pharma companies tell doctors and the regulatory authorities and the public. Sickness is a multibillion pay packet for these companies that's never-ending, and it doesn't benefit them to cure diseases or make us healthy.'

'But surely a drug is subject to rigorous testing before it's even available to the public. When I was looking up Caprixanine on the MHRA's website, it mentioned brief details of the trial information.'

He laughed humourlessly. 'If only. Let me explain how drugs are tested. Clinical trials for new drugs are only tested on several thousand people, or sometimes only a few hundred, before a drug is approved for marketing. Often the tests are only done over one to two months. When they're done ethically and independently, with clear prior protocols, you might get unbiased data being reported, but you still won't know the full effects of the drug – good or bad – until it's been on the market for years for two reasons. One: because of the low percentage of people trialled; and two: because trials done for approval involve "ideal" healthy patients, or patients who have the disease being studied. But in the real world, people have many health issues or are on many different drugs at the same time or have various lifestyle differences.'

'Wow.'

'Exactly. That's not the only problem, though. The thing is, most trials *aren't* independent. The drugs are tested by the very people who manufacture them, so of course they're predisposed to produce positive results. And what goes on behind the scenes is that unflattering, negative results that show a lack of efficacy or safety are often not published. Or they'll publish data that is often falsified or biased.'

'Wait. You're saying that clinical trial data can be *hidden* or *faked*?'

'It sounds incredible, doesn't it? But believe me, this is just the tip of the iceberg of what goes on.'

'How do they do it? I mean, surely there are rules they have to follow.'

'There are many ways to cover up, fabricate, bury, bias, cherry-pick, or misrepresent data that these companies don't want regulators or healthcare professionals to know. And the public, well, you're not deemed worthy enough to be able to see the results in case you misinterpret them! Even though the patient is the one taking all the potential health risks and being endangered in possibly irreparable ways.'

I tried to formulate the next question in my head, but I was too stunned to think straight.

The expression on my face must've given me away, because Daniel jumped in and said, 'Now, you mentioned off-label, which means doctors can prescribe *any* drug for *any* condition they think is appropriate, regardless of whether it's officially approved or trialled for that purpose. This can be a benefit, but it can also be a huge risk. The use of drugs in certain groups of the population – children, for example – is not adequately studied, so prescribing a drug to kids that was originally tested in adults can produce a whole range of potential problems.'

I rubbed a palm across my forehead. 'I was hoping when I spoke to you that you'd tell me I was wrong and I was just being paranoid and I could walk away from all this. Now I'm wondering what the hell I've got myself into.'

He laughed gently. 'Do you want to hear more, or walk away now while you're still relatively blissfully ignorant?'

'I'm not walking away. If Caprixanine is responsible – if Zoe was murdered because of it, or Dean and Rachel and Maria did what they did because of the drug – I want to expose it.'

He sat back and eyed me thoughtfully. 'What do you think causes depression?'

'You mean individual factors or physiologically?'

'Physiologically.' Daniel watched me intently, waiting for an answer.

'Depression is caused by a chemical imbalance in the brain,' I said.

He shook his head. 'The idea that it's caused by a chemical imbalance is unproven and simply pure speculation that's been carefully and cleverly fed to us by the industry as truth to market drugs. It's that old adage that if people are told something often enough, they believe it. And because people believe the hype as scientific truth, and due to clever and aggressive marketing by these drug companies, antidepressants are prescribed like candy. It's estimated that about ten per cent of the population are on them at any given time, so it's a lucrative earner for big pharma, particularly when a new so-called wonder drug enters the market. We're in the midst of a psychiatric drug epidemic, and these companies will do anything to protect their financial interests.'

Anything? I thought about Zoe's murder again and dug my nails into my palms, my jaw clenching tight.

'The psychiatric field of medicine has given us some of the most dangerous, addictive drugs in history. The old-type SSRIs, for instance – the wonder drug of the last decade – have had more adverse reactions reported to the US's Food and Drug Administration than any other drug type. Ever. And they're still being prescribed. Children are the most promising growth area for the industry – even kids younger than five are being prescribed psychiatric drugs!'

'That's what I read when I was researching it. I couldn't believe it.'

'Pets are on them now, too! If you look at other psychiatric drugs, as well – let's say for ADHD, or attention deficit hyperactivity disorder – that's a huge market. Tiazal, for example, was almost virtually identical to crystal meth. Can you imagine if a drug dealer offered a parent crystal meth to give their kids? They'd be livid! But package it up as a prescription drug and that's fine.'

'Wait a minute!' I held my hand up. 'Crystal meth?'

'Unfortunately, I'm not joking. Hook a child on those kinds of drugs and you've got a market for life, but the effects on brain functioning of taking psychiatric drugs – especially on vulnerable, developing brains – can be irreparable and deadly. The trouble is, by the time you start to question any side effects you've already been labelled with a psychiatric diagnosis, so anything you say becomes suspect, particularly when you've got doctors assuring you it can't possibly be the drug causing the problems because, as I've already explained, they are routinely relying on flawed and biased data from the drug companies.'

I thought about what Dr Baird had told Rachel's and Maria's parents. He'd blamed so-called depression and anxiety disorder for the suicides, rather than the drug, and they hadn't questioned it, even though none of the teenagers had previously had depression or suicidal and violent thoughts. It seemed that there was an inherent problem with the doctor–patient relationship because most patients – and, in this case, the parents – would generally trust their doctor and believe their advice. If a doctor told you a pill was going to help, you'd take it. Pete Tucker had seemed particularly worried to go against Dr Baird's advice in case it made his daughter worse. And these parents all thought they were doing the right thing for their children.

It struck me then that there was a common illusion and false sense of security that, just because a drug was legal and prescribed by a doctor, it was safe and effective.

Daniel tilted his head, watching me. It took a minute for me to realise I was staring at him and hadn't spoken.

'Did you have a question?' he asked.

'Sorry – I'm in shock, I think. I'm still stuck on doctors giving kids crystal meth. I'm finding it really hard to get my head around how they could prescribe this kind of stuff. I mean, the doctor's motto is "First, do no harm".'

'Doctors may know about diseases, human physiology, and psychology, but they don't know very much about the drugs designed to treat them. That's where the marketing muscle of drug companies comes in – and, I'm sorry to say, where my involvement in the murky world of bad pharma took place. As a drug sales rep, it was my job to convince clinical healthcare practitioners that my company's drugs were the best.'

'And how did you do that? What did it involve?'

'We'd give doctors only certain information about clinical trials if it suited our cause. If it didn't – if the studies showed potentially harmful side effects or a lack of efficacy – they weren't mentioned. The information doctors are given is designed to mislead, cover up or misrepresent potentially fatal risks of drugs while spinning and promoting benefits, whether real or not.' He spread his hands on the table and looked at them before closing his eyes for a moment. I knew from his pained expression that there was more – a lot more dirty tricks involved.

'What else went on?'

He opened his eyes and looked at me. 'There are many methods employed to make sure that a company's goal is achieved. Jaw-dropping kickbacks given to certain doctors and key opinion leaders – influential expert doctors in their field – to promote our drugs by strongly advocating one drug over another, or perverting a colleague's prescribing practices in favour of the company. Doctors are bought with gifts or corporate entertainment and hospitality, or maybe an all-expenses-paid trip to a conference at a golf hotel in Hawaii!

'The reps compile strategic notes on doctors' personal and professional habits to manipulate any weaknesses or combat objections to prescribing the company's drug. Good salespeople can work magic,' he said ruefully. 'They can also make a lot of money and are often paid on results. In the US, pharmacies sell their prescription data to certain companies, so sales reps get to see who's prescribing what and revamp their sales pitches and favours accordingly. Or carefully tailored pressure can be applied in different ways. In the UK, which doesn't yet allow the sale of data, reps employ other methods as simple as asking doctors or pharmacies to see their prescribing records, and plenty of them say yes.'

I thought about Miles evading the question when I'd asked him how he knew about Dr Baird's prescribing patterns. Anger punched me in the gut. Miles must've been involved in the same appalling behaviour for Tragatech and he was keeping it quiet. I wondered exactly when he'd found out about Caprixanine being harmful, because he definitely knew what it was doing – of that I had no doubt. I remembered Miles at the barbecue with that haunted look on his face, and his disproportionate anger and animosity towards me. Was that guilt? Fear? There was his new weird behaviour Tania had spoken about, and Tania and Hayley disappearing suddenly, too.

Another thought struck me then. Had Miles discovered something, like Daniel had, and then tried to do the right thing and confront Tragatech, only for them to threaten to do to his family what they'd done to Zoe? Is that what Tania had been keeping from me when she'd dropped off Leigh? Were they in hiding somewhere? Maybe what she hadn't said to me was more important than what she had.

Daniel's voice pulled me away from my thoughts as he carried on. 'After doctors qualify, any continuing medical education they receive is largely funded or sponsored by the pharma companies themselves.'

My head spun as I tried to keep up with all this information. 'So you're saying it's marketing disguised as education to influence or alter a doctor's treatment habits in their favour?'

'Got it in one. The pharma industry also regularly sponsors public service campaigns about certain illnesses. But of course they're not doing it out of the goodness of their heart. They expect a return on their investment and it's just another branch of their marketing campaigns. By increasing consumer awareness with large-scale media coverage, they create further demand for their products. In the US, people are bombarded with direct-to-consumer adverts of prescription drugs on TV, telling millions of potential customers to ask their doctor about certain drugs for certain conditions – conditions they didn't even know they had, but after watching these ads, they believe they need medication for them! When these companies spend probably twice as much on marketing and promoting their drugs as they do on research and development, that has to tell you something.'

A harassed-looking woman with three children barged into my chair just then as she walked past, knocking me sideways.

'Sorry.' She muttered a distracted apology and sat down at the next table.

The youngest girl with them burst into tears because she thought her juice tasted funny, wailing loudly. The boy with them moaned to his mum about how annoying his sister was and started kicking his sister's chair. The older girl complained that her shoes were rubbing her feet. The mum hissed at all of them to be quiet or they'd have no Internet privileges for a week. The threat didn't seem to work, and the noise reached deafening levels, causing many customers to look over at them. The mum seemed at the end of her tether.

Despite leaning closer to Daniel over the table, I had to strain to hear his next words.

'There are many wonderful doctors who are trying to do the right thing by their patients, but they're just human, like all of us. They're not gods. They're not infallible. They have weaknesses and motivations like everyone else. And with the flawed system we have, even good people can do a lot of harm without knowing it.

'But also, they're often very overworked with increasing patient loads, have very little time for doing their own research, and are deliberately misinformed by drug companies. Journals are the gatekeepers of medical knowledge, but even if HCPs do read them, it's standard operating procedure that the academic literature is written by ghostwriters who work for pharma companies. Then they put the name of a bought and paid-for expert in their field of medicine on it to give the illusion that they're independent literature.'

'I take it these medical journals don't check the validity of these articles?'

'Not usually, no.'

The boy kicking his sister's chair knocked his drink over then. It ran in a river all over the table.

'*Muuuuum! Look what he's done now!*' the older girl said, glaring at her brother and punching him on the arm.

The younger girl wailed even louder.

The mum looked like she was about to tear her hair out or join her daughter in crying. 'I can't take you lot anywhere, can I?' She glared at them all, standing up and tugging on her youngest's hand. 'Come on. We're going home!'

'You started it,' the boy said to his baby sister, poking her in the back as she was dragged out by her mum. That made her cry even harder.

I followed their movements out of the door with my eyes. When I looked back at Daniel, he was still watching them. 'What drug companies are doing now is disease-mongering – inventing disorders out of *normal* human experiences so that there's a whole new market for medication. They convince parents, teachers, media, doctors, the general public, and regulators that a new disorder is real and that millions of people suffer from it so they need this great new drug to treat a fabricated disease. Social anxiety disorder – which is really shyness. Mathematics disorder – having trouble with maths. Oppositional defiant disorder – your child annoying people, basically. Sibling relationship disorder – not getting on with your siblings. That family there would all be drugged up to the eyeballs if pharma companies had their way.' He pointed at them through the window as they walked down the street. 'Hell, we all would, even when there's nothing wrong with us! Just about every kid could be diagnosed with ADHD if they asked particular questions in a particular way, because it's a pass to print vast sums of money.' He turned back to me.

'But if this is common, then surely there must be a *lot* of drugs out there that are dangerous. Why haven't I heard of them? Or why couldn't I find much when I was researching on the Internet?'

He smiled knowingly. 'You're right. The bad side effects aren't just common to psychiatric drugs. You've got diabetes drugs, anti-inflammatories, statins, painkillers, osteoporosis drugs, cancer drugs, pills for weight loss – the list is endless. And it's easy for an industry as powerful as theirs to keep things hidden. They've got big money to line influential pockets, and they're protected.'

As I thought about every mind-blowing thing Daniel had said, he glanced at his watch.

'There's so much more I could tell you, but I'm sorry, I really have to get back for a client now, so I don't have any more time.' He held out the A4 envelope that was on the seat next to him. 'But I did put together some more research reading for you to look through in case it helps.'

'Thank you for all the information you've given me. This whole thing is a minefield.' I smiled gratefully and took the envelope. 'You've been a big help.'

'You're very welcome.' He stood and we made our way to the door.

I thought about telling Daniel that I'd been followed and threatened, but decided against it. He'd already been through one nightmare exposing Tiazal and Grafloxx; he didn't need another one. And I didn't want to put him in any kind of danger. Besides, I'd got myself into this on my own. I had to get myself out of it, too.

And that meant finding my own proof.

Somehow.

Because I didn't think staying silent would keep me safe.

Chapter 32

Give me an update.

The warning didn't work. The reporter's still asking questions.
The Golden Boy's wife and kids have disappeared.
Things are getting out of control.

Wait for the right time and fix them both.

Chapter 33

Daniel said goodbye to me outside the coffee shop with an offer to contact him anytime I needed to pick his brains. He told me to be careful, wished me luck, and gave me a hug. In the short time I'd spent in his company, it felt like I'd known him for ages.

It was almost five when I walked away through the crowds of people. My mind was in overdrive as I went over and over every abhorrent thing Daniel had told me. I watched the people rushing by, wondering how many of them were taking a deadly drug right now.

By the time I realised I was outside my old office at the *Daily Insider*, it was too late to turn around before I saw Richard exiting. Maybe it was a subconscious decision to go there – a need for some kind of closure, finally.

I was across the street from the rotating glass doors when I saw him coming out of the building, briefcase in hand, as immaculately dressed as always in an expensive grey suit, his fair hair ruffled slightly at the front where I knew he'd have been running his fingers through it during the day.

I stopped and leaned against the facade of the opposite building, watching, waiting to feel a tug in my heart, a gripping sense of loss all over again.

But I felt nothing like that. No twinge of love, no urge to rush towards him and beg him to change his mind. No stabbing regret at what might've been.

Instead, some unexpected realisation clicked in my head. He'd never really loved me. Had only been using me. So why was I destroying myself in still longing for something that had never been real in the first place? I'd thought letting Richard go in my head and heart, letting go of the grief, was a betrayal to my baby – that it meant I'd forget her or him – but it wasn't at all. Maybe sometimes the bad things that happen put us on the path to the best things in the future. Maybe the heartache I'd suffered had been shaping me all along, leading me to exactly where I was right now. I had to believe there was still hope for me to find love and have a family with the right person or I'd never move forward. And I shouldn't need someone else to validate me. I had to believe in my abilities and strengths, not my weaknesses. I had to move on. And to do that, I had to forgive. If I didn't, the only person I'd carry on hurting was me. I'd been holding myself hostage, unable to let go of resentment and blame and disappointment and anger. Now I had to forgive my mum and dad for not being the parents I thought they should be. I had to forgive Richard for not giving me the relationship I wanted or loving me like I'd loved him. But mostly, I had to forgive myself – for the choices I'd made, for my failures, for all the things I didn't live up to, for the things I was wrong about, for the guilt I felt.

I'd been stuck in limbo, wanting to get the old Holly back, but she didn't exist any more. She couldn't. I realised then that there was more than one story to write. And I'd forgotten about the most important one of all. My own.

And *I* would decide how it ended.

I touched my stomach gently and said a final goodbye to the life that was once there. I wasn't forgetting. I just wouldn't let the grief consume me any more. Happiness was in my hands alone.

Then I turned and headed back towards the station, a heavy weight unfolding within me and lifting away.

I sat on the train and opened the envelope Daniel had given me. He'd helpfully listed some links to websites and other information that he thought might be useful. I was halfway through it when a question suddenly burned in my head – a question I should've asked Daniel in the coffee shop, but the time had run away with us and I'd been too astounded to think of it then.

I dialled Daniel's number on my mobile, expecting he'd be with a client and the voicemail would kick in, but he answered on the fourth ring.

'I'm so sorry to bother you again,' I said after greeting him. 'I thought I'd have to leave a message.'

'One client's just left and I've got another in ten minutes so I'm all yours for the moment. You're not bothering me at all.' I sensed the warm smile in his voice. 'I take it you've thought of another question?'

'Yes. What about the drug regulators' responsibilities? The MHRA and FDA, for example. Surely *they* must see any clinical trial data before they approve a drug for the market, so how can the drug companies hide such data from them?'

'The bar is set pretty low, I'm afraid. Regulators fail to scrutinise raw data during applications and rely on summaries, which can easily be manipulated or bought. Sometimes all regulators require is for a company to show that their drug is better than a dummy placebo, not better than the best currently available treatment.'

'You mean they just have to show it's better than nothing?'

'Exactly.'

'So, say they approve a drug and later find out it's responsible for some deadly side effects, like Tiazal. How long does it take to get it off the market?'

He snorted with disgust. 'Once a drug's licensed it's very rare to take it off the market. Even when there are *deadly* side effects, the delay in removing it can take years and can be contested by the drug companies.'

'So in the meantime there could be a very dangerous drug out there?'

'Most definitely. Big pharma has long-reaching arms. Many experts on panels voting to approve drugs have financial ties to drug companies, so there can be massive conflicts of interest. Sometimes they're pressured by political intervention to approve drugs, because, of course, no one pays kickbacks like the trillion-dollar pharma industry! The regulatory bodies are almost entirely funded by drug companies from the fees paid to get drugs through the regulatory process, so effectively the customer isn't the public, but the corporations themselves. Some regulatory bodies' performance is measured by how many drugs it approves a year. They're also under pressure to approve drugs far more quickly than before.'

'There seems to be a huge parallel here between the pharma industry and the tobacco industry. You wonder how they could be allowed to mix deadly poisons with something as addictive as nicotine in cigarettes – why the government have allowed it to happen, and to carry on happening.'

'You're spot on. To do something so abhorrent at that level, just imagine the high-up people who have to be complicit. There's an entrenched, blatant disregard for public health from these corporate mafia, along with the government, who are profiting out of death and pain, basically. And if the public really knew what went on, they'd be enraged beyond belief. You might think from recent scandals being exposed that things would get better and regulations would be tightened, but it seems to be getting worse.' He sighed.

'It seems like Tragatech already has a bad reputation, but it's astounding that they're getting away with it.'

'Their corporation harms millions of people with pesticides and GM crops, dangerous chemicals and carcinogens in our food, then when people get sick because of it, the same corporation pumps them full of more poisons in the form of prescription drugs to make even more money. But they're not the only ones. They're all at it, because when one starts playing dirty and exploiting loopholes and regulations, the others have to employ the same methods to keep up. And when crime pays, it creates more crime.' He paused for a breath. 'You know, most of the leading pharma companies have been fined for fraud, but the fines are a mere drop in the ocean compared to the profits they make. There have been hundreds of civil cases against them, but there are ways to keep the details hushed up. Gagging orders on settlements, paying off plaintiffs to withhold crucial evidence at court so their dirty secrets don't get out. With the level of fraud and corruption going on, I'm sure some are not averse to even bumping off a few key witnesses.' His sympathy for Zoe was evident in his voice.

I thanked him again and we said our goodbyes. As I stared out of the window, I wondered briefly if I'd been wrong about Dr Baird. Maybe he was perfectly innocent in all this and really didn't suspect Caprixanine was responsible for his patients' actions. Maybe Tragatech had lied to him about the true side effects of the drug, or he was relying on faked data they'd given him.

But by the time the train pulled into Ashfield station, I'd come full circle with my suspicions, convinced now more than ever that Zoe must've been killed because she'd discovered a key piece of evidence about Caprixanine at Dr Baird's practice.

He *had* to be involved, but I doubted Dr Baird had acted alone to stage her murder so it looked like a mugging. He must've called upon someone from Tragatech to help him cover it up.

Either way, I wouldn't rest until I got justice for my sister.

Chapter 34

When I arrived home, I couldn't settle. I paced the flat aimlessly as my head swam, trying to think what to do next, muttering ideas to myself. Tragatech obviously thought they were above the law, so why should I act within its parameters? Not that the police believed me anyway. Will thought I was a raving lunatic.

I thought briefly about the possibility of breaking into Tragatech's huge headquarters fifty miles away, just outside Cambridge. I googled images of the building and, from what I saw, it was set within masses of high fencing. No doubt they'd have security cameras and state-of-the-art alarm systems. Probably security guards, too. There was no way anyone would get inside that building to dig anything up. And even if I did manage to get in, I wouldn't know where to look. That's why I needed Miles to gain access, but since he wouldn't help, I had to go with the next best thing.

Dr Baird. He had to be the weakest link. I thought about going to Dr Baird's house and confronting him directly, but I didn't want to tip him and Tragatech off that I was still trying to find evidence. And what Zoe had discovered about Caprixanine and Dr Baird's involvement she'd found at work, which meant I needed to somehow get inside his practice and search for it myself. The rational part of my brain said breaking in was madness, but the irrational part knew there was no way I was going to prove my theory without evidence. I chewed on my thumbnail, working out what to do.

I'd go for a run first, posing as a jogger who just happened to need a break to catch my breath when I reached Dr Baird's building. Then I'd have a look around at the security and form a plan before returning in the early hours when no one was around.

I pulled on my running leggings and top, stuffed my phone in my sports bra and the canister of self-defence spray in my pocket, and let myself out of the flat. It wasn't as good as pepper spray, but at least it might give me those vital few moments to disorientate any would-be attacker so I could get away.

It was only 9 p.m., and there were still people around, so even if I did spot that black car, it wasn't likely they'd be able to bundle me into it in the middle of the street without someone noticing and calling the police. Besides, I didn't really care much any more. Zoe was dead. Mum would fight me tooth and nail if I said I wanted custody of Leigh. I didn't know Miles any more and wasn't sure I even wanted to. I had no job. What was left for me? At least if they killed me, too, I'd have died doing something useful with my life.

I ran past a group of teenagers milling around outside the entrance to a housing estate, smoking and laughing. Past a businessman in a suit carrying a briefcase and talking loudly on the phone. Past a middle-aged woman walking her dog. They whirled by in a blur as my heart pounded and my muscles loosened. My trainers slapped quietly against the pavement and I counted my steps as a way to stop the fear closing in.

Twenty minutes later I was at Dr Baird's practice at the end of the high street. It was the last house in a terrace of similar properties that had all been converted into shops or business premises. After the practice, the high street ended and gave way to a long path under a canopy of thick trees that led to Cooper Park.

The property next to Dr Baird's was boarded up – an optician's practice that had gone out of business. The one next to that was an estate agent's office.

I stood in the entrance to the practice's private car park at the side of the building, hands on hips, breathing deeply, looking at the bricks and mortar and wishing it could tell me something about Zoe's last movements. Had Dr Baird killed her himself, or had he called in the big guns to do it for him? Will had said he'd seen CCTV from the practice that showed Zoe leaving the building at 5.32 p.m. If that were true, had someone followed her after she'd left? The council CCTV cameras stopped there. I doubted very much that Zoe had followed the path to Cooper Park, where her body was found, instead of walking in the opposite direction down the high street. It would've taken twice as long to get to the childminder's place that way.

I looked at the CCTV camera above the glossy black front door. There were no lights peeking through the slatted blinds at the window next to it. A burglar alarm high up on the wall blinked every few seconds with a blue light, seeming to taunt me. I wondered how much time I'd have before the police arrived if it was activated – if there were contacts on the glass at the rear of the property. If I smashed a pane of glass, would the alarm activate, or were there just motion sensors? I'd never broken into somewhere before, so I had no clue. Of course a doctor's practice would have a high response rate to the alarm being activated, and I couldn't do any good locked up in a police cell. But there had to be a way.

I thought of Miles in his home office, getting drunk, wallowing in self-pity, hiding things, denying and covering up, seeing the world only from his own perspective, and anger slapped me hard in the face. The thing was, I knew my brother too well. I knew when he was lying. I could understand if he was worried about someone from Tragatech coming after him or Tania or Hayley if he told what he knew. I could also understand that Miles would be worried he'd be implicated in a police investigation because he'd hidden something. But it was too late for that. At the moment, Tragatech probably thought they had him contained on a short leash, either through bribes or threats. Had they promised him money in return for his silence?

I turned around, looking at the neighbouring properties. Diagonally opposite were a couple of houses before the street ended and the path began. They were both in darkness. Further up the high street on the opposite side of the road was a pub, but it was set back from the pavement, so it was unlikely that someone coming or going would have seen Zoe.

I walked down the narrow driveway that ran along the side of the practice and turned into an L-shape as it opened up behind the building. It was in semi-darkness as the street lights didn't reach this far. There were tall, thick laurel bushes along its boundary that separated it from a cricket pitch behind the row of terraces. There was a double-glazed rear door in the building, probably leading to a kitchen or storage room. I pressed my face to the glass and peered in, cupping my hands around my eyes to get a better look. I could just about make out a sink and some wall units. The internal doorway was closed, but probably led to a corridor. I stood back and looked at the glass in the door. I couldn't see any motion sensors or contacts from this side. I'd need to bring something to smash it with later.

A noise sounded from the thick laurels in the very corner of the car park where it met the cricket pitch.

Something was there. An animal? A person?

My head whipped around, terror ricocheting through me. I ran back up the driveway and was almost at the entrance to the car park and rejoining the high street when it registered what I'd heard.

A cough. Hacking and phlegmy. It sounded like someone old. Possibly injured or sick.

I stopped, pulled out the self-defence spray and held it in my outstretched hand, then turned back and walked cautiously back down the drive.

I couldn't make out at first if they were male or female, the figure being just a blurry darker patch beneath the laurel bushes.

'Hello?' I said, taking small tentative steps forwards, my heart hammering. 'Who's there?'

The figure coughed again, a horrible, wheezy sound.

I pulled my phone from inside my sports bra and turned on the torch app, holding it out in front of me with my other hand.

I saw him properly then. It was a homeless guy – the same homeless guy I'd seen picking through rubbish bins on the night Zoe disappeared when I was searching for her. 'Are you OK?'

He was curled up on his side, a filthy padded coat underneath him, a ripped rucksack under his head being used for a pillow. Long, matted hair frizzed around a lined face and dark eyes. He could've been any age from thirty to sixty. It was hard to tell.

He put his hand in front of his face to shield him from the light, and I stuffed the phone back in my sports bra and the spray in my pocket.

He sat up then with what looked like a great effort. 'I'm not causing any trouble. I never do. Don't call the police.' He coughed again, his whole body wracking with short, sharp bursts of effort.

I was about to ask if he needed a doctor when I realised the irony that we were in the car park of Dr Baird's practice. And anyway, I didn't think anyone needed Dr Baird's particular brand of so-called healthcare.

'Can I get you something? Some water maybe?'

'I'm OK.' He tilted his head towards a white plastic shopping bag on the ground with a big bottle of water poking out the top.

I didn't know whether to be scared of him or not. He could be a violent psycho for all I knew, but there were plenty of those around disguised as upstanding members of society, as I was finding out to my cost, so I decided to take a chance and stepped closer.

'Do you . . . um . . . is this where you usually sleep?' I asked. It was as good a place as any, I thought, if you were living on the streets. The building shielded the car park from the high street. It was dark back here, and if anyone did come in to look around, they probably wouldn't see this man unless he made a noise.

'Yeah. Why? I don't ever do anything except spend the night. I'm gone in the morning. Don't call the police. I'm just minding my own business.'

'No, no, don't worry, it's OK. I just . . .' My mind raced with possibilities. 'I saw you three nights ago along the high street, rummaging in some bins.'

'It's not a crime. It's rubbish,' he said defensively.

'Were you here that night? Did you see anything suspicious? My sister worked here.' I pointed back to the surgery. 'That night, she was murdered. They said she left work at five-thirty, but I don't believe them.' I held my breath and chewed my lip, waiting for a response.

His gaze slid away from me and he didn't reply.

'Did you see her leave? Did you see anything at all?' I said urgently.

'I don't need no trouble. I just mind my own business.'

I crouched down in front of him, sitting on my haunches, trying to catch his eyes. '*Please!* She was my sister! She had a four-year-old daughter!'

'I'm not talking to the police. They'll chuck me in a cell. They'll blame me.'

I studied his makeshift bed of coat and rucksack, wondering if that was better than sleeping underneath a bush in the mud and cold. 'Blame you for what?'

His mouth twisted with contempt. 'You people have no idea, do you?'

'About what?'

He didn't answer.

'How did you end up here?'

'You wouldn't want to know,' he scoffed.

I stood up, my knees aching. 'Look, I'm sorry. No, I can't even begin to imagine how you ended up on the streets. But isn't there a hostel or something you can stay in? Can't the police help you with that?'

'There ain't no hostel round here.' He laughed like I was stupid. I felt stupid, too. I was one of those people who'd spotted plenty of homeless men and women in London, sleeping in shop doorways with a ratty dog or a single bag holding their worldly possessions. I didn't cross the street to avoid having to confront the reality, though. I'd always give them a few pounds, although I was never sure how much went on food and how much on alcohol or fags, but it wasn't enough. They'd gone from my mind the minute I was further along the street and I was back to thinking about work and self-pity and general busyness. When this nightmare with Caprixanine was over, I was going to rectify that. I'd write a human interest piece about it. *If* the nightmare was ever over.

'I do want to know how you ended up here,' I said. 'I'd like to help, if I can.'

He snorted. 'Most people don't give a shit about someone like me.'

'No, *really*. I'd like to know. What's your story?'

He stared at me for a moment. 'I'm an ex-veteran, all right? I fought on the front line and now I'm forced to *beg* from the people I defended. I had post-traumatic stress when my tour finished. I couldn't adjust to life on civvy street. Couldn't get a job. My wife and I broke up. I lost my house. Started using drugs. And now I'm here. *That's* my story. You satisfied now?' His voice was bitter and defensive.

'I'm so sorry.'

'Yeah. Sorry doesn't really help, does it?' He looked away.

I undid the zip on the pocket of my leggings. I had an emergency fiver kept in there for if I needed to grab a drink when I was running. I held it out towards him. 'Here.'

He looked from my face to the note.

'Take it. Please.' I waved it in the air.

He reached out and took it, tucking it carefully into the pocket of his ripped trousers. 'Thanks.'

'I'm sorry,' I said again.

'What for?'

I shrugged. 'Life,' I said quietly. 'Look, maybe we can help each other. If you saw something that night, then tell me. I'm a writer, so I can tell your story for you in return, if you want me to. Maybe it'll get you some help – raise awareness.'

He studied me for a moment, pensive, as if weighing up a decision. Eventually, he said, 'I saw them bundle a woman into the boot of a car that night. I only come back here when it's dark and I know he's gone. Except that night, he came back really late – early hours of the morning. He didn't have his lights on when he drove down the drive and parked here so he didn't see me lying at the bottom of the bushes right in the corner.'

'Oh, my God!' The breath was sucked from my lungs. I stepped closer. 'Who did you see?'

'That doctor bloke. The one who works here. He arrived in his car with another guy and they went into the building. When they came out, the other guy had the girl draped over his shoulder. She might've been unconscious, but I'm pretty sure she was dead. He put her in the boot then the car drove off.'

I tried to steady my wobbly legs, bent over, tried to breathe. I felt my legs collapse as I fell to my knees. Tears bloomed in my eyes. 'Zoe,' I whispered, agony crushing my insides.

It was his turn to say he was sorry.

My brain swam in a sea of questions as the tears fell. 'Had you seen the other man before?'

'Nah. But he was stocky – thickset, about five eight, maybe thirteen stone. The light wasn't good so I didn't see his face. The doc

241

was panicking, telling him to hurry up. The other guy kept telling him to shut up.'

'Why didn't you say anything before? Call the police?' I shrieked, raw grief swelling in my chest. It felt like my heart was about to stop.

'Like I said, the police don't take too kindly to people like me. Knowing my luck, they would've tried to pin it on me! Or they wouldn't have believed a word I said. I should've said something, but I was worried about what would happen to me. Besides, I'm saying something now, aren't I?'

I didn't know whether to be glad or angry. There was no room for either emotion to filter through my shattered heart. I wiped my eyes with my hands. 'Will you tell the police what you told me? I've got a friend. Someone who you can trust. He won't try to pin this on you, I swear. I know who's involved. I just need evidence. I need an eyewitness.'

He made a noise at the back of his throat, but I couldn't tell if it was a sigh or an angry snarl.

'Please! I'll pay you! I'll give you money!' I said desperately.

He twisted his lips again, maybe wrestling with his conscience. 'Who's this friend?'

'He's a detective investigating Zoe's murder.'

He stared at the ground. The seconds crept into a minute.

'Please! You've got to help me catch my sister's killers!' I held my breath, my lips trembling, while he made a decision.

'OK. I'll speak to him.'

I wanted to hug him but I didn't. I just cried out a thank you, took my phone out again and dialled Will's number.

'Holly? Is everything OK?' he said before I could get a word out.

'No,' I said breathlessly. 'There's a homeless guy – an ex-veteran – and he saw everything! And Dr Baird's involved. I knew he was, but no one listened. I was right, Will. He—'

'What? Wait. Slow down a minute. What's happening?'

I took a deep breath and tried to speak more slowly. My brain wanted to spew everything out too quickly, and in my rush it sounded like garbled nonsense. 'I found a witness, Will! A homeless man who sleeps at the back of the surgery. He saw Dr Baird and another guy bundle Zoe into the boot of Dr Baird's car and drive off the night she was killed. He said she looked unconscious, but she must've been already dead by then. Then they must've dumped her in Cooper Park.'

'A homeless guy? Where is he now?'

'We're both at the back of Dr Baird's practice. Can you come down and talk to him? Take a statement? Dr Baird killed my sister!'

'I'm on my way. I'll be there as soon as I can. Stay where you are, OK?'

I hung up and sat down on the ground next to . . . what was his name? 'I'm Holly.' I held my hand out. 'What's your name?'

His eyebrows rose with surprise, as if no one had bothered to ask his name in a long time. 'Colin.' He stared at my hand, then slowly reached out and shook it with dirt-ingrained fingers.

'Thank you, Colin. My friend Will is on his way. He'll look after you.'

'So . . . your sister . . . what did she do to get herself killed?' He shuffled into a cross-legged position.

Where did I start? I sniffed and said, 'She found out something she wasn't supposed to. It's a really long story.' As the tears fell again, I started telling him about Dean and Jess and Stephen. I'd got up to Rachel Tucker and how I'd first started suspecting Caprixanine when a car swerved into the car park and stopped in front of us, halogen lights on full beam, illuminating us, blinding us.

I leapt to my feet. 'Will's here!' I bent down to help Colin up as the driver's door opened.

A shadowy figure got out and stood next to the car.

Then the passenger door opened and someone else stepped out.

'Will, this is Colin. I . . .' But I never got to finish my sentence. Because the driver wasn't Will.

And I'd seen the passenger before, at Miles's barbecue. The one who'd chatted me up. The one who'd introduced himself as Martin.

It took a few seconds for my brain to connect the dots – to realise the danger.

And in those seconds Colin called out 'Gun!' and pushed me behind him, into the laurel bushes.

I heard a *whoosh* from the gunshot.

Heard Colin grunt out a sound.

Felt the weight of him as he fell backwards on to me.

And then Martin turned the gun on me.

Chapter 35

I scrabbled manically through the rough trunks and thick branches of laurel, leaves slapping at my face, getting swamped in them, fighting my way through.

And then I was out the other side, running alongside the edge of the cricket pitch, panic like white noise in my ears, trying to hug the boundary of bushes to shield me from their view as much as possible.

A stitch in my side. Lungs heaving with pressure. My mind shrieking, *They killed him! They killed Colin!*

I fumbled in my pocket to pull out the self-defence spray but it was gone. Had probably fallen out when I was scrambling through the bushes.

Shit! Shit! Shit!

At the other end of the cricket pitch was a housing estate but it seemed so far away, like one of those dreams where you're running and running and you never get anywhere. I wanted to shout out for help, but there was no one else around. No one would hear me except those men. I didn't dare look back, but I sensed them there, like a rabbit senses a wolf on its tail. I thought I could hear heavy breathing, but maybe it was mine.

I pumped my arms and legs faster, the housing estate finally getting closer. I ran through the entrance and swung a left on to the quiet street with no idea in which direction I was heading. I couldn't work out where I should go or where I could hide. The only thing I knew was that I had to keep running.

An explosion sounded in the distance. Bright red and white light lit up the sky. I had no time to consider what had happened; I was too busy concentrating on trying to keep my body moving forwards without collapsing.

I risked a glance behind me. One of the men was there, maybe seventy metres behind. I pushed myself harder, a thought slamming into my head. My new phone had been bugged somehow. They'd listened to my conversation with Will and knew where to find me. Did that mean they'd also put some kind of tracking device on it? But Andrew hadn't been near my new mobile, so it couldn't have been him.

The blank texts! Was that how they'd done it? By sending some kind of software to my phone? Had those texts contained a Trojan that had also deleted the threatening call from my incoming log and Zoe's voicemail message?

I slid my hand into my sports bra and pulled out my phone. I threw it on the ground, hearing it smash as I ploughed on forwards, chest heaving, cramp spasming in my hamstring.

I ran through the housing estate, rounded a corner and realised where I was. Howard Becker's cul-de-sac.

A dead end.

I'd have to turn back and run straight into the man chasing me.

A blast of panic detonated in my chest before I remembered the small alleyway between the two houses I'd walked through with Howard. It led to Cooper Park. From there I could go . . . where?

Think! Think!

The police station was in the other direction. But if I carried on this way I could make it through the park to the opposite end of the high street from Dr Baird's practice and head to Will's house.

As long as I could lose the man behind.

I heard sirens wailing in the distance. A vehicle speeding up behind me. Was that the other guy chasing by car?

The alley was closer now.

Twenty metres.

Fifteen.

Ten.

A shrieking of brakes.

Then I bombed through the entrance to the alley and carried on going.

Somewhere behind, the vehicle reversed loudly.

I ran blindly through the park, making for the trees at the far end. I'd run in a big circle.

I willed my legs to carry on as the trees got closer. Closer.

I could hear a sound behind me but didn't dare turn around. Whoever was still there, I had to lose them.

I scrambled through the patch of woodland and came out into the beer garden and car park of Fredos wine bar. I pushed my way through its rear door, past the groups of people drinking and laughing, to the toilets.

I burst into the ladies' room. Thankfully, it was empty.

I rushed inside one of the stalls and locked the door, trying to suck in enough air before I passed out, sinking to the floor as my legs gave way.

Chapter 36

The sweat cooled on my face as I took deep breaths and closed my eyes. What to do? What to do?

Did they see me come in here? Was someone waiting outside?

I heard a couple of women enter the toilets, one chatting about some guy called Jim who looked hot and the other asking her mate whether her hair was too blonde.

I tried to get my wobbly legs to cooperate so I could stand up. I was about to unlock the door and ask them if they could scout around outside for someone matching Martin's description, but by the time I stepped out of the stall they'd gone.

I turned on the cold tap, cupped my hands underneath the stream, and filled them with water, gulping thirstily. In my head I saw Colin being shot and bile rose to my mouth.

The door opened. I jumped, my heartbeat rocketing again.

It was a middle-aged woman with an expensively cut skirt suit on. She glanced at my hot face and my hair plastered to my head with sweat, taking in the panic in my eyes, and said, 'Are you all right?'

'I was being chased by a guy,' I said. 'Can I borrow your mobile? I need to call the police.'

'Uh . . . yeah, sure.' She dug inside a huge handbag and handed me her phone, watching me with a mixture of suspicion and concern.

I realised then I didn't have Will's number. It had been on my phone, but that was now roadkill. I chewed on my lip, wondering whether to call 999. But what would I say that didn't sound crazy? No, it had to be Will I spoke to.

I handed her phone back. 'Never mind. Thanks.'

'Are you sure? You look a bit peaky.'

I nodded. 'I'm sure. But could you do me a favour? The guy who followed me . . . could you just have a look outside and see if he's waiting for me?'

She studied my face for a second. The terror must've been evident because she said, 'Bastard!' Her eyes narrowed. 'Us women have to stick together with abusive men. Course I'll help you.'

Tears pricked behind my eyes. I almost laughed hysterically. If only it was as simple as that.

'What does he look like?' she asked.

I described Martin, although I hadn't had time to notice what he'd been wearing. I didn't have a clue who the other guy from the car was, as I hadn't seen his face, but I hoped she'd be observant enough to notice anyone else suspicious hanging around. 'Be careful, though, he's dangerous.' Although I doubted he'd try to shoot anyone in a pub full of witnesses.

She went outside to check and five minutes later she was back. 'He's not there.'

'Did you see anyone else who looked dodgy? He may have sent a mate to find me instead.'

She shook her head. 'No, I didn't spot anyone else who's not part of a crowd or a couple. Look, I can tell you're scared. I'm about to head off in a minute. Do you want a lift somewhere? I can take you to the police station, if you like.'

'Will's,' I said.

'Sorry?'

'Uh, could you take me to a friend's house?'

'Yeah, just give me a minute to pee.'

I waited for her by the sinks, running my nails against my mouth, tugging at my lips, scratching my arms, manically fidgeting.

She came out and smiled at me as she washed her hands. 'All set!' She opened the door and peered out, having a good look into the bar area. 'Still can't see anyone suspicious.' She beckoned me out.

I followed her to the rear of the wine bar, glancing around the car park area and small beer garden. Lattice fencing separated it from the side road that fed into the front of the high street. Through the gaps in the woodwork I spied their black car parked just on the other side, waiting, the shapes of two men inside.

I gulped in a breath, my scalp prickling with terror, and followed the woman to her car, head turned away from the fence, praying they wouldn't spot me.

I got in her vehicle and sank down low in the seat. 'I think he's still out there somewhere,' I said to her, willing myself to stop shivering.

'There's a blanket in the back seat. It's for the dog but you could put it over you if you want, in case he's hanging about.' She twisted around and yanked on a tartan blanket. 'Here.'

'Thanks.' I sank lower in the seat and pulled it over my head.

'So, where to?'

'Cromwell Street. Do you know where that is?'

'No.'

'If you take a right at the high street and then go straight. There's a turn into Keller Road a little further up. Take that and then I'll tell you where to go next.'

She hit the ignition button and the engine sprang to life. I couldn't see beneath the blanket that smelled of wet dog, but in my mind's eye I pictured her coming out of the car park, going left past the parked black car to get to the T-junction with the high street, swinging right and travelling along the main road.

I held my breath and didn't exhale until I thought I'd left those men safely in the distance.

Chapter 37

Will's house was in darkness. I glanced up and down the street but no one was there. No one was watching out for me. Of course not. They couldn't have known where I'd go. They hadn't followed me in the woman's car; I'd checked when I thought it was safe to do so, constantly looking behind me and in the side mirror. Even so, I didn't want to wait on Will's front doorstep in full view.

I walked round to the side gate, but it was locked, so I hoisted myself up and over the other side into the small garden that backed on to his neighbours' houses. I tried the back door, my hands shaking uncontrollably, but it was locked.

All I could see in my head was Colin falling lifelessly to the ground. Then the image mingled with Zoe lying on the mortuary trolley. Dean, Jess, Stephen, Rachel Tucker, and Maria Butterworth. It was horrifyingly surreal, the lengths Tragatech and Dr Baird would go to in order to stop this coming out. I'd narrowly escaped – this time. What would happen next time? How long did I have left before they silenced me?

But now Colin had been killed, Will would *have* to believe me. I was an eyewitness to Colin's murder. And after what he'd told me about Dr Baird's involvement in Zoe's death, Will could get a warrant to search Dr Baird's practice and find the evidence of what had been going on with Caprixanine and how it was being covered up.

I slid down to the ground and curled my knees up to my chest, wrapping my arms around them, trying to stop the shivering, trying to stop the images and to think clearly about what I would tell Will, but my mind was a panicked jumble.

A noise from the house next door made me freeze, but it was only a neighbour going into their back garden for a cigarette. I smelled the smoke, heard his conversation with someone inside, a woman's muffled replies. I breathed quietly and rubbed my hands up and down my arms. I was bone-numbingly cold now from a combination of the sweat that had cooled on my skin and fear and shock.

The man went back inside. The sky darkened. An owl cried out. A bat did a loop of the garden. A lone star twinkled. And I cried. Fat, hot tears streaked down my cheeks that I didn't even bother wiping away.

I don't know how much later it was when I heard a noise and saw a light go on in Will's house downstairs. I got to my feet, my limbs stiff and unwieldy, and banged on the back door.

The kitchen light turned on and he was there, by the back door, peering out at me, my own deranged reflection in the glass looking back at me, too, like some wild maniac. His initial frown of confusion turned to surprise, then worry and relief.

He opened the door and I was suddenly in his arms, pressed tight against his chest, his lips in my hair, muttering my name. He felt like solid ground and safety.

'Shit, I was so worried about you. What happened?'

He smelled of smoke, like a bonfire. I gripped the back of his jacket tight between my fingertips until he pulled back, took my hand and led me inside.

He sat me down at the tiny breakfast bar and stood above me, his hands gripping mine, his eyes intense and questioning. 'Do you want a drink?'

I nodded, unable to speak just yet. My throat was dry and I still didn't know what words to use to explain. It all seemed so unreal. So unexplainable.

Turning his back to me, he reached up high into one of the cupboards. He pulled out a couple of tumblers and filled them with a good splash of brandy before placing one in my hand.

I took a sip. Took a bigger sip. The alcohol burned my throat and warmed my insides. I'd promised myself no more alcohol, but a near-death experience trumped abstinence.

He sat next to me, one leg on the floor, one propped up on the footrest of the stool, watching me as he drank his own brandy. He put his glass down and said, 'Can you tell me what happened?'

I took another drink and cupped the glass in my hands for comfort. 'It was awful. I saw him get shot.'

'Who?'

'Colin. The witness I told you about on the phone. The homeless guy. I went to the surgery to have a look around. I wanted to—' I stopped abruptly, wondering whether to tell him I'd been thinking of breaking in. Probably not a good idea. I took another drink to give me a few seconds while my mind raced. 'I wanted to see if there was something you might've missed somehow about Zoe. Anyway, I found Colin sleeping rough, right at the back corner of the car park. It's dark back there, so I nearly missed him.' I inhaled, fighting against the images pouring into my head. 'He said he was there the night Zoe was killed. She didn't leave the building at five-thirty. She couldn't have. He said Dr Baird came back in the early hours of the morning with another man. They went inside, and when they came out, the other man was carrying Zoe over his shoulder like a deadweight. Colin saw them put her in the boot of Dr Baird's car and then they both got in and drove off. That CCTV footage Dr Baird gave you showing Zoe leaving the building must've been from a different day. That's why the CCTV on the high street didn't capture her afterwards. Not because she walked towards where the cameras stopped. It couldn't have been that, because she was in the boot of Dr Baird's car! He must've doctored the date on the CCTV.'

Will's brow furrowed as he looked at me with a peculiar expression.

There was something – a feeling – niggling at me that seemed important but was just out of reach, too mixed up with the jumble in my head. I didn't have time to try to work out what it was then. I needed to explain to Will what had happened as quickly as I could so he believed me. 'Anyway, then I managed to get Colin to agree to speak to you and tell you what he'd seen. But after I phoned you two men arrived in a vehicle. They must've bugged my phone and listened to our conversation. One of the men was called Martin and works for Tragatech. He was at Miles's barbecue and I met him there. I didn't see the other one. He was shielded by the full beam of the car's headlights. But Martin . . .' I inhaled, then exhaled loudly through my mouth. 'Martin shot Colin!' I shrieked. 'In the car park by the hedging. There was some kind of silencer on the gun because it hardly made a sound! Colin just went down in front of me. It was . . .' I shook my head manically. 'I was so scared. I managed to run through the laurel hedge and someone was chasing me, but I got away and came here. I didn't know what else to do. Do you believe me? You have to believe me now!'

He took my hand and held on tight. 'After you ran, there was an explosion. Someone doused the outside of the building in accelerant, smashed a few windows at the rear and poured more in. By the time I got there, the fire was well under way. I thought you were in the car park where I told you to wait so I looked frantically for you until the fire brigade arrived and moved me out because it was unsafe. Then part of the building exploded. We can't go back inside until everything's settled down tomorrow, but from the look of it so far, the place will be wrecked inside. But this guy . . . this Colin you spoke to . . . the one you said was killed.' He paused for a moment, scanning my face with a look I couldn't work out. 'There was no sign of him.'

I blinked once. Twice. 'How could that . . .' I stopped when it hit me. 'They got rid of the body to make it look like I'm lying, to cover up what they did. Then they set the surgery on fire so there would be no evidence of Dr Baird's involvement in any of this. Probably to destroy his patient records, too.'

I felt the weight of the situation like a punch to the stomach. No evidence. No witnesses. No anything. They were cleaning house. 'Look, I'm not crazy. I'm not! I'm telling the truth. Colin was real! What he told me was real! And the arson – it's very convenient that Dr Baird's records and CCTV evidence have now been destroyed!'

He looked away, uncomfortable. 'But no one else saw this Colin. And I've been through the CCTV in the high street tonight. He wasn't on the camera.'

'Well . . . maybe he . . . maybe he got into the car park from the cricket pitch, through the bushes behind. The ones I escaped through.'

'You were seen acting suspiciously around the front of the building on the cameras. Then you disappear into the car park at the back and *then* the building explodes. You can see how that looks, can't you? I'm trying my best to protect you here, but my colleagues want to talk to you about the arson.'

'What! But . . . but that's ridiculous. What about the car? The black car with Martin in? It pulled into the car park, too, before they killed Colin and started the fire.'

'We got the plate number. The car's a clone. My colleagues think you were working together.'

'But what possible reason would I have for starting the fire?' My mouth gaped open.

'Revenge, Holly.' He took my hand in his and squeezed it. 'They're working on the assumption that you blame Dr Baird for Zoe's death, that you've got some kind of misguided vendetta against him. You *have* been acting irrationally lately, Holly. You've been coming up with wild theories about him.'

'That's because he *was* involved! Colin told me before he was killed. He saved my life! He—'

'But there was no body,' Will said calmly. 'There is *no* Colin.'

'But there must be some forensic evidence that Colin was shot if you look!'

Will shook his head. 'The fire spread to the hedge, and the car park was awash with water and foam from the fire engine. It's a mess up there. Even *if* there was any evidence, it would've been destroyed.'

I leapt to my feet, confused, pacing. What was happening here? Was I going mad? Having a breakdown like everyone seemed to think? Had I imagined the conversation with Colin? Conjured him up out of thin air? Imagined seeing him shot in front of me? Was I making connections when there weren't any? Had I been doing that all along? I closed my eyes and pinched the bridge of my nose.

Will stood in front of me, placed his hands on my shoulders and stooped his neck to my eye level. 'They wanted me to bring you in for an interview tonight. I went to your flat, but obviously you were here, waiting for me.'

'And then what? Tragatech's trying to pin the arson on me, aren't they? They'll have friends in high places who can twist things and make me look guilty and set me up. What if the police lock me up? What if I'm remanded until a trial? How long a sentence does arson carry?'

'In some circumstances it's a life sentence, but don't worry about that now. No one's setting you up. We'll sort things out together. I'll help you. We'll get to the bottom of this, I promise.'

'Oh, God!' A twitch started in the corner of my right eye. I pressed a fingertip to it. 'But surely you don't think I did it, right?'

He rubbed at his forehead. 'I really don't know what to believe. But, look, why don't you come in voluntarily to the police station and talk to my boss. I promise I'll help you fix this. If you don't . . . if they find you and arrest you, it will make things look much worse.'

I slumped on to the stool, picked up my drink and drained it, feeling my life draining away, too. I had no choice. I couldn't run forever. Somehow, I'd have to get the police to believe me.

And maybe I'd be safer with them.

Chapter 38

'Can I go to the police station tomorrow?' I pleaded. 'I can hardly keep my eyes open and think straight right now.'

Will studied me for a moment, his lips pursed as he thought.

'I don't want to get you into trouble, but I know I'm going to need my wits about me to explain everything properly, and I'm just . . .' I rubbed my forehead. 'I'm just so tired.'

He pulled me towards him, and I melted against his chest, my limbs impossibly heavy.

'OK,' he said. 'Why don't you get some sleep and I'll take you there in the morning? I'll make sure DCI Turnbull listens to you. I'll do what I can to protect you.'

I nodded because I didn't know what to say any more. Will was the only possible person who could help me sort things out. I knew he was only doing his job. He was a dedicated policeman, after all. And even if he still didn't believe me, I had to trust in him – trust that he'd help me fix everything and prove my innocence before Martin or someone else got to me.

He gently held my elbow and guided me upstairs to his bedroom. So much had happened, and I was so tired that my mind wouldn't work properly. My brain felt like slush.

'You can stay here. I'll sleep in the spare room,' he said.

I sat down on the bed and he removed my trainers before lifting my legs up on to the duvet. I sank my head into the soft pillow and watched him as he sat beside me, the weight of his body dipping the mattress.

'It'll be OK,' he said. 'We'll get it sorted.'

'Don't leave me.' I wrapped my arms around his neck and pulled him closer, so his lips were on mine, gently at first, and then my tongue pushed into his mouth and it felt like I was floating. He plunged a hand into my hair as our lips ground against each other urgently, greedily. And then the past collided with the present, and I was lost in my eighteen-year-old self again, in this very room before I'd left for London, and I was ripping his clothes off, touching him, tasting him, exploring him. Only this time, at the end, I'd tell him I wanted to stay with him. I'd rewrite history and never leave Ashfield for London. I'd marry Will and we'd have a couple of kids and be happy.

I wanted to lose myself in that fantasy, in his gentleness and kindness and brooding eyes. I wanted him to wrap me up in warmth and make me forget everything. The bad choices and mistakes I'd made and the hollowness inside me. To chase away the loneliness and grief.

I closed my eyes and clung on tight, my nails scratching against his back as I wrapped my legs around him and drew him inside.

Chapter 39

I lay in the darkness, eyes wide open, staring at the ceiling, listening to my heart beating. I needed sleep, but every time I felt its fingers clawing at me, my brain refused to switch off and allow me any respite. I still had the feeling that there was something wrong – something I should know that was just out of reach.

Will breathed in a slow rhythm beside me, deep in sleep. I lifted my head to look at the digital clock on the bedside table next to him: 3.31 a.m.

Will moved on to his side, facing away from me. The mattress shifted. He let out a sleepy moan.

And that's when I worked it out.

Zoe had been moved! If she'd been murdered in Dr Baird's office and not taken to Cooper Park until the early hours of the following morning, the police would've been able to tell. I'd watched crime films before. There was a telltale sign when a body was moved after death. Lividity. Zoe's blood would've pooled in the lowest parts of her body after she was killed, indicating the position she'd been in when she'd died. If she was transported later by car from Dr Baird's practice and dumped in Cooper Park, the pathologist doing the post-mortem would've spotted that anomaly.

So why hadn't Will told me that?

And now I thought about it, Will was the *only* one I'd given my new phone number to. Those blank texts I was now convinced transferred some kind of listening or tracking system on to my phone could surely only have been sent to me if someone knew my number. Maybe Will had even told them to find me at Dr Baird's office when I'd got off the phone to him.

My heart froze as the realisation kicked in.

Will was involved. They'd got to him, too.

I held my breath as I turned my head on the pillow to check he was definitely asleep.

Slowly, I swung my legs off the bed. Waited. Beads of sweat broke out on my skin.

Will didn't stir.

I sat up, then stood and silently picked up my discarded clothes and trainers from the floor. I crept out of the room and down the stairs and dressed in the kitchen, my heart thudding loudly in my ears.

I spied Will's wallet and took out fifty-five pounds, tucking the money into the pocket of my leggings. Then I grabbed a black fleece and navy baseball cap from Will's downstairs cupboard and put them on.

My stomach muscles clenched tight as I unlocked the front door. The click sounded so loud in the silent house that I flinched. I waited a second, but there was no noise from upstairs, so I let myself out into the dark night.

The air was cold against my face as I ran up the street and away.

Away to where? I didn't know. Somewhere I could sit and think and make a plan where no one would find me.

I thought about going straight to the police station. Will had been lying to me about Zoe, but that didn't mean he was lying about his colleagues thinking I was involved in the arson. And without Colin's body, my story did sound ridiculous. If I went to them without any kind of proof about what was really going on, they'd probably still lock me up. Or section me.

I thought about heading for Miles's house, because he was the only one who could help me get the truth out into the world – the only one who could prove I wasn't going mad. But if they'd bugged my phone, they'd probably bugged his, too, and most likely his house and mine. They were probably even watching his place to see if I showed up there.

I kept looking around, eyes alert, as I walked the deserted streets. I couldn't go to Mum's house – couldn't bring them to her door with Leigh there. I couldn't go to Barbara's and get her killed. So where could I go to wait it out until the morning when I could somehow get in touch with Miles?

Chapter 40

I woke up just as dawn was breaking on another new day. I peeled myself off the hard, concrete floor, stood up and stretched, instantly feeling dizzy with blood rushing to my head. When had I last eaten? I couldn't remember.

I was inside an abandoned building at the edge of town. At one time, it had been a cottage hospital, but it had been empty for years after it was closed. Zoe and I had played inside it, spooking each other out with ghost stories as we roamed from room to room. Now it was earmarked for development into fancy apartments. There was evidence of other people who'd slept rough in here before. Luckily, none of them had returned while I was asleep.

I held my hand against the wall until the black and white stars in my vision disappeared, then walked up and down, trying to bring some warmth to my muscles. I had a plan now, but I'd have to wait several more hours to put it into action, and even then I'd have to wait longer for Miles to hopefully meet up with me.

I needed something to eat and drink before I passed out, but I couldn't go to the shops in the high street in case the police or Martin's gang were looking for me. There was a small cluster of neighbourhood shops near one of the housing estates with a newsagent, a florist, a betting shop, and an Indian takeaway.

I picked up Will's fleece that I'd folded into a pillow, shook it out and put it on. I pulled the baseball cap down low over my face and climbed out of the broken window at the rear of the building. As I made my way to the shops, I watched everyone carefully in case they were about to grab me.

The newsagent's roller shutter door was halfway up, with light from inside spilling out. I ducked underneath the shutter and called out, 'Are you open?'

A man emerged from a doorway out the back, lugging a bundle of newspapers tied together with plastic cabling. 'Give us five minutes, love.'

He dropped the bundle on the floor by the side of the counter and snipped the plastic ties, removing newspapers and putting them on a shelf next to the till.

I went back outside and sat on a small brick wall, my back to the row of shops, watching the street, watching the world wake up, watching for signs of someone watching me, until I heard the roller shutter open fully and went back inside the shop.

I bought two bottles of water, a can of iced coffee, a prawn sandwich that looked limp and soggy, and two packets of crisps. Glancing around as I exited the shop, I didn't see Martin or any police, so I crossed the road and headed back towards the building where I'd slept.

I climbed through the window and sat on the dirty floor, where I ripped open the sandwich packaging and devoured half of it in one bite, my stomach rumbling loudly. I finished the rest of it in between gulps of water. Then I ate both packets of crisps and drank the coffee as I stared at the graffitied wall in front of me, waiting for the time to tick by.

Traffic rumbled in the distance. Horns beeped. Aeroplanes flew overhead.

I got to my feet, left the safety of the building once more and retraced my steps back to the shops.

The door to the florist jangled as I opened it. A young, fresh-faced girl stood behind the counter, cutting lengths of red ribbon. She smiled as I walked in.

'Morning,' I said, as normally as I could.

'Hi. Can I help you?'

'Can you do a flower delivery today?'

'Is it a local address?'

'Yes.'

'In that case, yes, we can. Um . . .' She tapped on the computer screen in front of her. 'Let me just see what slots we have left.' More tapping. 'We could do a delivery for between one and two this afternoon. Is that any good?'

I hoped Miles was still sitting at home drinking. If he'd gone to work, then my plan would be ruined. *Would* he have gone back to work knowing what they'd done to Zoe? I had no idea. I didn't know who my brother was any more. I just had to pray he hadn't. 'That would be great.'

'Did you have a particular arrangement in mind?' She tilted her head, smiling.

'Something inexpensive.'

She rounded the counter and stood next to displays of various flowers in buckets of water. 'How about these? I can do a bouquet for eight pounds. Delivery will be another two pounds.'

'Perfect. I need a card to write a message.'

She pointed to a display rack with various small cards the size of business cards. 'You can choose anything on there.'

I ignored the 'Happy Birthday' and 'Congratulations' cards and took a blank one while the girl busied herself behind me, picking out flowers. I took a pen from the counter and scrawled a message with a cryptic location on it that only Miles would understand:

Miles, I need your help urgently. They tried to kill me last night!! Tania and Hayley can't hide forever, and neither can I! Meet me where we used to play pirates as kids. The roadside entrance. 9 p.m. Make sure you're not followed. Holly X

I tucked the card inside an envelope, sealed it, and wrote Miles's name on the front before putting it on the counter.

Now I just had to hope Miles would get the flowers in time.

Chapter 41

The day slid by in anguished slowness as I waited in the building. Sometimes I was hyper-aware of every sound, senses alert to the slightest detail as every minute slipped by, but at others the drowning wave of sadness and racing thoughts pushed away everything from the outside world until it was just me and my head. I had no watch, so I could only estimate the time edging forwards.

Just as dusk was turning the world outside into smudges of purpley-orange, I rose from the concrete floor, stiff-backed. It took a good few steps to bring the blood back to my numb buttocks and seized-up muscles. Pulling the baseball cap's peak low over my face, I walked, head down, to the meeting point.

Zoe, Miles, and I had played in Downs Wood often when we were younger, when Mum wanted us out of the house to stop annoying her or when she and Dad were reading the Sunday papers quietly at the breakfast table. Mum was always on at us to stop getting under her feet and to run off our energy elsewhere because she and Dad needed some peace and quiet. I guess some people just aren't maternal.

There was one main entrance to the woods, which was where I would meet Miles, off the main road that went from Ashfield to Bloomfield via a narrow track leading to a gravel car parking area before the woods began. But the woods also butted up against the golf course, the industrial estate, and several housing estates, so you could gain access to it from many points. I didn't dare walk along the main road while it was still light, so I made my way through the backstreets to one of the housing estates and entered through there, my stomach churning with nerves.

Inside the woods were a few dog walkers – a thin woman with a well-trained German shepherd that was almost glued to her side and an elderly man with a Jack Russell that ran towards me, yapping around my heels. It wouldn't leave me alone, so, with an apology from the owner, he put it on the lead until they were out of sight.

I stepped off the path, worn with years' worth of use, and walked through the thick, protective layer of trees and bushes. At one time I knew every inch of these woods, but I hadn't been here since I was about sixteen. It was slowly coming back to me, though, as I headed deeper inside.

I'd almost reached the main entrance and gravel parking area when I saw a flash of red through the trees. A stationary car was parked up.

I approached slowly, using the cover of the foliage as a shield, my eyes straining through the leaves. The car was empty. Another dog walker? Or one of the thugs working for Tragatech? Unless Miles had told them where to find me, they couldn't have discovered where I'd be, but I couldn't afford to take any chances.

I tried to keep my breathing under control as I glanced around in a circle. I couldn't see anyone, but the sky was darkening now and the shadows growing bigger. Was someone hiding out there, waiting for me?

I pushed my way inside a huge rhododendron bush, hands protecting my face from the leaves and branches scraping at my eyes, my skin. Normally I'd be freaking out about spiders in my hair, but that was the least of my worries.

I crouched, rigid, listening for sounds. In the distance I heard a dog barking. I took slow deep breaths to stop myself dissolving into panic. Panic would get me killed.

A little while later the barking was a lot closer, and I could hear a man talking to his dog, hear his footsteps crunching on the debris of the path.

I peered through the dense bush and watched the man I'd seen earlier with the Jack Russell walking towards the red car. The shoulders I'd been holding tense relaxed a little. He opened the back seat for the dog and it jumped inside. The engine fired and then they were driving away.

It was almost dark as I fought my way back out of the bush and stood behind a tree right at the edge of the woods where I would see any cars arriving in advance.

It had been the longest day of my life and it wasn't over yet.

Chapter 42

Miles's Porsche Cayenne pulled into the car park at speed and crunched to a stop. I peered around the old tree trunk to make sure he was alone before approaching him.

He got out of the car, looked around and spotted me. His usual immaculate presentation had fallen apart. His hair was greasy and flat against his scalp, and he hadn't shaved. His eyes were swollen with bags underneath. His jeans and shirt were creased.

He stood there, waiting for me to come to him. Despite his appearance, I still expected to see the usual arrogance in his face, but it was gone. He looked tired and sad – distraught, even. I felt a flash of anger towards him, but pushed it away. Now wasn't the time for a fight. I had a bigger fight on my hands.

If we'd had a close relationship, maybe he would've hugged me then. Maybe I would've gripped on to him, hoping he'd save and protect me. But instead of offering words of comfort, he simply said, 'Get in the car.'

'Thanks for coming,' I replied as I opened the passenger door and sank into the plush, comfy seat, the leather moulding against my back and thighs. I wanted to let my head relax on to the headrest and close my eyes, but I didn't have time for such luxuries.

He stared out of the windscreen in front of him into the darkness and said, 'I'm sorry.'

'It's too late for apologies, Miles. They killed Zoe. They murdered a witness right in front of me, and they were going to kill me, too.' I told him about everything that had happened – meeting Colin, seeing him get shot, running, the explosion at the surgery, Will's involvement, how the police probably thought I was unhinged and involved. 'The only witness to Dr Baird's part in Zoe's murder is dead. Any evidence that could've proved he knew about the side effects of Caprixanine and had covered it up has gone up in smoke. You're the only one who can stop this now. I know you know more than you're saying. Tania even hinted you'd told her things, and I think you've sent her and Hayley away somewhere to protect them. But they'll find them at some point. You know they will. They seem to have ears and eyes everywhere. Now you need to tell me, and then we can go to the police together before we all get killed.'

He ran a shaking hand over his forehead. 'I had no idea things would end up like this. If I had, I never would've kept quiet.' He paused, as if he wanted me to reassure him somehow, or say he wasn't to blame. Well, he'd be waiting a long time. When I stayed silent, he carried on. 'At first, I had no idea what was happening with Caprixanine. It was being hailed as the new, non-addictive wonder antidepressant that didn't have any of the horrible side effects associated with so many of them.'

I thought about what Daniel had told me – how drug sales reps were supposed to omit the bad trial data and pump up the good. I couldn't believe Miles hadn't known, too. 'I don't believe you,' I said flatly.

'It's true! The clinical trial data I saw before the drug was approved by the MHRA was all positive. The problem was Tragatech got greedy.

Caprixanine was making them so much money from the start, but they wanted more. There was a massive growth market they wanted to exploit – children. They got Dr Baird to carry out secret post-marketing research on adolescents by prescribing it off-label and monitoring the results. He was already on their payroll, so they paid him vast amounts of money to be the first one to test the waters and report back with his opinions before they went all out on marketing it to other healthcare practitioners.' He paused, looked at his hands trembling in his lap. 'Then Dr Baird called me about a couple of patients – Maria Butterworth, who'd taken an overdose, and Robert Holloway, a fifteen-year-old who was being bullied at school and became agoraphobic. A week after taking the Caprixanine Dr Baird gave him, he hung himself. Dr Baird told me he thought this could be a side effect of the drug. I went to Tragatech and they denied it could be. They said it was safer than aspirin – that no one in any of the previous trials in adults had had a psychotic or suicidal reaction. I believed them and shrugged it off until Dean, which, of course, you know all about. Then there was another teenager who killed herself called Rachel—'

'Rachel Tucker.'

He nodded. 'None of these kids were suicidal or violent prior to taking Caprixanine.'

My stomach twisted. All those lost lives, families destroyed, and for what? For money. Greed. Power. 'So what happened? Did you confront people at Tragatech again?'

'Yes. I was in a meeting with the CEO, Phillip Gregson, and his "security" team.' He made quote marks in the air when he said 'security'.

'Martin was one of the security team?'

'Yes.'

'Why did you invite that kind of person to your barbecue?' I snapped.

'He wasn't at the meetings. And at first I thought he was just a good guy at work who I played squash with, but I realised a day or two ago he'd been sent to keep an eye on me – make sure I was toeing the line.'

'But you tried to set me up with him! How could you have done that when you knew what he was capable of?'

'I didn't know who he was then! I thought he worked in the accounts department!'

I sucked in a furious breath. 'What about Andrew? He engineered meeting me in the car park. Whose idea was that?'

'Andrew?' Miles looked blank.

I described him.

Miles shrugged. 'I don't know who that is. And before that meeting with Gregson, I'd never met any of the other security people. But it became apparent after Dean that Tragatech would stop at nothing to keep the deadly side effects covered up. They wouldn't let anything get in the way of their plan. It would take *years* for people to realise the *true* effects of the drug, and it's very unusual for regulators to take a drug off the market once it's approved. By the time that happened, if it ever did, Tragatech would've made billions. And even if they were prosecuted over it, the fine they'd get would be nothing compared to what they'd already made. The system's designed so they don't lose. The only losers are the unsuspecting patients.' He blew out a breath. 'They knew it wasn't safe for adolescents, but instead of raising the alarm, the CEO, top-level execs, and the marketing and PR teams cooked up a scheme to deceive by aggressively promoting Caprixanine for under-eighteens.' He closed his eyes for a moment, then opened them again, staring out into the night without looking at me. 'They told Dr Baird to change the patients' records to show they were depressed or suicidal when they consulted with him at the beginning, so it would look like their mental health disorders were to blame and not the drug.'

'That's what Zoe found out.'

'Yes. But I didn't know she was poking her nose into everything.'

'She was doing it for me, Miles! You knew I was looking into what happened with the Hudsons, why didn't you fucking warn me! Why didn't you say something?'

He swallowed hard, his jaw a tight line. 'I tried to get you to stop asking questions, but you wouldn't listen.'

'Yes, by making out I was crazy!'

'And besides, you have all these ideas and never follow through on them. At the beginning, how was I supposed to know you were that serious about writing a story?'

'So you swept it under the carpet, too? Why would you do that? Did they threaten you?'

He didn't say a word, but his silence said everything.

'They bribed you, didn't they?' Anger set my body on fire. 'I don't fucking believe this! How much was it worth to keep quiet, eh? How much for Zoe's life? For Dean or Jess or Stephen or any of the others? How much, Miles?' I grabbed his arm and squeezed it, but he still wouldn't look at me.

'Two million,' he said quietly.

I let his arm go like it was diseased, my hand flying back to my thigh with a loud slap.

'They said they'd discredit me if I spoke out. It was either take the money from them and keep my mouth shut, or be ruined with no job and no possibility of working for another pharma company. I didn't know they'd murder my own sister! And after Zoe, they threatened me. They said if I exposed what was going on they'd kill Tania and Hayley. I couldn't let anything happen to them, so I sent them away, trying to protect them. But I had to go along with what Tragatech wanted! They said I had to keep you in line or they'd kill you, too!' he yelled. 'And I was implicated in the cover-up by then for taking the bribe.' His face crumpled, tears slipping down his cheeks. 'Yes, I took the money at first, but then I was in too deep. Everything I did was to protect you and my family!'

'Not everything. You bastard! You're complicit in all this! You should never have let it get that far. As soon as you knew what was going on, you should've blown the whistle. You wanted to keep the good life and profit from it all as well. You're as bad as Tragatech.'

'I didn't kill anyone!'

'You as good as did by keeping quiet, so don't pretend you're Mr Fucking Innocent.'

'I've got evidence.' He twisted in his seat to look at me, his eyes pleading for forgiveness. 'After the meeting, I started digging around. I found secret emails and internal memos about the original hidden trial data. Covert off-label marketing strategies cooked up by the PR department and Phillip Gregson to mislead doctors about the deadly adverse reactions. Strategies to discredit or neutralise any doctors who criticised Caprixanine.

'The literature written in the medical journals about Caprixanine was all bought and paid for, written by Tragatech's ghostwriters, but with the names of well-respected experts on them. I've got records of how much the experts were paid to make it look like they'd written them. It was my insurance in case they went back on their word.'

'You mean in case they didn't give you the money?' I fired at him with disgust.

'I'm trying to do the right thing now, give me some fucking credit!'

I glared at him. He didn't deserve credit. He deserved a smack in the face. But that could wait. 'Are you saying the original trial data was fabricated?'

'Some of it was. There was already evidence from those trials that Caprixanine wasn't safe for young adults. In the adult trial, twenty-five per cent of people aged between eighteen and twenty-three became either suicidal or psychotic and violent, and none of them had any previous suicidal or violent ideation. But that got covered up so they could get the drug approved.'

'Why didn't anyone else notice that patients taking part in the trials were becoming psychotic or violent or killing themselves?'

'The trials were outsourced to a CRO, a clinical research organisation, in India.'

'India?'

'It's a growing trend to outsource trials to developing or Third World countries because it's cheaper than running a trial in the US or UK. Regulatory oversight is a lot poorer, as is the standard of clinical care, and passing on incentives for massaging data is far higher due to corruption. And since Tragatech was paying the CRO, of course their main aim was to make the drug look good enough to get it on the market.'

I rubbed my hands over my face. Daniel had told me pretty much the same story, but it was still so hard to believe the lengths that these people would go to with such blatant disregard for people's lives.

'We can go to the police with everything I've got. I'll get a good lawyer and cut a deal: a whistle-blower's evidence and testimony in return for not pressing any charges against me.'

I was about to scream at him that he was still trying to protect his own back after everything that had happened, but I was more concerned with the evidence he had. 'Where is this evidence?'

He rummaged in his pocket and pulled out a memory stick. 'It's all on here.'

I took it from his hand.

Then I heard a car. The squealing of tyres out on the main road. The crunch of gravel. I twisted around in my seat as a sickeningly familiar black car swung into the narrow entrance to the car park behind us, blocking our exit, the beam of its headlights bouncing and lighting up the dark sky.

I pushed open the Porsche's door and yelled, 'Run!'

Chapter 43

I wasn't aware of the scraping of branches across my face or the direction we were going. All I could feel was my heart hammering in my chest and blind panic squeezing the breath from my lungs as we navigated the uneven ground, tree limbs and brambles tugging at us as we sped past.

Sometimes I was in the lead, sometimes Miles was, the memory stick clutched tight in my hand as I listened for the sounds of footfalls behind us.

Deep in the woods, we came upon a circle of eight-foot bushes that I recognised – the exact spot Zoe, Miles, and I had hidden inside as kids, pretending we were pirates on a secret desert island. The bushes had grown a lot denser since I was a little girl. All the better for hiding in.

I pushed my way through the thick branches, Miles following behind. Twigs tugged at my hair, ripping it from the roots. Inside we were completely hidden from view.

Miles leaned over, hands on his thighs, heaving for breath.

'Shut up!' I hissed, eyes wide open, training my ears to the sounds of the men out there.

'What are we doing here?' Miles whispered. 'We should just keep running. Get out through the housing estate side. That's closest to the police station.'

'They'll probably have someone waiting at that entrance, too.'

'Then we should double back to the car park and take my car.'

'They've probably disabled it by now. They . . .' I heard a crashing of branches close by and heavy breathing. Saw a beam of light filtering through the darkness of the night sky.

I clutched Miles's arm tight and we stood, frozen, trying not to breathe.

The men stopped right outside our circle.

'Any sign of them?' one voice said.

'No. If they come out the other entrance Martin will be there to get them. They're in here somewhere. Just keep looking.'

Footsteps ran in opposite directions then. I waited until I couldn't hear anything else and breathed out.

Miles looked at me, his face twisted with fear. 'What do we do?'

I tried to think, but my head was thick with panic.

'What?' Miles hissed.

'Hide the evidence and split up,' I whispered. 'At least that way if they catch one of us, they can't destroy the evidence. Whoever makes it to the police station first can bring the police back here.'

'Right. OK.' Miles nodded madly.

'We can't use the main entrances, so we need to cut through where the . . .' I stood still, picturing exactly where I was in relation to the rest of the woods, my brain scrambling to recall all those times I'd been here as a kid, our lives depending on it now. A ball of pressure squeezed against my sternum.

'Where? Which way?' Miles almost shrieked.

'Shut up! I'm thinking.' I clenched my fists. 'You go that way.' I pointed left. 'Head in a straight line and you'll come out at a bramble hedge at the golf course. Cut through the course and then keep going to the police station. I'll go this way.' I pointed right. 'It comes out at the back of the industrial estate. Hopefully one of us will make it out of here alive.'

I crouched down and pushed the memory stick into the soil, covering it with a rock and moving some dry leaves and broken twigs around it until it just looked like a patch of uneven, undisturbed ground similar to the rest of the forest floor. Then I eased my head out through the bushes, straining my ears to hear anything. I saw a torchlight streaking in the distance, but not in the direction either of us would be heading.

So far so good.

Chapter 44

I hurt everywhere, but I kept on going, over uneven ground, the night air stinging the cuts on my face made by branches and twigs.

I jumped over a fallen log, not seeing the dip in the ground on the other side until it was too late.

I missed my footing. Staggered. Went over on my ankle, twisting it sharply to the side. A stab of pain shook me to my core, but I gritted my teeth and kept on going in a half-jog, half-hop until the pain subsided to a throbbing ache.

I wondered how they'd found us. Had Miles told them? I still didn't know if I could trust him any more. Or had they put some kind of tracking device in his car? On his phone? I should've told him not to bring his phone – to come by foot. How stupid of me!

I could see the street lights of the industrial estate in front of me flickering through the trees. I heard a shout some distance behind me but didn't turn around. I prayed they hadn't got to Miles, even though I could've quite easily fed him to them myself right now.

I was slowing down. I hadn't eaten since the morning and I'd long since burned off any energy that food had provided. A fog swam in my head. The edges of my vision clouded with blackness. My limbs felt simultaneously heavy and light. Panic was ringing in my ears and the back of my throat felt raw and scratchy.

Come on! Come on! Keep going!

I slapped myself lightly on the cheeks to stay alert. The street lights came closer. I could make out buildings now. Warehouses.

Another shout from somewhere behind me in the distance. A fox darted out of a bush to my right and ran away.

And then I was through the trees and vaulting over the chicken wire fence on to a tarmac road at the back of a warehouse.

My arms pumped hard.

Not far. Not far. Just a little bit more.

The world was wobbling in front of my eyes, my brain fuzzy. I tried to concentrate, the effort almost too much.

I was just rounding the corner of the warehouse when I saw the car – saw the two men rushing towards me, another shadowy figure behind.

All my momentum was still propelling me forwards, so by the time I stopped and turned around, one of them was grabbing my arm and pulling me backwards.

Chapter 45

A shard of pain in my shoulder so deep inside it almost made me pass out.

Someone swung me roughly around.

I came face-to-face with Martin, who squeezed me against him tightly, a gun pressed against my temple.

Part of me was frozen, a deer caught in the headlights. The other part was hyper-aware. Struggling for breath. Fear so desperate I could taste it in my mouth. My heart pounded against my ribcage. I recognised the second guy with bad acne-scarred skin. I'd seen him outside Jess and Stephen's house. Outside Barbara's. I'd assumed he was a reporter, but obviously not.

And the third guy . . . when I saw him my heart splintered, and I almost dropped to my knees. It was only Martin's vice-like grip that kept me upright.

Will.

I knew already that he'd lied to me – knew he was involved. But still, seeing him here with me so helpless, I couldn't believe I'd ever thought I'd known him at all.

I looked at him with pleading eyes. There was still a little sliver of hope that maybe he was undercover, infiltrating Tragatech's 'security' team. Maybe he was going to save me after all.

But that hope died when the hyper-aware part of me registered the look of cold detachment in his eyes, the determined set of his jaw.

'Where is it?' Martin pressed the gun harder against my head, squeezing my arm tighter so his fingernails dug into the skin on my arm.

I didn't speak. I couldn't speak.

My gaze locked on to Will's. His face was rigid, eyes boring into mine.

'Where is it? We know Miles took it now.' Acne Guy got in my face, spittle from his angry shout spraying over my skin.

I flinched.

'Where the *fuck* is it?' Martin squeezed me tighter against him.

I struggled to breathe.

'Where's Miles going?' Will asked, in a tone of voice I didn't recognise. Hard, calculating, lacking in any feeling or empathy.

I wanted to cry, but I was too scared to even do that. I tried to think of what to do. Should I say I'd hidden it but couldn't remember where in the dark? Would they keep me alive until it was light and bring me back into the woods to show them where it was? Every second's delay was a second still alive, a second in which Miles could make it to the police station. And then the police would come looking for me. Wouldn't they?

'We need to get that fucking evidence,' Martin snapped. 'We're not fucking around here.' His mouth was hot against my ear, the barrel of the silencer icy cold against my temple. 'Where is it?'

And then I heard the rumble of a car coming from somewhere over the other side of the industrial estate.

Will and Martin exchanged a look.

The car was coming closer.

Acne Guy ran to the boot of their car and opened it. 'Put her in here for now.'

Martin dragged me along to the boot. I tried to dig my heels into the crumbling old tarmac, but he was too strong.

It was a BMW. Dark blue. Funny the things that register when you're about to die.

Martin picked me up and threw me in the boot, Acne Guy pushing my legs inside.

They slammed it shut and I was in complete darkness, curled into a foetal position.

The car started. Wheels on tarmac. I tried to picture the layout of the industrial estate but couldn't. Couldn't see past my terror.

I scrabbled my hands around on the carpet flooring, searching for a weapon. A screwdriver or wrench or a wheel brace.

Nothing.

It was no use screaming. No one outside would hear me over the diesel engine.

It was hot. No air. Would I suffocate in here before they shot me?

I felt along the top of the boot, searching for some kind of release catch.

No, there was no catch. Nothing to pull or press to open the boot from the inside.

I forced myself to stay calm.

Think! Think!

Tears stung my eyes. Pressure built in my chest as I frantically started my search again in case I'd missed something the first time.

But there was nothing there. *Nothing!*

The car bumped over a speed hump, going fast. It jolted me upwards, my head banging into the roof of the boot. I cried out in pain.

The car swerved right, lurching me to the side. I banged my cheek against cold metal.

I tried searching again, hands skimming over every surface, then touching the plastic cover to the car's rear lights. There was a small hole in the plastic. I reached my forefinger inside and pulled off the cover with a popping sound. Light illuminated the boot.

I could see the bulbs and wiring and some clips keeping them fixed in position. I tugged the wires but the lights didn't move. I tugged again, but they remained in place.

The car swung left, tossing me sideways, ripping my grip away from the wires. I was disorientated, dizzy. My breath was jagged. I swallowed hard as the car straightened out and I reached for the wiring again. I squeezed the plastic clips and the bulbs came out. Now there was just the plastic outer covering of the lights left. If I could break it, I could wave my hand through the gap at any traffic behind.

I pressed the cover, but the plastic didn't move. There were only two small screws holding it in place, but they were strong.

I pressed it again, but nothing happened.

I leaned against the back of the boot, bracing myself with a hand on the carpet on either side and pushed at the plastic with my foot. It groaned and moved a bit. I pushed again and it went tumbling out on to the road behind.

I reached my hand through the gap where the lights had been into the night air, waving frantically, hoping someone would see.

Sweat poured down my temple and into my eyes. The car jerked left, almost tearing my hand at the wrist where it was stuck out of the hole. My elbow cracked against something. My head bounced off the roof again. And still I waved.

We went straight for some time. Then a left. Another right. And the car started slowing down. A different surface now. Gravel.

The car stopped. A door opened. Another door. Voices.

I tugged my hand back through the gap and into the car.

Then the boot opened and Martin loomed above me with a sneering smile on his face. 'Well, that didn't work, did it?' He laughed at me before gripping my arm and hauling me out of the boot.

I cried out with the sound of a dying animal.

No one had seen me. No one was coming to save me.

Chapter 46

I saw a big detached house ahead of me that was in complete darkness. The world was silent except for my heavy breathing.

I glanced around manically. The place was kept completely private from prying eyes by mature trees at the border of the plot. I tried to turn my head to look back down the gravel driveway, but all I saw was Will behind me, his eyes narrow and slightly panicked.

Acne Guy took hold of my other arm and he and Martin frogmarched me inside the house. Will flipped on lights behind us. I registered a quick flash of hallway, a kitchen, another closed doorway.

We went through the doorway and they manhandled me down some stairs.

A basement. Dark. The smell of damp and mould was overpowering.

At the bottom two steps, one of them pushed me. I toppled forwards, my right arm outstretched, trying to stop the fall that was inevitable. A pain surged in my back. My head bounced off the hard floor.

Then their footsteps receded up the stairs. A key turned in the lock with scary finality.

I sat up and rubbed at my arm, my back, my head, wildly looking around for . . . something. A window. A door. A weapon.

I forced myself to my knees, then to my feet. It was dark, but my eyes were adjusting slowly. A vague haze of light filtered down from a gap around the door at the top of the stairs. With outstretched hands, I walked forwards to the wall looming in front of me, mocking me. There was a dusty wooden bench attached to it, but nothing else. No sliver of light coming from the outside. No tools.

The only thing in the room was a tarpaulin that smelled of engine oil, crumpled in a heap on the floor. No windows. No means of escape. Nothing to attack them with when they came for me.

Somewhere outside I heard a car engine start.

I headed back up the stairs, wood creaking beneath my feet. I turned the door handle.

Locked. Of course it was.

Where the hell was I? I tried to calculate how much time had elapsed since Miles and I had separated. Had they got him, too? Were there other guys trudging him through the woods right now, making him tell them where the evidence was? Or had he safely managed to escape to the police station and was busy reciting a garbled and unbelievable story? And even if he was, he didn't know where they'd taken me.

No one did.

Chapter 47

I was crouched into a ball in the corner of the basement when the light came on and the door opened. I blinked rapidly to adjust my eyes to the sudden brightness.

Will entered and walked down the steps, stopping at the bottom one.

I pressed myself against the cold wall.

'I've got a bottle of water for you and something to eat.'

My head pounded with writhing hatred and anger. I pictured his face that night we'd slept together when I was eighteen. The happiness in his eyes. My words, excuses. *I won't have time for a long-distance relationship. I need to concentrate on my career.* The light in his eyes dulling as he'd realised that was it. There would never be an *us*. Realising his feelings for me weren't reciprocated. Was this what it was all about? Revenge? I pictured us together last night in his bed. He'd slept with me fully knowing they were still after me – knowing they'd kill me. What kind of callous person does that?

'Do you really hate me that much?' I said, my voice wobbly, my throat dry.

He snorted. 'It's not about you.'

'I'm locked in a basement. They'll kill me. How is it not about *me*? How could you?' I watched him warily. 'You're a *policeman*!'

'Yeah? Working my fucking arse off and getting passed over all the time? Well, I'm sick of doing everything the right way and getting nowhere! This was my way out. I deserved it!'

I wanted to ask him more. Had he approached Tragatech for a bribe or had they approached him? He obviously hadn't been intending to take me to the police station, so where had he been planning on taking me this morning? Straight to these guys to be disposed of? But I wouldn't give him the satisfaction of words. He was a liar and a calculating, evil bastard that I'd so misjudged. And in the end, did it matter? The truth wasn't going to save me now.

'Here.' He put the water and sandwich on the ground by his foot. 'Thought you might want these.'

'My last meal? And then what?' I glared at him.

He ignored the question. 'They've gone back out to look for Miles, but if they don't find him, they'll be back to ask questions about where that evidence is. You'd better tell them.'

'Or what, Will? They'll kill me anyway. Or are *you* going to pull the trigger? You can live with all these deaths on your conscience?'

He didn't reply – just turned and walked up the stairs.

I thought about hurtling towards him, pouncing on his back, scratching at his eyes, trying to get through that door, but I didn't have the strength left to get out before he would knock me unconscious. I couldn't fight him and win without a weapon.

I waited until the door was locked again before I stood on trembling legs and picked up the water. I unscrewed the cap and took long swallows. It was gone in seconds. With the way my stomach was roiling, I couldn't even think about eating. I didn't trust the food not to come back up again.

I paced the floor. I searched the basement again, even though I'd already scoured every inch. I chewed on my lip and fought more tears.

Then finally I collapsed to the floor again, hopelessly waiting. I didn't think they'd 'ask questions'. It would be more like torture. I tried to blot out images of them breaking my legs, pulling out my teeth, my fingernails, but they wouldn't go away. A wave of dizziness hit me, as if the ground were falling away beneath my feet and I was plunging into a dark hole I'd never escape.

I huddled in the corner of the room, burying my head in my hands as the agonising minutes ticked by, my life slipping through my fingers, waiting to die.

At some point I heard a car outside again – maybe it was Martin and Acne Guy returning. Had they found Miles and killed him? Had they found the evidence? How long would it be before they came for me?

I don't know how much later it was when the noise jolted through my body. A loudspeaker sounded from somewhere outside. I was too shocked to register the words at first before I caught 'Armed police!' and something about opening the door.

I heard a crash from upstairs and leapt to my feet, adrenaline pulsing through me.

Heavy footsteps above. Banging. Shouting. A crash. Something splintering. Glass shattering. More footfalls now and shouts of 'Stay where you are!'

A gunshot cracked out, followed by another.

I screamed as hard as my lungs allowed. 'Help! I'm down here! Help me!' And I kept screaming until the door to the basement burst open and a beam of light trailed across the floor, stopping on me, blinding me.

I blinked rapidly and someone rushed down the stairs.

Chapter 48

I sat in the interview room at the police station, a blanket round my shoulders and a half-empty bottle of water in front of me on the table. The walls were pale blue and made me feel even colder. They made me shiver just a bit more, even though the room was stuffy and hot.

DCI Turnbull sitting in front of me had kind eyes, but I was still wary. I'd been fooled before. By Richard. By Will. By Miles. I was a terrible judge of character.

'You're very lucky, Miss Gold,' DCI Turnbull said. 'A woman was driving behind their vehicle and saw your hand waving from the back of the car. She phoned us to report she thought someone had been kidnapped and followed at a discreet distance until we could get there.'

I stared at my hands in my lap. 'So many people are dead.'

'Your brother's told us what he knows, but I need to hear it from you.'

'I don't know where to start.' I shivered, rubbing my hands up and down my arms.

He leaned back in the plastic chair. 'It's OK. Take your time.'

I inhaled a deep breath and held it, grabbing on to the oxygenated energy. Then I told him everything.

He asked questions now and then, but his face didn't give anything away, so I carried on until everything was finally out in the open.

'I'm very sorry for your loss.' He shook his head sadly. 'I thought I'd seen it all doing this job for thirty years, but this takes things to a whole new level.' He sighed. 'You never were a suspect in the arson attack at Dr Baird's surgery. Will Jackson was lying about that.' He had a look of disgust and contempt on his face when he mentioned Will's name. 'He's in custody right now. He won't get away with his part in this.' He shook his head slightly. 'I'm sure he didn't keep you updated on Zoe's murder, either, did he?'

My head snapped up. 'Why? Have you found something?'

'We knew her body was made to look like a mugging and that she was killed somewhere other than Cooper Park.' He opened a buff-coloured file on the desk in front of him and picked out a piece of paper, reading through it. 'This DNA report just came back. We found evidence that Dr Baird killed Zoe and transported her body in his car, like this Colin told you. Dr Baird's skin was found underneath her fingernails as she fought back when he hit her on the head. His DNA was on her body. Fibres from inside the boot of his car had transferred on to her clothes. She died from blunt force trauma.'

I wrapped my arms around myself and let out a gasp as fresh tears welled up. 'Poor Zoe.' Splinters fractured my heart all over again.

He slid a box of tissues towards me. 'Once again, I'm very sorry. Dr Baird is being arrested right now.'

I ignored the tissues and he let me cry in silence for a while.

Finally, he said, 'We don't know where Colin's body is or *who* he is yet. But we'll obviously be trying to find out.'

'He saved my life.' I looked down at my hands, my neck trembling, as if it were almost too heavy to hold up any longer. Fat tears clouded my vision. 'I think . . . I think Will was going to deliver me to those men. They needed me silenced. They thought Miles was under their control.'

'Those other men at the house opened fire on our units. They were shot dead at the scene. But Will Jackson's not answering our questions.'

It had been pandemonium at the house where I'd been held when the police led me out of the building. Police cars and ambulances with their lights strobing through the night. People in uniforms everywhere.

I fought the bone-deep fatigue to keep my eyes open and focused. 'What will happen to Miles? If he'd exposed this sooner . . .' I trailed off as Zoe's face fluttered in front of my eyes.

'We'll be treating him as a whistle-blower. He'll be protected. He's out with some police officers in the woods at the moment, locating the evidence you hid.'

'Even though he took . . .' I stopped short of mentioning the two million pounds. The police would find out about it eventually and decide what to do. The money meant Miles couldn't claim to have kept quiet for so long because he'd been scared. In my mind, he'd colluded with them. He was still responsible for Zoe's death. For my almost-death. For Colin's and all Dr Baird's patients' deaths. He had to live with his own conscience.

It was hours later when I signed my long statement and DCI Turnbull said I could go. When I exited through the back of the police station with a young policewoman who was giving me a lift home, dawn was just breaking on the horizon. DCI Turnbull didn't think there would be another attempt on my life, not now we'd passed over the evidence to him, and Martin and Acne Guy were dead. But he did offer to have a police officer stationed outside the flats, which I didn't accept. I didn't think anyone would come after me now. It was over.

The policewoman drove me in silence back to my flat. I was all talked out. I wanted to sleep for a hundred years. Or maybe hibernate and never come out into the real world again.

She dropped me off with a smile and a goodbye, and I trudged up the communal stairway on legs that felt like deadweights.

I opened the door and, for once, welcomed the solitude and silence. I crawled into bed fully clothed, and closed my eyes.

Chapter 49

The intercom buzzing woke me some time later. I ignored it for a while. It was probably Mum, come to have a go at me. No doubt Miles had got to her first and given his own version of events that would render him blameless and me in the wrong somehow. There would be things to sort out and talk about with her later. Leigh. Miles. Zoe. But not now. Not yet. I couldn't deal with her at the moment.

I put the pillow over my head and willed her to go away, but the buzzing didn't stop. I threw the covers back and went to the intercom by the front door.

'Hello?'

'It's me.' Miles's voice was hesitant, full of guilt.

'What do you want?' I sighed. 'I can't talk to you right now.'

'Can I come up?'

'No.'

'Look, I don't want to say this down here. Just let me come up and apologise.'

I closed my eyes and rested my forehead against the wall.

'Please?'

I sighed again and pressed the entry system, waiting behind the front door for his knock.

I let him in and walked to the window, as far away from him as I could get. He closed the door and stood there with red eyes, looking dishevelled and haunted.

I looked away, unable to stand the sight of him. 'Just say what you want and go.'

'I am truly sorry about everything.'

'And you think that makes it OK?' I folded my arms across my chest, turned my back on him and stared out of the window. 'What about the money they gave you? You sold out to the devil.'

'I did a lot of things I shouldn't have. I know that. And you're right. I am responsible for some of it. If I'd been a better person, then Zoe wouldn't be dead. But I've done a lot of thinking. About my actions. About my life. Things are going to change. I've got a lot of making up to do.'

I watched a sparrow sitting on the roof of my car in the communal car park below, ruffling its feathers with its beak.

'I know I don't deserve your forgiveness, but I'm asking for it anyway.'

I looked at him then over my shoulder. 'Yeah, well, I know you're used to getting what you want, but it doesn't always work out like that. Maybe one day I'll forgive you, but right now I'm so fucking angry with you.'

'I don't know what you want me to say! I'm sorry. I can't change anything now. But I did do the right thing in the end.' He held his hands out by his sides.

'Just go, Miles,' I said wearily.

He nodded. 'Can I ask you a favour?'

I glared at him. 'Seriously? I'm not inclined to do you any frigging favours right now.'

'*Please.* I want to borrow your car. I need to go and see Tania and explain everything. I need to get her and Hayley back.'

'So you get to play happy families again while Zoe can't?' I snapped. 'What's wrong with your own car?'

'Those men slashed the tyres and it'll take too long for a garage to pick up my car and then replace them. I just . . . I need to explain to Tania *now*, before the press get involved. I don't want her to hear it all from someone else. And I need to do it face-to-face.'

I wanted to tell him to go to hell but, despite everything, I couldn't. It wasn't for his sake, though. It was for Tania and Hayley. I snatched up my car keys from the coffee table and threw them towards him.

He caught them in mid-air. 'Thank you.'

'You can let yourself out.' I turned my back on him again and looked out of the window – watched him exit the communal entrance and walk slowly to my car.

He unlocked the door with the remote control and then paused, glancing up at me. Our gazes locked.

He opened the door. Slid behind the wheel. Closed the door.

I don't know what happened first. The birds scattering a trail across the sky. The noise of the explosion vibrating through the window. Metal wrenching away from the bonnet. The flash of yellowy-white flames searing my eyeballs and engulfing the car.

I've replayed it in my head over and over again and I still can't tell. All I know is that the car bomb was meant for me.

In the end, Miles unwittingly sacrificed his life for mine. And I didn't know if that made it worse or better.

EPILOGUE

twelve months later

Chapter 50

A year is a long time, but it seemed that so much had happened, and not enough.

To avoid a trial, Will had pleaded guilty to his involvement in my kidnapping, along with bribery and corruption charges. He'd repeatedly given 'no comment' interviews. I wondered how much Tragatech had promised Will for his silence. He was now serving a fourteen-year sentence, and my only consolation was the fact that prisoners hated coppers. He'd lied to me about botching a high-profile case that risked his chances of promotion. That was all bullshit. The real reason he wanted to appear to be following his superiors' orders was revealed when the police searched his house after his arrest. They found a huge stash of drugs he'd stolen from a raid he'd been involved in. They had a street value of half a million pounds, and he was going to sell them back to a local dealer. He had been passed over for promotion a couple of months earlier, which apparently fuelled his decision to turn back to a life of crime, although outwardly he'd been keeping his head down so as not to raise any suspicion about himself. I guess after you cross that line, it's much easier to do it again, and when the opportunity of

Tragatech's bribe came knocking, Will was already a dirty policeman. Maybe you can never take the 'bad' out of the boy. His trial on the drug charges and further corruption charges was still pending. He wouldn't be out of prison for a long time.

At Dr Baird's trial for Zoe's murder, he pleaded not guilty, but was convicted and given a life sentence. He'd probably be out in twelve or so years with good behaviour.

He'd denied all knowledge of Caprixanine's deadly side effects and his involvement in secret research and collusion with Tragatech. The evidence Miles had given me didn't include any written correspondence specifically from or to Dr Baird, but his telephone records proved he was in contact with Miles and Phillip Gregson, the CEO of Tragatech, on many occasions. I didn't know if Tragatech had threatened his family or whether they'd paid him handsomely.

Colin's body has never been found. No one even knew his full name. DCI Turnbull and I were still looking for Colin's family. An image of him from CCTV cameras on Ashfield High Street had been made into a still and plastered in newspapers. I'd tried various British Army websites in an attempt to locate anyone who knew him, but so far I'd got nothing. In honour of the man who'd saved my life, I was going to write a social justice piece about the growing epidemic of homeless veterans and how there was a huge lack of support and assistance for our forgotten heroes. But Colin was my hero, and I wouldn't let him be forgotten.

Any evidence the police could've found from the car bomb that killed Miles had literally gone up in smoke, and DCI Turnbull had put the investigation into his death on hold unless new evidence came to light.

I'd learned that Andrew hadn't been involved. He'd just been in the wrong place at the wrong time.

In the end, I didn't write a freelance article for a newspaper. What had happened – what we'd all gone through – was too complex and astounding to capture in just a few thousand words. Instead, I'd written a book. It had been my new baby for the last twelve months. The fork in the road had led me here. It was all finished, apart from the ending that I would write today.

I sat in the car next to Daniel, fidgeting with my hands in my lap as I rested my forehead against the window on the drive down to the MHRA headquarters in London. The other families had travelled together in convoy and would meet us there. Barbara, Pete and Jenny Tucker, Mike and Sandra Holloway – Robert's parents who I'd since met – and Terri Butterworth. Terri's husband wouldn't come. The death of Maria had been too much for them to withstand as a couple, and they'd separated.

None of the families could get legal aid to sue Tragatech in a civil action for wrongful death, and none of them had the funds to pursue a case themselves. So the MHRA were our only hope for some form of justice.

I wanted Phillip Gregson to pay. His name was on those internal documents Miles had given me that withheld crucial original trial data that could've stopped so many deaths. He was the one who ordered Zoe, Miles, and me to be killed. I knew it. I just couldn't prove it. But no one had ever been able to sue a top-level executive of a pharmaceutical company before for covering up a deadly drug. They were never held accountable or personally responsible. And DCI Turnbull had found no evidence of his direct link to the murders of Zoe, Miles, and Colin.

'Are you OK?' Daniel glanced over as he navigated the London traffic. He reached out a palm to my cheek and I leaned into it, closing my eyes.

We'd grown close in the last twelve months. What started as me picking his brains for more information for my book had turned into something else. I was in love again, and this time, I knew Daniel loved me, too. It was in his every gesture and every word. It was right. He was an amazing man. A man with a huge heart.

Last night I'd told him about the baby, fearing his reaction. Fearing another rejection. But I should've had more faith in him. He'd spun me around the room, alternating between crying with joy and laughing. We hadn't worked out the logistics of everything yet. With him in London and me in Ashfield, it had been a long-distance relationship, with us only having time to see each other at weekends. But somehow it had worked. All those late-night calls had meant us getting to know each other as friends before we fell deeper for each other. It had forged a strong bond that was the foundation of our romantic relationship.

But I had custody of Leigh now, so it wasn't just me I had to think about. Mum had obviously forgotten her previous lack of maternalism until it came to the crunch of looking after Leigh day in, day out. I fought Mum on the custody issue, and she gave in without much of a fight. Now I was Leigh's legal guardian, I didn't really want to drag her away from her friends in Ashfield – away from Tania and Hayley. I didn't want to unsettle her any more than she had been with a move to London with Daniel. She'd been through too much already. While I'd spent most of my life hating that town and dying to get away, much of my association with it had been tainted by my parents. Now I thought that a small town was the best place for my niece to grow up in. And last night Daniel had said he'd move his naturopathic practice to Ashfield if it meant building our new life together as a family.

Leigh and Daniel had been my saviours over the last year. Paradoxically, something so good and life-changing had come from something so bad and life-shattering. The darkness of catastrophe had shone a light in me again.

'Here we are.' Daniel drove into an underground car park near to the MHRA building. He pulled into a space and turned off the ignition.

I sat there, breathing deeply, my stomach twisting in knots. The MHRA had been investigating all the evidence I'd passed on from Miles. Today was the day they'd let us know their decision about whether to prosecute Tragatech, but I wasn't confident justice would be done.

While the FDA had prosecuted or fined pharma companies for their deadly drugs in the US, the MHRA never had in the UK. And both of these bodies hardly ever removed a drug from the market. I was hoping the MHRA would do both, but deep down, I wasn't holding out much hope. Realistically, the most I could wish for would be that this case led to huge publicity, warning people of the dangers before it was too late. Daniel and I had been ringing round the press in advance to let them know what was happening, but the response hadn't been great.

Daniel twisted in his seat to look at me. He clasped my hands in his. 'You know, even if it doesn't go in our favour, your book's going to raise awareness. I'm so proud of you.'

I nodded and smiled, trying to remain positive. No one had ever said they were proud of me before and it made my heart flutter a little in my chest.

'Have you worked out a title yet?'

I'd been back and forth with a few ideas. I wanted something hard-hitting, maybe a play on words. I'd decided that morning on the drive down what it would finally be. '*Licence to Kill*,' I told him.

'I love it.' He squeezed my hand and grinned, trying to keep my spirits up. 'Come on. We'd better go.'

We walked the short distance to the building hand in hand.

This tragedy had all the makings of a headline-grabbing story for the press – corruption, fraud, scandal, murder – but there were only a few medical journalists there. No doubt anything they wrote would be carefully spun in favour of Tragatech since their salaries from the medical journals were effectively paid for by the drug companies. As I'd found out to my cost, the pockets of bad pharma ran deep. There were no reporters from the mainstream media. They didn't seem to be interested in four deaths from one drug, and I wondered how many people had to die before it was worthy of a public outcry? Ten? A hundred? A thousand? Did they really care more about which celebrity was getting new breast implants and fillers than a silent killer in our midst?

The MHRA had said they weren't making a formal announcement about their decision today – which didn't sound good to me – so the medical journalists had to be here for the statement we'd make when we came out, but they didn't seem all that interested in us – they didn't shout out questions as we approached the entrance. I wanted to scream at them, tell them of the lives torn apart, the trail of destruction Caprixanine had left in its wake. But that would come later. In my book. In my own words, not ones that could be distorted and played down.

Instead, I told them we'd talk to them after our meeting, holding my head high as we stepped inside.

We were given visitors' passes and led to a conference room. DCI Turnbull was already there, chatting with Barbara and the other families. In the centre of the room was a long table laden with jugs of water. A bored-looking security guard stood next to the door.

DCI Turnbull gave me a grave smile, shook my hand, and then stood aside for me to hug Barbara. She'd aged so much in the last year. Her face had sagged with sorrow and fatigue, her eyes puffy from a lack of sleep. As I wrapped my arms around her, I felt the contours of her spine and ribs beneath my fingers. She was literally wasting away, disintegrating a little more each day. I knew she'd been holding on for this moment to get justice, but I feared what she'd do after today.

I didn't ask her if she was OK. It would've been a stupid question.

I hugged the other families in turn and we stood in silence, waiting an eternal wait.

Then three members of staff entered the room: two men in suits who I'd never seen and one woman, Angela Clarke, the MHRA legal representative whom I'd been liaising with. I'd found her brusque and insensitive in the past, and my stomach knotted into a tight ball.

Angela gave everyone a flimsy smile, thanked us for coming, and sat down, flanked by the two men, before inviting us all to do the same. She clasped her hands together on the table in front of us and started speaking.

'As you know, we've been investigating allegations of withholding new and important safety data regarding Caprixanine, withholding or falsifying clinical trial data, and unlawful promotion of the drug. After much consideration, we've concluded that there will be no prosecution in this case.'

There was a collective outburst in the room.

'What?!' I cried.

'You can't be serious!' Pete Tucker shouted. 'They killed our children with that drug. They knew about lethal side effects before it came on the market! And *you*' – he pointed a shaky finger at Angela – '*you* should've stopped it ever being approved in the first place.'

'Yes!' Barbara shouted. 'My whole family was killed because of Caprixanine!'

Angela lifted her chin, remaining calm and aloof. 'As sad as I am about the deaths of your loved ones, we found no direct evidence that links Caprixanine to those incidents.'

'Incidents!' Barbara shouted, eyes bulging. 'My family being wiped out is just an *incident* to you?!'

'Four out of twenty people prescribed Caprixanine by Dr Baird committed suicide,' I said as calmly as possible, trying to suppress the anger saturating me. We'd discovered that number during the MHRA's review of Dr Baird's prescribing data. 'That's twenty per cent! And he'd only just got started!'

'It's corporate murder!' Barbara's hands shook violently.

Angela shifted in her seat. 'We've found no new safety concerns regarding Caprixanine. The medicine is not licensed for adolescents and shouldn't have been prescribed to them.'

'But it was,' Daniel said. 'And it happens, off-label, all the time with all sorts of drugs. Do you really think—'

Angela butted in. 'We've concluded that the benefits of this drug outweigh the risks. And the only issue here today is our—'

'Are you saying you're *not* taking Caprixanine off the market?' I asked incredulously, heat building in my stomach, a coldness in my limbs.

'No, we're not. However, a warning will be issued to doctors not to prescribe it to adolescents, and a new addition will be added to the patient information leaflet. All side effects will also be carefully monitored by the MHRA.'

'There's already a warning in the leaflet! Who takes notice of them?' I shook my head and tried to keep breathing. 'I don't believe it. I gave you all the evidence about the dangers of Caprixanine. Evidence Tragatech had hidden or doctored. Evidence they were going to lie about to doctors so they could aggressively market a drug off-label to children that they *knew* was dangerous. How they lied about the results in medical journals. At the very least, it was massive fraud!' I glanced at Daniel as my blood pressure rose. He'd seen it all before with Grafloxx and Tiazal. He didn't look surprised, just resignedly disgusted.

'And what about the corruption and bribery? What are you doing about that?' Terri Butterworth spat, her pale cheeks flooding with colour.

Angela pressed her lips together and held a hand up for silence. I wanted to grab her by the shoulders and shake her, knock that aloof coldness off her face. The people who'd died were just statistics to her, not real flesh and bone.

'I understand this isn't the outcome you were looking for,' Angela said.

'It's a joke! We've lost our son and there's no way we can get justice! You're playing with people's *lives* here!' Mike Holloway stood up and stormed out of the room.

'What *are* you going to do?' Sandra Holloway cried in her husband's absence.

'Surely the *least* you can do is impose sanctions or fines against Tragatech,' I said.

'Tragatech has signed a binding legal agreement with the MHRA forcing them to publish all future clinical trial data in a timely manner and alert us of any known findings of adverse reactions, and they are required to ensure such data is dealt with in their routine pharmacovigilance activities.'

Pete Tucker threw his hands in the air.

'Right. And how do you enforce that?' I asked. 'When that's what they *should* be doing already anyway?'

'More to the point,' Daniel said. 'How can you guarantee that any trial data or adverse effects they're allegedly *forced* to publish are accurate?'

'I'm not going to go into the specific logistics of this agreement due to a privacy clause,' Angela said.

'And what privacy has my daughter got now?' Jenny Tucker shook as an angry red blotch crept up her neck. 'God, you should be ashamed of yourself! How can you people sleep at night?'

'So you won't be prosecuting for civil or criminal fraud? For bribery and corruption?' DCI Turnbull said, arms folded across his chest. Since the MHRA was the governing body for prosecutions in the life sciences sector, he could take no more police action than he'd already done. He looked as outraged as I and the other families felt.

'No,' Angela said.

'Not even a fine?' Barbara screeched.

'You are, of course, free to pursue a civil claim against Tragatech,' Angela said.

'And how can we do that when we can't even get legal aid?' Tears of frustration and fury ran down Jenny Tucker's cheeks.

'You want another parent to bury their child, do you?!' Barbara narrowed her eyes at Angela.

Daniel clenched his jaw. 'You're supposed to be protecting the public, but you've tragically failed. Your actions are just gross negligence and betrayal. You're putting lives at risk here. You—'

Angela pressed her hands against the table and stood up, cutting him off. 'Thank you all for coming. I thought I should give you the courtesy of announcing our decision in person, but I think it's best if we leave things here before matters get more heated.'

Pete screwed his hands into fists, looking like he was seriously considering hitting Angela.

She stalked away from the table, flanked by her two colleagues who hadn't said a word, and out the door.

We were dismissed.

'They've got away with murder,' Barbara said, looking around us all at the table, wild-eyed. 'Those bastards have got away with murder!'

'I'm very sorry,' DCI Turnbull announced to everyone. 'I wish I could do more, but I have no powers here.' He held his arms out in a placatory gesture.

I pressed a hand to my stomach. I felt sick.

Daniel put his arm around me and hugged me close, whispering in my ear, 'You did everything you could. You need to think of the baby now.'

I nodded, my eyes on Barbara. The tears sliding down her cheeks. The devastation on her face. How she clutched the edge of the table, her knuckles white. My gaze skimmed the others. There was so much pain and anger in the room I couldn't breathe. Everything I'd worked so hard to prove – had almost died to prove – was being dismissed with just a slap on the wrist for Tragatech. It was business as usual for them, while they left a trail of shattered lives. It felt like someone had ripped out my insides and left them trailing on the ground.

'Let's go out and tell those medical journalists the outcome,' I said, trying to stay strong and not fall apart. The only power we seemed to have in such a fucked-up, dangerous health system was our voice.

I forced one foot in front of the other as Daniel clutched my hand, the others following behind us in a wave as we walked down the corridor and out of the front entrance to the building.

A few people had gathered outside on the steps, and I stopped short when I recognised Phillip Gregson, the CEO of Tragatech, with some other men in suits, and his wife, Isabelle, at his side, who I'd seen in several press articles. He was talking to the few members of the medical press who'd bothered to turn up, a smug smile on his face.

'What's he doing here?' Daniel whispered in my ear.

And then it dawned on me that those medical journalists had never been waiting there for our statement at all. They were here to listen to Phillip spin his lines. The MHRA must've called Tragatech in earlier than us to give them their decision.

My every muscle tensed with seething anger. The man responsible for the murders of Zoe and Miles and Colin and the deaths of six more people, not to mention the others who'd died during the clinical trials, was talking with such arrogance and nonchalance that I wanted to kill him. If I'd had a gun in my hand I'd have shot him there and then.

'Patient safety is of paramount importance to Tragatech, and we're taking urgent action to rectify Tragatech's unfortunate oversight that some safety data was not passed on to the MHRA,' Phillip announced to the journalists. 'We understand there may be some concerns regarding the non-assessment of a handful of adverse events, but these were not intentional, and immediate steps are being taken to correct the oversight.' Another smug smile.

The Tuckers, Terri Butterworth, the Holloways, Barbara, and DCI Turnbull spilled past me as I stood frozen on the steps, not believing my eyes and ears.

I was vaguely aware of someone rushing past me, but I didn't register who it was. I was too busy concentrating on Phillip as one medical journalist called out, 'So what would you say to allegations that Caprixanine kills people?'

Phillip smiled again. 'Tragatech firmly maintains that Caprixanine did not cause the recent tragic deaths of four patients, and the MHRA have, of course, concurred with those findings. Patients should continue to take their medication as usual.'

I saw Pete then, rushing towards Phillip, his arm swinging as his fist raced towards Phillip's head. Security guards rushed over and grabbed Pete. People screamed and shouted. Daniel pulled me out of the way. DCI Turnbull yelled at the security guards to stop manhandling Pete.

Phillip and Isabelle Gregson were hurriedly escorted away by the suited men to a shiny black Jaguar waiting in the front car park. Just before Isabelle got into the car, she looked over at me. There was something in her expression I couldn't work out.

And then I realised she wasn't looking at me at all. She was looking at Barbara.

Barbara watched the Jaguar speed out of the gate on to the main road. Then she turned and walked away towards the car park entrance and the street beyond without saying a word.

'Wait! Barbara!' I ran after her. I caught up to her on the street, with Daniel close on my heels. 'Let us give you a lift home.'

She stopped and turned around, her whole body sagging, as if staying upright were a huge effort. 'I'm sorry how this all turned out, Holly. Sorry I dragged you into this, and you've had your own terrible family losses to deal with as a result.'

'It wasn't your fault,' I said. 'None of this was your fault.'

'Jess would've been so proud of you, you know.'

I choked back a sob.

'I've got nothing to live for any more, but you have. You've got your baby and Daniel. You've got your family.' She smiled at Daniel warmly. 'Now all I can do is wait for karma to take its course.'

I wanted to ask her not to do anything stupid, but I couldn't. She'd lost her whole family. I knew carrying on for her was impossible these days. I couldn't tell her how to live her life – or not.

'Come with us,' Daniel said. 'I don't think you should be on your own at the moment.'

'But I am now, aren't I?' She blinked quickly, patting my hand. 'Don't you worry about me.' She turned and walked away.

Short of kidnapping her, I didn't know what else we could do, but I worried about her all the way home, and in the days that followed when she wouldn't answer her door, leaving me standing on the doorstep while she shouted from within that she wanted to be alone, and when she wouldn't return my calls.

And on that last day, when I went to her house and my knocks were unanswered, I spotted Barbara's cat in her neighbour's window, looking out at me curiously, and I knew Barbara wouldn't have let go until she'd made sure the cat had a new home.

All I could do was go home and wait for the inevitable news.

Chapter 51

I'll always remember exactly what I was doing when I heard it: a Saturday morning and Leigh was on a sleepover with Hayley at Tania's house. In the last year, Tania had become a rock for me. She'd kicked off her old materialistic lifestyle and become more humble. We'd turned to each other for support.

I was in the bedroom of my new rental two-bed home, sitting cross-legged in bed, reading through the final proofs of *Licence to Kill* before it was published. It would be out in e-book in the next few days, and the paperback and hardback would follow shortly after. My eyes watered as I reread the events we'd all lived through, worrying again about Barbara. Worrying about *all* of the families.

Daniel's footsteps rushed up the stairs and he burst into the room. He stood, panting, in the doorway. 'You need to come and watch the news.'

'Oh my God, Barbara's killed herself, hasn't she?' I cupped my hands to my mouth.

He didn't reply, just walked towards me and took my hand. He pulled me downstairs as a shudder rose up my spine.

The TV was on in the lounge, tuned to BBC News. An anchorwoman was stood outside a hotel in London. I pressed my fist to my lips as she told us the breaking news . . .

'*Phillip Gregson, the CEO of pharmaceutical giant Tragatech, was found dead in one of the suites at the Claremont Hotel behind me. Last night, Mr Gregson attended an industry conference dinner here with his wife. He was a key speaker and, according to witnesses, he gave a speech regarding Tragatech's new wonder antidepressant Caprixanine, which is revolutionising the treatment of depression.*

'*It appears that while Mrs Gregson left the dinner early due to another prior engagement, Mr Gregson stayed in the pre-booked suite, and his body was found when Mrs Gregson contacted the hotel this morning after failing to reach her husband by phone.*

'*We're still waiting for more details from the police, and it's not clear at this time whether this was a suicide or something more suspicious. But in a bizarre twist, a second body was later discovered in another bedroom in the hotel.*

'*The deceased was female and the room was booked in the name of a Mrs Barbara Acres. Cause of death is also unknown at this stage, but sources say the woman left a suicide note blaming Phillip Gregson for the death of her family due to deadly side effects caused by Caprixanine.*

'*We'll update you with more information when we can. Back to you in the studio, John.*'

Daniel's arms enveloped me from behind. I leaned against him and closed my eyes.

'Christ. Somehow she managed to murder Phillip Gregson and then killed herself,' I whispered, still trying to take it all in.

'Not just that. She's given Caprixanine the most damaging publicity it could ever get. The press have finally taken notice now. That's Barbara's legacy. Now you need to do what the drug companies do: market it. If the MHRA won't name and shame them, it's up to us.'

Chapter 52

The details emerged in the coming days. Phillip Gregson had been drinking heavily after the conference and presumably was in a deep drunken sleep when Barbara entered his room. He'd been issued with two key cards when he'd checked in and somehow Barbara had managed to get hold of one. It was speculated that Phillip had lost the key at some point during the dinner.

Barbara had also booked a room at the Claremont so she could strike in the middle of the night, entering his suite, and injecting him with a fatal dose of Ventaphen, a drug Tragatech manufactured for the euthanasia of animals. Murdered by his own drug – a bittersweet irony that was a message in itself. Afterwards, Barbara had gone back to her room, left a very detailed note about Caprixanine and what we'd all been through, then injected herself with a massive amount of the same drug.

I was devastated about Barbara's death, but at the same time I'd known she'd never carry on. There could be no closure for her. No resolution. No justice good enough. No healing. She was at peace now that her suffering had ended, which made it more bearable. And Daniel was right. We all do what we can. I'd written the book to raise awareness, but Barbara had done the same thing in her own spectacular way.

And it had worked. Her suicide note was published in several papers. Journalists started calling me for information, which, of course, I exploited to the nth degree. I was going to market it for all it was worth. It wasn't justice, but maybe it was the next best thing. The press was going crazy with it. I and the other families went on numerous talk shows. The story went viral. *Licence to Kill* hit the number one spot on Amazon Kindle in the UK and the USA. Inquests into the deaths of the Hudsons, Maria, Rachel, and Robert were about to be reopened. Shares in Tragatech plummeted. More stories emerged about patients who'd become suicidal or violent whilst taking Caprixanine, stories not just of other adolescents who it had been prescribed to off-label. There were thousands of adults who'd been affected, too. In the nineteen months in which Caprixanine had been on the market, reports of sixteen thousand deaths and adverse effects had come out so far following the publicity. That figure was still rising. It was looking likely that data from the clinical trials Tragatech had carried out in adults had also been fabricated or hidden. The public began boycotting Caprixanine and other Tragatech drugs as panic took hold. The MHRA changed their tune and were blustering about prosecution and possible fines for Tragatech.

It was a Thursday when the phone call came. I was in the middle of an email interview for a national paper and the story was still going strong.

'Hello?' I picked up the phone, expecting it to be another journalist.

'Hello. Is this Holly Gold?'

'Yes.'

'My name is Isabelle Gregson.'

I thought I'd misheard at first. Why would Phillip Gregson's wife be calling me? To give me a tirade of abuse? By the time I'd recovered enough to ask how I could help her, she was talking again.

'I have a story for you. But it's exclusive. For your ears only,' her voice was calm and neutral. 'I wondered if we could meet.'

I frowned, trying to decide if this was some kind of trap – if she blamed me for the death of her husband somehow because I was the one who'd started it all. Was she going to fake some information she thought I'd want to hear so she could attack me? Did she want revenge? But, of course, I wanted to hear what she had to say. I *had* to. 'Yes, we can meet.'

'Good.'

'When did you have in mind?'

'Are you free tomorrow?'

'I can be. Can you give me any idea what this is about?'

'Not on the phone, no.'

We arranged to meet in the early afternoon at Syon Park, a historic house and garden in south-west London. I hung up and pressed the handset to my lips.

The look she'd given Barbara that day in the MHRA car park swam into my head then, and I thought I knew what it had meant now.

Chapter 53

When I arrived at Syon Park at the prearranged spot, Isabelle was already there, sitting on one of the benches, although I had to look twice to make sure it was really her. She looked nothing like the polished, expensively dressed woman I'd seen in the press articles or at the MHRA building. Her long hair was scooped up inside a tatty baseball cap. She wore an old grey hoodie, jeans, and trainers. Her eyes were hidden behind square-framed glasses.

She stood when I reached her and shook my hand. 'Thank you for coming.'

'Thank you for contacting me. You said you had a story.' I tilted my head questioningly.

'Shall we sit?'

I sat next to her, watching her carefully.

'This is off the record,' she said. 'Not a story for the press. Just for you.'

'OK.'

She paused, rubbing her palms against her thighs. 'My husband wasn't who I thought.' She turned away from me, fixing her gaze on a young mum in the distance holding her daughter's hand as they meandered through the grounds. 'I met him five years ago at a charity function. He was charismatic, charming, attractive – wealthy, obviously. That was the side he showed me for a long time until, over the years, I realised slowly what he was really all about. He was a narcissist – only interested in power and money. He . . .' She paused and shook her head briefly. 'You don't need to know all the details. Just the ones that matter to you.' She clenched her fists. 'He lied to me repeatedly about this Caprixanine scandal when he found out the MHRA were investigating Tragatech over it. He told me the people who'd died were all teenagers who'd taken illegal recreational drugs at the same time as Caprixanine and that's why they'd had those reactions. He said their families were out-of-work benefits scroungers who were just after compensation. And, stupidly, I believed him. Until I found a mobile phone in his car.'

My forehead knotted in a frown as I wondered where she was going with this and how it related to me, but I didn't interrupt.

'I borrowed his car one day and I heard a text message arrive. I couldn't find the phone at first. It was hidden. But, eventually, I did. My first thought was that he was having an affair again. He had many over the years.' She laughed bitterly. 'God, if only it *was* that. It turned out to be much worse.' She took a quick sidelong glance at me, then watched the mum and child again. The little girl was running, arms splayed out behind her, as if she were trying to fly. 'My husband ordered someone to murder you and your brother.'

I sucked in a jagged breath. It felt as if someone had poured a bucket of icy water over me, every nerve ending firing madly. Even though I'd known this all along, hearing it somehow made it worse. I clutched the arm of the bench between my fingers.

'I managed to correctly guess his PIN code for the phone and looked at the many texts on it – how they were watching you, listening to you. He ordered the same person to threaten your brother's family. That car bomb was a direct result of Phillip's orders. He paid off the

policeman, Will Jackson, and others higher up. He paid off Dr Baird.'
She picked at a thread of cotton on one knee of her jeans.

My eyes widened. 'Why are you telling me this?'

She took a deep breath, flattened down the thread, and looked at
me. 'Because you deserve the truth. And I couldn't tell the police, could
I? Not when he'd bribed key people. You already know any investigation
goes nowhere. Tragatech is at the heart of the biggest organised crime
and corruption industry in the world. They make the mafia look like
pussycats. They've got so much power and influence and they're all
protected. They've bought everyone. Nothing would've been done
about it. They get away with murder all the time. And the order to kill
you and your brother was sufficiently ambiguous that he would've got
away with it anyway.' She pressed her lips together for a moment. 'But
after I discovered that phone, I started searching his laptop and papers
in his office at home. I found secret memos and documents. The same
kind of things you found and passed to the MHRA.'

I snorted. 'Yes. And they did nothing to protect people. While
they spent a year on their so-called investigation, thousands more
people died.'

'Industry payroll is a cavernous, deep hole.' Isabelle shook her head,
as if I shouldn't expect anything else. 'Anyway, after what I discovered, I
was devastated. I wanted to meet Barbara. I wanted to tell her how sorry
I was. I knew Caprixanine was responsible for her family dying. It was
responsible for your loss and those of the other families, too.'

'Barbara never told me.'

'No. It was our secret, and you'll understand why soon. Meeting
her was heartbreaking. She was nothing like the lowlife Phillip had
described. She was a wonderful, compassionate, and empathetic
woman. She'd worked hard all her life and had good family values.
When she talked about Dean and Jess and Stephen, who she'd loved
so much, and told me what had been done to them – to everyone – I
wanted to find some way to make amends for what Phillip had done.'

She rubbed at a lone tear in the corner of her eye threatening to fall. 'Barbara said she couldn't carry on any more. She'd tried but . . .' Isabelle reached into the pocket of her jeans, pulled out a handkerchief and dabbed at her eyes. 'Well, you know. She couldn't get over the loss. I understand that completely.'

'I know.' Of course I knew how that felt as well.

'She told me quite frankly that she wanted to kill my husband for what he'd done and got away with. I didn't blame her.' Isabelle looked at the young mum and child again. 'You don't have children, do you?'

I touched the life growing in my stomach. 'Not yet. But I have custody of my niece.'

She nodded. 'Of course. Dr Baird panicked when he realised Zoe had found some documents that would've implicated him. He did act alone when he killed her, but it never would've happened if he hadn't been involved with my husband.' She sighed, a note of sadness and regret in the undertones.

Tears welled in my eyes as I thought of my sister again, dying so violently. A searing pain stabbed at my heart.

'I'm so sorry,' Isabelle said.

I wiped my eyes and nodded as she carried on talking.

'I had a miscarriage early on in our marriage. I desperately wanted children, but then . . . well, obviously, it didn't happen.'

I stroked my stomach gently. 'It happened to me, too. I'm very sorry.'

She nodded my words away. 'So I know what it feels like to lose a child, even though it's not the same situation as you and Barbara and all the other families. And I couldn't let it happen again to another child. They're precious.' She bit her bottom lip. 'The thing is, my husband was evil. He didn't care about all the lives lost. He was remorseless. All he ever cared about was profit and control. He made sure he always got what he wanted, but there's a price to pay for that.' She laughed bitterly. 'He wouldn't stop, because he was driven by power and money.

He'd do it all again in the future. And he would get away with it again. No one's ever accountable, as you've discovered yourself. My husband messed with *real lives*. Not just numbers, statistics on a page he wanted erasing. He's not God. He doesn't get to decide their lives don't matter. So there was only one way to make him stop. Because a man who kills people doesn't deserve to live.'

'So . . . what . . . you helped Barbara to kill him?' Maybe I should've been incredulous, disgusted, shocked. But I wasn't. Isabelle's husband had stolen lives. He'd nearly stolen mine. I wouldn't shed a single tear for him. The world was a better place without him in it.

'Yes. She wanted him dead and so did I, before he did it again. Barbara wanted to leave this world, anyway. And there was a way to guarantee it gave Caprixanine the maximum amount of bad publicity. It was an unlikely pact, but . . . well, let's just say Phillip deserved a taste of his own medicine.'

I smiled sadly as I thought of Barbara, the determined, strong woman I'd known growing up. I'd thought she'd lost her fighting spirit that day at the MHRA, but she hadn't in the end.

'I knew he was going to be at the industry dinner in advance. I knew he was staying the night, that he'd drink too much, celebrating he'd got away with everything again, and that he'd fall into a deep sleep – he always did. I took the second key card for the room and passed it to Barbara in secret. And I had a convenient alibi. I had to leave the function to collect my parents from Gatwick Airport. They were returning from a holiday and their flight was due in at 5 a.m., but I told the police I'd got the time wrong and thought it was two. I made sure I was caught on various cameras while I waited for them to arrive.'

'How did Barbara get the Ventaphen?'

'She had some left at her house from when she was a vet.'

I reached out and touched Isabelle's arm – for comfort, or as a thank you for Miles and Zoe, I wasn't sure which.

'Barbara wanted me to explain what we did, in case you didn't understand her reasons. She didn't want you to think badly of her. But it was the only way she could end things.'

'I think I understand perfectly.'

Isabelle leaned down to reach into her handbag nestled at her feet and pulled out a thick brown envelope. 'And she wanted me to give you these.' She held the envelope out to me.

Puzzled, I took it and looked inside. It contained photos.

I emptied them on to my lap and, my heart clutching with sadness, I was overwhelmed with the memories that came flooding back as I looked at the first image: Jess and me in Barbara's garden with her old dog Scrappy. We'd been playing bat and ball, and I was sprawled on the ground after Scrappy had knocked me flying when he'd chased after the ball. Jess was bent over double, laughing, her eyes sparkling with hilarity.

I flicked through the others: Jess and me when we were eighteen, before I'd left Ashfield, wearing witch fancy-dress costumes, our arms around each other, trying to pull spooky faces. Jess and me swimming in the sea when Barbara and her husband had taken us to Brighton one summer's day. Me holding Dean in my arms in a hospital ward after Jess had given birth.

I closed my eyes and pressed the photos to my chest. 'I think . . . I think I'll look at these at home,' I said, my voice cracking as I put them carefully back in the envelope and transferred them to my bag.

Isabelle laid her hand on my arm. 'In a few days there'll be an announcement. The backlash of this story has meant it's all come out. Reports of deaths and adverse reactions are now well into the mid-twenty thousands. Tragatech is being forced to withdraw Caprixanine from the market.'

I gasped with relief. 'Thank God for that!'

'I doubt if it will be long, though, before it's tweaked slightly and renamed and approved again for marketing. They'll be up to the same dirty tricks. They'll just get even better at hiding it. And, of course, all the other drug companies are doing the same.' She stood up, facing me. 'We have to do what we can, but we're just a drop in the ocean, aren't we?'

I stood, too, my hand touching my stomach lightly, letting the words sink in for a moment. 'Thank you for telling me the truth.'

'It's the least I could do, and I promised Barbara I would. I admire you, you know. You're an incredibly strong and courageous woman.'

'If you'd seen me a year ago, you wouldn't have said that.'

'Well, I suppose you never know what strength you have until being strong is the only choice there is.' She hugged me awkwardly then stepped back. Her lips parted, as if she were about to say more, but then she turned and walked away.

I knew I'd never see her again, and I watched her for a while, lost in thought and with emotions fighting for space inside me: regret, sadness, grief. But I began to feel a small sense of closure.

My mobile phone rang, jerking me away from these thoughts.

'Hello?' I answered.

'Hi, is this Holly Gold?'

'Yes.'

'You exposed the Caprixanine scandal, and I wondered if you could help me expose something, too. My daughter has got autism and I *know* it stems from her flu vaccination. But no one's taking me seriously – no one's listening. I thought you might.'

'OK. Please tell me about what happened.'

'I've found some new studies showing that the vaccination was never tested properly and doesn't even work against the virus or give any benefits for complications from flu. And the company who made it withheld crucial safety information from the public about serious side effects.'

I recognised the devastation and loss in her voice as she carried on.

'I found out the government signed a deal with the drug company so they'd be immune to prosecution because they wanted to stockpile the vaccination urgently in case of an epidemic. They lied to me! It was all about making huge amounts of money! And if I'd known the real risks, I *never* would've let my daughter have that jab. But the biggest scandal is that this drug company hasn't even broken any laws by withholding this vital information! I mean, how is that possible? And I found out they destroyed evidence that . . .'

Anger and heartache bubbled to the surface as I gripped the phone tightly in my hands and listened to her story. Caprixanine had been just a superficial cut. How deep did the rancid wound really go?

I touched my stomach again and thought about my unborn child growing inside me – depending on me, needing my protection. If I didn't try to make this world a better place for her or him, then what kind of a mother was I? I had to stand up for what I believed in, even if I was standing alone.

And I didn't think we were just a drop in the ocean. Maybe we were really the whole ocean in one drop.

A NOTE FROM THE AUTHOR

Although all events and characters in this book are entirely fictional, *Beneath the Surface* was inspired by many real-life pharmaceutical scandals. When researching for this novel, I worked my way through too many online articles to mention here, but if you're interested in reading more about the subject, as a place to start I can recommend the following eye-opening books, which are pretty terrifying and jaw-dropping, considering they're non-fiction and not thrillers: *Bad Pharma* by Ben Goldacre, *Let Them Eat Prozac* by David Healy, *Deadly Medicines and Organised Crime* by Peter Gøtzsche, and *Confessions of an Rx Drug Pusher* by Gwen Olsen.

I'd like to say a huge thanks to my readers from the bottom of my heart for choosing my books! I really hope you enjoyed *Beneath the Surface*. If you did, I would be so grateful if you could leave a review or recommend it to family and friends. I always love to hear from readers, so please keep your emails and Facebook messages coming (contact details are on my website: www.sibelhodge.com). They make my day!

Massive thanks go out to my husband Brad for supporting me, being my chief beta reader, fleshing out ideas with me, and generally putting up with me ignoring him when I'm writing!

Thanks so much to Tarquin Schumacher for his pharma advice and input, and for answering all of my annoying questions.

A huge thank you goes to Jenny Parrott for all of her editing suggestions, and to John Marr for catching all of the things I didn't. Big thanks go to Emilie Marneur for all of her help, advice, and support over the last few years, along with Sammia, Sana, Hatty, and the rest of the Thomas & Mercer team.

And finally, a loud shout-out and hugs go to all the peeps at The Book Club on Facebook and to all of the amazing book bloggers and reviewers who enthusiastically support us authors with their passion for reading.

Sibel xx